Some Call
Me Eve

by

T. Pike

Cover Art by *Teddi Black*

The Wild Rose Press, Inc.
PO Box 708
Adams Basin, NY 14410-0708
Visit us at www.thewildrosepress.com

Publishing History
First Edition, 2025
Trade Paperback ISBN 978-1-5092-6199-4
Digital ISBN 978-1-5092-6200-7

Published in the United States of America

Dedication

For the women who taught me how to be a warrior.

Chapter 1

Our two swords clashed with a violent clank, reverberating through my body like a turbulent wave. Its power rolled through my limbs, its force colliding with my core. The commanding thrust of my rival's weapon was enough to set a common warrior off-balance, to easily send them to the ground, spiraling uncontrollably to their imminent death.

But I was no common warrior.

I utilized the strength of his blow to my advantage. Using the pressure of his attack, I propelled my body into a 360° spin. Then, harnessing the momentum of my twist, I launched my sword into his side. The strike was fatal, rattling his armor and sending a sharp ring across the training field.

I spun to face my next opponent without a moment's hesitation. He, however, was prepared for my swift attack, aimed at his poorly guarded stomach. He parried my charge with ease, promptly swinging his weapon in a slanted arch towards my open chest. But my reflexes were too quick for his blade to find its target. I smoothly dodged his assault as well as the subsequent swing toward my knees.

His swings were too aggressive, leaving him defenseless, vulnerable. Before he could recover his footing for the next jab, I sprang forward and shoved him backward with my elbow, sending him stumbling on his heels. Seizing his brief moment of imbalance, I stabbed him mockingly in the stomach, just enough to make him double over then trudge away in defeat.

I heard the growl of my next enemy at once. He approached at a run, his sword hanging over the back of his head as he leveled his weapon for a forceful downward chop. It was a poorly chosen technique, a clear sign of inexperience, making my defense a simple one. I effortlessly dodged his first blow then knocked him forward with the base of my boot before he could recover, sending him face-down into the dirt. Holding him in place with my foot, I dropped the tip of my sword into his armored buttocks and laughed to myself when he flopped helplessly on the ground.

From the corner of my eye, I saw my commander. His arms were raised in frustration, his eyes rolled angrily to the back of his head. "Haynes, you cannot defeat your opponent if you are eating dirt. Perhaps if you focused more on keeping a balanced stance and less on raging like a bull, you would not make such an ass of yourself."

The knights lining the battleground snickered at the blushing Haynes who ambled towards them with his head tucked shamefully. The commander shot his eyes toward the steel-plated knights. "You have some nerve laughing after your own pitiful performance, Fischer," he continued with a snarl. "Even a novice swordsman knows not to leave his abdomen exposed." The men quickly fell into silence. No one dared risk another verbal beating from their ruthless leader.

One by one, the soldiers approached, gambling their hand at the undefeated champion. I soon fell into a groove, blocking each strike, dodging each jab, hitting each mark. The nimble movements came to me naturally. My primal instincts rushed through my veins in a constant flow. It was as if my feet were moving independently from my body, stepping in time to the moves of my competitors like a choreographed dance, a perfected rhythm of knight and blade.

My commander desperately attempted to correct the technique of my endless string of opponents——"Keep your feet light…Never take your eyes off your challenger…For God's sake, Payne, use your shield!" ——but to no avail. No matter their size, skill, or strategy, no man could land a blow on this untouchable moving target.

Some might say I was at an advantage, my small, slender stature too low to the ground for their most powerful hits. But the ease in which I could slide beneath a flying sword and knock a man double my size off his feet would stun even the craftiest of fighters.

Before long, the line of awaiting opponents began to wear thin. The commander brought his hands to his hair and pulled in exasperation, his temper piquing. "Can no one defeat this puny warrior?"

As if summoned from the depths of the earth, my final challenger stepped forward. He towered over me like the great castle walls, his shadow engulfing me in darkness. I watched his sword intently as it swayed like a feather between his fingers.

He struck without warning. I was sent stumbling backward after a weak parry, underestimating the power of his swing. But speed was my greatest strength, and I recovered my balance almost instantly. The sheer force of his assaults far overpowered my own, restricting me to the defensive. Each slash of his blade flew by my head at frightful speeds, backed by a guttural grunt. I inched my way backward as each slice brought him a step closer. Without hesitation, my instincts took over, leading me into my signature move.

Gradually lowering myself to the ground, I bent into a squatted shuffle. My competitor's attacks persisted, unrelenting. He leaned downward to better reach my chest. At just the right moment, when he carried his weight on the ends of his toes, I leapt over his low arcing swing, twisted through the air over his outstretched arm, and landed smoothly behind his hunched frame. Before he could regain his stance and turn to face me once more, I delivered a lethal blow to the back of his knees.

My rival released a monstrous howl as he fell forward, dropping into a kneel. The heavy pound of his knees shook the ground, a quake that silenced the entire training field. All watched in awe as their star fighter lay helpless by my feet.

I looked expectantly at my commander, my racing heart beating in my ears. It was clear by his crossed arms and knitted brow that he was disappointed in his disgraceful brigade, but from the slight twitch at the corner of his mouth, I knew he was pleased with my performance. "Finish the job," he said in a low voice.

I turned back to face my statuesque adversary. No longer was he the invincible beast he was just minutes before. Down on his knees, he became a shell of his former self, humbled and abashed by defeat. Through his face guard, I could just make out his pleading eyes, ashamed before his peers, begging me for mercy.

With that look, a flood of heat filled my core. A yearning. A hunger. A lustful rage.

I chuckled coldly. *How pathetic.*

With a skillful twist of my blade, I struck the base of his neck with the flat of my sword, simulating a dramatic beheading and sending his helmet soaring through the air. It bounced through the dirt theatrically, spinning on its edge with a clatter before finding its final place of rest before the feet of the crowd, its hollow interior facing the huddle of defeated men.

A slow clap broke through the deafening silence, echoing across the training field. I lifted my gaze to see none other than King Ricard, ruler of Vitalia. He was adorned in a violet tunic lined with golden thread, a puffed silver surcoat that augmented his considerable physique, and a long, draping cloak exhibiting an intricate design of the royal crest. His threatening stature was only deepened by his austere visage——a thick nose framing a set of demanding brown eyes; a bushy, graying beard matching the shade of his thick, protruding brows; and his lips, normally forming a thin, sober line, now curved in a sly side smile.

The cluster of knights immediately fell to their knees, dropping their heads in a respectful bow. Even the commander knelt upon the dusty ground before his crowned ruler.

But I did not kneel. Instead, I stood boldly, facing my king with my head held high. The monarch stilled his hands. All waited expectantly for him to break the silence once more, this time with his booming voice. "Well done, Princess Evangeline."

At his declaration, I sheathed my sword and doffed my helmet to reveal my face. I released the pin from my hair and let it flow down my back in long copper waves, shining like the silver armor it lay upon. My crimson lips wore their own smug grin, perfectly matching that of the king.

"Thank you, Father."

Chapter 2

Eve

I am a roaring river.
I evade every obstacle in my way.
I command the land to part at my passing.
I rush boldly over the edge, raging into the unknown.
You may try to build a dam to stop my forward progress.
But, eventually, dams break.

I gently rapped my knuckles on the door, careful not to rouse the residents of any neighboring cottages. My fingers were bare, my fighting gauntlets long since removed to reveal my pale hand, now unprotected as I knocked against the splintered wood. It felt exposed in the early morning breeze, stripped of its enclosure of armor.

In fact, I was practically unrecognizable from the ironclad girl I was just hours before. My metal sabatons had been replaced by leather riding boots, my chainmail traded for a long wool cloak and a pair of close-fitting breeches. As the door slowly creaked open, I removed my hood to reveal my chestnut hair, no longer hidden within my cumbersome knight's helmet. Now the long strands were fastened in braids, the roots laced to the sides of my head, wrapped delicately around my ears, and floating effortlessly down my neck. The ends were knotted in forest green ribbons resting lightly upon my chest. Once uncovered, they caught the light of the fireplace from within the house, flashing their bronze hue.

As a princess, I had to be many women, playing different parts in a royal play, switching seamlessly between roles before the audience could notice. Sometimes I was a brave knight, others a devoted daughter or a trusted leader. Today, I was a woman of the people.

On the other side of the door was a middle-aged woman who, upon identifying her visitor in the dim light of the morning, inhaled sharply, staring at me wide-eyed. She was exceedingly short, my own meager stature towering over her. Her simple dress complemented her figure, tastefully displaying her hips while still covering her modestly. Silky brown locks peeked from the sides of her gray head scarf, and despite the startled blush in her cheeks, I discerned her handsome natural coloring.

"Princess Evangeline!" she finally blurted. "What a pleasant surprise. I am afraid we were not expecting any visitors this morning." Her voice shook nervously.

I replied with a gentle grin. "That is no problem, Mrs. Manfield. I hope I am not interrupting anything."

"Heavens, no!" she squeaked despite her best efforts to remain composed. She flung the door open to clear a path for my entry. Nodding my head graciously, I stepped inside.

Although the sun had not yet made its appearance, the Manfield house was already bustling with life. I was arrested at once by the sweet aroma of fruit tarts that drifted through the cottage, the pleasant scent fused with the unmistakable fragrance of freshly brewed coffee. The clanking of pots in the kitchen was muffled by the playful laughter of two young girls racing around the living room. A quick glance at Mrs. Manfield revealed her horror, her face contorted with humiliation at the sight of her children's rowdy behavior, and before a princess no less.

When the girls noticed me standing by the door, they instantly stilled, no commands needed from their mother. They stared at me, motionless, wearing the same expression Mrs. Manfield had donned just moments before. They flashed their eyes nervously between their mother and myself, soon regaining their senses and dipping into a curtsy. "Good morning, Princess Evangeline," they softly uttered in unison.

I smiled. "Good morning, girls. I pray you are behaving well." I held back the smirk that threatened to overtake my cheeks.

The children looked at each other hesitantly before nodding. I stepped forward before their bowed heads and knelt to meet them face to face. Sensing my closeness, they lifted their eyes to meet my own. "You two are very lucky. You know your mother and father work very hard to care for you, don't you?" The children nodded again, more forcefully this time.

I stood back to my full height. "Run along now," Mrs. Manfield said. The girls promptly lowered their heads and curtsied once more before scurrying out of the room.

I turned back to Mrs. Manfield who hastily swapped her nervous expression for a wide hostess grin. "Can I offer you any refreshments, your majesty? Some coffee perhaps?"

I humbly accepted, and she led me into a narrow kitchen. Beside the stove was a younger woman of striking similarity to the former. They shared the same shapely figure, but this woman's dark locks were displayed openly along her shoulders, her perfect auburn ringlets the same glowing shade as her eyes. Hearing our entrance, the girl turned. Her brows lifted in surprise, making the skin of her forehead crinkle.

"Evangeline!" In her consternation, a wooden serving spoon flung from her hand and clattered noisily on the ground, leaving a messy puddle of brown liquid on the floor. She ducked down to retrieve it, keeping her head bowed to conceal the redness in her cheeks as she rose. "What are you doing here...your grace?" She hastily added this last part after noticing her mother's commanding stare.

Mrs. Manfield flinched beside me. "That is no way to address our guest, Margaret!" she hissed. "Why don't you make the princess something to drink?"

The girl nodded, clearly flustered by her mother's reproach. She cleaned off the serving spoon in a basin of water before dipping it back into the boiling pot. The ceramic cup she placed before me became hot to the touch as soon as she scooped the steaming coffee inside. I lightly lifted the beverage to my nose, inhaling its pleasant scent before taking a cautious sip. I smiled at the girl in approval, sneaking in a quick wink her mother could not see.

"I apologize for intruding on your day off, Mary." I delicately placed the mug back on the table and rested my hands in my lap, regaining my formal persona.

Before the girl could respond, Mrs. Manfield protested. "It is no trouble at all, my lady!" She plopped down into the seat beside me. "In fact, I would like to thank you personally for giving our Margaret the honor of serving in your court."

I turned my gaze towards Mary who stood by the stove, fidgeting awkwardly with her dress. It had only been a few months since I promoted her to my lady-in-waiting, but Mary and I had been close friends since she first started working in the palace years ago. In our younger days, we would run recklessly through the castle halls, always hand-in-hand, causing mischief at every corner. She was the only person who did not treat me like a precious glass vase, delicate and breakable, meant to be honored and admired only at a distance. When I spoke with Mary, she spoke back, freely and candidly. With her, I could share my most intimate stories, could tell my darkest secrets, could be my true self. She was more like a sister than a servant.

So the choice was simple when I selected her to be my head lady's maid. In reality, it was just a formal title for being by my side at all hours of the day. Mary had always been my constant companion. Now, it was simply part of her job description.

Of course, Mrs. Manfield would never approve of such informalities, so I played along in the most imperial tone I could muster. "The pleasure is all mine, Mrs. Manfield." I caught Mary's eye in a sideways glance. She was tightly squeezing her lips together to hold back a flood of giggles. "She is more than qualified for the role. She knows what I need even before I do. I am not sure what I would do without her." The honest truth was that I would likely go mad from boredom in that massive, empty castle and would surely die of unbearable loneliness if it were not for Mary's companionship. She had come to mean a great deal to me, undoubtedly the closest friend I would ever have. Now lifting her head, hearing the sincerity behind my words, she met my eyes with a soft smile.

Mrs. Manfield's sharp voice cut back in, disrupting our private moment as she continued her rambling. "We are so proud of our little Margaret. If not for her, we would hardly be able to put food on the table." She sighed. "After Mr. Manfield's tragic accident, I have been forced to spend most of my time aiding his recovery and caring for the children."

She paused, momentarily losing herself in a silent reflection before snapping back into focus. "What I mean to say is that we are immensely grateful for your great kindness." She pasted the postcard smile back on her mouth, but this time it appeared genuine.

I reached out and lightly touched her hand. "Actually, that is why I have come today."

Mrs. Manfield sat upright. "Oh?"

"Mary has recently informed me of her father's terrible injury. Would it be alright if I spoke with Mr. Manfield?"

"Of course! Let me take you to him." She scuttled through the kitchen, and I rose to follow toward a small bedroom at the back of the house. The room was bare apart from the cobblestone walls, a beige nightstand holding a dimly lit candle, and a bed, sagging slightly in the middle, just big enough for two. Upon it lay Mr. Manfield. He was leaning back against the frame with one leg elevated upon a mountain of pillows. He held a pair of thick spectacles before his eyes and his other hand thumbed at the pages of a scuffed leather Bible resting on his lap.

His eyes slowly lifted upon our entrance, and he jolted in shock. His sudden movements launched his book into the air, sailing through space then flopping face-down on the floor. Completely ignoring this mishap, he slid his legs to the edge of the bed, wincing as he did so, then dropped them painstakingly to the ground as he attempted a respectful bow. I quickly stepped forward to stop him, leading him back onto the bed at once and insisting he not strain himself on my account. He graciously accepted my help, allowing me to guide him onto the tattered mattress. He sat upright with his back rigid and his hands folded tensely before him. "To what do I owe the pleasure, your majesty?" His voice was raspy, timid.

"I heard your leg has been troubling you." I gazed down at the injury in question and leaned forward to examine it from a closer angle.

"Surely this is no matter for a lady of your standing to worry about." His eyes flashed uneasily between my scrutinizing gaze and his precariously balanced leg.

"Of course it is." I paused my inspection to peer into his eyes. "The suffering of my people is always a concern of mine, especially when they are not provided sufficient care." The man's lips tightened. Nodding, he swallowed down any further objections.

I turned toward his leg once more, further assessing the injury. His knee was clearly swollen, the skin bulging and concerningly dark. "Tell me how this happened."

Mr. Manfield sighed. "I was helping repair the tower at the west end of the castle, the one damaged in last month's storm. As I was applying mortar to the wall, I tripped from the scaffolding and fell several stories to the ground, landing awkwardly on my right leg." He peered up at me with a careful grin, his expression grateful despite the circumstances. "I am quite lucky to be alive."

He twisted his lips and continued with a sigh. "The leg was set and bandaged by the village physician, but I am afraid it did not heal properly. It gives me greater pain today than it did on the day of the accident." He squinted at his bum leg and cringed at its unnatural protrusion.

I carefully rolled my fingertips over the wound, sensing the heat of the excess tissue. I bent the joint upward just slightly but stopped when I saw Mr. Manfield gritting his teeth in agony. After gently placing his leg back onto the cushions, I reached into my satchel and removed a long leather contraption. It was a complicated tangle of straps, some circular and some straight, some with holes and some with buckles.

Mr. Manfield eyed the device skeptically as I began loosening the belts. "This is a brace. It will keep your knee stable as you begin using it again and help prevent further strain." I cautiously pulled the apparatus over his foot and slid the straps along his shin. He gripped the sheets firmly and squeezed his eyes shut as I tightened it into place.

"And for the sting," I said, dropping my hand back into my bag, "I brought you this." In my palm was a white cream encased in a glass vial. "Rub this on the swollen area and the pain will dissipate in no time."

He took the small container from my hands and stared at it, mystified. After a while he set his heavy gaze on mine, his face blank. "I am not sure what to say."

"You need not say anything." I returned the satchel to my shoulder and stood. It had been easy enough to obtain the supplies. All it took was a quick trip to the palace infirmary and a short discussion with the castle doctor, and seeing the relief on Mr. Manfield's face made it well worth the effort. "Wear the brace for a few weeks and apply the cream as needed. I will send the castle physician to see you if I hear there is no improvement."

His eyes were still bound to mine, my words going unperceived. "Thank you."

It shook me, that simple phrase. I was used to extravagant greetings and exaggerated expressions of gratitude. But Mr. Manfield's words were rewarding in their authenticity.

I offered a small grin in return. "You are welcome."

****

The sun had just peeked over the distant hills when I left the cottage. A shower of pink light poured over the valley, blanketing the village in its rosy glow. The little town had come alive since I arrived at the Manfield home this morning. The cheerful sounds of birds chirping, the soft mumble of carts bumping along the cobblestone path, and the sharp cry of a rooster alerted me to the quickly approaching day.

I bit my lip. I had not realized how late it was.

I replaced my hood to conceal my features as I hastened to retrieve my horse from a nearby stable, but to no avail. A passing child skipping along the road recognized me with ease. "Look, Mama! It's Princess Evangeline!"

All heads within earshot spun to meet the object of the boy's pointed finger. I halted my purposeful walk, my identity now compromised, and unveiled myself. There was no point hiding anymore. The boy ran from his mother's side to meet me, soon followed by a flock of eager children, rushing toward me from all corners of the street. A small wave of panic swept through my chest as the small creatures surrounded me, barring any chance of escape. But I slowly relented to the smile that crept onto my lips as their cheerful faces came into view.

"Princess Evangeline!" two young girls cried out in high pitched voices as they sprinted toward me. I knelt to meet them face to face.

"Good morning, Sylvia. Good morning, Eleanor." I kept my hands folded on one knee as I observed the cluster of freckles sprinkled across their cheeks. "Are you helping your mama with chores this morning?"

The girls smiled widely. "We are delivering bread to the villagers," said one, holding up a wicker basket teeming with baked goods. Their matching pigtails bounced excitedly by their ears.

"Princess Evangeline!" a small boy interrupted before I could reply. "Look!" He gritted his teeth in an exaggerated grin to reveal a small gap.

"You lost a tooth!" I exclaimed, trying to replicate the enthusiasm in his voice.

"I put it under my pillow, and when I woke up in the morning, it was gone! Mama said a fairy took it and left me a fresh orange." He relayed his tale wildly as he jumped up and down, unable to contain his excitement.

"That is wonderful, Elric! You are becoming quite the young man now, aren't you?" He nodded fervently as he spun around in a joyful dance.

I reached back into my satchel and carefully withdrew a basket of small pastries. I knew I would likely run into a pack of hungry children this morning, and I stealthily swiped a few treats from the palace kitchen before sweeping out the door. Now the little ones eyed the sweets ardently.

I presented one pastry to each child then sent them on their way. They accepted the gift graciously, thanking me with a bow before running back down the road. Elric's mother had finally caught up to her son, now stuffing his mouth zealously with every crumb he could fit of the rich tart. "My sincerest apologies, Princess," the woman said breathlessly. "We did not mean to disturb your morning activities." She lifted Elric onto her hip, wiped the pink frosting from his face with her apron before plopping him back to the ground.

"It is no problem at all, Mrs. Walters." I returned my satchel to my shoulder before rising back to my feet. "How is the cobbler shop?"

Mrs. Walters brightened at the mention of her family's small business. "Very good, thank you."

"I am glad to hear it. These riding boots you sold me are unmatched. I have never had such a fine pair in my life." Without meaning to, I wiggled my toes, noting how comfortable my feet were within the shoes. "I would be remiss if I did not purchase a second set. Could I trouble you to craft me the same pair in black?"

Mrs. Walters beamed. "Of course, my lady! I will see to it personally that they are delivered to you by the end of the week."

"No need to rush." I pointed down at my feet, clad in the unblemished leather boots. "These will surely last me a while."

She chuckled amiably. "Bless you, Princess Evangeline." With a mannerly curtsy, the woman turned back toward the road with little Elric in tow, the boy waving to me madly. I chuckled as I waved back and watched as the duo skipped off.

Suddenly remembering that I was due at the castle, I spun my head around to inspect the rising sun. It was now completely visible, illuminating the valley with the full glory of the morning. I cringed, confident that my tardiness was now inevitable, then sped into the village stables. Inside, I retrieved my horse and hastily guided her from the stall. She broke into a gallop as soon as I mounted her saddle, racing us home.

The journey back to the castle was a short one. I had taken the same route countless times before: over the stone bridge, through the iron gates, around the palace walls, across the training fields, and into the palace stables. If I looked closely, I could just make out a trail of hoof prints in the ground, marking our well-trodden path.

As we approached the stables, I slowed my horse to a trot and hopped off my saddle, leading her the rest of the way by foot. The morning light beamed brightly upon the east end of the castle, seeping obstinately through the cracks in the stable walls. Once I removed her bridle, I swept a few brush strokes through her long silver hair while she drank eagerly from her water trough. Across the room, I spotted a bin of bright red apples, likely picked in the early hours of the morning from the palace orchards. I found the shiniest one and fed it to my loyal mare by hand, rewarding her for tolerating my ceaseless antics.

As I turned to leave, my eye caught a flash of light reflecting off of a slumped stack of hay in the corner of the room. At the sight of the pile, I felt my chest warm and the space between my legs start to tingle, suddenly immersed by the innumerable memories it contained. I was defenseless to the visions that came rushing through my mind.

Late at night, when the darkness had enveloped the whole of the kingdom, I would come here, bringing with me the men I had chosen in secret. The men I desired: knights in my father's guard, servants in the palace kitchen, men I closely examined when no one was watching. I did not choose those who loudly boasted of their great swordsmanship or those who trudged away in bitter defeat after a friendly spar with their princess. Not those who eyed me critically in the castle halls when I failed yet again to don the traditional royal dress.

I chose the men who lost with dignity, who humbly raised their arms in surrender when my sword had snuck its way to their necks, who knew they were no match for my power and skill. Those who dropped their eyes modestly to the floor when I passed, who tried and failed to hide the blush that crept onto their cheeks. Those who watched me, studied me, in what I knew was unspoken adoration.

They were the ones who I knew would accept what I was willing to give them. Who would grant me the control I craved. The men who admitted their defeat on the training field would always welcome my conquering on the earthen stable floor.

It was here that I would bring the latest one I had chosen and command him to strip bare. I would chuckle softly at the way his body shivered in the chill air and stare hungrily at his bulging flesh, erect despite the cold wind that crept through the cracks in the stable walls. He needed no touch to harden, only my strict demands. I knew he would be unable to resist arousal when I gently rolled my fingertips down his chest, across his abdomen, along the warm skin between his thighs.

I teased his body mercilessly until I could see the desperation in his eyes. Gripping him by the shoulders, I forced him to his knees before me and tilted his chin upward to see his face. Now towering above him, I leaned forward and rolled my tongue along the sides of his neck, savoring the taste of salty sweat, dried there after hours of hard labor. Without fail, he released a low groan in my ear, lighting a fire within me that burned along with the hot moisture between my legs.

My licks soon became more urgent. Increasing the pressure of my tongue, I wrapped my hand around the other side of his neck, taking long, hard bites until his skin turned red. With each nibble, I sensed a growing yearning, the animal within me threatening to break from its cage and take over my body.

When I could hold back no longer, I placed my hand over his naked chest and pushed him violently to the ground, forcing him flat with a loud thud. I took him in my mouth, bringing the fullness of him between my lips while I swiftly removed my own garments. I could feel him throb, and I swept my tongue upward to taste his own warmth pooled there. He swept his head back into the hay as he moaned. His body writhed wildly while at my mercy. But with a tight grip of his side with my free hand, I forced him into stillness.

Once my clothes were piled beside me, I released him and moved my hips to hover over his torso, feeling my own body tremble with need. Slowly, I would take him within me, rolling my head back with pleasure as I pulled him deeper still. I gradually quickened my movements, digging my nails into his arms as a growing ecstasy overwhelmed my senses.

Now the groans were mine, the sound rattling the stable walls as I rode him faster still. I leaned my chest down until my face was just an inch from his, still rocking back and forth as I effortlessly slid him within me. He moved his head upward, trying to steal a kiss from my open mouth. But I seized his throat and shoved his head back into the dirt. Then, sitting upright, I grasped him by the hair, wrenching his face forward until he was nose-deep in my breasts. "Suck," I commanded. The only moans I wanted to hear were my own.

The slickness of his lips against my nipples carried me dangerously close to the edge, and I slowed my hips to regain control. Occasionally, he lifted his arm and attempted to roll his hand up my thigh. In an instant, I pinned his wrists to the ground. I was not his to kiss or caress. He was mine to control.

Finally, I rolled my neck back, releasing all my restraints, no longer fighting the desire that raged through my body. I tugged at his hips with growing intensity until I sensed my approaching climax. Suddenly, I was overtaken by an explosion of euphoria. My lips pulsed around him, feeling an eruption of warmth. As we both cried out in rapture, I pulled his head upward and squeezed his face tightly against my chest. I could barely hear his muffled sighs over my own, reverberating through the stables.

Adrenaline flooded my veins at the host of memories—the nights I played out my darkest sexual fantasies. A shiver rolled down my spine, leaving the space between my thighs aching with want. But there was no time for reminiscing. Reluctantly, I snapped myself out of my reverie and rushed from the stable.

My path through the castle to my bedroom, located

at the far end of the main hall, normally took me several minutes to traverse. But time was of the essence this morning, so I took every shortcut I knew. I practically ran through each hall, ignoring any offending stares that were thrown my way, before finally arriving at my destination.

I stood for a moment by the entrance and peered through the door as I labored to catch my breath. At first glance, few would suspect my room was that of a princess. Although the room itself was vast, replete with an expansive vanity table and an opulent king-sized bed, dozens of feather cushions, and a sheer canopy hanging around the edges, any resemblance to a royal bedchamber stopped there.

The delicate pastels of a typical regal woman were absent within the dark interior design. Black furniture dominated the scene, accented by the occasional splash of silver or violet. The entirety of the east wall was covered in book shelves filled with my lengthy collection of combat guides, sword fighting strategies, and war histories—with a small corner dedicated to the various methods of diplomacy, volumes my father insisted I read. The bulky couches originally occupying the lounging area of my chamber were stripped away and replaced by my cherished collection of war prizes, keepsakes from battles I had fought and won: the sword I had wielded to kill my first enemy; the helmet of a fallen adversary, obtained after the first battle I had ever commanded; the wooden training sword, now warped and chipped along the edges, gifted by my father on my eighth birthday. Each object was pinned to the wall, forming an extensive gallery in honor of my triumphs.

To a stranger, the place was entirely unsettling, its

eerie darkness menacing and uninviting—just as I intended. I had no shame in establishing what was mine, even if it came at the cost of frightening away the rest of the world.

I hurried through the dimly lit room toward my closet tucked around the back corner. Inside hung an endless array of clothing. Along one wall were dozens of finely sewn dresses of all colors and fabrics, gifted to me by neighboring kingdoms as symbols of peace. They were practically untouched. The rest of the space was occupied by an assortment of simple cloth shirts and cotton pants intended for everyday use. I stared longingly at the comfortable attire. This morning was one of the few times I would be forced to wear my formal garments, a burden I loathed.

I grumbled aloud as I stripped out of my riding gear and prepared to don one of the many gawdy dresses that lined the wall. But before I did, I noticed a stack of perfectly folded clothing lying on a wooden chest. Upon closer look, I realized it was a custom outfit set aside for just this occasion. Relief flooded my chest, and I inwardly blessed Mary for her thoughtfulness. Even on her day off, she knew I would be in desperate need of assistance. I was utterly clueless when it came to royal fashion, whereas Mary was an expert with a needle and thread.

Lifting the lavish outfit from the chest, I threw on the selected attire without a second thought. After hastily removing my braids, I rushed toward the door but came to a halt when I caught a glimpse of myself in the vanity mirror, unable to resist the smirk that formed on my lips. Mary had left me an inky black corset that dipped dangerously between my breasts, a pair of slim silk slacks, a set of dark leather flats that laced around my ankles, and a shining regal cape that flowed majestically from my shoulders and left a stark pool of violet about my feet.

Someone had once told me that purple was the color of royalty, and even though I was no traditional princess, it soon became my signature shade: the color of power. I wanted everyone, from faithful servants to distant foreigners, to know from just a brief glimpse that I was a woman of great authority, a princess not to be messed with.

I lifted my gaze upward to meet my own eyes in the mirror. My hair was untamed, its frizzy ringlets spiraling out at odd angles. My face was completely bare of makeup, but I did not dare chance my hand at the threatening assortment of powders, brushes, and dyes lying on the table before me. Besides, I despised the unnatural look of a painted face, caked like a porcelain doll. I found the practice of hiding my features counterintuitive to establishing myself as a respected ruler.

Thus, I avoided the piles of makeup upon the vanity, instead electing to take on my nemesis: the hairbrush. I forced the prongs through my stubborn locks, replacing the knots and curls with umber waves but frizzing each strand in the process. Eventually, I conceded to my unruly mane and plopped the brush back onto the table, defeated.

Before slipping away, I took one final moment to observe myself. I was not the woman most people expected. I was far from the obedient princess they all desired me to be. But now, I smiled at the fierce retaliation in my reflection. I had no intention of fitting into their mold. This was who I was, and I would be damned if I let them believe I was anything less.

Finally withdrawing from my room, I raced toward the great hall. Castle servants froze at my passing, caught off guard by my formal attire, then bowed lowly to the ground. I hastily acknowledged their gesture with a nod before continuing on. The clank of my shoes on the granite floor rang through the hall to the beat of my rapid stride. As I walked, I gazed out through a set of large windows beside me. The castle orchards stretched out for miles, their leaves blazing with the morning's golden glow. However, my own reflection obstructed this stunning view. I peered sideways to observe my gait. My shoulders were pulled back, my chin held high, my lavender cape floating elegantly behind me as if possessed by the wind.

Soon, I arrived at the great hall, and without bothering to slow down, I threw the massive mahogany doors open with both hands. I far overestimated their weight, however, and sent them sailing into the walls. The wood and stone collided with an ear-piercing crash that echoed through the massive hall.

As if on cue, the heads of the men seated around the long table turned to find the source of the thud, and their eyes came to rest on me. I froze in place, my entire body tensing under their paralyzing stares. A powerful stillness overtook the room as everyone waited for my next move. I could have cowered. I could have scampered over to my seat in humiliation with my head hung low.

But I was Princess Evangeline. Instead, I stood taller, raised my head higher, and met their looks with my own cool gaze.

I took my time walking to my empty chair, the last remaining seat at the table, and let the sound of each footstep resonate through the hall. I embraced their starstruck gapes, glued to my exposed chest displayed above my lacy corset. Their eyes drifted down my shapely legs beneath my flowing pants, drifting all the way to the end of my cape, hovering weightlessly in the air behind me.

By the time I took my seat at the head of the table, I had every man transfixed, their prior conversations long forgotten. Their expressions were mixed: some disapproving, some amazed. Either way, each one had fallen into my trap. None of them could take their eyes off me. And it was not just because I was beautiful—it was much more than that. It was the dominance that diffused from my body, a power unlike any they had ever seen.

I absorbed their admiration greedily until I heard King Ricard clear his throat, breaking my spell and shifting their focus back toward his side of the table. "I am glad you could join us, Princess." He controlled his voice so masterfully, sounding authentically pleased at my arrival. But he was also my father, and I detected in his tone a subtle note of irritation at my tardiness. Silently acknowledging this private rebuke, I lowered my chin to avoid his reproachful gaze.

"As I was saying, gentlemen," he continued, the tension I had created dissolving under his warm tone, "I am pleased to welcome you all to the annual summit of the Western Alliance, and I am greatly honored to host you in our kingdom." With just one sentence, my father could make a room full of noblemen feel like they were in the presence of family, like they were seated in the comfort of their own homes rather than hundreds of miles from their respective kingdoms. Clearly, it was not a skill I had inherited as evidenced by the unsettling effect I had on the visitors.

"On behalf of Princess Evangeline and myself, we welcome you to Vitalia." At the mention of my name, a few heads turned back in my direction. I met their eyes shamelessly. My poor attempt at a graceful smile came out more like a self-righteous smirk that led my uneasy observers to turn away in discomfort.

"Fortunately, there appear to be no dire matters in need of discussion," the king said. "Our kingdoms have been blessed with peace for many months now, with few serious threats to our union."

"Apart from the string of invasions in the northern provinces," one man interrupted.

The king sighed. "Thank you, Lord Cassius. I was just getting to that," my father said with a tinge of irritation. Although he was the head of the Western Alliance, King Ricard hated discussing war or any conflict for that matter. He set his folded hands upon the table before continuing. "As most of you know, an unknown power has taken possession of a small number of territories in the far north."

My heart dropped, a cold dread settling over me. *Invasions in the northern provinces?* Amity had governed our realms for nearly a year with no incentive for war of any kind. But my father had told me nothing of these attacks. This changed everything.

"Nevertheless, the threat does not seem to be pressing at this time. As of yet, the invaded lands have been insubstantial in size and influence." Several men nodded in agreement with the king, but a few grumbled audibly.

"Regardless of the severity of these attacks, the invasion of occupied territory is a direct violation of the Treaty of Bastien, binding all kingdoms east of the Great Sea to respect the sovereignty of any self-governed domain." The nobleman spoke with concern, seemingly bothered by the casual way in which the matter was being addressed.

At the long end of the table, Lord Cassius stood. "And allowing any invasions to take place by a foreign power sends a message to all other kingdoms, friend or foe, that the illegal conquering of lands will be tolerated. If you ask me, we should send a message of our own, rebuking these actions." He spoke with a tone of authority, and several men mumbled in agreement at his suggestion.

"Let us also remember that these *insubstantial lands*," said another concerned delegate, citing the king's own words, "are our allies. I believe it is our duty to defend their freedom, no matter how small they may be." At my own end of the table, I fervently nodded my head in support.

Before I could voice my agreement, however, the Duke of Norburrow entered the discussion. I bit my tongue to keep from grumbling aloud, bracing myself for another of his infamously cavalier speeches. "The Treaty of Bastien was dissolved years ago after the Lockidian War. Besides, shipping men to battle just to assert our power is a waste of human lives when the possession is so minimal."

I forced my way into the conversation before anyone else could interrupt. "*Minimal* is a drastic understatement, Duke. Let's not forget the numerous attempted invasions that these territories thwarted only a few years ago." I lifted my hands above the table, counting off examples with each finger. "Azov defeated both Navarre and Koda under the reign of King Augustus. Nivia overtook the Simeon Empire in the Battle of Avgard under the leadership of the honorable Commander Henrich. And no rational force has even attempted to invade Thera in over fifty years." This seemed to impress some of the nobles, now eyeing each other with raised brows. Others, likely ignoring the bulk of my speech, gawked at the indecency of my boldness. Their inward criticism burned a hole in my chest, quickly sparking my short temper.

"Nonetheless, it is fruitless to get involved in a war that does not directly concern us," the Duke replied, scowling directly at me. "And although we are all aware that you are quite an…" he paused, choosing his words carefully, "*accomplished* lady, I believe I speak for everyone when I say that your opinion is not appropriate on the topic of war."

The burners within me turned to full blast. My rage instantly boiled over. I gripped the edge of the table tightly, my ears burned red. My father, well accustomed to my spurts of fury, stepped in before I could give the Duke a real piece of my mind, which we both knew would undoubtedly trigger gasps of shock and disgust from around the table.

"I will remind you, Duke, that I am head of this council and I have approved my daughter's attendance." He was so collected, a stark opposite to my unbridled ferocity. "Princess Evangeline is an intelligent and noble voice in my court whose opinions are to be respected." My father was the one who eyed me now. His expression conveyed the authenticity of his words while simultaneously attempting to douse the flames within me. "Besides, there will soon come a day when I am no longer able to lead Vitalia, and Evangeline will be the one to take my place."

"But even a queen should not be invested in such violent matters. Per tradition, the military affairs are to be dealt with by her husband," said the Duke.

"Who said anything about a husband?" I shouted, finally releasing my pent-up fury.

The room erupted in disgruntled murmurs. Before more men could protest, the king calmly addressed the council, raising his voice above the uproar. "Royal women are given greater power in my kingdom." He cleared his throat. "I am sure you all remember the honorable reign of the late Queen Genevieve." The king's manner became grim at the mention of my mother, his thoughts seeming to drift away. The men detected the somber change in the atmosphere and quickly fell into a hush.

In a few seconds, my father pulled himself out of a distant memory and resumed. "My wife was a remarkable woman. She led our people with more strength and dignity than any queen this kingdom has ever seen. I know most of you knew and respected her deeply, as I did." A few of the nobles lowered their heads, ashamed for implying any disrespect toward the late queen. Others, however, were not so convinced.

"Besides," he continued, regaining his stoic persona, "Princess Evangeline is the highest ranking officer in my brigade. She is entirely qualified to speak on matters of war."

This set the men off again, their respectful silence

shifting into total commotion. The momentary pride I felt at my father's defense was squandered by the guffaws of the group.

"We have all heard about your daughter's *unique gifts*." The Duke emphasized his words with sarcasm and contempt. I had to bury my nails in my palms to keep from throwing a nearby gauntlet at his head. "But do you really expect us to believe that this girl is some kind of expert swordswoman?"

I slammed my fists into the table. The force shot through the hall with a thunderous bang, shaking the men into silence. "I would be happy to prove my talents to you myself if you would be so bold as to raise your own sword."

"That is enough!" The king's voice boomed through my eardrums, instantly regaining the attention of the nobles. "Let's keep this civil, shall we?" His eyes flashed between the Duke, still blushing after my menacing threat, and myself. I met his glare with my own defensive scowl, unwilling to acknowledge any wrongful behavior on my part.

The king continued with his jaw clenched. "Despite your opinions, I will rule my kingdom as I see fit." He was addressing the entire council now. His tone had grown more assertive, evincing his intolerance for any contempt toward his rule. "My daughter is more than fit to rule in my place if and when that time comes."

The Duke rose to his feet in outrage, the loud scrape of his chair drawing the attention of the other nobles. "I, for one, do not feel compelled to follow your guidance when you are clearly incapable of properly governing your own kingdom." He turned to face me, his piercing glare filled with scorn. "Not to mention your inability to rein in your unruly daughter."

The room lay perfectly still. A heavy tension hung in the air as all waited breathlessly for the king's response. His face formed a hard grimace. His brows furrowed harshly, and his mouth fixed into a firm line. His eyes penetrated the Duke like spears. "Where do you find the audacity to question my rule?" He spoke in a low growl barely louder than a whisper yet more intimidating than any yell I could ever muster. "Where do you get the nerve to talk down to the ruler of the most respected kingdom in this realm?"

A biting chill rolled down my spine. Pride rippled through my body with a shiver.

"Let us not forget all the times *your* province would have suffered defeat if it were not for the involvement of the Vitalian army. I am sure that everyone in this council would agree that your own kingdom would cease to exist if not for the persistent and selfless support we have provided you." The king lifted his hand from its place on the table to point at the Duke's chest. "So I suggest you think twice before insulting my rule or my family. I have more public influence and loyal followers than you could ever hope to obtain."

The silence in the hall was deafening. I was certain that everyone in the room could hear the pounding of my heart against my rib cage. The Duke's features turned ashen. With every eye in the room now directed at him, he fumbled his way back into his chair with a nervous swallow.

"Now that the matter is settled," the king said, smoothly regaining his composure, "let us return to the subject at hand." I leaned back and crossed my arms before me, balancing carelessly on the back legs of my chair. A smug grin covered my lips as I waited for my father to berate the Duke once more. "It is my opinion that, due to the distant and mostly minimal threat from this unknown power, our kingdoms should remain neutral at this time."

My jaw dropped open. I leaned forward sharply in surprise, forgetting about my precarious position and slamming the front legs of my chair loudly onto the granite floor. Once again, I had unintentionally drawn the attention of the entire room. Utilizing the opportunity, I spoke. "You wish to stand by while innocent people are unlawfully attacked?" There was an added spite to my words. I took my father's disagreement on such a critical subject as a personal offense, and I was unable to conceal the betrayal I felt.

The king responded coolly, unmoved by my hysterics. "This is not our battle to fight—"

"But doesn't our great influence come with a responsibility to fight for those who cannot fight for themselves?"

"Not when the cost is the lives of countless men!" the king roared.

I was shaken, caught off-guard by my father's outburst. A surge of unfamiliar emotion blossomed in my throat before I choked it down. This time, his attempts to appear calm were less successful. A line of sweat glistened along his forehead, and his left eye twitched in frustration. "The members of this alliance will continue to exclude their respective kingdoms from this conflict until a change of circumstances necessitates our involvement."

My panic rose as I felt myself growing invisible. "But—"

"And as head of this council, that is my final decision." His eyes bore into mine with that same razor-sharp stare he had used against the Duke. I winced under its blistering sting.

Before I knew it, the king began thanking the nobles for their attendance, the summit quickly coming to an end. But I could barely hear him over the buzzing in my ears, my thoughts overwhelmed by humiliation and rage.

My father soon dismissed the nobles, but before they could rise from their seats, I leapt to my feet. The force of my spring pitched my chair backward, causing it to teeter dangerously on one leg. I did not wait to see its fate. Without another word, I stormed from the great hall and let it clatter to the ground behind me.

****

Watching as the setting sun dipped beneath the rolling hills far in the distance, I finally concluded that dusk in Vitalia was even more spectacular than dawn. The light's intensity slowly waned as evening approached. The bright blue sky gently faded into a vibrant orange. On the western end of the valley, the sun casually descended into the far-off peaks, still sparkling with last winter's snow. The changing hue ignited the village in a blinding inferno. It enveloped every home, shop, and street, illuminating the world below with a beaming halo.

I used to spend every night up here, seated atop the highest point of the castle's tallest tower, watching nature's majestic display on my homeland. As the spectacle of colors gradually dimmed, I laid my back flat on the ground and stared up at the legions of stars that conquered the night sky.

I could not remember the last time I visited this

place. I used to lie here and dream about the kingdom I would one day rule, the league of citizens I would one day lead. But for the past few years, I had been too busy with my royal duties to sneak away. I rarely found the time to relive the pleasures I often enjoyed as a child.

But today was different. After the morning's unpleasant events, I knew I had to get away, and atop the secluded castle balcony, high enough to view every acre of my kingdom, I prayed I would never be found. Although the stone floor was rugged and much more uncomfortable than I remembered, the brilliance of the starry night had not changed, its immensity as breathtaking as ever.

Following the disaster at the summit of the Western Alliance, I vanished, evading any further conversation or forged cordiality with the noblemen, disappearing into my bedroom and locking the door behind me. But no attempts to distract myself could slow my racing thoughts, constantly replaying the course of events in the great hall. Eventually, I declared my efforts fruitless, and as soon as the coast was clear, I dashed through the twisting corridors to the north tower and climbed straight to the top. I had hoped the fresh air would bring me some much needed relief, but even the dazzling view of distant galaxies could not quiet my rebellious mind.

Sighing aloud, I stood, wincing at the sharp ache in my back from the uneven ground. I walked to the edge of the terrace and propped my elbows on the railing. I rested my head in both hands as I peered out at the quiet village, surrendering to the newest wave of thoughts that rushed through my mind.

How could my father be so unfeeling? It seemed so unlike him, ignoring such a grave injustice to protect his own interests. Years ago, well before I was born, my father had been known for his courage. He was a man whose fearlessness practically radiated from his body, who stopped at nothing to defend the rights of others. All who knew him said he was the most honorable of warriors, a dauntless hero. He was everything I had ever wanted to be.

So why this? Why now did he refuse to aid those in great need? What had changed? What would make the king, whose valiant acts were those of legends, choose to turn his back on the world? It was selfish, ignoble, cowardly.

I tilted my neck upward to gaze out beyond the valley, toward a distant land I could not see. Could we truly be a kingdom of honor, the powerful dynasty we claimed to be, if we sat idly by as another stole the peace we had toiled to preserve?

From behind me, I heard a muffled shuffling of boots against stone. My limbs instantly tensed, my senses instinctively shifting into high alert, on guard against any potential threat. I stilled and listened for whoever was hidden in the shadows.

But just as I assumed my defensive stance, I relaxed my muscles and slumped back over the railing. Years of training had made me keen to my surroundings, able to identify a friend or foe by their tread alone. These footsteps I knew well.

I remained motionless, trying my best to ignore my father's slow approach. When he plodded onto the terrace, I kept my features neutral, not bothering to move my vision from the valley below. I was well-versed in this game we played: keeping my guard up, refusing to speak first, never making my feelings known. I had forgotten, however, that I was contending with the master.

He sauntered to the edge of the balcony like I was not even there, ignoring my presence completely. Bitterness flooded my chest at his disregard of my very existence, and I knew then that I had already lost.

I sighed aloud, signaling my surrender. "You are making the wrong choice." It was a partial submission, but I was still unwilling to meet his eyes.

"How so?" His question was simple, but I was no idiot. I detected his psychological tricks and rolled my eyes. Even in the most serious situations, my father spoke more like a prophet than a king.

"Strong leaders fight for the weak, even if sacrifices must be made." I finally wrenched my cold eyes from the darkening hills to face him. "You taught me that."

At my resignation, he turned to regard me with his heavy downward gaze. I anticipated his next attack, doubtless a seemingly simple statement coated with his fatherly wisdom. But to my surprise, the terrace erupted with his explosive laughter. When he finally spoke, his mouth was still curved in a smile. "Classic Evie. Using my own words against me."

And just like that, the anger boiling within me floated away like autumn leaves. There was some kind of magic in that simple name, a charm I could not explain. *Evie*. I had never been a fan of nicknames. I insisted on being addressed by nothing but my full royal title. But for as long as I could remember, my father had called me Evie. It was his favorite pet name for me, his one and only child. He knew how much I loved it, especially coming from his deep, comforting baritone. By just uttering it aloud, he could bring my rising temper crashing to the ground.

He watched me openly now with his wide, regal grin, amplified by his fatherly pride. Despite my best efforts to resist, my own smile crept onto my lips. I turned my face back into the night in a sorry attempt to conceal the powerful effect he had on me.

He chuckled again. "You are just as stubborn as your mother was."

My body stiffened. My mother, the woman I came from but never knew. I stared uneasily at my hands, my fingers firmly gripping the stone barrier. My mind was engulfed by a torrent of emotions I did not understand, a confusing web of grief, anger, and pain. "She was always determined to accompany me when we set off for war," he continued, the smile still in his voice, "even when she was pregnant with you."

I had heard this story dozens of times. As a child, I used to ask about her often, curious to know more about this mysterious woman whom everyone seemed to worship, even in death. And every time I raised the subject, my father's cheeks would twist into that same sad grin.

"Your mother was fearless," he always said. "She cared for the townspeople when there was horrible sickness in the village. She traveled throughout the land to make peace with our enemies. She even refused to stay home when our men went off to fight."

"When I was still in her belly!" I used to exclaim, having memorized every line by heart.

"That's right," my father would reply with a laugh. "She insisted on joining us for every battle. To stay at home when we were at war: that was never an option for her." He would stare off into the distance with a sparkle in his eye. "She nursed our injured men back to health and encouraged us to fight with honor. Even with you growing inside her, she was still our most relentless warrior."

Then came the part of the story when his face turned grim. For a moment, he would grow quiet, the painful memories choking him into silence.

"Then what happened?" I would ask delicately. I knew he was reliving the scene, once again suffering through the heartache that seized his throat in its death grip. But I could not let him stop there. Despite the pain of remembering, I never left the story unfinished.

After a steadying breath, he would let out a deep exhale, pulling himself back to the present before speaking again. "You were born early. We were not expecting you for at least another month. We thought we had more time, enough to get your mother home before you arrived. But you have never been one to follow expectations."

He would tousle my hair with this little joke. I would giggle lightly then brace myself for what I knew came next.

"But after you were born, your mother got sick. No one knew what was wrong with her, and when things took a turn for the worst, it was already too late." Glossy pools would form in my father's eyes, and each time, I could not help but dive inside to see what treasures they held.

In their depths, I would see myself, an infant cradled in my mother's frail arms, my tiny head beating along with the faint pound of her fading heart. Even in sickness, I knew she was beautiful, her ragged locks still rolling elegantly down her back, hair the same copper shade as my own.

Beside her knelt my father, stroking her hand lovingly, burying his pain deep within himself as he held my mother close. I had never seen my father cry, had never seen those clear pools overflow. And although he always told me this story with a steady face, I imagined that in her final moments, a single tear had finally spilled. Even he was unable to stop the stream that rolled down his cheek as he told my mother goodbye.

"What did she say before she left?" I would ask gingerly, saving the most important part for last.

Despite the pain in his voice, he would comply, sinking deeper into the memory to recite my mother's dying words. "She told me that you would be special," he said, the tremble in his voice so slight that I could have imagined it. "That one day you would bloom like the brightest sunflower. That I had to protect you from all the people who would try to chop you down."

When the story was over, my father would smile, peering over as if he saw me anew. "And now here you are, the most radiant flower in all of Vitalia. My little Evie."

I grew up hearing the legend of my mother from all who remembered her. People told me she was a strong leader, a selfless servant, and, often times, a continuing presence, living on in me. Everyone who knew my mother never hesitated to relay all they remembered of her. They told me how much they loved her, how much they missed her. And without fail, how alike we were.

My father believed this more than anyone. Most young girls who wanted to fight would be punished for simply possessing such unladylike interests. And most princesses would be laughed back into the castle, back into their lives of dignified obedience and silent submission. But when I first told my father of my desire to wield a sword, I knew it was my mother he saw looking back at him. He recognized that passion, that same unquenchable fire he had come to love, and he melted into my open palm.

I learned the art of combat from the most skilled swordsmen in the land. When my father noticed the rare talent that I possessed, he sent for the very best trainers from every known kingdom. Over time, I painstakingly cultivated my craft, and before long, sword fighting became my life. I lived each day to stand out on the training field, sparring with Vitalia's bravest knights. Holding my own weapon felt like destiny, like I was finally complete when it was gripped in my gauntleted hand.

As soon as I defeated my first enemy, I knew that I was born to fight. I was certain that my duty to my people was not any kind of graceful presence or quiet beauty. I was the chosen champion of Vitalia, and I would bring my kingdom glory.

There were many who disapproved of the woman I had become. Many looked down upon my refusal to hold my tongue, to follow their rules, to be the submissive princess they wanted. To play the role I was doomed to play by birth. But my father would squash my critics in an instant. With a cold scowl and an icy word, he sent them all running. I knew he took pride in who I was. He saw the blaze that roared within me, and unlike the rest of the world who tried to squander it to ashes, he helped it burn brighter.

As I got older, growing more into a warrior than a woman, people often told the king that it was obvious I was my father's daughter. But he would simply shake his head. "No," he would say with a thoughtful grin. "She is her mother's."

"And just like with you, it was hard to tell her no." My father's words snapped me back to the present. I finally abandoned all reserve and turned to face him head-on, my resentment swept away with the flow of memories.

"I used to think that bravery and sacrifice were always the right answer until I lost your mother." There was hurt in his voice, but his gentle gaze still held softly to my own. "But then I learned that blind courage often comes with devastating consequences."

I stared down at my hands as I considered his words. My father had expressed great pride each time I went off to battle, but I could always sense a hidden reluctance to let me go.

He placed a finger beneath my chin and lifted, forcing my eyes to meet his. Within them, I detected something I had never seen there before: fear.

"There will always be injustice in this world," he said, the insistence in his voice begging me to see reason. "But the best rulers have the wisdom to place the value of human lives over justice or glory." His words hovered in the space between us like thick smoke, an ominous invitation waiting patiently for my acceptance.

But before I could respond, my father leaned forward and planted a soft kiss on my forehead. Then, he turned towards the castle and walked away, leaving as quietly as he had come. With the warmth of his lips still on my skin, I watched each of his weighty steps drift away, farther and farther until he was out of sight.

A chill suddenly filled the balcony in my father's

absence. What remained of the sun's light had disappeared entirely during our conversation. The village seemed so small now, nearly invisible beneath the faint moonlight. The cottages were shrouded in darkness. The only thing that prevented a perfect blanket of blackness over the valley was the beaming of thousands of stars seemingly inches above my head, just out of reach, and a few candles yet to be extinguished.

As I stared out, I heard my father's words once more. *The best rulers have the wisdom to place the value of human lives over justice or glory.* I could not deny how much I cared for my people. I may not have been the type of princess who hosted lavish gatherings or gave grand public speeches, but I loved the citizens of Vitalia personally. I was proud to lead good-hearted, loyal people who gave me the respect even I did not think I deserved. Our kingdom was united, and I had always felt more like one of them than their crown princess. And I knew that I would gladly bear their pain upon myself if I could. I would share the grief of mothers who lost their sons or of children who lost their fathers, just as my father had grieved for my mother.

Nevertheless, guilt pierced my core at the thought of leaving the people of the northern provinces to fend for themselves against a foreign invader. And I still wrestled with allowing a corrupt empire to grow slowly more powerful. I heard a far-off alarm in the back of my mind, a troublesome feeling I could not shake. What if we were just foolishly waiting for the rise of a new power? What if, rather than wisely opting to protect our own people, we were simply turning our backs as they took everything we had built from right under our noses?

I sighed, too exhausted to come to any sensible

conclusion that night. I started to move away from the balcony's edge then paused at a rogue thought, peering out at the village once more. Everything in my view would someday be under my leadership. One day, I would be the sole ruler of Vitalia, with the lives of thousands in my hands. I had been dreaming of that day since I was young, striving constantly to establish my merit as a sovereign ruler. But was I ready? Although I was known for my confidence, there were times I feared I would never be the ruler my kingdom needed. That I would not be able to lead with the wisdom of my father or the grace of my mother. That I would never be enough.

As the last few flames were finally put out and the valley was left in an eerie darkness, I could not shake the feeling that my own strength would soon be put to the test.

Chapter 3

Eve

I peered out my window and grumbled at the lively bustle of people below. Throngs of castle attendants scurried along the cobblestone path encircling the palace. Each one weaved hurriedly through the masses, carefully evading any disastrous collision. Gardeners carried flower pots, blacksmiths held boxes of tools, chefs balanced plates piled high with pastries. All of them rushed about the castle grounds, completely oblivious to the radiance of the afternoon sky. The sun's rays covered every square inch of land with golden beams of light. I knew it was likely the last of these perfect summer days before the coming autumn, but I would not get to enjoy a single second of it. Instead, I was trapped in my room, observing the inviting glow from afar.

I tilted my head upward to gaze into the sun, squinting at its commanding glare. I sighed longingly. It was hovering directly over the north tower, signifying the start of the castle guards' daily sword training. All of Vitalia's best knights were meeting at the training fields to sharpen their combat skills. All except me.

Instead of a silver sword in my hands, I was gripping the arms of my vanity chair with all my might. My knuckles were white as I gritted my teeth in agony. Mary stood behind me forcing an ivory comb through my unruly hair, her own breaths ragged as she wrestled each stubborn snarl.

Through squinted eyes, I peeked at our reflection in the vanity mirror. We looked simply miserable. Every muscle in my body was stiffened, braced for the next excruciating tug. My face was contorted, my brow deeply furrowed, my forehead wrinkled, making me appear practically deformed.

Mary looked just as pitiful as I did. Her face was coated in a thick layer of sweat. Her bottom lip glowed bright pink from her harsh bite, and her arms shook with fatigue from the near impossible task of detangling my wild mane. She gripped the comb with both hands as she worked through one particularly willful knot, grunting with effort.

I was not sure what was worse: being denied the opportunity to shame Vitalia's finest warriors in combat training or suffering through the torment of Mary's hair styling.

After several agonizing yanks, the knot finally gave way. Mary dropped the comb to her side, giving her exhausted arms and my aching head a much needed rest. I loosened my death grip on the chair, finally able to breathe again. "Whoever invented that wretched comb better be rotting in their grave." I wiped the back of my hand across my forehead, unsurprised to feel my own layer of perspiration there.

Mary waited until she caught her breath before answering. "It was likely not intended for ungodly rats' nests like yours." She tossed the device onto the vanity table with a dramatic clatter. I chuckled. Any trace of yesterday's feigned formalities was now long gone.

"You can blame my family's long history of thick

waves for that," I said, "and this damned prince for his thoughtless intrusion on my day."

Mary did not respond, only sighed as she began separating my frizzy mess into sections. She winced as a few stubborn tangles persisted. I grunted aloud at the stinging pain that shot through my sore scalp then exhaled in relief as she exchanged her ceaseless tugging for gentle braiding. "Sometimes, I struggle to fathom why we entertain these helpless men." I tried to sit tall, but my thick shoulders weighed my chest down into a hunch-backed slump.

Mary looked up from the clumps of hair in her hands to meet my eyes in the mirror. "If you are so sure you will reject them, why even invite them into the castle?"

I rolled my eyes. "My father wants to ensure we remain on good terms with the other kingdoms. Better to keep old friends than to make new enemies." Truth be told, I was unsure whether any alliance was worth the painstaking process of preparing for their arrival.

Earlier that morning, a servant had rushed to my door and requested immediate entry, which I knew could only mean one thing. After waking me from my first late morning rest in weeks, the young messenger delivered the news that sent me into an instant rage: a prince was on his way to Vitalia to ask for my hand in marriage. The servant boy was lucky my wall of daggers was on the opposite side of the room. The only weapons I had at my disposal were the mounds of pillows upon my bed, which I proceeded to hurl at him indignantly.

Any plans I might have had for the day were to be abandoned immediately. There would be no time for reading, no visits to the village, and worst of all, no sword training. I would be forced to join the rest of the

47

castle in preparing for the prince's arrival.

Everyone, servants and nobles alike, was well-rehearsed in this ritual, having gone through the process countless times in the last ten years. The announcement of a coming prince would often come unexpectedly, sometimes with less than a day's notice. The entire castle would spiral into chaos, hastily making the appropriate preparations for the visiting nobleman and his court. Lavish decorations were set about the halls, sumptuous feasts were assembled at record speeds, and our finest silver was polished to a spotless sheen.

Frankly, I did not see what all the fuss was about. Rulers from all corners of the world had come to present their sons to me. They showered me with gifts and put on theatrical displays of adoration, all in the hopes that I accept their offer of marriage. That I join our two kingdoms under the guise of imperial unity. That I grant him the honor of becoming the next king of Vitalia, effectively making him the most powerful man this side of the Great Sea.

I denied every one of them.

As far as I knew, there was no prince who had not already made his desperate plea, falling to his knees before me and vowing his undying love. Large and small, young and old, he would come, seated upon an opulent throne carried on the shoulders of his servants. He would be adorned with a shining silk tunic, a long fur cape draped over his shoulders and dragging along the ground behind him, and a golden crown glistening with jewels. And, of course, a self-righteous smirk on his lips. He would saunter through the tall castle doors with his chin held so high I was surprised he did not trip over his own feet.

Despite the inconvenience, I always relished the moment when I would reject him. I could hardly conceal my own satisfied smile when I saw his baffled face. Some men would slump their shoulders in humiliation. Others would grow red with rage. But all would eventually veer away and storm out the same way they came in, their dismal procession in tow.

"Who is the helpless suitor this time?" Mary asked as she weaved my hair along the back of my head.

"Who knows?" I slumped over the side of my chair and rested my cheek on a closed fist. It had been years since a new prince had traveled to Vitalia to entice me into marriage. I was almost certain that every noble bachelor on the continent had already made his attempt. Now stubborn princes would return to our kingdom with renewed vigor, confident that a bigger, bolder display would spark a change of heart in me. In reality, as their attempts became more absurd, I grew to despise them even more.

As if reading my thoughts, Mary scoffed aloud and lifted her eyes from her detailed work. "You don't think it could be Prince Alcott *again*, do you?"

I let out an exaggerated groan and rolled my eyes. "Don't you mean Sir Smolder?" Mary choked on a laugh as I continued. "I pray to God we are withheld the blessing of yet another one of his toothy grins." She broke into a full-on howl then, barely keeping her hold on the thick strands of hair between her fingers as she doubled over in laughter.

She struggled to take in a breath before spitting out her own jab. "Not even all the silver on his crown could block out those blinding fangs." Now I was the one cackling, the laughter leaving my throat in short croaking gasps. Soon, we had worked ourselves into a frenzy, both of us roaring uncontrollably. Mary rolled on the floor, spittle flying from her mouth with each breathless chortle, and I gripped the vanity with all my might to keep from collapsing under the intensity of my blaring snorts.

Eventually, Mary picked herself up off the ground, and I settled back into my chair. I wiped the remnants of stray tears from my eyes as Mary stifled a few persistent giggles. "But seriously," she finally said, "assuming this is not Lord Horse Teeth, would you never even consider accepting a prince?"

My lips tightened into a line before I answered. "Under no circumstances will I agree to live under the control of a self-righteous nobleman, especially under the deceptive promise of marriage." A sly grin crept across my mouth. "Let's just say I am not particularly fond of *submission*."

Another wave of laughter sprung from Mary's lips, along with a knowing blush. As my best friend and closest confidant, she was the only woman in the castle who knew about my scandalous affairs. She was the only person in the world with whom I shared my private and, many would say, indecent desires, along with tales of the men I chose to endure them.

She continued her braiding absentmindedly for a moment before speaking again. "What about love?" she mumbled, almost to herself.

I snickered. "What about it?"

Mary swallowed, concentrating on the movements of her hands. "Have you ever considered marrying a prince because…you admire him?"

I laughed again, this time a deep, humorless chuckle.

"I am not interested in any heartfelt romance, if that is what you are saying."

She squinted her eyes and nodded, humming skeptically. "I think I could name *several* men who would say otherwise." Her hands paused as she locked eyes with my reflection. Her lips curved slightly. She thought she had me cornered.

I twisted in my chair to face her head-on. "There is a big difference between love and sex."

Mary rolled her eyes and twisted my head back around. "Sex is about holding power," I continued. "Love is about losing it. And that is a risk I would never take." I shifted my gaze to my wall of war trophies and felt a surge of ambition. "If someone like me were to fall in love, I would not only lose myself. I would lose everything I have ever worked to gain."

Recognizing my serious tone, Mary lowered hers to match. "I think you are forgetting the benefits of love." I pulled myself from my introspective trance and listened dubiously. She rested her elbows on the top of my chair as she stared into the mirror, her task forgotten.

"Sometimes, love is a sacrifice we make for something greater than ourselves. Something more freeing." She cocked her head, peering at me sideways. "Take your parents, for example."

I would be lying if I said I had not considered this myself. My father often told me of his undying love for my mother, how she had drastically changed him for the better. As a young prince, he had been a brutal tyrant. He was famous for his uncontrollable fury, getting into fights at every turn, taking out his anger on those he was supposed to protect.

But then he met my mother: the beautiful Princess

Genevieve of Vitalia. He said that just the sound of her voice could douse the roaring wildfire in his soul. That her words had the magnitude of an endless canyon that made every violent impulse within him drift away like dust. Not long after they married, his cruel temper was reformed into an intense passion for her, his sole desire to make her happy.

But that was just it. My mother could have had everything. She was an only child, next in line to wear the crown. Praised for both her elegance and determination, she was highly favored by her people. Her long list of accomplishments proved she was more than qualified to rule Vitalia single-handedly.

And yet, when my father came to beg for her hand, proclaiming his profound love and eternal devotion, she accepted. She forfeited her throne, gave up the crown she should have worn herself, and stepped aside as he took what was rightfully hers. She could have denied him, preserving the role she had toiled for her entire life, but instead she sacrificed it all for him.

And for what? Love?

When it came down to it, marriage was just another way to imprison women into a life of complacency and obedience. After you are tempted by lofty dreams of true love and eternal devotion, the excitement fades and the truth reveals itself: the life you strove to gain has been lost, never to be reclaimed.

That was why I preferred brief periods of passion over such foolish risks. Short but steamy affairs. These intense moments of lust, although fleeting, were by far the safer choice in my mind. No commitment, no danger, no loss.

Mary laid down my finished braids, intricately

twined in a violet ribbon. She then moved to the assortment of makeup scattered about the vanity, carefully considering her options before selecting a translucent powder and a feather applicator. "You are one to know about love," I said with a smirk, crossing my arms and eyeing her devilishly. She twitched, awkwardly toying with the bristles on the brush as her cheeks colored.

It was not often that Mary opened up about her own love life, but eventually, through my power of coercion, I would pry the details out of her. The two of us were starkly different: Mary, a young woman experiencing love for the first time, on the cusp of her sexual awakening; and me, older and experienced, consumed by an insatiable lust for all things physical.

But our dissimilarities made for fascinating conversation. I would listen in keen interest as Mary told me everything, describing sentimental experiences that I had never had, or wanted, but that bewitched me nonetheless. And although I was sure my lifestyle was far from appealing to her—sex with no strings attached, a dirty play of power and greed—she was undeniably captivated when I relayed my own vulgar stories.

Mary dipped the brush into the bowl of translucent powder and twisted it mindlessly as a helpless grin spread across her cheeks. "Arthur is different. What he and I have is…special."

For once, I did not argue with her. There was no denying the two had a unique bond. Mary and Arthur had met when they were children, young servants raised within the castle walls. Then just a laundry maid and a humble scullion, they slowly developed feelings for each other, feelings they tried to keep hidden. As they grew older, they began a secret relationship, one that only I knew about. Sworn to secrecy, I was granted each juicy detail of their young love affair, and I hungrily ate up every last drop.

Both had done well for themselves in their respective roles within the palace. They had each been promoted to some of the most prestigious positions in the castle. When Mary advanced to head lady's maid and Arthur started his training to become a knight in Vitalia's royal guard, they were left with little time for each other, forcing them to meet in secret late at night. Sometimes, she told me of their midnight encounters, of the short but passionate moments they shared when no one was watching.

Beside me, she stood beaming with blurred eyes, lost in thoughtful bliss. But despite the joy that enveloped her now, I could not help feeling like she was setting herself up for a painful end. The more her smile grew when she talked about Arthur, the louder the alarm bells sounded in my head. She was giving herself away to a boy I knew she loved, whether she had admitted it to herself or not, and it was just a matter of time before it all came crashing down, as love always does. She would become yet another lost casualty in the inevitable destruction.

As Mary absent-mindedly applied powder to my cheeks, I gently expressed my concern. "Just promise me you won't get too attached. I do not want to see you get hurt."

The brush tickled my nose as it twirled across my skin. She nodded but showed no sign of grasping my warning. I bit the inside of my cheek nervously. My fears had been confirmed: she was lost in the well of her own heart, far too deep to pull herself out.

A sharp knock on the door interrupted my thoughts. Mary jumped at the sound, almost dropping the brush as it fumbled between her fingers. I sat upright before I spoke. "Enter!"

A tall, thin lady's maid timidly opened the door. She peeked her head inside before hesitantly stepping into the room. She cleared her throat. "The prince's procession will be arriving shortly," she muttered feebly. "You are—"

"I know," I interrupted with an annoyed eye roll. "I am expected in the throne room forthwith." The girl blushed at my annoyed outburst, and guilt pinched my stomach. "Thank you, Gwendolyn. We will be out shortly," I said in the most cordial tone I could muster. She nodded with a curtsy and scurried from the room.

Mary swiftly applied the last of my makeup, dying my lips a deep maroon with just a few nimble flicks of her wrist. She then snatched a pair of silk gloves from a nearby stool and slid them delicately over my hands. The smooth fabric was of the finest quality, feeling like ocean waves rolling down my forearms.

Finally, she knelt to the ground to place my best pair of silver slippers onto my feet, expertly fitting each one over my heels. They were no comparison to my leather riding boots, but they were comfortable enough.

After each shoe was fastened into place, she stood to her feet, and I rose beside her. I caught a glimpse of myself in the vanity mirror and paused, transfixed by my own reflection. Mary noticed my observation and pulled my chair aside. I stepped back to inspect my entire frame. As always, she had done an exceptional job. My hair was elaborately braided, crisscrossing along my head with each piece meeting in the middle, the ends tied in a tight knot. Any mark or blemish on my face was hidden beneath the layer of powder clinging to my cheeks, and my eyes were sharpened by a dark outline. I looked like a different person, indistinguishable from a finely crafted wax doll—if you liked that sort of thing.

As I rolled my eyes down to my dress, I scrunched my nose in disgust. It was one of my most lavish gowns, gifted as a peace offering by a neighboring province a few years prior. I would have preferred a flax sack with arm holes. Even that would have been more comfortable than this contraption. What I wore now was a man-made torture device, a cruel method of torment specially devised for women of royalty.

I shifted side to side, fidgeting uncomfortably as I tried to release the dress's tight grip around my chest. I sighed as I relinquished my efforts, concluding that the harsh fabric was not designed to be worn by a human being. The corset was as hard as stone, unnaturally shaped to feature a pair of oversized breasts, ones I did not possess. It successfully removed four inches from my waist, squeezing my stomach to appear unnaturally slender and covering my upper body with a sheet of gaudy gems. Stitched to the arm and neck holes were strips of a rough mesh-like fabric. Each time I shifted my shoulders, the material scratched against my skin, and I clawed at my neck in response.

My skirts contained so many layers that it was impossible to make out my figure within. Instead, the piles of fabric made my hips appear unnaturally wide, framing my body in an awkward pear shape. The hem of the dress dragged along the ground, my long train requiring several attendants to carry.

It was garish, absurd. But at least it was purple.

Mary fiddled with the lavender ruffles around my waist, attempting to smooth the rebellious layers that stuck out. I watched her through the mirror as she made small adjustments to the sleeves and pinned down loose strands of hair. She finally caught me staring and halted her trifling to smile back at me. "You look beautiful, Evangeline."

I sighed softly as I returned my gaze to my pale face, no smile forming in return. "I suppose so." The woman in the mirror looked so sophisticated, so pristine, but I knew it was a false façade. Even if the prince liked what he saw, it would not have been me that he was attracted to. The real me was buried deep beneath the clothes and cosmetics, beneath this carefully crafted exterior.

I inhaled as I took one final look at myself. Then, I firmly pulled my eyes away and turned toward the door. "We had better get going." I grabbed two handfuls of my skirts and lifted them as high as I could before stepping away from the vanity. But the bulky material was too much for me to carry, and I immediately tripped on my skirt, barely catching myself in time to avoid tumbling to the floor.

Mary's eyes widened in terror as she rushed to my side. "Please, let me," she insisted. I dropped the dress reluctantly while she delicately gathered my train, careful not to form any wrinkles. The path before me now cleared, I cautiously stepped forward, moving one foot at a time until we reached the bedroom door.

A jumble of voices emanated from the hall, but when I stepped out, each one fell silent. Clusters of maids turned from their conversations and stared at me open mouthed. It was not often they saw me adorned in the attire of a traditional princess. From their astonished expressions, I guessed that I was hardly recognizable to them in this rare form. Their shock was undeniable, their gaze scrutinizing. I did not take it as a compliment.

That familiar fire began to burn in me. I lowered my arms to my sides with clenched fists. "Are we just going to stand here or are we going to meet this damned prince?" A few girls balked at the harshness of my tone, and all instantly dropped their eyes to the floor in deference. Unappeased, I stormed forward without warning. The group quickly parted. Some had to leap backward to avoid colliding with me as I raged onward. Mary sprinted around them to catch up to me, nearly tripping over her own feet as she tried to regather my fallen skirts. Behind me, the ladies hastily arranged themselves into the proper formation and scurried along as we proceeded to the throne room.

The mountains of fabric flapped against my shins with every step as I marched purposefully toward the front of the castle. Passing attendants still bustled through the halls as they made their final preparations but stopped in their tracks when they spotted me strutting before my entourage. Their tasks momentarily forgotten, they gaped at me with that same stunned expression. I lifted my head higher.

"Evangeline," Mary whispered over the parade of tapping footsteps. I shifted my head sideways to hear her better.

"What is it?" I whispered back.

"I think you should consider this one." I was halfway through another agitated eye roll before she hissed, "I am serious!"

"And why would I do that?" I could barely suppress

my irritation.

"People are more than they seem from the outside. We can only truly know who they are if we let them show us." We made our final turn toward the great hall, the tall wooden doors coming into sight. Mary spoke even softer now, leaning forward to whisper into my ear. "Just think about it."

We finally arrived at the head of the castle. I halted as a set of guards heaved open the mahogany doors towering over us, sending a rush of wind over me. The flowing air blew loose curls from my face and made my skirts float around me. A soft chill rolled down my spine.

As the path before me cleared and the throne room became visible, I chuckled silently, my lips curved in a wicked smile. I mumbled under my breath so only I could hear. "Not a chance."

Chapter 4

Eve

"Presenting Her Royal Highness, Princess Evangeline of Vitalia."

My name rang out across the throne room. The great hall was so large that the announcer's voice bounced from the front wall and back again in an ominous echo. Heads all throughout the room turned in my direction, and as I entered, the mass of spectators dropped to their knees, bowing to the floor in unison.

Despite the triviality of the occasion, I felt a spark of pride. The full attendance of Vitalia's royal court was typically paired with obnoxious frivolities, fake courtesies, and whispered judgments, their disapproving stares poorly concealed. Now as they knelt before me, I knew their deference was purely customary, an artificial display of respect. But for just a moment, I welcomed the satisfaction that swept over me.

Still scanning the room, I stepped forward. My dress suddenly felt lighter, like a bubble floating me into the great hall. I walked slowly, placing each foot carefully, knowing my every movement was being closely observed by the surrounding crowd. The click of my shoes against the floor was the only sound to cut through the silence.

I finally stole my gaze from the mass of people and

turned my head toward the pair of thrones. The chairs were massive, lavishly adorned with crimson velvet and lined with a gold trim interlaced in geometric designs. The arms were made of varnished wood, intricately carved to depict the royal family seal. Every inch was painted in gold.

I took my time strolling toward the empty throne, slightly smaller than the one beside it. Standing before them, tall and regal, was my father. He was dressed in his most stately attire including his signature violet cape and a sizable crown littered with jewels of every color. Although I did not think it possible, somehow the splendor made him appear even more imposing.

As I stepped closer, I noticed a collection of wrinkles across his forehead and at the corners of his eyes. They were deep creases, formed by the inevitable passage of time. I had never noticed them before, but perhaps I had simply not been looking, unwilling to accept that my father was anything but immortal.

Beneath his fixed gaze, a flush of heat filled my cheeks. Unlike the others, his stare was not aimed at my elegant gown or styled hair but directly into my eyes. The left side of his mouth curved into a knowing smile.

With just that look, I knew I had been caught. Only he could sense my pride at seeing the whole of my kingdom bow down before me. My features were firm. Not even a twitch of my lips could reveal what I was thinking, but my eyes betrayed my pride and my father read right through them. I approached my throne with my face turned, but his stare remained unmoved. His rooted glare held mine so steadily, I had to drop my eyes to the floor, watching my final steps along with the crowd.

I hardened my demeanor as I took my place beside

him, donning the same expression I wore leading men into battle. But I could still feel my father's gaze burning into the side of my face, his glib smile unwavering.

"I am not an apparition. You need not stare at me as though I may disappear." My words were as cold as my features, holding an icy glare at the rows of lowered heads across from me.

"You are allowed to enjoy it, you know," he said with a chuckle. "You are a princess after all." I clenched my jaw, compelling my cheeks to return to their natural temperature. "We both know you deserve their respect more than anyone."

A weight I did not know I was carrying lifted from my shoulders. He was right, of course. The noble men and women may have been bowing to me now out of custom, but I knew their reverence was well-earned. With each battle won and every new enemy defeated, I had secured their right to live freely in my kingdom. They owed me much more than they were willing to admit. Steadily, that same pleased smirk that my father wore became my own.

Without a word, the king and I took our seats, signaling that the rest of the room stand back to their feet. Excited murmurs resumed as the court and attending villagers waited anxiously for the prince's arrival. I knew they were predicting the identity of the unnamed nobleman as Mary and I had done just minutes before.

"Any report as to who this mysterious suitor is?" I spoke softly but knew we were seated too far from any spectators to be overheard. I maintained my formal tone but found it impossible to disguise my sarcasm.

"None at all," the king responded. Even his hushed voice reminded me of thunder. I tilted my head toward him. His throne greatly outsized my own, the wooden armrests at least two feet longer and the back towering well above my head. Yet somehow, he made the chair look small, filling the spacious seat with his expansive figure.

I, on the other hand, was utterly consumed by my throne. Although several sizes smaller, the cushions on my seat practically consumed me. My hands only reached halfway across the golden arm rests. My thick legs sunk into the padding, and my feet hovered awkwardly over the ground.

I groaned aloud, my patience already wearing thin. "Are we simply to wait in expectation for this *charming cavalier* to arrive?" Dropping my head into my hand, I hunched my shoulders forward. I had been sitting here for mere minutes, and already I had abandoned my proper posture, returning to my natural state.

The king sighed. "We must respect their visits, Evie." He turned to speak in my direction. "You know I would never force you to marry. But our top priority is and always will be to keep the peace between our nations. And if that means letting every prince in the realm make his case for your hand, then so be it."

Even though I was no less than twenty-four years old, I grumbled loudly and rolled my eyes like a dramatic teenager. "I might agree with you if this was their first visit, but most of these princes have proposed to me several times already." I shook my head, exasperated. "How many times must I deny them before they accept my refusal? Don't you think this is becoming somewhat ridiculous?"

This time, my father's sigh sounded like mine, and he sank back into his throne with the same irritated slump. "I agree with you. You would think ten years of rejections would be enough to deter their efforts, but they only seem to be pushing harder. Nonetheless," he said, his resolve slightly weakened, "we must maintain harmony amongst our kingdoms, especially with the troubling invasions in the North."

I opened my mouth to protest but quickly bit my tongue. I had not considered how welcoming neighboring princes could help affirm our alliances in a time of political turbulence. I knew firsthand that having these men on our side during a war was critical. But that did not mean I had to enjoy their absurd presentations. I would not pretend to be impressed or moved by their feigned adoration. They could say their piece and be on their way, and no matter how striking their display, I would not smile or laugh or show any reaction for that matter. I refused to give them any reason to return.

Suddenly, the unmistakable blare of trumpets blasted through the castle walls. A hush passed over the crowd as they eagerly prepared for the grandiose procession of this nameless prince. The music gradually swelled, the melody now integrated with bagpipes and drums. The song overtook the great hall, its rhythm surging through me in time with the quickening beat of my heart. I held my breath as the volume reached its apex, the instruments quickly closing in. I lifted my chin high, fixing my features into a callous scowl.

As the tall doors swung open, the palace exposed to the world beyond, the music burst into the room with an abrupt explosion of sound, so loud that anyone unprepared for the blast would surely jump. Fortunately, I was ready.

The drum line entered first. A row of uniformed men

beat their massive snare drums in unison as they paraded into the castle. Behind them were the trumpeters, holding their instruments upward so their timbres echoed through the room. Following were several rows of armored men who marched in perfect synchrony to the beat of the drums.

A covered processional litter finally came into view. The cart was draped in maroon velvet, the sides more thinly woven to reveal the silhouette of a passenger within. The corners of the litter balanced upon the shoulders of four ironclad men. I squinted as the distant cart neared, looking for any clue as to the identity of its rider. Sparkling gems shrouded the thick curtain that hid the traveler, and the roof of the vehicle touted a flaring silver statue.

To my surprise, a second, albeit much smaller, litter then came into view. This one was topped with a dark green curtain but lacked the myriad jewels that brandished the first. The crowd exchanged puzzled glances, caught off guard by this breach of custom. Like the former, this cart hid its passenger within its dull walls. The spectators waited restlessly for the mysterious foreigners to reveal themselves.

After what seemed like an eternity, the drummers finally reached the far end of the hall. Standing before our thrones, they halted, pounding a few more beats before snapping their drumsticks to their sides in one stiff motion. The procession suddenly split apart. The musicians and guards moved aside to make room for the first litter. Each man stood at attention as the lavish vehicle advanced, halting only a few feet before us. The men carrying the cart carefully lowered it to the floor then reached forward to cast the curtain aside.

Astonished whispers were exchanged throughout the room. I stared in wonder at the character before me, not a prince but a woman. She rose from her seated position and glided gingerly down a small set of steps leading to the floor. The whole of the castle held its breath as she slowly came into view.

What struck me first was her size. This woman was no less than six feet tall, rivaling the height of the steel-plated men surrounding her. She was wrapped in a thick fur cloak that made her chest and shoulders bulk outward. But after a few graceful steps forward, she paused, raising her arms outward like a porcelain swan.

A trailing guard stripped the cloak from her shoulders to reveal a slick black gown. Sparkling gems covered her bust and speckled the lining of her skirt. Her raven-colored dress was a stark contrast to the snowy hue of her skin, glowing brightly beneath the afternoon light streaming through the windows. Atop her head sat a silver crown encrusted with broad columns of glistening jewels. The headdress played as an optical illusion, its hue blending seamlessly with the long gray hair that sprawled down her back. Although there were a few visible wrinkles on her face and neck, her ashen locks acted not as a symbol of lost youth. Instead, each strand flowed from her head in a silvery shimmer, encircling her in a commanding aura.

Without the cloak around her arms, the woman was pure bone. Her translucent skin displayed each joint within, and her face was practically gaunt. Her cheeks sunk into her skull, harshly defining each feature. Her long nose carved her face with perfect symmetry; her thin lips squeezed together in a rigid line. And her dark eyes were all-consuming, staunchly fixed on the set of thrones before her like a lioness eyeing her prey.

She floated slowly forward, hovering delicately over the floor like a ghost. If not for the swarm of awestruck eyes set upon her, I would have wondered if she was, in fact, a specter. She was a flash of light and dark. The contrasting colors along her figure shined alternately as she ambled her way in and out of the intermittent rays of sunlight. She was an enchantress, dazzling and unsettling me equally.

A hurried shuffle from the back of the procession finally broke me from her spell. The second traveler had emerged from the smaller litter and was hastily scurrying forward. From the shape of his body, I deduced that this was no woman. But upon viewing his thin limbs and frail figure, I doubted that this was the strapping prince who had come to woo me into marriage. Once he arrived at the woman's side, he kept his chin lowered. His long, sandy hair shadowed his face, his features yet to be seen.

He was taller than I first perceived. Even in his slouched stance, he stood a few inches over the adjacent woman's staggering height. He wore a dark blue tunic, markedly oversized. It practically swallowed his slim chest and slender arms. He bore no fur cloak over his shoulders, his skin the color of parchment. His breeches barely spanned the length of his long legs. The pants strained to reach his ankles, peeking out above his scuffed boots. It was by far the most modest princely attire I had ever seen. The man's face remained hidden behind a row of perfect ringlets that hung over his forehead, his gaze glued to the floor.

The sight of the clashing pair was transfixing. So odd was the duo that I became lost in my study of them. Who were these curious characters, their dynamic so bizarre it hypnotized the entire hall?

Seeming not to notice our puzzlement, the woman smiled. Her thin lips curled up into an eerie grin, straining the tight skin of her cheeks to reveal a wide set of teeth.

A heavy weight formed in my stomach. I heard a soft voice in my mind, an inner alarm growing slowly more urgent.

"King Ricard." The woman's voice was much deeper than I expected, raspy. "It is an honor to make your acquaintance." Her words scraped harshly from her thin throat, wedging through her stiff smile.

An awkward pause ensued. I could sense the growing unease in the room. It was customary for any foreigner, royalty or not, to bow before the ruler of the kingdom in which they were visiting, but this woman remained motionless, standing at her full height without moving an inch. Her gaze was immovable, deadlocked on the king.

My father showed no acknowledgment of the insult and greeted them with his warm demeanor. "Welcome to Vitalia!" he declared amicably. "Princess Evangeline and I are pleased to host you. Both of you." He hesitated before adding this last part, clearly intending to instigate some kind of response from the man beside her. But he remained stock-still, showing no indication of returning my father's greeting.

The king chuckled lightly under his breath, attempting unsuccessfully to ease the tension in the room. "Do forgive me, but I do not believe we have met."

"Of course!" Half of the crowd jolted in surprise, caught off guard by the woman's shrill response. "How rude of me! Let me introduce myself. I am Ingrid, Queen of Kreagan." The statuesque illusion was finally broken when she took her skirts in one hand and lightly poised the other behind her back, sinking her chest to the ground in a low curtsy. Despite the gesture, the tense atmosphere remained. Her slow, exaggerated bow included all but her head which she kept stiffly upright. With every movement, she never took her eyes off the king.

Rising back to her full height after this dramatic display, she held her chin a few inches higher. "And this is my son, Prince Rune." The man in question kept his hands clasped tightly behind his back, and even at the mention of his name, the tip of his chin remained fixed to his chest in a perpetual bow. Not until the queen administered a firm shove to his side did the prince dare to lift his head. He was knocked off balance for a moment but then hastily snapped back to attention, instantly straightening his spine to stand erect.

I stifled a gasp. At his full height, the prince was a narrow spire, a towering pillar. But my surprise was not due to his lanky stature but rather my first glimpse of his face. His skin was impossibly smooth. If he had any marks or blemishes, they were imperceptible. His eyes were the color of the noon sky, glowing like the ripples of a softly flowing stream. The azure orbs overtook the fullness of his face, dwarfing his nose and mouth. His hair was a mudslide, rolling from his head in thick ringlets and falling along his shoulders like an avalanche. Hints of matching blond were scattered around his chin and upper lip, signs of new growth.

He was young. Very young. He could not have been more than eighteen years old. This was no man. This prince was just a boy.

He cleared his throat, a sound nearly devoured by

the spacious hall. "It is a pleasure to meet you, King Ricard. Princess Evangeline." He turned to look at me then, and our eyes locked for a moment. For an eternity. I felt like I was drowning in those aquamarine pools, lost in their cool depths. But within seconds, I reset my stern demeanor, and he dropped his head back to the floor, this time his cheeks flushed pink.

The queen coughed uncomfortably before replacing her toothy grin. "Prince Rune is here to ask for your daughter's hand in marriage." My jaw tightened out of instinct. The queen addressed my father alone, without even a glance in my direction. She spoke as if I had no say in the matter, as if I was incapable of making my own decision.

In fact, she had not shifted her eyes from the king since their arrival. She acted as if I were invisible. Just an object. A measly obstacle to her son's throne. I ground my teeth in an attempt to subdue my anger.

The king and I stared at the prince. As we waited for him to make his offer, the queen eyed us expectantly. But the boy remained silent. A few confused murmurs trickled through the crowd. I peered over to see perturbed nobles whispering behind open palms, veiled ladies fanning themselves uncomfortably. My eyebrows furrowed, my patience waning. The sooner this sorry prince made his case, the sooner I could refuse him. And the sooner I refused him, the sooner I could relish in his disappointment.

I turned towards my father, wearing the same puzzled expression as the rest of the observers. "Well," he said, finally breaking the painful silence, "go on then." He eyed the prince darkly, his own annoyance becoming evident.

This time, the queen failed to hide her scowl. With one quick stride, she jammed her heel into the prince's foot. He jolted upright upon impact, his face turning deathly pale. I tried to read his secretive eyes. What I saw was not the anxious face of a man about to put his pride on the line. What I saw was fear. Pure, unmistakable fear. And somehow I knew that it was not I who was the source of his despair.

Sinking his head once more, he scrambled forward until he stood just a few steps in front of me. His long body curved forward like a fishhook. His fingers intertwined behind his back, fidgeting restlessly. He hesitated as he considered his next move, finally deciding to drop one knee to the ground. Behind him, the queen tapped her foot irritably.

"Princess Evangeline," the prince started. A slight crack in his voice betrayed his unease, and he promptly cleared his throat before starting again, his tone a bit deeper. "I have heard of your beauty from across the seas, but now that I stand before you, I can see your splendor surpasses any description." He spoke in a low monotone, reciting what was clearly a rehearsed speech while staring awkwardly at his own feet. "It would be a great honor if you would grant me the privilege of being your husband to unite our kingdoms and rule together in holy matrimony."

It was the most pitiful proposal I had ever heard. There was not a single strain of genuine affection in his voice. Not a trace of sentiment. He offered me no gifts or empty promises. But one thing was undeniable: like all the others, this prince was lying through his teeth.

His deplorable offer hung weakly in the air as all eyes turned to me, cringing as they prepared for the inevitable. I bit my tongue in a desperate attempt to keep my poise, but the urge was too strong. A torrent of laughter leapt from my throat, flying freely through my lips.

Was this a joke? This prince could not possibly believe I would accept him after that pathetic display. I had seen men ride into my castle upon pristine white stallions, their servants forming astonishing acts like fire breathing and sword swallowing. Men who had offered me troves of jewels and rings of pure gold. And this boy thought a sad bow and a few hollow words could convince me?

I did not even need to turn my head to sense my father's furious glare. I could feel his wrath piercing my skin like a bayonet. I gritted my teeth to stifle what remained of my laughter, but my cruel smile remained. Leaning forward in my chair, I stared straight into the prince's glossy eyes. "No." My declaration was clear, unquestionable, well-practiced after many years of denials.

The hall of onlookers stewed in an awkward silence, one they had become accustomed to over the last decade. I leaned back in my throne and folded my arms smugly over my chest. The entirety of the prince's face had turned a ghostly white, and the queen's fixed jaw revealed her displeasure. "Princess Evangeline," she said. My stomach clenched at the way she addressed me, uttering my name like it left a bad taste in her mouth. "I beg you to reconsider."

I scoffed. "My decision is final, Queen Ingrid." I spat her own name in the same tone she had pronounced mine, and a thrill ran down my spine at her insulted grimace. "I am afraid your son is unqualified to rule

Vitalia and entirely unfit to be my husband." I turned my gaze toward the prince to watch as my biting words made impact. But rather than a wince of pain or a swell of anger, there was a desperation in his eyes, an urgent pleading that replaced my satisfaction with unease.

Without warning, the queen dropped her amiable façade. Any fragment of her cordial persona disappeared in a flash, traded for a dark glare and a malicious smile. My stomach twisted. I knew that smile. It was one I had worn myself many times. The haunting grin of a villainous secret. I tightened my grip on the arms of my chair.

"Fine," she hissed. "Have it your way." She lifted her arm slowly. Her hand hanging perilously in the air, she snapped her fingers. At the sound, my world was turned to slow motion. Time stopped. My heart paused its beating, and my body became paralyzed.

Before anyone could register what was happening, a Kreagan guard darted from his place from within the mass of knights, racing to the queen's side. In one swift motion, he withdrew a wooden longbow and pulled a single arrow from the quiver along his hip. He nimbly drew his weapon and pulled his elbow backward at the ready.

The arrow left his fingers as quickly as it was set. I watched helplessly as it hovered in the air between us, time and gravity seemingly forgotten. It hung like a question, a daunting challenge, asking me if I was prepared for my fate. But before I could form an answer, my destiny was fixed into place.

The arrow found its mark at the center of my father's chest. I did not hear the spear pierce its target. I did not hear the iron tip sink into his flesh, spewing a shower of blood over his velvet tunic. Instead, a piercing scream filled my ears. A shrill cry of horror, its source unknown.

Suddenly, I was on my feet, racing like a falcon to the king as he hunched forward and collapsed to the ground. I threw myself to my knees before him and unfurled his crumpled body. I now recognized the screams as my own, wracking through my chest in painful surges. I rolled my father onto his back and gasped. A dark, wet stain was quickly forming along his front, instantly staining my hands red. He was losing blood fast, his gaping wound forming a thick puddle on the floor. My desperation spread to my trembling hands. I rested his head on my shoulder and peered down into his pale face.

At last, I discerned the words that were shooting from my mouth, an endless string of agonizing shrieks: no, no, no, no, *NO*.

My father choked out a few weak coughs. I stifled my cries when I saw his lips moving and lowered my ear toward his mouth. His voice had turned to a gravelly whisper, barely audible over the chaos that ensued around us. Or perhaps it was merely muffled by the blaring pound of my heart in my ears.

"Evie," he croaked. Everything within me broke at the feeble way he uttered my name. My wells of tears finally overflowed, leaving a damp trail along my cheeks. "Evie," he said again, more forcefully this time.

I lifted his head closer to my face so he could meet my eyes. "Yes, Father?"

Raising a quivering arm, he grasped the top of my head and pulled me closer still. When his lips grazed the edge of my ear, he mumbled, "Remember your people."

I squeezed my eyes shut, cutting off my stream of

tears. *No*, I thought, shaking my head mutely. *This cannot be the end.*

A surge of panic drove me into action. Through my blurred vision, I tried to stop the bleeding. With one quick yank, I removed the arrow from his body, wincing as he recoiled. I hastily tore off strips of fabric from my skirts, tossing them on a patch of dry ground beside me until they formed a thick pile. I took the stack of lacy material and tied each piece around my father's chest. His blood soaked through the cloth before I could even fasten the knot, dying the lavender a dark scarlet.

Flailing his weak arms, he tried to stop my frantic cycle of ripping and tying, tearing my dress to shreds, each strand becoming drenched with blood. My father finally caught my wrists at the peak of my frenzy. When my eyes were again locked to his, he repeated his words. "Remember your people."

There was no need for him to explain. I knew exactly whom he spoke of: the citizens of Vitalia. The men and women we cherished. Those we were born to lead and protect. "They are in your hands now," he continued. "You must put them first. Lead them with strength, like only you can."

I bit my lip as another flood of tears rushed down my face. I could not bear to hear him speak this way, like he would not be there when I rose to the throne. Like he would not be the one to place his own crown upon my head. Like he would not be there standing proudly by my side when I became Vitalia's first queen regnant, ruling my kingdom in my own right. He was all I had, and I refused to accept a world without him in it.

"Please, Father." My speech was cut off by the sobs clogging my throat, making my words almost imperceptible. "Please don't go."

He rolled his hand from behind my head down to my cheek. I felt its warmth slowly fading. He gently caressed my face with his palm. I wrapped both of my hands around his wrist to feel what was left of his faint pulse. "You are ready, Evie." From the pained look on his face, I knew he was using every last ounce of energy he had to speak.

My tears flowed freely now, landing on his ashen face then rolling down his cheeks as if they were his own. But he kept his eyes fixed on mine, using all of his strength to keep them from closing. They gleamed with undying compassion but also something deeper, something urgent. A commanding fervency. A call to power.

And within a moment, it was gone. The tenderness. The ardor. All that was left drained from his face, leaving his body limp and lifeless in my arms.

My hands started to shake uncontrollably. My vision faded beneath a dark fog. I forgot how to breathe. A wave of anguish rippled through my body, debilitating. It felt like my entire being was about to burst, like my limbs were ripping at the seams. I squeezed my eyelids tightly, tensing every muscle in my body. But there was nothing I could do to stop the pain from overtaking me.

Finally, I took a deep breath and let it blow. From the depths of my soul, I released a screeching howl. The ground shook with my deafening roar. Spit flew from my open mouth and landed on my father's stiff corpse, mixing with the blood still seeping from his wound. I buried my face in his open chest, desperate for the steadiness of his beating heart. But all that was left was a cold, wet stillness, lacking the comfort it once gave.

When my lungs ran out of air, the rest of the room suddenly came back into view. The entire hall had erupted into madness. Noblemen ran panicked toward the front entrance before being tackled to the ground by Kreagan guards. The cries of women rang out as scrambling aristocrats were beaten senseless before their eyes. The shrill clatter of shattering glass blended with their screams. It was a scene of total anarchy.

I remained fixed to my place on the floor, incapable of leaving my father behind. I could only sit and watch as the foreign guards turned what was once our pristine throne room into lawless disarray. My body felt numb, powerless against the weight of my grief, the born fighter within me stunted.

A burst of movement flashed beside me, and I was pulled from my oblivion at last. Three Kreagan guards were sprinting toward me. My eyes dashed to the swords that clanked in their sheaths with each approaching stride.

I tried to stand, to ready myself for their attack, but I was trapped beneath my father's limp body. I swiftly slid my legs out from under him, on my feet within seconds but not quickly enough. Before I knew it, the soldiers were on top of me. I cried out as two guards grabbed my hands and whipped them behind my back. The other reached for my feet and started dragging me toward the exit. I jolted with all my might to escape their grasp. Twisting my wrists from their fingers, I expertly maneuvered out of their trap.

I hurtled back towards my father and thrust my body back toward the floor, refusing to abandon him there. But the third guard, predicting my retreat, snatched me from behind. I frantically tried to wriggle away from his hold, but once the others had regained their clasp on my arms, my efforts were fruitless.

As they began dragging me away once more, I shouted every curse I could muster. But their grip became too tight for me to evade, and when the fallen king grew distant, my rage turned to desperation. I squirmed violently as I called his name, shouting over the groans of the guards as they struggled to contain me. When we reached the far end of the hall, I strained my neck to get one final glimpse of my father before he was taken from me forever. But instead, something else caught my eye.

Still standing in the center of the hall was Queen Ingrid. She had not moved since ordering the fatal shot. And unlike before, she was now watching me straight on, wearing that same sinister smile as I was dragged out of sight.

Chapter 5

Eve

The dark cell was much colder than I expected. The stone floor was like ice against my skin. I curled my body into a tight ball and tried to suppress the next wave of shivers that tore through me.

With each subtle movement, pain shot through my limbs, making me wince. Scattered around my arms and legs were bruises made by the harsh grip of the Kreagan guards as I was dragged down to the castle's base floor. A deep aching swept through my veins like a flood, bringing with it memories of yesterday's horrific events: rough hands wrapped around my wrists and shoulders, armored guards tugging me backward as my father's body was stripped from view. The only thing left of him was his name on my lips, bellowed toward heaven.

It was one thing to be ambushed by a foreign power; it was another to be locked away in your own dungeon. I had no idea how long I had been down here, how long ago the faceless men had tossed me to the ground and bolted me within these metal bars, ignoring my screaming curses until they were out of sight. I had tried to keep track of the time, but eventually fatigue won out. Now I did not know if I had been trapped there for hours or days, unsure if I would ever be released.

And yet, I lay awake. Any trace of sleep was

instantly abolished by fresh waves of anxiety. The massive dungeon was like a vacuum: the sounds from the floors above were muffled by the thick walls lining the dark hall. Meanwhile, my mind raced with questions for which I had no answer. What was happening up there? What would I find when—or if—I was finally freed? Who would remain? Would there be anything left of Vitalia?

A surge of guilt pierced my stomach. My father, along with countless other knights and nobles, was dead, killed just a few feet above where I now sat captive. Instead of fighting honorably by their side, I was trapped here, barred from joining in their final battle. As they bravely defended my kingdom until their dying breath, I was forced to sit in wait, safe from their suffering, prevented from sharing in their hardship. They would go down with pride—sword in hand, the king's name on their lips—while I remained here, awaiting my own hero to free me from my cell. I groaned. *How stereotypical.*

I could not help feeling like this was somehow my fault. Was it my stubborn arrogance that put my people in this situation? Was this why I was constantly pressured to accept a prince's offer of marriage? Because they knew one day a man would come along who would not take no for an answer? That my rejections would lead to our inevitable doom?

But as I reflected further on the situation, I realized that accepting the Kreagan prince would have made no difference. It had all been a trap: the impromptu arrival, the unimpressive display, the bizarre presentation. The Kreagan army must have surrounded the castle during the procession, secretly taking out our guards until there was no one left to block their attack. The graceless proposal was just a diversion to leave our kingdom powerless when they made their move.

Nevertheless, I could not conceive how it was possible. How could an unknown empire bring the realm's most powerful kingdom to its knees with a single arrow? How could everything we had ever built come crashing to the ground with just the snap of a white-haired woman's fingers?

And what did any of this have to do with me? Why had I been singled out, removed from the scene instead of being slain with the rest of them? Clearly, any hope I had of one day ruling Vitalia was long gone, evaporating into thin air. But why not kill me with the others? What could they possibly want from me that they did not already have? I had no clue what they were planning, but I sure as hell would not go down without a fight. They could try to bend me to their will, but I would choose death over submission. I would resist their demands until they had no choice but to kill me too. At least then I would not have to live under the hand of that conniving witch. Anything was better than being a slave in my own kingdom.

Interrupting my thoughts was a rumbling clatter. I jolted upright, listening more closely. Slowly approaching was the unmistakable sound of metal against stone. Footsteps. I shuffled from the corner of my cell to peer through the bars, twisting my neck to catch a glimpse of the approaching visitors. Marching down the stairwell came a group of Kreagan guards. Their armor clanged between their legs in time with each other. When they reached the ground floor, the men organized themselves into two lines and strode forward in unison. The crash of their boots upon the ground grew louder as they neared, their steps an ominous drumbeat that sent tremors through my chest. They were coming for me.

Despite my aching legs, I shot to my feet, struggling to steady my wobbly knees. I willed any fear to the back of my mind. Crossing my arms firmly across my front, I donned the most menacing scowl I could muster.

The parade halted just outside the thick metal door, standing at attention. Before they had a chance to address me, I spoke out in a commanding tone. I refused to let them have the first word. "Release me from this cell at once!" I demanded. My imposing voice reverberated through the dungeon, surprising even myself with its severity.

But the guards did not acknowledge my outburst. They were unmoved, unfazed. I recognized a few of the men who had pried me from the throne room. One of them sported a black eye. Another nursed a misshapen nose, dried blood caked to his nostrils. Both of these, I knew, were my doing. I smiled at my fine work.

To my surprise, the closest guard, rather than refusing my order, pulled out a ring of keys from his hip and approached the cell. Frozen in place, I remained skeptical as he unlocked the door and swung open the iron gate. There was no way I would be discharged that easily.

At my stillness, the acting guard spoke. "The queen has requested your presence in her throne room." An icy shiver rolled down my spine. I was not sure if it was the man's dark tone or his reference to *her* throne room—like it had not been mine just a few hours before—but I had to swallow hard to settle the panic that crept up my throat.

It was all moving too fast. Yesterday, I was one of

the most powerful women in existence. Now I was a captive in the place I called home, forced to consent to the authority of a kingdom I did not know.

I bit my lip as I considered my options. In no circumstance would I obey the orders of that cruel monster, but my band of chaperons had doubled in size, likely due to their great difficulty in detaining me the first time. To challenge a group of six trained men while unarmed would be unwise, even for me. Instead, I stepped cautiously out of the cell, saving my resistance for a battle more worthy of my efforts.

All of a sudden, two guards flung my body to one side and yanked my hands behind my back. I cried out in protest, recoiling at the pain that exploded in my wrists as they pressed their thumbs into my still-forming bruises. The men jerked me forward, leading me like an untrained horse toward the long spiral staircase. At their demeaning treatment, anger shot through my veins. I wrenched my arms and grounded my feet stubbornly. "I am perfectly capable of walking myself," I spat. But they ignored my objections, thrusting me violently onward and resuming their collective march.

As I was hauled up the stairs toward the throne room, I could not help but notice the cruel irony. Yesterday, I had tread through these very halls followed by a procession of my own servants. Now I was being ushered through a dim corridor, not a servant in sight, to what I could only assume would be my demise. In just one night, I had gone from Vitalia's most prominent royal to its most valuable prisoner.

I felt my heart beating in my throat as we walked through what remained of yesterday's onslaught. I carefully stepped over fallen paintings and overturned chairs, broken tiles and shattered glass, our fine décor strewn across the floor. Apart from my escorts, the hall was deserted. Fear rose in my chest as I considered where everyone could be. All of the maids and servants, nobles and guards—had they been taken captive? Killed? Was I, perhaps, the only Vitalian left alive? Fearing the worst, I ground my teeth until my jaw ached and imagined what I would find when I walked back into the throne room.

I held back the bile that scaled my throat as the great wooden doors came into view. *It isn't supposed to end like this. What kind of warrior was executed in her own kingdom?* But then I considered my father, how he had fearlessly faced every trial, how even though he had been shot down in this very room, he would be remembered as nothing less than a hero. No, I would face this wicked queen head-on, as I had all the enemies I faced before. Just as my father would have done.

Once more, the tall mahogany doors were torn open, this time by a set of guards I did not know. Once more, I strode inside without breaking my stride, refusing to succumb to fear.

The throne room was nearly unrecognizable. What used to be a bright, open hall was shrouded in darkness and disarray. Women I did not recognize, dressed head-to-toe in navy and black, busily swept the floors and removed any trace of Vitalian regalia, replacing each one with what I could only assume were Kreagan banners. I peered at the floor and walls. Cracks were visible in some places, residual blood stains in others. The few windows that remained intact revealed a dark night sky with no sign of the moon. I guessed it was somewhere between two and four in the morning, at least twelve hours since the prince and his procession first arrived.

A violent shove to the center of my back sent me toppling forward. I was barely able to catch myself before I could land face-first on the hard ground. "Keep moving," a guard growled from behind me. I turned to pierce the offending knight with a dangerous glare then continued forward.

The guards led me to the center of the hall, the same place, I noticed, where the queen and her son had stood the last time I was in this room. I was once again dragged into the tormenting flashback. My eyes remained transfixed to the space on the ground before the golden thrones, the place my father had fallen, breathing his last in a pool of his own blood. His body was gone now— God only knows in what cruel manner they had disposed of him—but lingering in the dead space was a grim shadow, a black stain that tainted my memory. His final words echoed through my mind in the voice of a ghost. *Remember your people.* As my grief blossomed anew, a thick film settled over my eyes. The path before me became nearly imperceptible by the dewy glaze blocking my vision.

I blinked away the mist when two cloudy figures came into view. Upon my father's throne sat the frail queen. Her spine was held stiffly upright, her arms taut along the arm rests, her claws digging into the velvet cover. Upon her face, she wore a sickening sneer. Her eyes, smug and pretentious, were bound to mine. I took my final steps toward the center of the room, completing my death march, and returned her stare with my own bitter scowl. Neither of us dared drop the savage glare we held upon the other.

In my father's massive throne, Ingrid looked

exceptionally scrawny. Her limbs were like twigs obscured by the chair's bulking width. Nevertheless, her visage was just as callous as I remembered. Her eyes were like daggers that twisted in my stomach along with her haughty grin. She was undoubtably satisfied with this favorable turn of events, the roles of ruler and outsider mercilessly switched.

Another swell of outrage swirled in my chest when I saw who sat upon my own throne. The spindly Prince Rune sat hunched forward, his head hung in its perpetual downward curve. With his hands clasped tightly on his lap, he seemed awkward and out of place. His leg twitched restlessly, his discomfort evident. I knew he would not dare meet my eye, not while I stood fuming before him. Not while he sat on the throne he knew belonged to me.

The guards finally released their grip on my arms, sending another painful ache through my wrists. The men took a few steps back to properly present their battle prize but remained close enough to restrain me if needed. Ingrid leaned forward and rested her chin in her palms, her elbows on her knees. Her villainous smile overtook her gaunt face. I released a low growl.

"Well, well, Princess Evangeline." Her snakelike voice sizzled in my eardrums. "You are looking rather hideous if I may say so." I did not need to peer down at my grisly appearance to understand her insult. My gown was in shreds and spotted with dried splotches of my father's blood. Bruises and cuts enshrouded my arms and legs, and I could only imagine the wretched state of my face and hair. I gritted my teeth like fangs and allowed my growl to grow louder.

Ingrid tilted her head to the side, her smirk still

tugging at her cheeks. "Why, Princess, don't you know it is customary to bow before your queen?" At this, she released a peal of laughter.

My body now trembled with rage which only seemed to further amuse her. Despite the storm of fury within me, I kept my voice steady. My words issued from my lips in a sinister whisper. "I will never bow down to you."

Surprisingly, my contempt did not seem to faze her. In fact, her thin smile widened, and her eyebrows shot up expectantly. "Is that so?" For the first time since I entered the hall, she released her threatening glower and peered over my shoulder, nodding her head.

Four hands clasped onto the tops of my shoulders as two guards attempted to plunge me to the ground. I successfully resisted them for all of two seconds before my knees buckled and my shins crashed to the earth, cracking loudly against the stone. A third guard wrapped his fingers around the nape of my neck and pressed down with all his weight. My face was shoved to the ground, my nose scraping against the coarse rock. All at once, the men released their forceful hold. But when I attempted to rise back to my feet, I was once again propelled to my knees. It was there, I understood, I was to stay.

Ingrid stood and stared down her pointed nose at me. I had forgotten how tall she was. Seated on my father's throne, she looked skeletal, like the cushions could have swallowed her whole. But standing upright, she was like a thin spire, slender but towering.

She shifted her hands behind her back, clasping them together as our eyes locked once more. "There are going to be a few changes around here." She took one step down from the dais, beginning her slow descent. "In fact, much has been changed already." I took a quick scan of the hall, noting all the ways it had been altered since I had last seen it.

She halted just a few feet before my kneeling frame. "And my next order of business," she said, bending at the waist until her face was mere inches from mine, "is you."

I met her sinful gaze without blinking. My hatred was only fueled by her hot breath on my skin. We stayed that way, frozen in place, for a few seconds—she eyeing me patronizingly, my unwavering glare full of spite.

Retaking her full stance, she turned to pace before me. "It was no challenge taking down your prized army," she said with a scoff. "How easy it is to seize a kingdom too busy trifling over the arrival of a worthless prince to defend themselves." I shifted my gaze over her shoulder to catch a glimpse of Prince Rune. He had not moved an inch since I entered the hall, his head still tilted toward his bony legs. But I detected a red tint along his temples, as if he had been slapped across the face by her words.

When I turned back to face her, Ingrid wore a nasty grin, her eyes full of venom. "And how effortlessly an empire falls once its *fearless leader* has been slain." She let out a horrible cackle.

Her laughter bit into my very flesh. Just the mention of my father made my entire body stiffen. I squeezed my fists until my knuckles lost all color. My vision blurred beneath a crimson veil, my fury taking over. In an instant, I was on my feet. I leapt from my knees and reached my hand toward her open throat. Before anyone realized what I was doing, my fingers made impact with her cold skin, and I squeezed until I could feel the ligaments bending, her windpipe closing in. Just before

I could snap her neck, the Kreagan guards ripped me away. I wriggled like a wild boar within their grasp. "Never speak of my father!" I snarled before being shoved back to the floor, bearing a few kicks to the back of my head along the way. I groaned under the new weight that pressed sharply into my calves: two boot heels pinning me into place.

Ingrid rubbed at her sore throat as she attempted to regain the color in her cheeks. Her smug grin was traded for an angry scowl. But she soon regained her composure and curled her lips back into a wicked smile. Despite my attack, she dared to step closer, meeting me face-to-face. "You are quite a fighter, aren't you?" she chuckled humorlessly. "I will soon change that."

Twisting away, she continued her pacing as though nothing had happened. "I was once like you," she started again. "Young, passionate, foolish. But the difference between you and me is that you have a fatal flaw, one that allowed me to take your miserable kingdom without even lifting a finger." She halted midstride to glare straight into me. I swallowed. "You see, Princess, you are too compassionate. You care too much about those peasants." She flicked her wrist haphazardly in the direction of the village. "You may put on a tough act, but I see right through you. You are weak, Evangeline."

"You do not know me," I interrupted. "You know nothing about who I am or what I can do." I stared through her icy scowl, wearing my most threatening grimace. "And I can promise you this: one day, I will take back my kingdom and avenge my father."

Ingrid laughed aloud, a thunderous roar that filled the room and tore at my insides. "Then it will come at the cost of everyone you love. Trust me, once I take control of your feeble heart, it will not be long before you break."

With my eyes like flames, one word barked in my mind: *never*. From the look on her face, I knew she had heard my silent defiance.

She spun on her heels and began her effortless stroll back to the throne. "From now on, you will do as I command." She did not even bother to face me as she stated her edict. "If you fail to obey my orders, you will suffer the consequences. Is that simple enough for you?" She paused in her walk as she waited for my response, one I refused to give. She twisted her neck slightly to glare at me over her shoulder. "Am I understood?" I could sense her patience waning. Unable to curb the wrath that boiled within me, I felt my muscles start to shake.

I gritted my teeth. "No."

She settled back into the chair and sighed. "Then we will start your first lesson." Once again, she caught the eye of my pack of wardens, still pressing their body weight into my calves. Without hesitation, one guard sent his elbow into the back of my head, knocking me flat on the ground. My forehead smashed into the floor, and a cluster of black spots clouded my vision. A barrage of fists and knees struck my sides and back, the rest of the guards soon joining in the beating. Pain traveled through my body in excruciating waves as my consciousness wavered. I squeezed my lips together, refusing to let them hear my cries.

Chapter 6

Eve

My heels scraped against the floor as I was once again dragged through the castle halls. The trauma to my head made my vision fade in and out, but I still jerked my arms away viciously. If I was to be forcefully hauled from one room to another by a nameless band of knights, I certainly would not make it easy for them. My entire body writhed to escape their clutches, but their grip on my wrists was like shackles. I had officially run out of patience and could no longer suppress my rage. Every profane word I knew leapt from my throat with a murderous snarl. I was pure savage, my wrath possessing me like a demon. I hissed and squirmed and gnashed my teeth until I was sure my jailers thought I had lost all sanity.

The men finally halted when we reached a closed door at the end of the main hall. I took the moment's opportunity to try to wriggle free, but a quick elbow to the side of my head sent me spiraling to the floor. Sparks exploded in my eyes as I was temporarily blinded. Just as light started to reenter my vision, the guards hurled me into the room. I crashed to the floor, smashing my already bruised ribs. Free from their grasp, I scrambled to my feet and charged toward them with my arms outstretched. But before I could sink my nails into their eye sockets, the door was slammed in my face and promptly locked from the outside. I banged my fists against the door. "Bastards!" I howled, bashing my knuckles into the wood until their footsteps faded into the distance.

My pounding gradually slowed, growing softer and softer as I sank to the ground, utterly exhausted. I closed my eyes and let my forehead rest briefly on the cool floor. But within seconds, I sprang back to my feet. I knew any time I had alone would be limited. I had to act now, before the soldiers returned.

I turned around and inspected my surroundings, surprised to discover that I had been locked in my own room. Like the rest of the castle, the space had been greatly altered. Much to my chagrin, my collection of weaponry had been stripped from the wall. My stomach twisted at the thought of some Kreagan guard going through my belongings, confiscating my most valuable possessions. I frantically searched through my drawers, under my bed, between books on my shelves. But every blade I kept stashed had been removed, leaving me defenseless.

I sighed in frustration as I slammed the last drawer shut. I began pacing across the room, considering my next move. Despite the aching pain in my head and spine, I knew I had to act fast. I would not stay here another minute. I refused to be thrown around my own kingdom like a rag doll. But my options were slim. There was no way I could unlock the door, and even if I could, the halls were teeming with guards.

I paused my pacing at the sight of a faint ray of light shining through the window: the first hint of sunrise. A new escape plan slowly formed in my mind. It was risky, highly impractical, but it was my only choice.

I dashed into my closet and began yanking every article of clothing I could find off its hanger, forming a tall pile of garments by my feet. I rapidly collected every cloth item within my reach and tossed it into the growing clump. Once the stack was hip-high, I gathered the apparel in my arms and carried it into my bedroom, plopping the stack down by the window. I spun back around, ready to race back into the closet for another load, but I stopped when I caught a glimpse of myself in the vanity mirror.

I was taken aback by my frightening reflection. Now I fully understood Ingrid's insult to my appearance. The beast that stared back at me now was disquieting to say the least. All that was left of my dress was a crumpled mess of tulle, frayed and blood-stained, its sequins dangling precariously from the bust. My hair looked like I had been through a windstorm; loose strands flew in every direction, and what remained of my braids was sprawled sloppily across the top of my head. The sight of my battered face would make a young child scream in horror. The white powder Mary had applied was splotched about my nose and chin. Dried blood caked my cheeks and forehead, and long streaks of black blotted the baggy space below my eyes. On top of that, a dark ring was starting to form across my left cheek bone, and my busted lip was swelling like a balloon.

With one quick tug, I stripped the dress from my body, ripping the seams around the waist before tossing it across the room in a messy bundle. My chest could finally return to its normal position, and I sighed in relief, letting my ribs expand outward. It was my first full breath in hours.

I opened a nearby dresser and took out a pair of linen trousers along with my long brown cloak. The bulky cloth covered my skin, effectively masking the slew of bruises and gashes along my arms and legs. I unraveled what remained of my braids and pulled my hair back into a tight knot. Then, I sped to a nearby basin of water and harshly scrubbed at my face until the last of my makeup had dissolved.

Returning to the vanity mirror, I now saw the true Evangeline. No adornments or fancy frills. Just a woman ready for battle. I lifted the hood of my cloak over my head, concealing my face within a dark shadow.

Snapping back to the task at hand, I dropped to my knees beside the mountain of clothes. I hastily knotted together sleeves and pantlegs, steadily building a chain of fabric.

A soft click sounded from the bedroom door, and my fingers froze. Frantically, I tossed the cloth rope beneath my bed. Just as I tucked away the last tunic, the door swung open. An unknown figure was cast inside, landing on the floor with a thud. Once again, the Kreagan guards slammed the door closed and bolted the lock, leaving me alone with the stranger. I scanned my fellow prisoner thoroughly. I could tell she was a woman by her long skirt. She was slow to move from her position on the ground, and as she stumbled to her feet and I caught a glimpse of her face, my guard instantly dropped. I leapt from my place on the floor and raced to her side.

"Mary!" I yelled as I threw my arms around her. She stumbled backward with the force of my body thrown against hers, but I would never let her fall. I pulled her tightly against my chest, only loosening my grip when I heard a muffled wince.

Releasing my firm embrace, I studied her. My anger surged when I saw the dark bruises scattered around her arms and a purple mark shadowing her right eye. "What happened?" I traced the wounds lightly, careful not to apply too much pressure. "Who did this to you?"

She took my hands in her own and pushed them away. "I'm fine." And although the thought of anyone hurting Mary made me want to snap their spine, I knew any further questioning could wait. There was no time to waste.

"Come on." I pulled her along behind me as I rushed back to my bedside. Falling to my knees, I pulled the makeshift rope out from beneath my bed and continued adding to its length.

Mary peered at my work curiously. "What are you doing?"

I looked up at her without slowing my hands. "I am getting us out of here."

Fear flashed across her face. She opened her mouth, but no words came out, just a rhythmic stutter. Eventually, she managed to speak. "But how will we—"

"I'm not sure yet," I interrupted. "But we have to try." This did not seem to alleviate her anxiety, so I told her what I had been plotting from the moment the arrow had struck my father's chest.

"I will not spend another second under the same roof as that monster." I stilled my fingers for just a moment and held her eyes steadily with my own, urging her to hear the words I had left unsaid: I was leaving here with or without her.

She bit her lip hesitantly, but within seconds, she nodded and stepped forward. "How can I help?"

I picked up a few loose shirts and tossed them her

way. "Hurry. Tie those together." Mary quickly linked the two items. Then, following my lead, she sank to the ground to collect more and constructed her own chain.

Once all the garments had been secured together in one long rope, I rushed back into the closet, returning with another dark cloak. "Put this on." She hastily threw it over her shoulders. I placed the hood over her head and tucked in the stray hairs sticking out the front. Satisfied with her disguise, I looked into her face. She was wide-eyed, terrified. I squeezed her hand tight, trying to impart some of my own courage.

Taking up one end of our cloth chain, I wrapped it firmly around my bed post and tugged hard to ensure it was secure. Then, I slid the window open and scanned the ground below. The area was temporarily deserted. I tossed the other end of the rope outside and watched as it settled a few feet above the ground. I took a deep breath. It was now or never.

I looked back at Mary. She was frozen in place, paralyzed with fright. "Let's go," I said. With an audible gulp, she willed herself forward, her hands shaking.

Without another word, I jumped out into the crisp morning air. The breeze rushed through my cloak as I glided down the wall, easily rappelling toward the earth as the rope ran through my fingers. I reached the ground within seconds, sticking the landing with a light tap of my boots on the cobblestone. When I glanced back up, I cringed. Mary was gripping the rope with all her strength, inching down the wall at a snail's pace. The trembling had spread throughout her entire body. She took a fearful peek toward the ground, only adding to her dismay. The muscles in her arms tensed, and the color drained from her face.

"Don't look down!" I whispered. "Just keep going!" Gritting her teeth, she resumed her slow descent. From the ground, I stayed vigilant, peering to my left and right, anticipating a Kreagan guard to round the corner at any moment. At last, Mary made it to the end of the rope. She hesitated, unwilling to loosen her tight grip. "Jump! I will catch you!" I held my arms out wide and stood directly below her, hanging perilously in the air. She squeezed her eyes shut as she willed herself to let go. After a silent prayer, she released her hands and dropped backward, falling directly into my arms. I only gave her a second to settle her feet on the ground before grabbing her hand and taking off at a run.

Treading as lightly as I could, I raced through the castle grounds with Mary in tow. At each turn, I carefully peeked around the wall to check that the coast was clear. At the first sound of approaching footsteps, I slammed my heels into the ground and came to a halt. Mary crashed into my back. "What's wrong?"

I threw my hand against her mouth and pulled her into a small nook in the castle wall. I held her still and kept my palm pressed to her lips as a group of guards marched by. Neither of us dared breathe, not until they had rounded the corner and sauntered out of sight. Alone once more, Mary relaxed her grip on my hand. I exhaled in relief and checked our path again. Not a soldier in sight. I grabbed Mary by the wrist and bolted onward.

At last, we made it to the back of the castle. Beyond the stables and armory lay the training fields, a long open plot of land where knights gathered to practice their combat skills. The field went on for nearly half a mile before a line of trees marked the end of the castle grounds. Every day for the past ten years I had come here, preparing myself for a war that I knew could come at any time. This was where I had molded into my true form, where I had learned what it meant to lead my people. Now it was a barren wasteland, a bloody patch of grass and dirt littered with fallen swords and shields. A battle had taken place here, but this time, I had not been there to defend my kingdom.

Beside me, Mary stared at the field, dread engulfing her features. I was not sure what terrified her more: the piles of bloody weaponry or the soaring watch tower located just a few yards away. "What do we do now?"

"There is only one thing we can do." I set my jaw and tightened my fingers around Mary's knuckles. "Run."

Ducking my chin to hide my face, I darted into the sunrise. My feet moved swiftly across the lawn, covering several yards in mere seconds. From afar, I might have looked like a dark blur shooting across the grass. But dragging Mary behind me greatly reduced my speed. I kept my eyes glued to the tree line, resisting the urge to look back at the castle lest I should find a group of Kreagan guards trailing us. Sure enough, shouts from atop the watch tower carried across the field, and I knew we had been spotted. Mary's pace slowed, her weight growing in my hand. "Keep going!" I cried. The forest was nearly within our reach.

Suddenly, a shooting pain exploded in my left calf. I roared in agony and tumbled forward. Mary tripped over my body and collapsed to the ground beside me, rolling through the grass. I sprang back upright but instantly fell to my knees. My heart flooded with despair as I glimpsed back at the source of my pain. An arrow was deeply burrowed in my calf, paralyzing my left leg.

Mary frantically rose, a dark grass stain across the front of her skirt, but instead of running for the safety of the trees, she rushed to my side, attempting to lift me to my feet. I threw her hands away. "Leave me!" I shouted. "Get out of here!"

She hesitated, looking over her shoulder at escape, now just a few yards away, then back at me. "Go!" I demanded. She winced, pain filling her eyes, then swung back around, heading for the trees. But her moment's hesitation had cost her her freedom. Right before she could cross into the forest, a pack of Kreagan guards caught up to her and tackled her to the ground.

Frustration and anguish mingled in my chest, culminating in a harrowing scream. The dam within me finally broke, and the swelling heartache burst from my chest: all the hurt, all the grief, spilling from my mouth in a gut-wrenching wail I did not bother to contain.

Someone lifted me from the dirt, holding my arms stiffly behind my back. But just the light pressure of my foot on the ground sent another wave of torment tearing through my calf, and I fell back toward the earth. With my body limp, the Kreagan guards took both of my arms and started dragging me back toward the castle.

My freedom slipping from my fingers, I panicked. I yanked my body in every direction. I became untamed, doing everything I could to escape their clutches. I would crawl into the forest on my hands and knees if I had to. But these guards had dealt with me before. Their grip was unyielding around my wrists. They groaned in frustration, struggling to keep hold of my contorting body. "Knock her out!" someone yelled.

Without hesitation, one of the soldiers lifted his boot and launched his heel into my temple. First, a sharp pain.

Then, darkness.

****

When I woke, my world was shrouded in black. I feared I had been permanently blinded by the guard's kick to my skull. The only proof I had of my consciousness was the sharp pounding in my head and the clamor of orders from unknown voices circled around me. Another stern command sounded from my right, and I swung my head around. I flinched when I felt something scrape across my cheek then relaxed my shoulders as understanding dawned on me. I was not blind after all. A gunny sack covered my head. I shifted sideways to find my arms and legs restrained; my wrists were tied at the center of my back, and a rope was wrapped around my ankles, confining me to my knees.

From the slight breeze and the heat of the sun's rays on my skin, I determined I was somewhere outdoors. Then, my memory came rushing back: Mary, the training field, the immobilizing shot to my leg. Right on cue, my calf stung anew. The pain was staggering, making me gasp.

The commotion around me quieted. I held my breath as I sensed a dozen eyes resting on me. "She's awake," said a man. Clanking footsteps approached then a large hand settled over the crown of my head. In one yank, the sack was removed, along with a few strands of my hair. The brightness of day scorched my eyes. Unable to shade my face, I squinted and recoiled into my shoulder.

When my eyes adjusted, I saw that I was on the cobblestone path encircling the castle, the same one Mary and I had slipped across to get to the training field. The area was now stocked with Kreagan guards, surrounding me in an ocean of navy uniforms. Between them was a line of kneeling men. They were blindfolded, their faces masked, each wearing a matching tan surcoat. I swallowed. These men were Vitalian knights. I suddenly came to understand the gravity of my situation.

"I warned you what would happen if you disobeyed." The voice was so close I jumped. Ingrid stood just a few feet from my left. She was a stone column, a marble statue with eyes like glass that scanned the hooded men, never blinking once. Behind the prisoners, her Kreagan soldiers had formed a line, their bodies stiff and at attention.

I heard a slight shuffling of boots and searched for the source of the sound around Ingrid's skirt. Prince Rune was almost completely hidden behind her, his thin figure seamlessly blending into his surroundings. He looked more unsettled than ever, tormented by some invisible phantom. Although he tried to keep his eyes focused on the ground below him, I occasionally saw him peel his gaze upward at the row of Vitalian captives, his face deadly pale. My cheeks burned red with hatred. I clenched my fists so hard, I thought the bindings would surely snap.

"You could have made this easy for everyone, but I suppose we will have to do it the hard way," Ingrid continued. "Unveil them."

At her command, the guards stripped the kneeling Vitalians of their hoods. My heart jolted as I identified each hostage, but my blood ran cold when I set my eyes on the final prisoner, his long, blond hair unmistakable: Arthur.

A frantic shriek rang from my right, and I swung my head around. There was Mary, somehow going unnoticed until now, bound and restricted to her knees just as I was. The utter despair that covered her face was enough to shake my soul. Thick tears rolled down her cheeks as she screamed hysterically through the gag in her mouth. My own distress was growing into terror. "No," I exhaled, the word barely leaving my lips.

"It is simple, Evangeline. You do as I command and keep what little you have left of your crumbling kingdom, or I will kill your dear Vitalians one by one." Before I could say a word, Ingrid turned to face the nearest guard and delivered a fatal nod.

"No," I said, louder this time. But I already knew it was too late.

In mere seconds, the Kreagan knights unsheathed their swords and swiftly beheaded the men kneeling before them.

I could not hear the slice of their blades against flesh or the thump of their severed heads against the stone. Mary's piercing scream drowned it all out. I could only watch as their limp torsos plopped heavily to the ground.

I was speechless, breathless, staring in shock at the row of corpses. My body went numb. Even the aching pain in my calf melted away as my head began to spin. I worried I might pass out again.

But Ingrid's voice drew me back into consciousness. "This is only the beginning, Evangeline." I turned to stare into her unfeeling eyes, seemingly unaffected by the ruthless slaughter.

Without a moment's pause, she spun around and floated toward the castle doors. "Come, Rune."

But the prince did not move. He stood, frozen in place, staring at my kneeling figure. As he watched me, I watched him, searching his face for the same cruelty his mother's held. But I found nothing of the sort.

Instead, I noticed something deep within his eyes, buried too far down to see clearly. A strange feeling swirled in my chest as I studied him closer. I could not put a name to it, but there was something familiar concealed in those depths. Something visceral.

But as soon as I saw it, the prince dashed behind his mother and disappeared into the castle.

Chapter 7

Rune

I am a drizzling rain.
You call me darkness,
A depressing burden,
An unwanted disturbance to the sun's light.
But you forget that it is I
Who brings life down to Earth.

Being a prince does not make you unbroken. Bearing a crown does not make you free. All the riches, all the power, all the fame—they were like gold-plated shackles binding me to life's cruel fate. A castle of confinement. A copper-clad prison with no hope of escape.

I had been a slave in my mother's kingdom for as long as I could remember. My whole life was spent in silver palaces replete with endless servants, but even they were freer than I.

I learned early that my life was not my own. I had no choice, no independence, no purpose. I was born to be another tool in my mother's arsenal. She told me I was worthless, that I didn't deserve the title of prince. And I believed her. After all, she was right about me. I was weak, shameful, powerless. I was prince only in name, and all of Kreagan knew it.

I used to feel fortunate that my mother let me live as she ravaged the world, that she had bestowed upon me some gift of unearned kindness. But now I knew that my existence was but a bitter joke, just another of her heartless ploys.

****

Since the day I was born, I was enveloped in ice. I came into this world two months early, frail and underweight, in the midst of an unforgiving blizzard. My kingdom was no stranger to freezing temperatures, but this storm was one of the most brutal we had ever endured. Homes were destroyed; families were frozen to death; and then came me, carrying the weight of disappointment before I could even take my first breath.

Doctors were sure I would not survive the freeze, not in my feeble condition. But somehow, I managed to survive.

As an infant, I cried constantly from the aching in my sickly body. No matter how many blankets they wrapped me in, I was always shivering within the castle walls. So eventually, my incessant wails were ignored, and I was left to suffer on my own, to brave the cold alone.

As a prince, I was thrown into the arms of servants immediately following my birth. For the first twelve years of my life I rarely saw my parents. Only on special occasions would I be asked to dine with them. My guardians would anxiously prep my clothes and hair, imploring me to be on my best behavior around the king and queen. I would be filled with excitement, sure my parents would be thrilled to see me. But in their presence, my father barely acknowledged me, and my mother would only glare, her face full of disgust, and complain of my unnatural scrawniness. And if I ever dared cry before her, she would slap me across the face, startling me into silence.

My mother told me I was too quiet, too timid. I thought through perfect obedience I might gain favor with her. But the more I conformed to her wishes, the harsher her gaze. My deference was like a taper candle, always burning but never bright enough. And yet I persisted. I submitted to her tyranny, hoping that one day my efforts would be rewarded. Instead, she trod over me like a frayed doormat.

Every once in a while, I would snap. I would stand to my full height, shouldering past the iron weight of her displeasure. I would tell her I was not weak or worthless, thinking that perhaps she would respect me for my boldness. But my outburst left her unfazed. Her cold features remained unmoved as she casually ordered her guards to escort me to the dungeon—a dingy one-room cell she dubbed the Reflection Chamber. She would leave me there, sometimes for hours, sometimes for days, always without food or water or light. The air in the narrow room would become putrid with the smell of my own filth, making it almost impossible to breathe. I would become convinced that she had finally left me to die, a notion I was not particularly opposed to.

Then, I would be released. Hardly able to move, I was ordered to stand before the queen. She would act as if nothing happened, as if she had not locked me away and left me for dead. Her message was clear: defiance was futile. My survival depended only on my quiet submission to her will.

Sometimes I wished I were a peasant. I wished I was

just another Kreagan subject in our decrepit village, living in one of the run-down turf houses I saw through my bedroom window. I would dream of being a carpenter or a farmer, working tirelessly to provide for a hungry family with too many mouths to feed. Because even though most people would kill to be the son of royalty, I would choose to live a life of poverty if it meant I could mean something to someone.

****

My mother hated the way I dissected my food. Every meal, I would take my fork and knife and cut my meat into tiny pieces, meticulously carving them into cubes no bigger than a gumdrop. I would place each bite, one at a time, upon my tongue and thoroughly chew until the food became mush. Then, I would swallow it down with a small sip of water and repeat. She told me I ate like a bird, that a true prince ate like a man. But nothing ever changed, because, to my mother's dismay and my own, I would always be this way.

I looked down at my plate. My steak had been sculpted into an assortment of game dice, mostly untouched. I dared a glance upward. I was seated at the end of the longest table I had ever seen, enough for at least thirty people to comfortably dine. I was grateful for its length, allowing a considerable distance between me and the opposite side where the queen and her advisors sat. I would prefer to eat alone, but years ago, when our reign of terror began, my mother had given me a choice: dine with the royal court or eat nothing at all. I scolded myself for not skipping the meal.

Each time we invaded a new kingdom, the queen insisted on keeping her tradition of a celebratory evening feast. She and her top attendants would dine exorbitantly as they planned their next move. For reasons unbeknownst to me, I had always been required to attend these intimate meetings. I knew the last thing she wanted was my input on anything pertaining to the running of the empire. For the most part, she had kept me majorly uninvolved in her exploits, rarely taking the time to inform me of her plans.

But my mother had made it clear when Kreagan had started to expand that my role was to follow and obey, no questions asked. I was her pawn, a small piece on her chessboard to be moved at her convenience. I was to stay out of the way as she and her army took over each new domain. That is until we reached Vitalia.

From the beginning, she planned to gradually build the size and influence of our kingdom, gaining more men and power with each invasion, until we were strong enough to seize the most dominant force in the realm: the Imperial Kingdom of Vitalia.

There was no point trying to argue with her. Anyone who attempted to dissuade her efforts would be promptly banished or put to death. Her hunger for power was insatiable. She would not be content until Kreagan ruled all.

So I learned to keep my head down, to look away from the atrocities I was forced to play a part in. Because here, the key to survival was to simply close your eyes and follow, trying not to think too much about your small role in the world's destruction.

I kept to myself as much as I could, not a difficult task when you are blatantly unwanted. Most of the time I stowed away in my room and hid inside my sketchbooks. Something about putting my visions of a better life on paper gave me a sort of ease I could not feel anywhere else. With pencil in hand, I could create the places I had never known, the ones I had always longed to see. I had never shown my drawings to anyone. I received enough criticism as it was. But my mother knew what I did behind closed doors, and she ridiculed my idle interest like she did everything else.

But for once, I did not care what she thought. My sketches were the only thing that made me feel alive. They were my sole escape in her twisted universe.

Now I waited patiently for their conference to end, anxious to return to my room—the new chamber I had been assigned in the colossal Vitalian palace. I used my fork to sweep the uneaten food around my plate. I spread the juices of the steak around my dish like paint, my fork the paintbrush, and watched the liquid swirl across the platter.

Normally, I blocked out the conversations between my mother and her advisors. But today, I chose to listen. I was genuinely curious as to what my mother was planning next. She had already obtained the land she had long hoped to possess. What more could she possibly want?

"The final renovations must be made quickly," she said between sips from a silver goblet, her upper lip stained red from the wine. "Our time is limited." I glanced across the room where maids were sweeping what remained of the wreckage from the recent battle and mounting oversized portraits of the queen to the walls.

Barely twenty-four hours had passed since we arrived in Vitalia, and the castle was already drastically altered, molded and shaped to my mother's liking. But this was no surprise. She had every detail painstakingly planned before our arrival. My mother had been this way for as long as I could remember: thorough, stringent, and scheming. Without her obsessive attention to detail, her rigid systems and rule, and the undying loyalty of her army, we never would have escaped our paltry homeland, a frigid island a hundred miles north of the Great Sea.

Each time she seized a new kingdom, no time was wasted in planning her next invasion. I learned to never let myself settle in one place, for I knew it would not be long before we moved on somewhere else. But now that she had finally obtained her greatest prize, she was establishing herself permanently. The Vitalian castle was to become our new home.

"After that, we can commence preparations for the wedding," she continued. I spun my head back around. I had heard nothing before about a wedding. My mother finally had the entire world in her hands, and I knew she would never share it with anyone.

"The ceremony will be held outside the castle gates, and I want every servant and villager in attendance." A nearby consultant frantically recorded the details of her requests on a scroll.

"But how will we ever convince Princess Evangeline to comply?" an advisor asked.

My stomach clenched at the mention of her name. I still did not know what to think about Princess Evangeline. I had never met any woman quite like her. She was drastically different from the other noblewomen I had met, the ones whom my mother had ordered killed once their land had been successfully confiscated. They had stayed silent apart from desperately begging for their lives, but this woman did nothing of the sort. She did not hide behind a sheer veil. She was not quiet or modest. No, this princess was terrifying.

Never had a man or woman ever dared stand up to the queen as she had repeatedly done. I had come to believe that there was no one in existence more threatening than my mother, but this cutthroat princess must have been the most menacing woman on Earth.

While I was lost in thought, I scarcely heard the queen's response. "The princess will learn the consequences of her rebellious ways soon enough. I will break her in no time." A dark smile snuck up the side of her mouth. "Trust me, Rune and Evangeline will be wed by the end of the week."

My fork slipped from my hands, the metal clattering noisily against my plate. *Me? Married to Princess Evangeline?* My mother had told me nothing about this. For the first time that evening, I opened my mouth to object. "I-I-I am not sure that's the best idea," I stuttered.

The queen glared at me out of the corner of her eye, clearly irritated by my intrusion. "Must I remind you again of your role in this conquest?"

I swallowed, my chest compressing inward. I felt the sting of a thousand knives when she stared at me that way. Out of instinct, I bowed my head and fell back into silence.

She sighed aloud, then spoke again, again in an exaggerated monotone. "Upon reaching Vitalia, it was your job to ask for the princess's hand in marriage."

I shifted my gaze slightly upward. "Yes, but she refused me." And hadn't the proposal been a ruse? A ploy to distract the castle staff while our army surrounded the palace.

Realizing she would have to explain herself entirely,

she leaned back in her chair and crossed her arms over her chest in annoyance. "Rune, why do you think I have kept that girl alive?" It was a question I had considered myself, one I honestly did not know the answer to. My mother had always commanded the total execution of the ruling family whenever we seized a new kingdom, ensuring her authority would stand unquestioned. I had no idea why she chose to spare this princess, especially one who so fiercely resisted her command.

When I failed to answer her question, the queen rolled her eyes. "Your stupidity never ceases to amaze me." She slowed her words as if she were speaking to a toddler. "Who is one person an entire kingdom will listen to, one whom they will trust until the end of time?"

I swallowed. "Their...princess?"

"Their damn princess!" she shouted suddenly. I flinched, heat rushing to my cheeks in humiliation. "There are no less than ten thousand Vitalian peasants out there, and we can avoid a disastrous civilian uprising if we join our two kingdoms through your eternal unity. They would never dare oppose their beloved princess."

"But what makes you think she would want to marry me?"

At this, the queen burst into a cold laugh, an ominous cackle that unsettled me even more. "Do you really think I care about her consent?"

I bit the inside of my lip and slowly shook my head. "Then it is settled." She positioned herself back toward her advisors. "You and the princess will wed within the next fortnight. Then, we can start making arrangements for your heir."

The blood drained from my face. "My heir?" I blurted breathily.

She angled her face my way again, growing exasperated. "Yes, your heir. If we are going to maintain their fidelity, we must prove the legitimacy of your union. And what better way to do that than with a royal child of both Kreagan and Vitalian descent?"

"But I can't—"

The queen slammed her palms against the table. "You will do as I command, or I will have you locked in the dungeon, you useless wretch!"

I leapt back in my chair. Goosebumps sprouted along my arms, and my entire body started to shake. Suddenly, it all made sense, why my mother had kept me around all this time. She did not need me to help expand her empire or lead her army. I was simply the means of continuing our royal lineage. My mother could do anything she wanted. She could command anyone to do her bidding, but she could not compel a princess to conceive. This was a duty only I could fulfill.

For years, I had wondered why she had not just done away with me. It was obvious she wanted nothing to do with me from the moment I was born. She could have easily made me disappear, the same way my father had years ago.

Without warning, the queen stood from the table, scraping the legs of her chair roughly across the floor. Her court quickly followed her lead and rose to their feet. "This conversation exhausts me," she said, regaining control of her temper. "We will finalize our plans in the morning." With that, she veered toward the door and drifted out of the dining hall, her gown gliding gently behind her.

Once she vanished from view, the tension withdrew from my shoulders. I waited until all her advisors had left the table before scurrying toward the exit. When I arrived in the main hall, I hastened to my new bedroom. But just as I reached the end of the corridor, my mother sprang out from behind a corner and backhanded me across the mouth.

I jerked backward in shock, barely maintaining my balance. My face stung where her gold rings had made impact with my cheek bone. She must have been waiting for me here, preferring to unleash her wrath on me without her attendants present. Her nostrils flared and her jaw clenched as she stared at me with her most threatening scowl, the one that made me want to melt into a puddle on the floor.

"I suggest you think twice the next time you decide to question my command," she hissed. Her face was so close that I could see red streaks in the whites of her eyes. She severed me with her razor-sharp glare then swung around and strutted down the hall.

I stood there for a moment, paralyzed in place. When she was out of sight, I stumbled into my room and shut the door.

Chapter 8

Eve

For the first time in my life, I welcomed the brutal tug of Mary's hairbrush. The sting was like a familiar friend. My hair was as wild as ever and, as always, she struggled to remove my unyielding knots. But this was a pain I knew well. A torment I had experienced before and knew I could withstand.

Mary swept the comb through my waves as gently as she could, but her delicate movements were painfully slow. There was no point in her soft touch anyway; I could barely feel the wooden teeth against my scalp, not since the numbness had started.

When I first heard the news, I nearly drowned in anguish, too wrecked with disbelief to form a sensible thought. But now my mind and body were unfeeling, my nerves deadened after hours of searing panic. I had transformed myself into an undead corpse. It was the only way, I knew, that I would survive this night.

The messenger came to my room early one morning. I had been sitting by my window peering down at the lines of Kreagan guards marching by. I studied them closely, memorizing their every move as they drilled around the castle. I used to know each of my soldiers by name, but these men were all strangers to me.

The lock on my door suddenly clicked open, and I

snapped my head around. I sprang to my feet to stand at high alert, clenching my fists by my waist. Without even a knock, a man I had not seen before entered my room. He was not dressed like the Kreagan soldiers. Instead of a military uniform, he wore a frilled jerkin atop a set of long stockings. His light hair was neatly brushed and parted in the center, dividing his head in perfect symmetry. He walked into my chamber uninvited, an air of superiority about him, but upon seeing me, stone-faced and at the ready, his shoulders fell slightly forward. I was fixed in place, gritting my teeth to mask any trace of fear.

The man coughed nervously then lifted his chin an inch higher. "Good morning, Princess Evangeline." I kept my lips sealed. No way would I participate in his feigned courtesies.

When I responded with only a hateful grimace, he let out a weak laugh and carried on. "I am here by order of Queen Ingrid to inform you of your mandated post." My stomach dropped as my mind raced through all the sadistic acts she could demand of me. "In three days' time," he continued, "you will be married to Prince Rune. You are to arrive properly attired outside the castle gates at sunset to commence the wedding ceremony."

My heart stopped. I sank into complete shock, falling mute. My eyes lost focus. I felt as though my throat was in a chokehold as I labored to speak. The vassal interrupted my stammering and continued his recitation.

"After the wedding, you are to birth an heir." He spoke too quickly for my frantic mind to keep up, my thoughts streaming through my brain at the speed of sound. My whole body was trembling, and I was not sure if it was from the terror that swelled in my chest or the growing mania that turned my vision red.

"No," I finally managed to choke out. I took one step forward, but the man persisted in his speech.

"If you fail to comply, the queen will begin ordering the execution of your citizens, starting with your lady's maid."

I froze, my eyes wide. *They were going to kill Mary.* "No," I said louder, taking another step toward him.

The vassal cautiously inched backward, rushing through the conclusion of his speech. "More details are to come, but for now, the queen would like to remind you that any defiance will have fatal consequen—"

"No!" I screeched as I sprinted toward him, my hands reaching for his open neck. I turned animal as I shot forward, eager to tear him to pieces.

He squealed and made a dash for the door. He had barely set the lock back in place when my fists slammed into the wood. "No! No! No! You cannot do this!" I was overcome by hysteria, pounding and scratching until my fingers bled. "I am the princess of Vitalia, goddamn it! You cannot do this to me, you sick son of a bitch!" I went on like this for God knows how long, eventually collapsing to the floor in exhaustion.

I spent the rest of the day racking my brain for a solution. There must have been something I could do to escape this fate. No way in Hell would I comply with Ingrid's vindictive demands. I rejected her orders with every ounce of my soul. In fact, I would rather die than marry that spineless boy.

All at once, I paused my restless pacing. *I would rather die.* My heart nearly stopped, the ugly truth becoming clear.

I scoured my room once again to uncover any weapons the Kreagan guards might have missed during their initial inspection. But my room was clean. Even my dull switchblade was gone from its place beneath my mattress. I searched every crevice of every drawer for anything that could possibly break skin. Then, at the bottom of my dresser, I finally found it. A small iron key I had almost forgotten about.

I withdrew the finely carved metal and stared at its shiny surface. Then, I walked to my bookshelf. Reaching above the top, I blindly searched until I recognized the texture of the glossy wood against my fingers. When I brought my arm back down, I held a tiny jewelry box, one I hadn't seen in ages. I took the key and inserted it into the lock—a perfect fit. Inside was a coin-shaped pendant edged with gold, thin copper loops coiled around the sides. In the center was a shimmering teal sapphire.

I carefully removed the pendant from the box and held it softly in my palm. I was too young to remember when it was first given to me. In my mind, it had always been here, guarding over me like a night watchman. It was my mother's, my father had told me. The old portraits that once adorned our walls often depicted the young Queen Genevieve with this exact pendant resting upon her chest.

Now, every time I thought of her, her image was filtered in a turquoise hue. To me, she would always be the color of the deepest ocean. I pressed the charm to my chest and squeezed it tightly in my hand. When the wire edges started cutting into my palm, I let them, the dew of fresh tears covering my eyes.

With a quick jerk, I thrust the medallion across the

room. It struck the wall with a crash then clanged to the stone floor. I pulled the key from the lock and held it up to my forearm. *It will only be a quick slash*, I told myself. *One wrist and then the other.*

Then, I would be free.

I pressed the key into my arm. The sharp edge pierced into my skin with a biting sting. But right before I could split the artery, I loosened my grip on the key, letting it clatter to the ground.

I could not leave my people to face that monster alone. I could not let them suffer while I took the easy way out. My father's voice was playing over and over in my head, his dying plea forcing me to forgo my death wish. I was no longer living for myself. I had to stay and fight for Vitalia.

I knew then that Ingrid had won. I would obey her orders. I would marry her prince. I would do whatever it took to protect my people.

Now, lifeless as I sat before my vanity, I was silent. In fact, ever since Mary arrived at my chamber that morning—my wedding day—neither of us had spoken a word. We both knew there was nothing to say.

As she had done countless times before, Mary tried her best to make me appear the proper princess. This time, as she braided my hair and applied my makeup, I did not complain. There were worse things than a tight dress and powdered cheeks.

After dying my lips a soft pink, Mary walked into my closet. I took a moment to consider my reflection. This time, I did not see the blush or the curls, just a dark puppet, a painted figurine without a soul.

"Evangeline?" Mary said quietly. I tore my heavy gaze from the mirror and turned her way. She was holding a long white dress. The thick bleached silk was covered by a layer of embroidered floral that swept across the neckline and along the sleeves.

I ignored the newest swell of grief that rolled through my abdomen and stood from my chair. Bowing slightly, I waited for her to place the gown over my head. But when she didn't, I looked up.

Now she was holding the top of the dress over her shoulder to display the details of the skirt. I gasped. A violet stripe had been stitched into the lace, a long purple streak that started at the right hip and traveled all the way to the floor. Mary had told me that the lady's maids were forced to design and sew my wedding dress in mere days, but Mary had still taken the time to ensure the gown was uniquely mine.

"You will always be our princess," she said, peeking her face around the bust. "You are the heart of Vitalia."

A raging storm of emotions dared to overtake me. For the first time that day, I almost let the tears flow over, but I hastily pulled myself together. I could not afford to break the dam I had built around my heart, unsure whether I could survive another flood. Nodding slowly, I dropped my eyes. "Thank you," I muttered softly.

Once she slipped the dress on—a perfect fit, no surprise—I shifted my gaze to the floor, holding it steadily on my toes. Never had I wanted to see myself in these garments, and I remained determined that I never would. With my chin tucked, I felt Mary place a jewel-encrusted tiara on my head.

Finally, she stilled her arms and met my eyes. Her lips were still, saying nothing, but her face said everything. A jumble of pain and sorrow, her cheeks still swelled from her own dried tears. Guilt filled my chest as I remembered that it was not only I who was grieving for love lost.

I sighed. There was no point stalling any longer. "Let's get this over with," I said dryly. I spun from the vanity and trudged toward the exit, throwing open the door as I marched into the hallway.

A crowd of Kreagan guards were waiting outside. They stared at me silently, their faces blank as they studied my regal attire. Two hands suddenly took hold of my wrists. I immediately whipped my arms away and caught the knight in my most dangerous scowl. "I can walk myself," I spit. The man lifted his hands defensively and backed away. No one dared come any closer. They only watched, waiting for me to make the next move. I twisted around and led the way toward the front of the castle.

Together we plodded down the long hall. I walked quickly, my arms crossed firmly across my chest. The footsteps of the trailing soldiers clanked in a rhythmic march. If I closed my eyes and listened, I could almost imagine I was leading them into battle rather than being ushered to my ruin. But when I opened them again, I was still a broken woman lumbering toward her fate. How cruel a reminder these halls had become of what once was and what would no longer be.

The palace doors were already open when we arrived. The glow of the evening sun poured through the entrance, painting the floor gold, but when I walked into the light, shivers rolled down my spine.

As I stepped through the towering castle doors, taking my first breath of fresh air since my sprint across the training fields, I felt a million eyes settle upon me, their stares like ants crawling along my skin. Through the sea of Kreagan guards, a path was formed. The soldiers, standing at attention, formed a fence around the make-shift aisle. At the end of the balcony stood a stern priest wearing silver robes and a satin cap. On his left was a band of well-dressed spectators, vassals, and dames I had never seen before.

Before them, clothed in a dazzling scarlet gown, was Ingrid. She stood perfectly erect, her hands clasped before her like the pompous royal she was. Her chin stuck out in its typical repugnant way, and upon her lips was a vile grin. Unlike me, this was a day she had long been waiting for. The day of her triumph.

Across from her, I saw Prince Rune. He had transformed into someone almost unrecognizable since I had last seen him. His chest was filled out with a white collared shirt and a thick black vest. A pair of kingly breeches hid his slender legs beneath their flowing velvet. Upon his head sat a tremendous gold crown, nearly double the size of his skull. The only tell-tale sign of his identity was the long blond hair that ran down his back in smooth ringlets.

Behind them all, beyond the castle gates and across the emerald fields, was a mass of Vitalian citizens. They clustered together behind the small wedding party, yet covered the distance from the castle grounds to the ends of the village. At this distance, I could not make out their faces, only a blur of what remained of my people spread throughout the valley. My chest stung as I imagined what they thought of me now, their crown princess turned traitor. I could only hope that they knew the truth.

A hush fell over the crowd as I began my long walk down the aisle. The prince swung his head my way, his blue eyes widening when they landed on me. He stared openly, but I was unable to read the expression on his face. Was it apprehension? Was it dread? Or was it awe?

I set my jaw and focused my gaze past them all, fixing my sights on the green hills in the distance, slowly dimming under the sinking sun. Still, I could sense Ingrid's glare burning into my skin. I wanted more than anything to match her stare, to show that she was far from breaking me, even now. But I feared if I did, the anger I desperately bottled down would pour over, and I had no doubt that my punishment would involve the villagers congregated behind her. Instead, I let my mind run beyond the valley, far from this place, pretending I was anywhere else as my pride was stripped away.

When I reached the end of the walkway, I took my place opposite the prince. Clasping my hands in front of my stomach, I stared down at my white knuckles, realizing with a bitter laugh that I finally looked like the obedient princess that Ingrid wanted me to be.

The priest cleared his throat and opened his large Bible. "We are gathered here," he began in an emphatic tone, "in the sight of God and His bounty of angels to join together this man and this woman in a binding of life."

"Make it quick, Father," Ingrid warned over my shoulder.

The priest reddened and hurriedly skipped a few pages. Straightening, he turned to face the prince. "Prince Rune, wilt though have this woman to be thy wedded wife, to live together after God's ordinance in the holy estate of matrimony? Wilt thou love her, comfort her, honor, and keep her, in sickness and in health; and forsaking all other, keep thee only unto her, so long as ye both shall live?"

He swallowed. "I will," he mumbled.

The priest nodded then turned toward me. But upon viewing my rigid jaw and piercing eyes, he paled and dipped his face back down to his script. "Princess Evangeline, wilt thou have this man to be thy wedded husband, to live together after God's ordinance in the holy estate of matrimony? Wilt thou obey him, and serve him, love, honor, and keep him in sickness and in health; and, forsaking all other, keep thee only unto him, so long as ye both shall live?"

The knots in my stomach twisted tighter. It was an oath to give my life away, a promise to abandon myself for a much crueler fate. I closed my eyes and inhaled. "I will."

He adorned an exaggerated smile. "I now pronounce you husband and wife." He turned around to address the throng of citizens. "May God bless our community and all here present. Go now, be of good cheer, and celebrate our happy couple!"

Dead silence swallowed the valley. The crowd only watched us with grim faces. They stared at the outlandish presentation through somber eyes. Their quiet persisted, and I realized they were waiting for something, waiting for me. I knew what I had to do.

Stepping past the priest, I approached the vast assembly of townspeople. A nearby Kreagan guard lunged forward to stop me, but Ingrid halted him with a light hand on his shoulder. "Let her go," she said lowly. "She knows what is at stake."

Every eye was fixed on me as I reached the end of the balcony, still contemplating my words. Like me, their entire world had been upended in a matter of days. I knew they were scared, lost. They were searching for the dimmest ray of hope, a hope only I could provide. I took a deep breath.

"We have endured many trials," I began, listening to the heavy timbre of my voice echo through the valley. "Much has changed in recent days. Several of us have lost those we love." I bit my lip, willing my voice to remain steady. "No doubt, we have faced our greatest challenges."

I lifted my chest higher and amplified my voice. "I know it may seem like the future is uncertain. But we must remember that together, we will not be broken. United, we shall not fall."

It was quiet at first, and I worried that they had indeed lost all trust in me. Then, a few hesitant claps rang out from the distant fields. Their uncertainty gradually fell away, and applause rolled through the crowd like a wave. A few spectators near the gates started to cheer, and slowly, the ovation grew louder. The energy spread across the valley, culminating in an impassioned roar.

"That is enough," Ingrid said. "Take them inside."

In less than a second, a pack of guards shoved me back, blocking me from the animated mob of citizens before urging me and the prince toward the castle. I obeyed willingly, striding coolly back down the aisle and through the open doors before the men could lay a hand on me. There was no point in resisting now. The damage had been done. The spark had been lit.

Chapter 9

Rune

I hurried along behind the lines of Kreagan knights ushering me through the palace halls alongside the stone-faced Princess Evangeline. The men were escorting us to our final destination of the evening: the royal bedroom. Behind me, I could hear the unmistakable click of my mother's quick gait followed by the hustling tread of her court. The parade pressed onward, not wasting a second on any frivolous conversation or trivial formalities. Even with my long stride, I had to rush to keep up with them. I knew if I slowed down, the queen and her attendants would not hesitate to trample over me.

The endless hallway was a blur. The air around me felt thin, like it had been sucked of oxygen. No matter how deeply I tried to breathe, my lungs still felt empty. My vision had grown hazy, and my head was spinning, making me dizzy. In a few seconds, I would have to race out of the procession to avoid vomiting all over my new wife.

My new wife. The phrase sounded utterly absurd in my mind. Never in a million years would I have guessed I would one day marry—let alone to the princess of Vitalia—and certainly not like this. I chanced a peek over my shoulder toward the woman in question. She carried herself gracefully, strutting forward with ease.

Despite standing an entire foot shorter than me, she held herself high with her chin lifted, her face rigid and unreadable.

No emotions were discernable from her stern features. I wondered how she always appeared so calm, so self-assured. She must have known what came next. I had been dreading the impending night more than the wedding itself. Just the thought of our compulsory act had made sleep impossible for the last three nights. Instead, I lay in constant apprehension. But I saw no trace of fear in her, no sign of the horror that threatened to overtake me now that the time had finally come. My hands trembled violently while she seemed unfazed. This woman was made of stone.

When I returned my gaze forward, I saw that we were closing in on the princess's bedroom, the one we were now to share as husband and wife. A single guard was patiently waiting by the door. As we approached, our entourage split apart, forming an open path. The men turned and stood at attention, watching as we traversed the remainder of the hall. The bedroom door was quickly drawn open. A swarm of eyes clung to me expectantly, the final task of the night placed delicately upon my shoulders, the inevitable finale to our wedding ceremony. I passed hesitantly through the passage of soldiers, nervously inching forward with the queen still on my heels.

Upon the knights' parting, the princess sped from her place beside me and stomped briskly into the bedroom, leaving me to cross the remaining distance alone. But when I reached the door, I froze. My limbs turned to ice. One more step and I feared I would shatter to pieces.

My mother's cool breath grated into the nape of my neck. I gritted my teeth and carefully turned to face her. The tip of her nose was mere inches from my face, her dark eyes penetrating as they bore into mine. "Are you sure that—?" I began.

In milliseconds, she grasped the front of my tunic and yanked me downward, our faces now even. Her cold lips scratched my ear. "Don't you dare screw this up," she snarled. "Either you fuck that girl or I will walk in there and make you."

My ears burned as I was flooded with terror. Yet, I still could not will myself to turn around. I was confronted by two of my worst nightmares, but at least the one standing before me was familiar. "Perhaps we can take some time first to—"

The queen threw all of her weight forward and shoved her palms into my chest, sending me stumbling backward. "I will see you both in the morning," she said calmly before slamming the door in my face. My head jerked backward as the hard oak collided with my nose.

I was not sure how long I stood there, too petrified to turn around. I stalled for as long as I could, biting my lip and trying to block out the harrowing silence. Finally, I took a deep inhale and turned.

Princess Evangeline stood along the wall opposite me, her arms folded stiffly along her chest and her menacing gaze piercing my soul. My heart was beating so fast that I feared it would leap from my body. I coughed awkwardly, unable to withstand the silence any longer. "So…"

Without a pause, the princess darted toward me. I instinctively slumped back, sinking into the closed door. "Let's get one thing straight," she said, thrusting her finger into my chest. "We might be married to the rest of the world, but in here, I will have nothing to do with you. I will play your games to keep my people safe, but I would not *obey* or *serve* you even if you held a knife to my neck."

"I—," I croaked before she silenced me with another jab to my sternum.

"If you even try to order me around, I will bring so much pain upon your head that you will be begging me for mercy."

She waited, her index finger still jammed into my ribs. "Understood," I mumbled. But the princess had not finished yet.

"And if you ever so much as *think* about laying a hand on me," she continued, pressing me firmly against the door, "I will slice off your cock and watch you bleed out on the floor."

I swallowed, my eyes wide. She was far from bluffing, that much was clear. We both knew she could tear me limb from limb, and she would do it without blinking an eye. "Any questions?" she asked softly, her mouth so close I could feel her spittle on my chin. I eagerly shook my head.

Satisfied, she backed away, keeping her stern glare fixed on my face. I kept my eyes up, trying not to drop them as I normally would under this kind of scrutiny, and for a moment, we stayed that way, watching each other in an electric silence. They were bewitching, those ember orbs. They held a light I had never seen, nearly blinding but somehow liberating. I did not want to let go and risk losing this unfamiliar feeling. But I could not hold her fiery gaze for long. Lowering my head to the floor, I wrung my hands together uncomfortably.

Evangeline exhaled, a sound somewhere between a sigh and a groan. She rolled her eyes as she spun around and stormed toward the other side of the room. "I thought I had seen it all." She stopped at the window and rested her elbows on the sill, staring out into the night. "I have fought and won more battles than I can count. I have defeated cruel tyrants, dethroned self-righteous monarchs, and dismantled entire empires."

Swinging her head back around, she locked eyes with me again. "Then you showed up." She walked toward an open closet at the corner of the room then turned, angrily pacing across the room as she continued her tirade. "You entered my kingdom on a lie, paraded yourself before my people, and feigned your courtesies with false intentions. And all the while, you were sending your army to sneak around my palace and take out my men. You took Vitalia without an ounce of dignity. You are murdering cowards, all of you. You destroyed my kingdom and stole the remains for yourselves."

She paused her rapid pacing, her forehead red with indignation as she turned my way once more. "You killed my father." This time, her words held more hurt than enmity. My stomach twisted with guilt.

In a flash, she regained her sharp scowl, deeper and more sinister than before. She began walking back toward me, her steps slow and foreboding. "And you," she said. "You are the worst of them all." My heart jolted in my chest, caught off guard by this harsh accusation.

"It may be your mother who commands your army and orders people killed." She took her final step, cornering me once again. "But you," she shoved me roughly with both hands, sending my back crashing into the door. "You watch it all happen and you do not do a goddamn thing. You are a prince, for Christ's sake. You could stand up, say something, try to do what is right. But you sit back and say nothing," she barked with a second shove, my aching shoulder blades connecting with wood once more.

"You are the weakest, most worthless man I have ever met."

Each of her insults was like a sharp knife puncturing my flesh, but these words stung the harshest. I flinched from the impact of this final blow, staring down at my bony legs and wishing more than anything that I was dead. "I know."

Confused, she twisted her features in irritation. "You know?"

I carefully lifted my head. "You are right." Not sure what else to say, I dropped my eyes in disgrace, my heart sunk.

After a pause, Evangeline scoffed. "Then you should also know that I will never forgive you for what you did to my father. He was the greatest king Vitalia had ever seen, the strongest, most loyal man to ever wear the crown. And it is your fault he is dead." For just a moment, she let her words hang in the air between us then started to walk away.

"She killed my father, too," I blurted. The princess froze. Slowly, she rotated back around, eyeing me questioningly.

"He just vanished one day," I continued, my faint voice barely cutting through the sudden stillness in the room. "My mother—she was not upset or worried. She was practically unfazed. You would think the disappearance of a king would throw a kingdom into chaos, but it was like he never existed."

I dared a quick glance upward to see if she was still listening, surprised to find her enraptured. "He was the only thing standing in her way, the only one who could stop her rampage. It was never proven, but…" I sighed. "We all knew that whoever dared search for the truth would be her next victim."

The princess studied me. I could not read her face, but the way she looked at me felt different somehow, almost softer. "Well, that is the difference between you and me," she said. "Unlike you, I do not stay silent when someone I love is murdered." She turned away, her braids swinging along her back, and stormed into the closet, slamming the door behind her.

I released a long breath, the tightness in my shoulders loosening. Finally alone, I used the opportunity to take in the room. It was nothing at all like I had imagined. It hardly resembled a princess's chambers. There were no bright walls or colorful décor. Instead, the entire room was blanketed in black. I gently unglued my feet from their place on the floor and tiptoed away from the door.

Her bed was colossal. Her obsidian sheets were further darkened beneath the shade of her sheer canopy. A slew of pillows lay strewn about the mattress and her crumpled blankets were left untucked.

Beside her towering bed frame was an ashen brown nightstand, covered by a hodgepodge of clutter: open books, hair clips, feather quills, and loose pages scrawled with unfinished notes. By the window was the largest bookshelf I had ever seen, filled to overflowing with assorted volumes. I stepped closer and read some of the titles: *Huxley's Guide to Swordplay*, *The Complete*

Combat Encyclopedia, Strategic Warfare. I whistled. It was not exactly what I would call light reading.

I turned to survey the silver vanity. Below an enormous mirror, the table was similarly littered with random objects like makeup brushes, lip dyes, and ribbon. Alongside it stood a large dresser. Clothing spilled from the drawers and hung down the sides like ivy. I stared with interest at the various articles, an odd collection of virile tunics and simple dresses. In the far corner of the room was a mountain of riding boots, all of different shades and designs, doubtlessly crafted from the finest leather.

Finally, I came to the open wall across from the bed. Considering the busy nature of the rest of the chamber, I was puzzled by this mostly empty space. The discoloration of the paint indicated that certain objects had once been displayed there but had since been removed, leaving the space mute and lifeless.

"She stole my war prizes," said a voice by my ear. I jumped and spun around, surprised to find Princess Evangeline standing close beside me. I had not heard the closet door open or her footsteps as she drew near. "This is where I used to keep all the weapons and armor I gathered from my fallen enemies," she continued. "Each one holds its own story, a memory I never let myself forget." She peered with longing at the naked wall then shifted her gaze my way, her expression mournful. "But you cannot trust the maniacal warrior princess with swords in her room, can you?"

I stared at her in wonder. It was the first time I had seen her without her rageful glower. She had exchanged her ivory wedding dress for a plain white nightgown. The fabric had no fancy frills or patterns, just sleeves that covered her arms and wrists. Her skirt draped just past her knees, leaving her feet and ankles exposed. Although the gown hung loosely around her, I could still see the curve of her body beneath, her bold shape molding the cotton into its form. She had unwoven her elaborate braids and now her long auburn hair flowed down her chest in waves. Gone was the thick makeup she had worn for the ceremony. I was surprised to find her skin a light bronze tint with a sprinkling of freckles about her cheeks, her face kissed by the sun.

When I finally arrived at her catlike eyes, my cheeks warmed. She had been watching me closely as I scanned her body. I waited for her reprimand, but rather than berate me for my gawking, the princess stared back at me, her head slightly tilted. It was almost as if she was searching for something.

"What are you looking at?" she asked. Her question was not hostile or threatening but curious.

I could have asked her the same thing. Instead, I hastily cleared my throat and tried to lighten my heavy gaze. "Your face—" I started, immediately regretting my poor choice of words.

Her brow furrowed. "Is there something wrong with it?"

"No, no," I stammered. "I mean, you look so different without all that…" I drew a blank and gestured with my hand around my own pale cheeks.

To my surprise, she chuckled, the left corner of her lips peeling upward. "I have always hated cosmetics. They are meant to make me look more regal, but I think I look no different than a common jester."

"Me too," I replied.

She cocked an eyebrow. "How generous of you,"

she said sarcastically.

I bit my lip. "I meant to say that I dislike them as well, all the powders and colors and such. But without them, you look—" I cut myself off, choosing my words with care. She watched me through squinted eyes as she waited for me to finish my sentence. I swallowed. "You look so real."

She scoffed, clearly amused. I laughed nervously, mostly to myself, and stared down at my feet.

The hint of a grin on her mouth only lasted so long. As if suddenly remembering her loathing, she snapped back to attention and reset her frown before quickly shuffling toward her bed. "If you don't mind, I have had a long day," she said as she climbed under the sheets.

I stiffened, not daring to move as I contemplated what she expected me to do next. She had made it abundantly clear, to my relief, that we would not be consummating our marriage that night. But whether we liked it or not, we were stuck in this room together until morning. Where did she want me to go? Lying on the mattress, she watched as I nervously ran through my options. Eventually, I risked a single step toward the other side of the bed.

"You must be out of your damn mind," Evangeline growled. I leapt back from the mattress as if it spewed flames. The princess grabbed at a pillow from the pile of cushions beside her and hurled it my way. I shot my arms up, barely catching it before it collided with my face.

"In my room, you will sleep on the ground," she commanded. I peered down at the empty space on the floor then looked back up at her in dismay, sure this was some kind of halfhearted jest. But I was no longer an object of interest to her. Before I could say a word, she blew out the candles on her bedside table and rolled onto her side, leaving me standing in darkness.

After a few minutes, I realized I had no choice but to settle on the hard floor. I carefully set the lone pillow beneath my head and, quietly so as not to disturb the sleeping princess, removed my vest and tunic, laying them over my torso like a blanket. As comfortable as I could hope to be, I leaned back and stared up at the ceiling. Despite my exhaustion after several days of debilitating dread, I knew sleep would evade me once again that night. Adrenaline still flowed rapidly through my veins, set to full speed by the most nerve-wracking few hours of my existence. But I closed my eyes nonetheless and lay perfectly still as I listened to Evangeline's steady breathing just a few feet above.

Chapter 10

Eve

I woke to the roar of distant thunder. Only when the fog of sleep cleared did I recognize the sound as snoring. In a flash, I jolted upright and scanned the room for the intruder, my limbs stiff and ready to attack.

Then, the memory of the previous night came flooding back to me, and I relaxed. The loud snoring was, of course, none other than Prince Rune sleeping soundly on the floor beside my bed. I rolled my eyes and turned over, plopping my head back onto my pillow.

Through the window, I saw the dim light of dawn. The sun was yet to rise, its edge just barely peeking over the horizon. I closed my eyes and pressed both sides of my pillow to my ears, but it was no use. I would never be able to fall back asleep with this racket. I sighed and rose from my bed, deciding to make use of the little time I had to myself.

I walked over to my dresser and snatched a few items hanging sloppily from an open drawer. I threw on the gray tunic and trousers I had selected, not caring when the cotton tousled my hair, and grabbed a cloak from a nearby hook. I snatched a stray ribbon from my vanity and tied my hair back in a tight knot then concealed my work within my hood.

I tiptoed toward my bedroom door but paused when

I saw Rune sprawled along the ground. Still snoring, his mouth hung open in the shape of a rose window. His limbs were splayed in all directions, his tunic settled like a thin sheet over his chest and neck. As if chilled by my breath, he curled into a ball with a slight shiver. I felt a twinge of guilt pinch my stomach but hastily dismissed it. He deserved no luxuries, let alone pity, from me. He could freeze for all I cared. I twisted back toward the door and fled the room, leaving him on the cold stone.

****

Kneeling on the gravel by the stream, I dipped my fingers into the cool water and swirled them in a long figure eight, temporarily stalling the river's natural flow. The surface was sparkling beneath the morning sun, the water so clear I could see the brownish green algae growing through the stony riverbed. Normally on a morning like this, I would take a quick dip, thankful for the chill against my bare skin, a welcome contrast to the blazing heat. But this morning the wind blew in frigid gusts, and I wrapped myself tightly in my wool cloak.

I was surprised to make it this far from the palace without getting caught, and if I was being honest with myself, it had been a fairly simple escape. When I first entered the main hall, buried within the folds of my cloak, I had shifted into stealth mode. Not many guards were moving about the castle at such an early hour, but a few were pacing leisurely along the corridor. I snuck carefully toward the exit, but as I rounded the last corner, a passing guard spotted me and I him.

He froze. I winced. Visions flashed through my mind of being dragged back to my room and locked inside. But to my surprise, the man casually turned his head away and walked toward the opposite side of the hall, acting as if he had not seen me. Confused but unwilling to press my luck, I skid out of the castle and hurried for the trees.

I jogged through the orchard, hopping over the fallen apples that lay in my path. After a while, the trees grew denser, and I had to lift my eyes from the ground to avoid crashing into the towering pines. Deep in the forest, confident that I was sufficiently hidden within the foliage, I slowed to a walk. I continued to follow the sound of water babbling against rocks, knowing I would soon reach the rolling stream.

Fall had come early this year. Memories of summer's heat still tickled my skin, but browning pine needles and leaves from the great oaks littered the forest floor, and the sun's warmth was blocked by a thick layer of clouds. I strolled down the hidden path, more so by instinct than by sight, and listened to the robins singing upon the branches, their song signaling the birth of day.

A clearing in the brush preceded the rumbling stream, and I was instantly enveloped by a sense of nostalgia. I had not been to this place since the invasion of the Kreagan Empire, and I soon felt the weight of my absence. It was the perfect place to find reprieve from the pressures within the castle walls. It was my safe haven, my personal oasis away from the long list of expectations piled on my shoulders.

I moved back from the water and hugged my knees to my chest. I could not stop thinking about the odd interaction I had with the Kreagan guard that morning. Why hadn't he stopped me? Why hadn't he run after me or sounded the alarms? If I wanted to, I could keep running, not looking back until I was miles from Vitalia's borders.

The realization dawned on me like a stab to the heart. I was not running. I was never going to run, and Ingrid knew it. They all knew it.

I could imagine it now: Ingrid instructing her leading knights on how to properly manage the unruly princess. "She will fight, kick, and bite. She will spit, scream, and curse. But she will never leave, not with all that she has to lose." No wonder the guard had let me walk right out the castle doors. Everyone knew that I was not going anywhere.

I buried my head in my knees and ground my teeth until my face shook. I hated everything about that cold-hearted queen. I loathed her egotistical smile and her cold stare. But I despised her most of all because she was right about me. Abandoning my people went against everything I knew. Leaving them behind was the one thing I could never do, even if I wanted to.

I sighed and leaned forward, daring to look down at my reflection in the water. I knew the woman I saw there was me, but I was finding it harder and harder to believe. Could this possibly be the same woman who had once fought off twenty trained men singlehandedly? The woman who had once killed an enemy with a single arrow to the eye? The woman who could get anything she wanted from any man she pleased?

Now all I saw was a helpless princess married to a child and forced to obey a frail queen or suffer consequences worse than death. This was not the same woman who had commanded armies of thousands. This was a fraud, a mockery of her people's strength and her parents' sacrifice.

I laughed dryly to myself and watched the girl in the water do the same. I used to believe that I would be the first woman to rule Vitalia, without a man in sight to interfere with my reign. I did not listen when they told me it would never happen, that no queen could ever lead her kingdom alone. But they had been right all along.

And the worst part was that I would not fight. I would not try to take back the kingdom that was rightfully mine. I would not stand up to Ingrid if it meant risking the lives of my people. I would never be the woman I once was. The broken girl before me now was who I would be for the rest of my life.

Dropping my face into my palms, I let my pain turn to sobs. Tears flowed down my face like rivers. My cries turned to wails as my sorrow turned helpless. I looked back at the water to get another look at my face, now swollen and red. I gritted my teeth and cursed the woman I now despised. I slammed my fist against the water repeatedly, forming ripple after ripple until she faded from view.

****

When I returned to find my bedroom door ajar, I immediately knew something was wrong. I hastened through the rest of the hall and flung the door wide. The first thing I noticed was the empty space on the floor beside my bed. Rune was gone, and the pillow I had loaned him was propped neatly against my bed frame.

Then, I saw three Kreagan guards congregated around my bookshelf. They waited in a single-file line as a fourth man stacked my books on their outstretched arms until the pile reached their chins. One by one, they withdrew, taking with them what little remained of my possessions.

I stomped toward them in four brisk strides, my fists clutched tightly by my waist. "What the hell do you think you are doing?" My arms shook with rage.

"Queen's orders," the last remaining guard said, his tone flat and uninterested. He lifted the final stack of books from the lowest shelf and began following the others out of the room, but I darted in front of him, blocking his path.

"You cannot just seize my belongings!" I yelled.

"Queen Ingrid requested the confiscation of all inappropriate literature from this room," the guard recited with an impatient sigh.

He tried to walk around me, but I cut him off with a swift sidestep, using my body as a living blockade. Heat swelled in my face, and my body trembled with fury. "I am the princess of Vitalia, and I demand you return my books at once!" I commanded with a sharp shove to his shoulder.

The stack of volumes teetered in his arms. He planted his feet and tensed to keep the pile upright. Upon regaining his balance, he stared down at me with an irritated frown. I stood my ground, holding his gaze and lifting my chin higher. "I said put them down!" I growled through my teeth.

Without warning, the guard thrust his elbow into my face. The power of his knock sent me crashing to the floor, my head smashing against stone. Covering my nose with my hand, I pressed myself onto my knees, but the guard was already crossing the doorway, the last of my books clung to his chest. "Bastard!" I yelled after him, my voice stifled by my palm.

I rose to my feet and carefully made my way to the vanity. At the mirror, I dropped my hand and groaned. My lips and chin were drenched with blood steadily flowing from my nose. I moved toward a nearby basket and pulled out a loose rag. After dipping the tip into the water basin, I pressed the cloth to my nostrils, wincing as my nose stung in response.

Just then, I heard the shuffle of approaching footsteps. I spun around to find Mary entering the room. At my blood-splotched face, her lips paled and her eyes widened. "What…how did…" she stuttered.

"Do not ask," I groaned into the rag. Mary closed her gaping mouth then hesitantly closed the distance between us. Peeling the rag from my hand, she tenderly dabbed at the blood already drying on my upper lip. "What are you doing here?" I asked, my mouth stiff.

"I am to dress you for your morning meal," she said as she rubbed at a particularly stubborn glob of blood on my chin. I frowned at her in puzzlement. No one had informed me of any formal occasion this morning.

Reading my face, Mary dropped the rag. "Queen Ingrid has requested your attendance at breakfast." She tilted her head questioningly. "I thought you knew."

I slumped lower in my chair. I had been notified that we would all be dining together once Rune and I were wed, but it never crossed my mind that these would be formal meals. My father and I had eaten together often, but these occasions had always been most casual. I would frequently show up to the table sweating after morning training, and my father would still be wearing his pajamas, having just rolled out of bed. Never once had we donned our formal attire for a meal unless we were hosting a nobleman for a feast.

Once my face was clear of blood, Mary picked up my brush and started the excruciating process of untangling my hair. I clenched my jaw and squeezed my eyes shut, quickly growing exasperated. If Ingrid expected me to appear preen and proper on the daily, I was not sure how long I could preserve my sanity.

****

The doormen lining the entrance to the dining hall chose wisely when they stepped aside as I approached. Using pure physical force, I flung the doors open myself and stomped hotly into the room. Without delay, I trudged to the only empty chair around the table, keeping my arms crossed. Once seated, I fixed my gaze on my cutlery to avoid Ingrid's critical glare, but I peeked up at her nonetheless. The long refectory table, once replete with nobles during our great Vitalian banquets, now had only three chairs along its edges. Prince Rune was seated at the center of the length of the table, several yards from the other two chairs. Meanwhile, Ingrid occupied the seat opposite mine, both of us placed at our own respective ends of the table. Her hands were neatly folded in her lap, but her embittered sneer betrayed her vexation.

I had hardly settled in my chair when she lifted her chin and projected her voice across the expanse. "You are late." Her lips twitched.

In an attempt to mirror her posture, I entwined my fingers and rested them with faux delicacy upon my legs. "Unfortunately," I started, the sarcasm in my tone unmistakable, "I was forced to extend my morning preparations after one of your *benevolent* guards gave me a bloody nose." To my right, I saw Rune fling his head upright and peer over at me. His fingers halted their fidgeting, now pressed stiffly into his lap. His eyes, usually flecked with lingering anxiety, now glowed with concern. But I heeded him no attention, my vision locked on the woman seated across from me.

She lifted an eyebrow, her expression revealing

more amusement than surprise. "I believe it is safe to assume his actions had just cause." The side of her lips curved upward.

I squinted my nose and punctured her with a resentful sneer. But before I could object, a well-dressed butler approached the table, interrupting our heated conversation. "Breakfast is served." His hands were clasped behind his back, and his chin was held upward, flaunting a pair of pursed lips. Lines of servants circled the table holding steaming plates and brimming pitchers. The dishes were placed in unison atop the three placemats, and a trailing server filled each empty chalice with a dark crimson wine.

All at once, my senses were overtaken by the delectable spread. The smokey scent of salmon permeated my nostrils, prompting a low growl from my stomach. At the sight of the rows of assorted breads and cheeses, my mouth began to water. Only then did I realize that I had not eaten a morsel in nearly 24 hours, too nervous to keep anything down since yesterday.

I reached eagerly for my fork and knife and began shoveling salmon into my mouth, moaning with delight at its sumptuous flavor. Once the fish had been devoured, I stacked several slices of cheese onto a piece of bread and swallowed it whole, washing it down with a swig of wine.

I leaned back for a moment to catch my breath. Then, with my elbow lifted, the bread hovering before my open mouth, I caught sight of Ingrid. She had yet to touch her food. In fact, she had not moved an inch since the lavish spread was presented. Instead, she was observing me closely, a thick film of disgust coating her features.

My face warmed. A combination of shame and annoyance swelled in my belly. I slowly set the bread back down and, lifting my napkin from its place beside my plate, I delicately dabbed at the corners of my lips. This seemed to pacify her. For now. At last, she gingerly lifted her fork and nibbled on a small bite of fish.

Once I had finished eating, I lifted a fist to my mouth and cleared my throat. Both Rune and Ingrid looked up from their plates, peering over at me questioningly. I knit my fingers together and rested my arms on the table with my head raised. "I would like to discuss the removal of my books."

Ingrid frowned at me in irritation, but I did not withdraw my gaze. She watched me thoughtfully as she finished chewing a bite of bread, contemplating its texture with distaste. When she finally swallowed, her grimace remained. "We like to withhold conversation until the conclusion of our meals," she said scathingly.

"Well, I find this topic of great importance and insist we discuss it forthwith." I crossed my arms stubbornly and tried to match her glower as I waited for her next move. Rune leaned slightly my way, his eyes wide with warning. I ignored him.

"It is not your place to determine when to speak and when to be silent," Ingrid asserted, annoyance edging her voice. "So I suggest we resume this conversation later."

"Or we could discuss it now." My words boomed across the table, my insistence now bordering on verbal assault.

Ingrid, her face twisted in a scowl, dropped her fork and let it clank loudly onto her plate. "Fine," she said. She laid her hands on the table and lifted her chest, glaring down her nose at me. "I have ordered all improper texts removed from your bedroom. A lady in my court does not associate herself with matters of war."

"And you found that reason enough to seize my belongings without my approval?" My eyebrows furrowed in indignation.

She stared at me sharply, carefully considering her words before she spoke again. "This is no longer your father's kingdom," she stated calmly. "I make the decisions now, and my decision is final."

I sprang from my chair and stood leaning over the table, gripping its edge so tightly my knuckles whitened. "I am still the princess and rightful heir of Vitalia. I deserve to be treated with respect," I bellowed, spittle flying from my mouth.

A faint smile formed along Ingrid's lips. "You are wrong." She leaned forward, resting her elbows on the wood. "Soon you will learn that being a princess in my kingdom grants you no privileges." She raised her eyebrows and tilted her head. "I suggest you take a good look in the mirror, Evangeline. Any influence you might have wielded in the past is long gone. It is time you accept that."

My face burned with fury. My arms and legs shook violently, my entire body steaming with a wild rage. Without thinking, I grabbed my empty plate and flung it across the table. Ingrid ducked, barely dodging the dish before it shattered on the floor behind her. "You callous bitch!" I roared. "You will not get away with this!"

I kicked the front leg of my chair, sending it toppling noisily to the ground. Then, with my shoulders hunched and my feet heavy, I stomped toward the door, avoiding Rune's dumbfounded gawking. The pounding of boots filled my ears as Ingrid's guards rushed to apprehend me.

But at the sound of her voice, the men halted in their tracks. "Let her go," she said dryly as she swept crumbs from my hurled breakfast off her cheek. "She will submit soon enough."

I did not stay to hear the rest. I rammed into the large doors, letting the handles slam noisily against the wall. Tearing through the castle halls, I felt my limbs quake with suppressed fury. Ingrid thought she could mold me into the perfect servant. Just like the Vitalian nobles who had tried and failed to restrain me, she wanted to bend me to her will. I had complied to marry her clod of a son, but this is where I drew the line. I would not allow her to change me. I would not let her cruel tyranny shape me into someone I was not.

Powered by a vengeful wrath, I hastened onward. Kreagan servants and soldiers alike jumped aside as I trudged down each corridor. Most stopped to stare. None dared meet my eye, fearing a single look might turn them to stone. I did not blame them. From the fire that built in my chest, I suspected I would soon breathe flames.

I had almost reached the backend of the palace when I noticed a scuttling of feet from behind me. Taking a quick turn over my shoulder, I was unsurprised to find a mob of Kreagan guards trailing me. I squeezed my fists tighter and picked up my pace. It was high time these knights learned who they were dealing with.

As I glided out the back door, I slid my hand imperceptibly behind a nearby guard and smoothly unsheathed his sword from the scabbard around his waist. The soldiers pursuing me suddenly shifted into high alert. Servants shrieked and ran from my path as I stormed toward the open training field. The weight of the blade in my hand was like an old friend, heavy but fitting. The sunlight shimmered along the steel, its sheen blinding. I pressed my thumb against the hilt and slid it across the smooth wood. A surge of energy rushed through me. If Ingrid truly believed she could tame me, wait until she saw my savagery in action.

One foot on the training field and an entire fleet of Kreagan soldiers had me surrounded. I lifted my sword and pointed it toward their eye line, my face set in a deadly scowl. With my weapon raised, the knights took a cautious step back. The guard nearest me reached for his weapon. I masterfully swung my blade downward, striking his wrist with the flat of my sword and sending his own soaring through the air. He gripped his forearm from the sting, but not a drop of blood seeped through his skin.

The other knights reacted quickly, but not quickly enough. Before they could reach their own weapons, I twisted my sword upward, the edge hovering just inches from their necks. Reluctantly, they lifted their hands in surrender and took a cautious step back.

Above me, I noticed a flash of green. Ingrid, her floor-length emerald gown now completely visible, stood upon the viewing balcony and stared down at me, her expression one of annoyed disinterest. Beside her, Prince Rune gazed down at me in dismay. He shifted his uneasy gaze between me and his mother. Clearly, he was unsure whom to fear more.

A smirk rolled up the side of my mouth. "May your bravest warrior step forward," I announced, now facing Ingrid. "Or are you afraid I will defeat them all and humiliate you in front of your servants?" I crossed my arms and widened my smug grin, letting the sword hang loosely by my side.

The crowd peered upward toward the balcony as they awaited her response. Ingrid darkened, contorting her face into a twisted grimace. Finally, she shooed a hand casually forward and rolled her eyes. "Amuse me."

My heart beat with anticipation, and I turned to set my sights upon my adversaries. They glimpsed at one another uncertainly. "Well," I said, "who is up to the challenge?" No one moved. Some stared at the ground while others fidgeted awkwardly. It was obvious none of them had ever fought a woman before, and none were willing to be the first.

"I knew it," I laughed. "Anyone can talk a big game until the princess has a sword in her hand. I see you are all too afraid to face a worthy opponent." A few men squinted toward me, their faces reddening with humiliation.

My patience was wearing thin, and I was about to select a competitor myself when a tall, sturdy knight squeezed through the crowd. "I will fight you," he grunted in a low voice. Unlike the guards beside him, he was not cowering with unease. His eyes beamed with bitter hatred. His bulking shoulders plunged through his leather jerkin, and his wide neck bulged outward beneath a sharp chin.

My mischievous smile widened as I crouched down, assuming my fighting stance. "With pleasure."

The man slipped a long blade from his sheath and began his approach, his fiery eyes adhered to mine. I backed away slowly and waited for his first strike. It came. I easily deflected it with an upward parry. He struck again, swinging his weapon toward my exposed hip. I leapt back and squeezed my belly inward. The sword glided through the air, missing its target entirely.

The force of his drive threw his body sideways, and he teetered slightly to the right.

Rushing at the opportunity, I lunged for his unguarded arm and carved a clean slash into his muscular bicep. The man howled and reached his free hand towards the wound. Still distracted, he did not notice as I angled my weapon and shoved its hilt into his chest. The impact sent him soaring backward and crashing to the ground with a grunt.

I spun back to the onlooking soldiers, resuming my ready position. "Who's next?"

The guards stared at their fallen comrade in disbclicf, some of them with their mouths slightly ajar. Suddenly, I sensed a rapid pounding of boots against the earth from my left. I pivoted swiftly to face my new opponent. His weapon was lifted above his head, preparing for a forceful downward strike. I twisted my body away from him and tilted my sword across my back, effortlessly blocking the blow from behind. Then, leaning into the pressure of his blade, I pressed upward, sending him off balance, and spun my body in a 180° turn to face him. Still wobbling, he spun his arms like windmills to try and regain his stability. But his movements lacked finesse. I concluded my twirl with a pommel to his knee. He collapsed onto his chest, wincing in pain. His weakness was terribly provoking, so I thrust the toe of my slipper into his Adam's apple. He groaned, burying his face in his hands before scurrying behind the line of knights.

Suddenly, a third man sped forward and jabbed his ax toward my chest. I swung my sword in a clockwise arc, curving the trajectory of his blow to the left. But his feet remained firmly planted. He charged onward, snapping the weapon toward my left breast. I spun my blade in the opposite direction to block his attack once more. His body pressed onward, forcing me into the defensive. With several quick strikes, he plunged his ax toward every corner of my body only to have each assault deflected. I tired quickly of following his lead. As he heaved a particularly strong blow, I darted to the side and let his ax swing through open air. He tumbled forward, tripping over his own feet and collapsing onto the dirt.

Satisfied, I ambled over to my fallen enemy and pressed the sole of my foot into his back. I tossed my sword aside and let it clatter obnoxiously onto the ground. Resting my hands on my hips, I stared up at the queen, my smirk now as pompous as ever. "You cannot defeat me, Ingrid," I announced. "I always win."

She was seething, her ears pink with frustration. "Enough," she growled. "Put an end to this." The command was directed at the remaining guards still huddled around me, albeit at a much greater distance than before. With that, she twisted away and plodded back into the castle, refusing to entertain my childish games any longer.

The rest of the knights suddenly recovered their nerves, each one slowly approaching with weapon in hand. I hunched down to prepare for their attack, but as I took my first step forward, my arms were seized by a group of soldiers who flanked me while I was not looking. I squirmed within their grasp, resisting with my whole being as they dragged me back toward the castle. "You cowards!" I screamed repeatedly as I thrashed my teeth and wrestled to escape their clutches.

The crowd that had gathered to watch my display

quickly scattered, resuming their respective tasks. Each observer sped away, trying their best to ignore my screeching expletives. All but one.

Hanging over the balcony, Prince Rune remained, gaping at me as my defiant gaze met his. His wide eyes bore into my own as I stared him down. His face, like his hair, was the color of ash. This time, there was no hiding the feelings he kept inside. He was utterly entranced.

Chapter 11

Rune

I watched her fight. I watched her seize my mother in the deadliest stare I had ever seen. I watched as she defeated the knights of our prized Kreagan army with ease.

Time went on. I did not stop watching.

Over the next few weeks, I watched her relentless struggle against the guards who tried to restrain her, stared as she mercilessly drove her elbow into their groins. I watched her challenge my mother at every turn, curtly interrupting the queen's stern commands, defending herself without a fear in the world. I watched the way she walked, her strides long and confident, her head held high. She carried herself like an all-powerful empress even though she no longer ruled a single soul. I watched her menacing glare aimed at the men who marched her around the castle. In her eyes was a thoughtful loathing, like she was planning out each detailed murder.

I watched her sleep. Every night, I lay perfectly still on the hard floor beside her massive bed, listening to the rhythm of her breathing. Once I was certain she was asleep, I would peek my eyes over the edge of the mattress. I studied her face, each distinct feature. I soon memorized the cadence of her breath, the slow rise and fall of her chest.

I often found it hard to recognize the ruthless woman I had seen on the training field—the one who had taken down a line of knights with a stolen sword—as this one, lying peacefully on her bed, delicately tucked in silken sheets. But sometimes I saw it, the other side of her she kept so carefully masked. I saw it in her smile when she spoke with her lady's maid. I saw it in her eyes when she stared out at the distant town, looking as if she could see each villager bustling down the cobblestone streets. In these short moments I found proof that her brief tenderness was not a fleeting effect of sleep but a hidden side of her, a kcy part of who she was, kept deeply buried beneath a thick cloak of resentment.

"How is the sex?"

I nearly choked on my tea and had to grip my cup firmly to keep it from slipping from my hand and shattering on the floor. The question had come from my mother, instantly pulling me from my thoughts.

She had called on me out of the blue, requesting I join her for her midmorning tea. It was a time she typically reserved for private meetings with her closest advisors, an appointment she religiously kept. So when she ordered me to meet her in her boudoir, alone, I grew instantly fearful. I was unsure what she sought to discuss with me, but I knew the main topic of our conversation for certain: Princess Evangeline. She was all anyone ever talked about in the castle. Her brutality, her insubordination. Her incessant attack on the very lifeblood of my mother's empire.

I cleared my throat and glanced up at her. "Hm?" I asked, certain I had misheard her.

"The sex," she repeated, casually sipping from her

teacup. "I trust we can expect a pregnancy announcement by next month?"

My cheeks started to burn. My heartbeat pounded in my fingertips, pulsing firmly against the porcelain. My mind was racing, and I floundered as I searched my brain for a satisfactory answer.

She lowered her cup to its saucer and eyed me skeptically. "You are sleeping with her, aren't you Rune?" Her gaze turned cold, and the longer I stayed silent, the more sinister her glare became.

"Of course," I squeaked, willing my face to cool.

"Good." She exhaled, bringing the cup back to her lips and taking another nonchalant drink. I tried to breathe normally, hoping against hope that she would not see through my blatant lie. "The sooner she becomes pregnant," she continued, glimpsing down at the liquid whirling in her cup, "the sooner we can be rid of her."

She plopped her beverage down. The impact rattled the table, making me flinch. She sighed. "She has proven to be more stubborn than I originally thought." She pursed her lips. "She is a menace. A relentless pest." I sensed her growing frustration, surging at the mere mention of the princess.

Shifting her gaze back to me, she relaxed her tense jaw and resumed her unbothered demeanor. "But as soon as she births your heir," she said, reaching for her teacup and lifting the rim to her mouth, "we will never have to see that wretch again."

I gulped as I slowly nodded, careful to avoid her eye. A wave of cold rushed over me, and I gripped my cup with both hands, seeking its warmth. But the tea was already tepid. I was not sure which reality frightened me more: my mother's wrath when she discovered there was not the slightest possibility of a child on the way or the gruesome fate of Princess Evangeline if she were to ever birth my heir.

My heir. The thought was practically laughable. As if there was any chance I would actually sleep with her. Since the wedding, when I had begun spending my nights in the princess's bedroom, she had kept her body carefully concealed. While changing out of her day clothes, she would lock herself in the closet, always undressing out of my view before emerging in her sleeping attire.

And I was more likely to sprout wings than to make any advances. Why would I? I remembered what she told me, the conversation still fresh in my mind. I had no doubt that she would dismember me for even bringing up the subject. And even if she consented, I would not have the faintest clue where to start and would likely suffer from a fatal heart attack.

But that did not stop me from thinking about her all the time. Although I would see her often—at the morning and evening meals my mother forced us to attend and, of course, in her bed chamber each night—most of the time she kept to herself, staying as far from me as possible. I had no idea where she went or what she did during those long hours alone, and I did not dare ask. She was never roaming the halls or lounging in one of the castle apartments. But whenever her presence was requested, she would simply…appear.

Meanwhile, I reverted to my old ways. I hid away in my own room for as long as possible, distracting myself with my drawings until I was called upon. For the last two weeks, the subject of my sketches had been the same: her. At first, I drew her as I first saw her, seated upon her throne, her long, sweeping dress spilled onto the floor, her legs and arms crossed. A silver crown sparkled atop her grim face.

I soon began experimenting with her poses and positions. Sometimes, I drew her with sword in hand, still wearing her morning gown as she drove a long saber into the stomach of a cowering knight, her scrunched features reading "revenge." Other times, I drew her as she was in her bedroom during our awkward nights together, her hair hanging freely down her back, her dress simple, her eyes a mystery.

Recently, however, my sketches had changed. Most of the time, I liked to draw only what I knew, what I had seen and memorized with my own eyes. But in my last few pieces, I took on a new venture. I drew the parts of Evangeline I had never seen before. As always, I would start with her face, carefully detailing her dark eyes and full lips, penciling each strand of hair flowing along her shoulders. Then, I would outline the shape of her body: the perfect curves around her waist, the tender spheres protruding from her chest, the supple front of her bare stomach. I would trace her legs, strong and thick, carrying her commanding figure with ease, and the space between them, a secret cavern that I could only imagine but took pleasure in imagining.

I always made sure to keep my sketches hidden, but I doubled my efforts when I started to draw Evangeline. And since crafting my newest pieces, I often contemplated throwing them into the fire, the only way I could be certain they would never be found. But for some reason, I could not will myself to get rid of them. There was something about those simple likenesses that I feared losing. Instead, I kept them neatly tucked in the folds of my sketchbook and prayed that no one would ever find them.

****

As the days passed and the castle eased into a routine, the nights started to blend together. Our evening ritual remained mostly unchanged: I would softly knock on the bedroom door then wait for her permission to enter. Most nights, I would find her sitting by her vanity, laboriously brushing out her hair. On this particular evening, the pattern continued.

When I slipped into the room, I was not surprised to find her seated by her dressing table, brush in hand. Draped over her shoulders and along the legs of her chair was her signature cotton nightgown, this one a navy blue. In long, slow strokes, she tugged the brush through her bronze waves, wincing as she did so. A thin coat of sweat gleamed on her forehead.

I angled my neck toward the empty space on the floor, my designated sleeping area. After a few nights, I came to the conclusion that the arrangement was all but permanent, so I left the loaned pillow there for the following night. As I expected, it remained exactly where I had left it. But rather than occupy this space right away, I remained standing by the bed post.

I was normally not the one for conversation. I could count on one hand the amount of times I had actually enjoyed speaking with another human being. But there was something about being in this room with her that made silence feel wrong. For the first time in my life, I felt my lips bursting to part, a string of words collecting in my throat. Alone with Evangeline, a foreign urge compelled me to speak, even if I only received a threatening scowl in return. Wringing my hands together, I glanced over at the princess as she wrenched her brush through what seemed like an endless array of knots.

"Why do you do that?" I asked, desperate to put an end to the excruciating silence. It was strange, hearing my own voice bounce between walls and feeling not a sense of dread but relief. I had never known the comfort of speaking and, perhaps, even being heard.

She halted the brush midway through her hair, watching me in the mirror through narrowed eyes. "Why do I do what?" she asked, a defensive edge to her voice.

"Brush your hair," I said. She twisted around in her chair and stared at me with furrowed brows. "I mean," I blabbered, "you obviously do not enjoy it." I tried to loosen the tension with a dull laugh, but her only response was an annoyed squint.

After a long pause, she sighed, dropping her critical gaze as she shifted back toward the mirror. "My lady's maid says I can prevent my hair from knotting if I detangle it every night," she said as she yanked on an especially relentless snag. She grunted when the brush finally broke free, taking a few loose strands with it. "Unfortunately, I have yet to see much improvement."

She threw the brush down on the counter, officially relinquishing the chore for the night. Spinning back around in her chair, she rested her chin on the top rail to observe me. "Don't you ever brush your own hair?"

I reached my hand up to feel one of my blond curls between my fingers. I was surprised to find it had grown well past my shoulders. "Well, yes but…" I racked my brain for a reply. "I do not seem to loathe the activity as much as you do."

I smiled uncomfortably but only received a dry

chuckle in return. "Must be nice," she mumbled, rising from her seat. She walked over to the bed and began peeling back her sheets.

Desperate to continue the conversation, I blurted, "I am sorry about your books." The princess gaped upward, both of her hands still pressed against the covers. This time, she responded with a questioning look. "I know they were important to you," I rambled, hating myself more with every word. But I was in too deep to quit now. "So I…"

I slid my hand from the pocket of my jerkin, bringing with it a thin manuscript. I stared down at the volume. It was one of the titles I had seen when first surveying the room.

Tilting my head upward, I found the princess gazing in astonishment at the object in my hand. "Where did you get that?" she asked.

"It was in the back of a dingy storage room in the east wing. I saw where the guards stashed all of your books and…" I tried to curve my mouth into a friendly smile. "I thought you might want it back."

I had hoped to find gratitude in her features, but all I saw was a deep mistrust. "Why are you doing this?" she asked skeptically.

I looked back down at the worn book and thought, nibbling at the inside of my cheek. "The queen has you under constant surveillance. She has ordered our knights to keep watch over you every waking second. If you were to try and rifle through deserted halls and locked rooms, you would be caught before you even reached the door."

"But me…" I smiled despite the slight sting in my chest. "No one cares enough to keep an eye on me. They never expect me to do a thing." I chuckled lowly, but the princess said nothing, only studied me through squinted eyes.

I exhaled, scratching at the nape of my neck. "I just figured we are both prisoners here, so…" I shrugged. "Why not suffer through our sentence together?"

Before she could protest, I shoved my arm forward and placed the book in her hand. She took it, fingering the parchment with uncertainty. "I do not need any favors," she finally mumbled.

"I know," I said, shuffling my feet uncomfortably. "But I thought this could be a sort of peace offering. A way for us to start over." My heart was beating rapidly in my chest. There, I had said it. I had tossed the olive branch her way. I winced and waited for the inevitable rejection followed by her embittered rebuke.

The princess was not looking at me but studied the folds of her comforter thoughtfully. After a long while, she nodded her head, almost imperceptibly. "I will consider it."

I exhaled, relieved. "Just—" I hesitated. "Just be careful what you say around my mother." I grimaced, already knowing my warning would not be well-received.

Her face grew dark. "And why is that?" she asked through gritted teeth.

"I know what she is capable of," I said, scrambling to explain myself, "what she is willing to do to get her way." I clenched my jaw and swallowed. "I have seen it firsthand."

Her sneer turned to a light frown. Eyeing me curiously, she asked in a low voice, "What does she do?"

I exhaled slowly, tightly gripping my forearms out

of habit. "She will do anything, whatever she has to, in order to get what she wants." I stared down at my feet, too ashamed to meet her gaze. "She will order her guards to flog you, to beat you until your vision goes dark. But when she is really displeased, she will…lock you away."

I lifted my head a few inches. She still looked unconvinced. "It does not seem so terrible until you have been trapped for days with no food or water, no contact with the outside world…" I trailed off, reluctant to give any further details. "And when she finally releases you," I continued after a breath, "she knows you will be too broken down to do anything but submit." I cringed at the confession, sickened by my mother's cruelty but mostly disgusted by my own weakness.

Before I looked back up at Evangeline, I prepared myself for her insults. I knew I would deserve it when she called me feeble, spineless, pathetic. I held my breath, bracing for impact. But when I caught her eye, she said none of these things. What appeared on her face was not a hateful grimace but instead the hidden tenderness she seldom revealed. Except this time, it was directed at me. Her eyes rested gently on mine, and perhaps I was wrong, but I thought I sensed a faint sympathy in her gaze.

But this strange look unsettled me more than her usual glower, and I scrambled to escape it. "I just," I quickly stammered, "I do not want that to happen to you."

Her mindful look vanished. She stood upright and narrowed her eyes at me. "I can take care of myself," she muttered darkly then swiftly lifted her sheets and slipped beneath them. Without another word, she snuffed out the candle on her nightstand, leaving me standing in darkness.

I sighed, feeling more humiliated than ever. Reluctantly, I settled onto the floor, resting my head on the thin pillow and curling my body into a tight ball, preparing for another frigid night. My heart was still racing, showing no sign of slowing down. But soon I heard Evangeline's deep breaths from above and felt my muscles soften. I listened to her steady inhales and exhales. Only then did I find rest.

****

The next morning when I woke, something felt different. The calming rhythm of Evangeline's breath was gone, but that was nothing new. She always disappeared by the time I rose.

Then, I sensed it: a subtle warmth. I was not shaking with cold, and the goosebumps normally coating my arms had dispersed. I opened my eyes and peered down. Stretched over my body was a thick wool blanket.

Chapter 12

Eve

For the third morning in a row, I awoke from the same dream. After the first night, I was sure it had only been a fluke. After the second, I started to worry. But now I knew I could ignore it no longer.

In the dream, I stood at the top of the west tower, peering down at the village below. The view from atop the highest point in the castle was unmatched. I could see the whole town along with the rolling hills and the snow-capped peaks in the distance. When I looked down at my feet and saw no floor, I thought perhaps I was flying. Only then did I notice that the palace was made of glass. I could see through several stories of fragile panels, and I knew I was alone. I finally had the castle to myself. To a distant observer, it may have looked like I was floating, hovering like a spirit above Vitalia's corpse, but my feet were firmly planted, and somehow I knew I would not fall.

My solitude did not last long, however. From behind me, a lone voice called my name, pulling me from my tranquility. I turned to find Prince Rune standing a few feet away. His light hair lay coiled over the front of his shoulders, but the rest of him remained uncovered, his body completely exposed. He stared at me, his expression mixed. In the wrinkles along his forehead, I saw uncertainty. But in his shimmering eyes was an unmistakable longing.

For some reason, I was not surprised by the sight of his naked body, or by my own, similarly unclad. Instead, I approached him readily, as if by instinct. I lightly brushed my fingers through his hair then traced them along his bare chest. He quivered beneath my touch. Slowly, I swept my hand down his stomach. When I heard his first low moan, something within me released.

I nimbly raised my right hand and drove my palm into his shoulder. He collapsed to his knees, his eyes still locked on mine. He seemed unsurprised by my forceful approach, almost as if he was expecting it. My fingers slowly found their way through his blonde curls, finding their grip near the back of his head. I pressed his face toward my open hips, the force in my hands gentle but uncompromising.

I paused for just a moment to look into his face, perhaps to tease him with the delay. There was no denying the timidity that reddened his features, but beneath it all was a deep hunger, silently pleading for more.

I kept my gaze steady as I pressed his lips between my legs. With the first flick of his tongue, I tossed my head back and sighed with relief. My moans grew louder as his mouth explored my innermost chamber, and just before his lips could take me over the clouds, my desperate groans stirred me from the dream. The glass palace vanished and in its place were the first hints of dawn seeping through my bedroom window.

For the third morning in a row, I awoke to an odd tingling sensation in my core, one that thrilled and disturbed me equally. I tossed my head back onto my pillow and peered up at the ceiling with a sigh. Once again, I berated my subconscious for the absurd vision, but I had to admit there was a part of me that was starting to enjoy it.

I rolled toward the edge of my bed and peeked over the side. Rune was lying on his back, his head tilted upward and his mouth agape. Wrapped tightly around his body was the wool blanket I had left him a few nights before. Squinting through the dark, I tried to make out his face. His long lashes rested against the tops of his cheeks, his nose rose-colored in the chill morning air, his chin dotted with specks of blond. There was no denying this was the man from the dream.

When I found myself running my eyes down the rest of his body, I whipped my head away, suddenly aware that the tingling sensation had yet to pass. At once, I sprang from my bed and threw on the first set of clothes I could find before racing out the door, certain some fresh air would restore my sanity.

****

Squeezing my eyes tightly shut, I turned my head away and tried to ignore the agonizing feeling in my leg. After four weeks, the castle doctor was finally removing the last of my stitches. My stomach churned as the string tugged through my skin. "How much longer is this going to take?" I asked through gritted teeth.

"Only a few more," the doctor replied casually. I groaned with impatience, covering the backs of my eyes with my palms.

"Come on, Evangeline," said a voice from over my shoulder. "It cannot be that bad."

I twisted my head around and frowned. Mary was standing a few feet from the front end of the table watching me with her arms crossed. "You were not the one struck in the calf with an arrow." She rolled her eyes.

Mary was right, of course; the pain was almost nonexistent. But something about pulling a thread through flesh deeply unsettled me. Mary never failed to point out the irony: I could take a punch to the nose without complaint but could not sit still anytime stitches were involved. Nonetheless, she never failed to stand by my side and provide emotional support, along with the occasional teasing commentary.

"Done," the doctor finally declared. I released the tension in my muscles and sat up, wiping the sheet of nervous sweat from my upper lip. I looked down at the scar on my calf, pleased to find it healing nicely. "No sign of infection," he confirmed as he tossed the last of the string into a waste basket.

After thanking the doctor, I hopped from the table and sauntered towards the open door with Mary following close behind. Together, we strolled along a tight corridor. What was commonly called "the servants' floor" was now home to all the palace residents who had been spared their lives after the Kreagan invasion. In other words, it was the gathering place for all who remained of Vitalia's castle staff. I had been spending the majority of my time here as of recent, speaking with the marshal about the goings-on in the village, gossiping with various maids, and, of course, strolling the halls with Mary. I much preferred socializing with my servants than pretending to be a Kreagan royal.

All around us, castle attendants were flitting about. A line of laundresses scurried by with armfuls of freshly folded towels while a few paces ahead of us walked a tall footman. In his gloved hand, he balanced a serving dish piled high with pastries. As we passed, each servant paused their respective tasks to bow and bid me a good afternoon. I greeted them in kind with a small curtsy.

"Good day, your majesty," said a short girl with hair weaved in long brown braids. She wore an ankle-length navy dress beneath a ruffled white apron, the new uniform for all castle maids.

"Good day, Muriel," I replied with a nod. "Where are you off to with that tray?"

The maid looked down at the silver platter in her hands. It held a steaming pewter teapot along with a cream-colored plate stacked with jam-filled tartlets. "I am delivering tea to Queen Ingrid."

My soft smile dissolved. I glared down at the tray and stifled the urge to knock it out of the maid's hands and send its contents splattering onto the floor, knowing this would accomplish little. Instead, a hideous grin spread across my mouth. "Do me a favor, will you Muriel?"

The maid brightened. "Anything, my lady," she said with another eager curtsy.

I removed the lid of the teapot then stared down at the simmering liquid. After a drawn out snort, I hacked a glob of snot into the kettle. Then, wiping my lips with the back of my hand, I replaced the lid with a smile. "Please present this to the queen with my deepest respects."

Muriel's jaw fell to the floor. The girl was completely dumbstruck, staring wide-eyed at the teapot. Eventually, she lifted her gaze, and her lips slowly curved upward. "Right away, ma'am!" she said ardently. She spun back around and quickened her pace as she ascended a set of steps to the main floor.

Mary and I continued our jaunt down the hall until

we reached a small dormitory. Inside, two twin-sized beds were dressed in matching beige sheets. Both beds were perfectly made, not a wrinkle in sight. Mary was a textbook perfectionist. I expected nothing less from her sleeping quarters despite the fact that she shared her room with one of the few notoriously messy servants.

"I see your neatness has rubbed off on Ava," I said, referencing the well-kept bed across from us as we both took a seat on the edge of her mattress.

She veered her head around to face me with an annoyed frown. "Not quite. I'm afraid I have grown exasperated of my dear roommate's sloppiness and have started organizing her space myself."

I chuckled and rolled my eyes in amusement. I knew firsthand that when it came to how things were arranged, it was Mary's way or no way at all. It was likely why she made such a great lady's maid. When anything needed to be done, Mary always made sure it was done right.

I sighed, the pleasant smirk fading from my lips. Any joy we shared nowadays was short-lived. "How are you?" I asked, holding her gaze gently and bracing myself for her tears.

Mary dropped her head, staring at her hands stiffly folded on her lap. "I've been better," she exhaled.

I gently rested my hand on her shoulder. "How is your family?"

"I'm not sure," she said with a sigh. "Queen Ingrid rarely lets us visit home."

She lifted her head. "Father's leg was healing well after your visit, but soon after the queen ordered the village masons to start constructing new barracks for her soldiers, his limp returned." She rested the side of her temple in her left palm, her body sinking gradually lower. "He tried to tell the guards that his knee was not yet fully healed, but they would not listen. The queen sends her men out to patrol the town around the clock, and anyone who refuses to work is flogged."

I shut my eyes and squeezed them tightly. My fists quaked with rage. I swore I would kill them all, every last one of those unfeeling Kreagan soldiers, starting with their heartless commander. I ground my teeth as I fantasized about tearing their limbs from their sockets, dismembering them one by one.

"Evangeline," Mary said suddenly, pulling me from my vengeful haze. "Vitalia needs you." I opened my eyes. Her gaze was no longer one of helpless defeat but of determination. "It's as if the entire kingdom is engulfed in a somber cloud." She paused, wringing her hands as she willed herself to continue. "Do you think you could go down to the village and offer them some encouragement?"

My blood, boiling only a second ago, turned cold. Now I was the one with my head drooped, peering uneasily at my fists. I knew she was right. A true leader reaches out to her people in their time of need, stands on the frontlines alongside them during their hardest battles.

But it was not that simple. I had often considered taking a trip to the village. Ingrid had never directly forbade it. But what was the point? I was no longer their symbol of hope. After my marriage to Rune, the son of the very woman who had killed their king, I was sure they deemed me a traitor. I could rebel against her all I wanted, but, in the end, Ingrid was right. The authority I once held was gone. I was no longer their princess. I was her puppet, and all the townspeople knew it.

Shame washed over me as I imagined showing my

face in the town. They would stare in disappointment at their traitorous heir. They would look at me like I was a fraud, a gutless sellout indifferent to their suffering. I could not bear to see the people who had once loved and admired me look at me with such pain.

Sensing my discomfort, Mary dropped the subject. "What about you?" she asked, sitting straighter. "How are you doing?"

"As well as I can be," I said thoughtfully. Neither of us spoke for a moment. Mary waited for me to go on, and I struggled to put my emotions into words. An unexpected swell of grief built up in my chest, and a haze fell over my eyes. "I miss him, Mary," I whispered. "My father was the only one who supported me. Now I feel completely alone, virtually invisible. I am an outcast in my own kingdom."

"What about Prince Rune?" Mary asked hesitantly.

I spun my head around, a humorless look on my face. "Very funny."

"He seems nice enough," she said, choosing her words carefully.

I snorted at what I assumed was a poor attempt at a joke. Surely she was not implying what I thought she was. "As if I would ever befriend Rune," I replied, my voice tainted with sarcasm.

Mary raised her eyebrows. "I am not suggesting you befriend him." I gawked at her, speechless. "Do not give me that look," she chuckled, eyeing me slyly.

My stomach dropped. She could not possibly know about the dreams. I had not told a single soul about them, not even her. "Evangeline, I have known you my whole life. I have heard all your stories, and I know your deepest secrets." She struck me with a knowing smile.

"Do not make me say it." It was quiet for a moment as she waited for me to confess. My lips stayed sealed.

She rolled her eyes. "You fancy the prince."

My face flooded with heat, and I instantly hated myself for it. I swiftly threw my head back, laughing at the ceiling to hide my features. "Where is this coming from?" I asked her playfully. "When did you become the matchmaker?"

Instead of the lighthearted smile I was expecting, Mary's face dropped. I felt my chest squeeze, immediately regretting my words. "Not a day passes that I don't think about Arthur." Her voice shook. "I know now how rare it is to meet someone who makes me feel the way he did." She turned to look at me with somber eyes. "I see the way you look at the prince." Although her words were caring, I could see the pain it caused her to say them. "You can still hold a grudge against him, but that does not change the way you feel." She chuckled with a slight shake of her head. "And it is hard to miss the way he constantly ogles over you."

I scoffed loudly. "That is ridiculous," I said, turning my head away, my lips curved in a nervous smile. Mary only lifted her eyebrows and tilted her head sideways.

I sighed. There was no fooling her. "I will admit I have thought about it. He is unlike any prince I have ever met, or any man for that matter. There is something about him so different from all the rest." Dropping my elbows to my knees, I rested my forehead in my hands. "But it could never happen," I muttered. "Being with Rune is exactly what Ingrid wants. I could never go so low as to consummate her marriage scheme. It would be an act of treason."

Mary shrugged, her resolve seemingly unaffected.

"It is your choice, but the Evangeline I know always takes what she wants and never cares what other people may think."

Reluctantly, I let my mind wander back to the dream. In the glass castle, there had been no complications or inhibitions. I had not stopped to contemplate the consequences. I simply acted—no hesitation, no uncertainty. Even though the thought of fooling around with the son of my father's killer left a vile taste in my mouth, the dream stuck with me. Maybe it was the way he said my name, his feeble voice cautious, servile. Or maybe it was the softness of his skin, the untouched flesh below his ribs that asked to be devoured.

I shook the thoughts from my head and jumped to my feet. "I have had enough of this absurd conversation," I announced irritably. "Ingrid will soon be expecting me for dinner." I quickly waved goodbye to Mary and scurried from the servants' quarters before she could stop me.

I shuffled up the stairs toward the main floor, my frustration lingering. I instantly regretted revealing my hidden feelings to Mary, feelings I had not even admitted to myself. I was filled with utter humiliation for even considering the prospect. How could I stoop so low as to sleep with the enemy? What would my father say?

Quickly striding through the corridor, I almost missed the sound of angry whispers from within a nearby room. I stopped and slowly crept toward the source of the noise to listen more closely. The speaker was undeniably Ingrid. I inched closer to the door, pressing my ear against the wood. "I am running out of patience," I heard her growl. An object crashed loudly against a nearby wall, making me jump.

"She is relentless!" Ingrid continued, her voice growing into a yell. "She insists on defying my every command. If this goes on much longer, I will be the laughingstock of my own servants. I am *this* close to throwing her to the wolves." A long pause. No reply.

She groaned aloud, her agitated footsteps thumping across the room. "I am tired of doing your job for you," she resumed. "Princess Evangeline is your wife and, therefore, your problem. It is time you got that shrew of yours under control. The woman needs strict discipline. Be a man for once and show her who is in charge!"

Again, silence. If it were not for the sound of my racing heart, I might have worried I had lost my hearing. Suddenly, Ingrid screamed. "Get out of my sight!"

I flinched. The sound of a chair scraping roughly against the floor was followed by rapidly approaching footsteps.

In a panic, I frantically searched for a place to hide. But there was no time. Just as I started to leap out of the way, the door swung open and knocked me in the back. I tumbled forward at the impact, landing face-first on the floor. "Watch where you are going!" I shouted. I contorted my face into a resentful glare, hoping my outrage would raise doubts to my eavesdropping.

"Princess Evangeline!" Rune exclaimed, his face of an exceptionally gray color. "I am so sorry! Are you all right?" He leaned forward, reaching an arm out to me, but upon seeing my hostile glare, he took a swift step back and threw his hands behind him.

"I am fine," I said, straightening the folds of my dress as I rose to my feet. "Just think twice the next time you so carelessly burst into the hallway."

He nodded stiffly, his eyes still wide with dismay. "It will not happen again." Then, before the awkward silence could set in, he turned and scuttled hastily toward the dining room.

I watched him closely, walking with his hands held tightly by his sides, his slender legs scampering down the corridor. If Ingrid truly believed this boy could control me, she was dumber than I thought. Did she seriously expect me to obey his feeble commands? It was practically comical—the idea that Rune would ever rule over me. It was obvious she knew nothing at all about me.

I thought about just how easy it would be to turn the tables. I could easily rule over him myself if I wanted to and show Ingrid how very wrong she was. Lost in the forbidden thought, a devilish smile spread across my cheeks. I studied the still recovering prince as he fled, a hint of muscle pressing through the arms of his tight doublet, the same shape it had been in my dream.

With a firm exhale, I banished the image from my mind. *Quit it, Evangeline. It is never going to happen.*

Chapter 13

Rune

When I arrived at the dining hall, I took my normal seat without a second thought, not paying a moment's attention to the assembly of vassals gathered about the other side of the table. I was too focused on bringing the blood back to my face to worry about anything else.

Princess Evangeline entered soon after I did. She passed by without a word, not acknowledging our awkward encounter in the hallway. She did not even bother to look at me for that matter. Instead, she plopped into her tall wooden chair, letting her shoulder blades slide downward until she was reclined at a 45° angle. With her left hand, she reached for her fork then fiddled with the prongs between her fingertips with an air of boredom.

After a few minutes, once Evangeline had deeply studied each centimeter of her utensil, the queen strolled into the hall. The vassals quickly hushed then stood to properly acknowledge her entry. I followed, noticing out of the corner of my eye that the princess did nothing of the sort. She kept her gaze glued to the fork between her fingers and sank a few inches deeper in her chair. My mother carried herself lightly, strolling effortlessly toward the final seat at the table. Any trace of our recent argument was almost imperceptible. Almost.

As the queen made her final few steps to the head of the table, a waiting butler pulled back her chair. She sat, her flowing movements nimble and refined. But her poise was a mere façade, for all the while, she stared coldly at the slumped figure across the table. I followed her gaze, unsurprised to find Evangeline squinting harshly back at her. Once the queen was seated, the rest of her court followed.

My mother lifted a hand, letting it dangle limply by the wrist. She snapped her fingers. The sound sent a chill down my spine. "Wine," she demanded in a shrill voice. From along the far wall, a footman hurried toward the table, carrying an oversized ewer. He started with the queen and quickly made his way around the table, filling each goblet with a dark red substance. When he poured the drink into my own glass, I noticed the subtle shaking of his hands, yet, somehow, the footman spilled not a single drop.

Her goblet now filled, the queen took a long swig before setting the glass back onto the table and resuming her icy glare. It was the same look that, when directed at me, felt like needles pricking my skin, the look I sought to evade at all costs. But when my mother's penetrating gaze was set upon Evangeline, the obstinate princess did not even flinch. She watched the queen steadily, enduring the daggers, her mouth set in a hard line.

"Evangeline," my mother began after lightly setting her goblet onto the table. "I've heard rumors of your frequent visits to the servants' quarters." Her tone was accusatory, not searching for an explanation but assembling the perfect target.

Evangeline carefully placed her own goblet back onto the table with a soft clink and used the back of her hand to wipe the crimson stain from her lip. Folding her arms casually across her front, she inspected her fingernails indifferently. "I might have made a few appearances there," she said, more interested in the state of her cuticles than anything the queen had to say. "What of it?"

My mother tapped her sharp fingernails rhythmically against the table. "I find it inappropriate for a lady in my court to associate herself with *peasants*."

I cringed. When I swung my head toward the opposite side of the table, I saw Evangeline clenching her jaw tightly, clearly growing vexed. Wordlessly, I willed the princess to let slide my mother's crude remark, to stand down just this once. But I knew her too well by then.

"I will spend my time with whomever I please," the princess snarled. "And to be frank, *your excellency*, my list of companions has grown rather thin since you had them executed." The fiery glare that she shot across the table showered me with embers.

From my mother's widening grimace, I could tell her tolerance for Evangeline's willful attitude was waning. Normally, she could withstand several of the princess's malignant comments before losing her temper. But it was obvious her ire had piqued early tonight. She sat up straighter in her high-backed chair, resting her folded hands on the table with feigned civility. "I have been lenient with you thus far." My stomach tightened. I counted down the seconds until their deadliest weapons were drawn. "But my patience is wearing thin. Either you learn where you stand in my kingdom, or you will suffer the consequences." She spoke slowly, exaggerating her words with an air of pretention.

"Do I make myself clear?" The corner of her lips curled upward, taking pleasure in her demeaning lecture. It was then, I knew, the fuse had been lit.

Turning back toward Evangeline, I saw her face darkening by the second. "Do you truly believe your threats scare me?" She chuckled to herself, a low, unsettling laugh. "I am one of the most ruthless warriors in the realm. I have fought countless battles alongside my own men." Her voice was growing louder, her words more insistent. "Nothing you do will ever break me. In fact, I think it is time *you* faced the truth, Ingrid." The princess lifted her chin, her nose a sharp point aimed directly at the queen's heart. "You will never be able to control me."

I was breathless, sure I was about to witness a full-blown war right there in the dining hall. The vassals shifted uneasily in their seats. The room sank into an excruciating silence. My mother fumed with a seething rage, her scowl so severe I thought her eyes would shoot out shards of pure ice. "We will see about that," she hissed. "Guards!"

My heart stopped. My hands and feet turned frigid. I knew what came next.

"Show Princess Evangeline to the Reflection Chamber. I believe she needs some time to reconsider her actions."

A band of soldiers marched over from across the hall. Without hesitation, Evangeline kicked her chair back and crouched into a ready position. She ducked beneath the first guard's arm as it swung in an arch toward her temple. She darted back upright then hurled her fist into his nose. The man stumbled backward, covering his face with both palms. The second guard lunged for the back of her neck. She twisted her body away before he could reach her and swung her legs around to knee him in the groin. But before she could turn to face the rest, three guards grabbed her by the wrists and yanked them behind her back. She jerked away violently, but their grip on her was firm. The princess kicked and screamed as she threw herself to the floor, refusing to walk on her own as they dragged her toward the door.

My heart raced with panic as I frantically looked from Evangeline to my mother, who watched the scene with a sadistic sneer. In the depths of my core, I felt a small fire ignite, spreading quickly through my body. It was all-consuming, a compelling heat that roused my soul from its slumber. Before I knew what I was doing, I was on my feet. "No!" yelled a voice I had never heard before.

The entire room froze. Princess Evangeline and the guards stilled, dumbfounded. The members of my mother's court gawked at me as though they had just witnessed the impossible. When I realized that it was I who had spoken, I peered down at my hands in disbelief. The fire had spread through my fingers, now clenched in tight fists. As the warmth reached my face, I gritted my teeth and glared at the static tableau. "Don't take her anywhere!" that same unfamiliar voice demanded.

I turned to face the queen. Her fury had been dulled by shock, her features frozen in astonishment. "This must stop," I said, my confidence slowly fading beneath her murderous glower. When I spun back toward the guards, I caught a glimpse of Evangeline. She was kneeling on the floor, her arms still held above her head, her eyes brimming with wonder. I puffed out my chest. "Let her go."

The guards, still fixed in place, not sure what to do next, gaped at the queen and awaited her next command. Costively, my mother rose to her feet, her glare so sharp it could pierce skin. "Sit down," she spat through closed teeth. "Keep your mouth shut, and maybe I will let you keep your tongue."

"No," I repeated, refusing to be silenced by her threats even though my throat was slowly closing in. "This is madness, Mother. I will no longer sit by and watch this abuse." I bit down hard on the inside of my mouth, the taste of iron tainting my tongue.

The queen leaned forward and gripped the sides of the dining table so tightly her arms shook, its legs rattling against the floor. All of a sudden, she relaxed. Still pressing her fingertips into the wood, she casually stood back to her full height. "Fine," she said. She shifted her gaze toward the nearest guard and nodded.

In an instant, the knights released their grip on Evangeline, letting her fall to the ground as they charged at me. I took a few steps back out of instinct but kept my arms pinned to my sides. When they took hold of me, their nails digging into my skin, I did not resist.

One guard wrapped his hand around the nape of my neck, forcing my head downward until my torso was parallel with the ground. A second man plunged his knee into my face. A sharp pain exploded in my nose, and blood gushed onto the floor. Before I could brace myself, the knight sent his knee skyward again, this time making impact with my right eye socket. After a few more blows, I collapsed to the ground. The soldiers surrounded me as I lay flat on my chest, their sabatons driving into my exposed sides. I cried out, my lips pressed into the stone floor, my fingernails scraping violently against the rock.

When I was sure one more kick to my head would render me unconscious, the men suddenly halted. Through the corner of my eye, I watched them turn to face my mother, still standing by the table, one arm now raised to command their attention. She turned and squinted at the princess, who was watching the scene from her place on the ground, her eyes wide with horror. "You were lucky today, Evangeline," my mother said. Her words sounded distorted through the throbbing in my head. "Rune may have suffered your punishment today but be warned. You are next."

I rested my eyes for a moment in the brief silence, taking quick shallow breaths to clear the dark spots from my vision. As the fog slowly dissolved, I heard my mother drop back into her chair. "Leave my presence at once, both of you," she ordered tiredly.

My arms aching, I pressed myself upward, struggling to my hands and knees. But before I could crawl away, the knights each delivered their final kicks, the last one bashing into my skull. I flopped back to the ground, motionless. Through the floor, I felt the brisk thumping of footsteps. When I finally gathered the strength to lift my head, Evangeline was already halfway out the door.

I ground my teeth through the pain as I carefully made my way onto my feet, taking a few seconds to establish my balance. Ignoring the splotches of blood on my tunic and the crimson puddle on the floor, I limped toward the exit. At no point did I turn back to face my mother, not to make some kind of bold gesture, but simply because I was too afraid to risk any more of her fury.

I exited the dining room and hobbled as quickly as I could through the dark corridor. The sun had set nearly an hour ago, and the hall was almost completely empty save for a few patrolling guards. I groaned inwardly, wincing at the pain that shot through my nerves with each step. Every corner of my body throbbed with agony, and worst of all, I was sure my punishment was far from over. I had dug myself a gaping hole with my reckless stunt, and I knew my mother's anger could not be tamed with a few swift kicks. No, my suffering had only begun.

But I could not let them take Evangeline. I could not watch them shatter her soul as they had done mine. No matter how strong she was, no one ever left the Reflection Chamber the same. And that was what scared me more than anything: that my mother would take the fiercest woman I had ever known and break her to pieces.

Without warning, a pair of hands wrapped themselves around the tops of my shoulders and thrust me backward, spinning my body around. Still whirling through the air, I felt the hands move to my chest, driving my back into the wall with a powerful force. I gawked, wide-eyed, at my assailant, my heart rate spiking once more. To my astonishment, I saw before me the face of Princess Evangeline, her eyes striking mine with their unrivaled intensity. The hands pinning me against the stone wall were hers, digging their thumbs mercilessly into my collar bone. From the way her mouth twitched, I was sure she was about to strike. I recoiled, closing my eyes tightly as I prepared for one of her lethal blows.

All at once, her lips collided with mine. Her mouth crashed into me with such force that the back of my head slammed against the wall. In no time at all, her lips found their rightful place entwined with my own. They stunned me into stillness, completely paralyzing, forcing me to surrender to their will. She lingered there, the warm insides of her mouth clasping onto me in a moment frozen in time. Her hands still shoved harshly into my ribs, pressing my body slightly downward to more easily reach my face. Easing back slightly, she kept her lips tightly wound with mine, ardently tugging me closer. They were like silk, like a set of cushions that gently but eagerly swallowed me whole.

I had no choice but to move my bottom lip upward and take in her open mouth. As soon as I did, the hands pressed into me harder, and her kiss grew more urgent. The softness of her lips was traded for the rough edge of her teeth, biting into my top lip ever so gently. I melted beneath her weight, yielding to her attack, surrendering to the power of her touch.

It ended as abruptly as it began. All at once, she tore herself away, unhooked her lips, and with a quick turn, bolted down the hall.

I was unprepared for her sudden departure, still hovering in midair as I caught my breath. When I finally made it back down to Earth, she was already gone. My mind still floated in a cloud. My legs no longer worked. Slowly, I sank, drifting through space until, eventually, I landed.

Chapter 14

Eve

I hiked briskly through the thinning forest, the ground gradually lightening beneath the pink glow of the rising sun, and heard the unmistakable sound of crunching leaves coming from behind me. In the quiet moment of stillness, I smiled to myself. Someone was following me. But I did not panic or turn to confront my pursuer. I had sensed him trailing me from the moment I left my bedroom.

Earlier that morning, before the rest of the palace woke, I had crept through the dim candlelight of the main hall. From the moment I left my room, I sensed his presence. I recognized his gait, the unmistakable click of his shoes against the floor. *Silly boy*. He thought he could move with my shadow, could sneak along without my noticing, but anyone within a mile radius could hear his clumsy tread.

Now in the woods I stood motionless. I taunted him with a quick scan through the trees, trying my best to look suspicious. At the snap of another twig, I rolled my eyes. His stealth was pitiful. He gave away his position with every other step. But rather than swing around to catch him in the act, I continued onward, resuming my feigned ignorance as I traveled deeper into the forest.

My deliberate disregard was nothing new. I had

caught him watching me on several occasions over the past few weeks: sitting at the dining table, standing on the balcony, lying in my bed. He was a terrible stalker, his staring always blatantly obvious. But for reasons I did not quite understand, I had never confronted him about it.

For the first time, he had followed me out of the castle, and once again, I had not said a word. He had been tailing me for several miles now, and still I played the fool. As we trudged along the rocky path, I reconsidered my choice to stay silent. If I wanted to, I could have exposed him before I had even reached the back door. I could have told him to scram, to leave me alone, to mind his own business. But I didn't. I let him follow me.

I knew I was partially to blame for his fixation. I was the one who cornered him in the dark. I was the one who kissed him in the vacant corner of the halls. A part of me regretted that night. I still worried that an affair with Rune would be a betrayal to my kingdom, to my father, to myself. I thought about putting a stop to whatever this was, ending it before it could go any further. But this morning, when I caught him lurking behind me, the opportunity came and went, and I said nothing. Now I was forced to admit the simple truth: I did not want it to end.

I ducked beneath the branches hanging over the trail, brushing them aside with the back of my arm. Before me appeared the rolling stream, deserted as always. I strolled forward and studied the ground as the terrain switched from packed dirt to polished stones. At the river's edge, I peered down at the running water and examined a small school of trout riding along with the current. From my left, I heard branches shuffling, and I knew he was hiding behind the trunk of a nearby oak tree.

The fish now gone, I stared down at my reflection rippling in the water. *This is a terrible idea, Evangeline.* But as I watched the sides of my mouth curve into a devilish grin, I knew that was just it. It was the forbidden nature of it all that made it so impossible to resist.

With a swift turn, I pulled myself away from the stream's edge. I saw the ends of his hair whip through the air as he darted behind the tree. Laughing inwardly, I sauntered toward a curved rock the height of my waist. Once there, I nimbly removed my clothes.

I started with my boots, the leather scuffed from a few too many walks through the thick brush; then my cloak, freeing my hair from the wool hood; then my cotton trousers; and, lastly, my ivory tunic. Luckily, it was one of the warmer fall mornings, making the chill on my exposed skin all the more inviting. I glimpsed down at my body. My nipples had hardened under the biting wind. A patch of goosebumps was emerging along my naked legs. With a single tug, I removed the ribbon from my hair, letting my copper waves flow down my bare back.

I twisted around and casually returned to the stream, making sure to display my backside in the direction of the lone oak. I dipped my toes into the water. A slight chill rolled up my spine. I kept walking, wading deeper and deeper until my breasts floated delicately on the surface. I spun myself around in slow, lazy circles, forming shallow ripples with my fingertips, creating a small whirlpool with the soft force of my hips.

When I stilled, the water continued orbiting around me like planets around the sun. I sank my body deeper and tilted my head back to let my hair soak in the moving stream. Water filled my ears, temporarily muting the world. I listened to the rush of the river against the stone walls, taking long, deep breaths as the current dared to carry me away.

When I finally lifted my head, my expression had changed into something more serious. A soft tingling was spreading through my chest as my body came alive. I was done playing games.

I fixed my gaze on the tree, the sleeve of an orange doublet peeking around the trunk. "I know you are over there," I said over the steady babble of the stream. He did not reply, likely paralyzed with horror. "Come out," I demanded teasingly.

Hobbling out from behind the tree came Prince Rune, his cheeks pink with mortification, his head bowed low. His gaze was fixed to the ground, and his hands fidgeted restlessly by his sides.

"Come closer," I said.

He looked up at me, taken aback. For a moment, his eyes lingered on my naked breasts. But in a few seconds, he shot them back down to his feet, the abashed color spreading to his ears. Carefully, he approached, sidestepping the brush that littered the forest floor. He neared the stream anxiously, still watching the ground with painstaking effort. When he reached my messy pile of clothes on the rock, he halted, wringing his hands nervously.

Slowly, I emerged from the water, letting each inch of my body hover above the surface before taking my next step. As my full figure became visible, the timidity in Rune's gaze faded away, and he shamelessly gawked at my uncovered body. By the time my knees reached the surface, his face was the color of a primrose, his mouth slightly ajar. Another shiver tore through me as a breeze caressed my wet skin. His eyes followed each subtle movement.

When I finally set my feet upon dry ground, I paused. He was watching me openly now, but I could still sense his quiet uncertainty. "Closer," I whispered.

His eyes widened. At first, he hesitated. Then, he took a small step forward. Then another. Then another, until he was standing just a few feet away.

With one arm, I reached out to him, taking his hand in my own. It shook between my fingers. I steadied it with a soft brush of my thumb. Gently, I pulled his open palm toward me, letting it hover expectantly over my breast. At long last, we connected. The cold of his fingers was like a frigid wave crashing into my chest. Rune exhaled softly, his tension dissolving with the first touch. He let his arm hang loosely to give me full reign, and I tenderly guided his hand around each breast. My body fluttered beneath the brush of his fingers on my skin. When I led him to the hard tip, he gently took my nipple between his thumb and forefinger, lightly massaging the smooth flesh.

I pulled his hand away. From the disappointment in his face, I knew he was reluctant to withdraw, but relief flooded his features when I began guiding his fingers down my side. His hand quivered as it slid over my stomach, his wrist twitching nervously as he rounded my hips. I watched him closely, his breath hitching with each shy touch. I stared into his face as I swept his fingers across my abdomen. I wallowed in the humble desperation in his eyes. They desired more, I knew, but he did not dare permit them. He graciously accepted what I allowed and nothing more.

When I inched his hand between my legs, his arm stiffened. His eyes flashed upward, holding onto mine with a new fear. His lips were moving, but only broken syllables escaped his throat. Finally, he managed a few words, a sequence of unfinished phrases, his jaw tense from the effort. "I can't…I don't…I've never…"

I pressed a finger to his mouth, silencing him instantly. His lips tightened beneath my touch. "I know," I whispered. "I'll teach you."

With a sigh, he loosened his wrist, and I guided him into the unknown. I danced his fingers between my hips, letting them graze the subtle heat that emanated there. In time, they glided across the surface effortlessly, coated with my moisture. His breaths were shallow in my ear, and he let out a faint gasp when I lightly dipped him between my folds.

Soon, I felt a sigh of my own building, the tips of his fingers causing a mild throb in my center. But before it could release, I dropped his hand. It fell limply by his side. He glanced up at my face, wordlessly urging me for more. But I shook my head. "Not yet."

Without another word, I reached around his legs and snatched my clothes. I threw them on hurriedly as I darted back toward the castle, replacing my hood over my damp hair. I left him in a daze, standing motionless by the water as I hastened for the tree line.

Before long, I heard the soft plod of his footsteps behind me. I swung myself around and met him with a stern glare. He froze, the unease returning to his features. "Do not follow me," I mumbled lowly. "No one can know."

****

I was in my closet when he came into my room that

night. I was changing out of my evening dress. It was the first thing I always did after dinner, yanking off the itchy gown and tossing it onto the floor. I knew I would never get used to wearing such irritating garments.

Dinner that evening had been especially unpleasant. After the utter chaos of the other night, Ingrid and I had adopted an unspoken truce of silence toward each other: I would not lash out as long she did not give me a reason to. It seemed to be working for the time being. Ingrid had ignored Rune as well, not commenting on his black eye or split lip. It had been a quiet meal to say the least, each of us pretending we were the only guest at the table, the only sound the occasional nervous sniffle of her vassals.

After what felt like an eternity, she finally dismissed us from the dining hall. I had marched straight to my room, desperately needing some time to myself. Even an uneventful evening was draining with Ingrid sitting across from me. Just as I expected, however, Rune arrived at my door soon after I did. When I heard his timid knock, I groaned aloud. I had not even had time to remove my skirts yet. Quickly, I tore off my undergarments and threw on a wrinkled night gown hanging on the door.

When I exited the closet, Rune was standing by the foot of my bed, restlessly rubbing his thumb against the wooden frame. His face shot up when he saw me. His lips curved into a nervous smile. "Good evening, Princess Evangeline." I heard a slight crack in his voice as he spoke my name. He hurriedly cleared his throat then scratched at the back of his hand.

Through narrowed eyes, I studied him. He fidgeted uncomfortably beneath my gaze. "Sit," I demanded, pointing toward my vanity chair. He looked uncertain, peering at me with a crinkled brow. I nudged my head toward the open seat, my movement more assertive this time. He sprang into action, hustling over and flopping into the seat. He sat with his back stiff and his hands pressed on his legs, his thumbs lightly rubbing the tops of his knees.

"We need to set a few ground rules," I said, looking down my nose at him.

Rune nodded fervently. "Of course!"

I narrowed my eyes. There was no way this boy knew what he was getting himself into. It was high time he learned the truth about his dear wife. "First, I need you to understand something."

Rune tilted his head curiously. "Okay."

I inhaled, my jaw tense. "I am not sure what you think you know about women, but I promise I am nothing like any of them. As you have likely surmised by now, I do not accept the meek position of a lady that my station demands. I refuse to act the part of the complacent, docile princess when it could not be further from the truth. Everyone knows I am the one in charge. I lead the way. I take what I want, no questions asked. And when I choose to be with a man, I take full control."

Rune was silent, his eyes a set of large blue spheres. I could not tell if he was frightened by my words or merely transfixed.

"I assume we understand each other." I raised my eyebrows and waited for a reply. Eventually, he nodded.

At last, I felt my chest unclench, and I dropped my imposing stare. Spinning toward the far wall, I started to pace along the floor in front of him. "So," I began again. "Here is how this will work. I will decide when we meet. I will dictate what we do. And you will follow along and thank God that I chose not to kill you in your sleep." I paused midstride and eyed him sharply. "Any questions?" He shook his head vigorously, his yellow curls swinging across his chest.

I smiled, a stiff side smile more menacing than reassuring. Rune's face brightened, but when I hastily resumed my severe glare, his grin vanished. "Do not think this changes anything," I snapped. "I still despise you and your hellborn mother, and I will never forgive you for what you have done to my kingdom." Rune swallowed and dropped his head under the weight of my scowl.

With a quick turn, I dashed toward him, taking his chin and wrenching it upward so our faces were just inches apart. He blanched in alarm. "And to be clear, I do not like you. You and all of Kreagan disgust me. Frankly, I would rather be run over by a fleet of horses than be married to you." He sat motionless, pain flashing in his eyes.

I released my grip and took a step back, crossing my arms over my chest. "But it is undeniable we are attracted to each other, and it is time we did something about it." I sighed and resumed my thoughtful pacing. "I mean, what's the harm? We are married. It is what everyone expects from us anyway." I said this last part mostly to myself, doing my best to rationalize what I was about to say next. I lifted my chest and turned to catch his fervent gaze. "So we fuck," I resolved. "We get whatever this is out of our system, and then we go back to hating each other."

Rune nodded eagerly like this was the greatest idea he had ever heard. "That sounds like a sensible plan to me," he said, barely managing to restrain his enthusiasm.

I responded with a dark frown. "No one can know about this," I said coldly.

His giddy grin dissolved. "I know," he said cautiously. "You told me by the stream."

"And I mean no one," I continued, ignoring his interruption. "Especially not the queen." My face tightened. "I refuse to do anything to please that tyrant. I could not stand the look on her face if she found out what we were doing, if she knew we consummated this reprehensible marriage."

Rune's lips tightened. "I understand," he uttered weakly.

"And that includes fooling around in my room." His eyebrows scrunched together in puzzlement. Tightening my arms around my front, I tilted my head higher. "I meant what I said before. You have no right to sleep in my bed, let alone do anything else in it."

He gawked at me, his mouth open but speechless. I smirked at his consternation. "I suggest you get used to sleeping on the floor. As long as I'm still alive, you will never set foot on this bed."

Chapter 15

Rune

I peered down from the edge of the balcony at the rows of praying villagers knelt before their pews. The morning's light poured through the stained glass windows encasing the chapel, showering its attendants with a glow of fuchsia, mauve, and indigo. Above the towering nave was a mesmerizing ribbed vault. How easy it was to get lost in the labyrinth of shapes formed by those intersecting beams if you looked for too long.

The varnished pulpit was covered by a wooden canopy in the shape of a hexagon, and within it stood the castle priest dressed in a light brown cassock and hood. It was the same priest who had officiated our wedding ceremony, who had served as the official Kreagan chaplain for decades. He was reciting the closing invocation in his theatrical vibrato as the service neared its conclusion.

At least, that's what I assumed was happening. Like the rest of the congregation, my head was bowed low, and my hands were folded. But unlike them, my eyes were open.

Through the corner of my vision, I watched Princess Evangeline. I was surprised by how angelic she looked. It was a rare moment of stillness, one that brought out her gentler features. Her palms were lightly pressed together, the tips of her thumbs resting against her nose, and with her chin tucked humbly, her eyes settled shut.

She had been ignoring me all morning, which was hardly abnormal; in fact, it would have been more unusual for her to acknowledge my presence than to disregard it all together. But since our weighty conversation in her bedroom the night before, the princess had not once looked my way. I was restless, unsure what to expect, impatiently waiting for whatever came next.

When the priest finally ended the lengthy prayer, I watched the faint movements of her lips as she silently mouthed the final words. She lifted her head to sit erect, her neck held tall. She was nearly a foot shorter than I was, but I rarely noticed. She always carried herself like the tallest woman in the room. Although I had to tilt my head slightly downward to meet her eye when I was talking to her, it always felt like she was the one looking down at me.

This morning, she wore a modest black gown. The dark linen hugged her chest and clung tightly around her throat, making her neck appear unnaturally long. The hand-woven fabric covered the entirety of her arms, hiding every inch of her tan skin, and ended in a mass of ruffles around her wrists. Her skirt was thin: a simple shift that concealed all but her toes, which were clad in strappy black sandals. It was her hair that fascinated me most. Her brown locks were interwoven in complex braids that crisscrossed along the back of her head. I took my time studying their intricate pattern, entranced by the optical illusion until I reached their end, tied off by a set of matching obsidian ribbons.

The princess soon detected my sideways glance.

Twisting her face so that only I could see, she pierced me with her sharp side eye. I recognized the warning and turned my head away to face the crowded pews. The priest had closed his Bible and was now addressing the entire congregation with his excruciatingly gleeful smile.

"Blessed are we to be gathered here in this time of great joy!" he declared loudly enough for the back row to cower. As he shifted toward the royal balcony, I felt my stomach drop. All eyes in the chapel followed his gaze, settling on me. "Today we celebrate, for our noble Prince Rune and Princess Evangeline have been wed for a month's time." His exaggerated joviality was like nails on a chalk board.

At the mention of my name, a bony elbow plunged into my side. I knew without looking that it was my mother's, urging me to acknowledge his recognition. I jolted to my feet and gritted my teeth into a wide toothy grin, the one I had practiced with my mother for occasions such as this one. From my other side, I heard a dispassionate sigh before Evangeline reluctantly rose from her chair. She twisted her mouth into a forced grin that was nearly indecipherable from her hateful smirk.

"Grateful are we to take part in your honorable union!" the chaplain proclaimed. The lines of peasants stared up at us in the silence following the priest's commendation. I took a deep, calming breath through my nose. Before I could change my mind, I slipped my hand into Evangeline's. Her arm stiffened as I entwined my fingers with hers. I lowered my chest toward the floor, bending into a dramatic bow. The princess eyed me uncertainly. After a long, thoughtful moment, she loosened the tension in her wrist, relaxing her fingers around my hand. Then, taking up the length of her skirt, she dipped into a graceful curtsy.

Our performance seemed to appease the crowd. A few sporadic claps bounced through the chapel. Others grinned softly up at us in approval. When the congregation was finally dismissed, the princess snatched her hand away. She spun around, the hem of her skirt slapping against my shin, and stormed out of the chapel.

I sighed and dropped my own arm to my side. Before I could follow, my mother grabbed me stiffly by the shoulder. I froze then slowly turned to face her. Her arms were folded across her chest. She wore a hardened frown, but her eyes lacked their usual coldness. "The princess has been more docile of late," she began. "Am I right to assume this is your doing?" There was genuine curiosity in her voice.

"Um," I started, scanning my brain for an acceptable answer. "Yes, she has been more"—I swallowed— "*compliant* than usual." I cringed inwardly, knowing nothing could be further from the truth.

She raised her eyebrows. "I will admit, I did not think you had it in you. But I must say I am pleasantly surprised by your ability to tame that she-wolf." Her lips curved into an unpleasant smile. "Now we just wait for the birth of your heir, and then we can finally be free of her." My chest tightened. I squeezed my lips together as I nodded. Cautiously peeling myself away, I scurried from the balcony.

It was extremely rare to find the palace halls vacant. Only when the entirety of the castle staff was attending mass did I ever find myself walking through them alone. I listened to the click-clack of my boots bouncing through the long empty corridor. The echoey chamber was dim through the morning's storm clouds, the atmosphere eerie.

I closed my eyes and tried to reimagine the static image of Evangeline that I had witnessed that morning. I had memorized every detail of her posture: her forehead slightly bowed, her flowing eyelashes resting against the tops of her cheeks. I could already feel the pencil in my hand, could sense the coiling strokes of my wrist as I sketched her hair, the light pressure of the lead against the paper creating the subtle blush of her cheeks. My fingers tingled. This would be my finest piece yet.

With an abrupt jerk, I was swept from the daydream by a firm hand gripping my arm. The nameless fingers tugged me into a nearby room, tearing the barren hallway from view and entrapping me behind a closed door. My lungs emptied. The hand suddenly doubled in number, swinging me around and gripping the front of my jerkin.

Face-to-face with my kidnapper, I sighed. It was Princess Evangeline. I was still not used to her abrupt greetings. Her cheeks radiated heat. Her lips, slightly parted, formed a thin gap through which I could barely see her teeth, and her eyes penetrated mine with a savage hunger. Her gaze hypnotized me, and I found myself studying their innermost colors—light brown patches, gleaming through her syrupy irises. Her wide pupils grew in size as she dragged me into the darkness.

For just a moment, I shifted my gaze to inspect the room. It was an old library, one I had never seen before. The walls were covered with bookshelves, filled with stacks of untouched volumes. A few couches were spread across the floor, their leather surfaces coated with dust. No candles were lit to brighten the interior. Only the faint sunlight that bled through the dingy windows kept us from being shrouded in blackness.

I opened my mouth to speak, but before I could say anything, her hands tightened their grip on my shirt and yanked me forward. I stumbled, tripping over my feet and crashing into her, our chests colliding as her back slammed into a nearby wall. Our lips snapped together like magnets. I leaned in closer, captivated by the warmth of her mouth. The tip of her tongue rolled smoothly across my upper lip.

My knees grew weak, and I pressed my palms into the shelves behind her to steady myself. I graciously accepted each passionate kiss and responded with my own gentle tug around her bottom lip. My body pressed closely into hers, impossibly close. My legs were tucked into the thin folds of her dress. My chest was enwrapped in her supple breasts.

Removing her right hand from my vest, she slid her fingers beneath my doublet and pawed eagerly at my bare chest. I quivered as they brushed against my skin, and I groaned into her open mouth. Beneath her hand, we both felt the nervous pulsing of my heart. She rested her palm there, holding it still until the racing beat gradually slowed, calmed by the power of her touch.

Without warning, she tore her lips away, leaving mine parted. My mouth desperately searched the space she had just left. Fervently, she slid her tongue down my neck, planting firm pecks upon each inch of the tender skin. I could no longer stifle my moans within the deep chasm of her mouth. I tried to hold back, sighing quietly as her teeth grazed the sides of my throat.

My heart jumped when I felt the new placement of her hands. They had moved from my ribs down to my waist, clawing impatiently at the string around my breeches. Below my navel, I felt a surging pulse. Once the knot was undone, she pulled her mouth from my neck. Her eyes darted upward, once again making contact with mine. Her hunger was now visibly ravenous. My chest ached with a yearning I had never felt before. I loosened my limbs, relinquishing myself to her will.

Lifting her hands back to my ribs, she drove my body backward. I staggered aimlessly away from the wall, entrusting myself completely to her guidance. Soon, my calves struck what felt like leather. I stumbled back, landing on one of the couches with a soft thud. She crouched to the floor and swiftly tugged my trousers down to my ankles. All at once, I was exposed before her, my entire manhood the sole focus of her gaze. She paused and stared, studying my protruding flesh with a lustful leer.

Finally, she ended the agonizing wait and sunk my fullness into her mouth. Unable to hold back any longer, I released the deep groan that had been lingering in my throat. I threw my head back, pressing my crown into the head rest. I swore I saw stars twinkling on the ceiling.

Through her lips, delicately enveloping my most fragile appendage, she growled and put her hands back to use. She skimmed her fingertips along my bare legs, their movements giving me chills as they circled my tender orbs.

My entire body quaked as pleasure swelled through me. But just before it could overflow, she pulled back, unbinding her lips. Standing to her feet, she gripped the hem of her skirt with both hands. In an instant, she wrenched the dress over her head and threw it carelessly to the floor behind her. Around her chest was a tight corset, carrying the fullness of her breasts while pinching the sides of her waist inward. The lacy top ended just above her hips, unveiling her lower half.

I stared longingly at her body with my mouth hung low. Her luscious curves left me just as entranced as they had the day before when I had watched her casually wading through the stream. To my delight, her legs were just as silky as I remembered. Her hips veered outward and back again around her slender middle. I lost myself in her thighs, bewitched by their voluptuous form. She was a sorceress, and I was defenseless against her charms.

When my wandering eyes reached her face, she was smirking at me, pleased by my reverent stares. She inched herself forward and reached for my hand, directing it to the space between her legs. Gingerly, she introduced my fingers to her depths, spinning them in the oozing wetness that resided there. She expertly angled my hand downward, inserting my forefinger within her and gently rubbing my thumb over her protruding button.

Once I was positioned to her liking, she took hold of my own hardness and tenderly stroked. I was again overwhelmed by her masterful touch and groaned desperately toward heaven. Lost in a trance under her skilled caress, my fingers slowed. With her free hand, she seized my chin and plunged me back down to earth. "Don't stop," she demanded.

I hastily obeyed her stern order. Over time, I felt the tension drift from her body. Her hand stroked me faster in response. Again, I was reeling, floating into another world, but this time I did not dare slow my fingers.

Unthinking, I lifted my free hand and swept it across the smoothness of her hips. Like lightning, she snatched my wrist and pinned it to the arm of the chair. She leaned so close I could feel her hot breath in my ear. "You will only touch when I tell you to touch." Her hiss was severe, making me shiver. I welcomed the feeling.

I nodded obediently and kept my arm glued to the chair even when she removed her strong hold. Closing my eyes, I focused on the motion of my fingers, slightly increasing my pace. For the first time, she tossed her own head back and groaned. The sound was carnal, making me throb. Her strokes became more forceful. I moaned desperately, she urgently. I tried to match her speed, keeping the delicate pressure on her mound and permeating her more intensely. Her thumb snuck to my tip, making me convulse with increased fervor.

Her ecstasy broke just seconds before mine. Feeling the violent throbbing in her core, I erupted with my own rapture. Both of us cried out in relief, our moans harmonized in a frantic melody.

With a final sigh, she collapsed onto the couch beside me. Her breath was heavy as she slumped her body into the cushions. I observed the pink hue of her cheeks, the quick pulsing of her chest. A line of sweat traveled down her neck. She turned toward me, and for the first time, I saw her true smile, a wide, unbridled grin. "Well done," she said between breaths, brushing away loose strands of hair that had escaped her braids.

I rested my head back as I relished the foreign heat that surged through me. I knew instantly that the feeling was her fire. For the first time, I was experiencing her flames, a sensation I had never before known and had longed to discover for myself.

As I caught my breath, my throbs fading away, I closed my eyes and embraced the last of the euphoria. I sighed inwardly, admitting to myself what I had feared most from the moment she first set her lips on mine: I would never get enough of this woman.

And I would never get over her.

Chapter 16

Eve

Sweat rolled down my temples as I stared longingly at the endless collection of weapons lining the walls. It was an immeasurable arsenal of bludgeons and maces, spears and crossbows, lances and sabers. The powerful heat of the hearth fueled the flames within me, and at the sight of the untouched metal, I felt a suppressed fury resurge.

For just a moment, I allowed myself to slip into a daydream. I imagined how easy it would be to snatch the nearest sword from its mount and rush from the forge with the weapon held tightly in my grasp. To chop off the arm of every guard who tried to stop me or dared stand in my way as I raced toward the castle doors. To climb the north tower at the speed of sound, headed straight for Ingrid's bedroom. To kick down the door and catch her lounging by the fire, stunned by my sudden ambush. To force her to her knees and tell her how long I had waited for this moment, to avenge my father at last. And when she begged me to spare her life, I would heave the blade directly through her neck, letting her blood splatter on the walls and windows, watching with delight as her severed head rolled across the floor.

"You know Queen Ingrid would never allow you to purchase that." The voice was Mary's, coming from the far end of the forge. Reluctantly, I abandoned the fantasy and pulled my gaze from the shimmering sword. Mary was standing by the entrance, her hands twisted stiffly around her front. I screwed my face into an irritated sneer.

"She is right, Princess," another voice said from behind me. I spun around and peered at its source. The brawny blacksmith stood by the hearth, pausing his hammering to confirm Mary's claim. His cheeks were coated in ash, his apron splotched with dark fingerprints. His long hair was tied back to reveal his rugged chest-length beard. His eyes were as black as soot, but they peered at me with a gleam of regret. "The queen forbade me from loaning you any items from the armory," he sighed, biting his bottom lip. "She threatened to chop off my hands if I did." Although his tone was remorseful, I heard genuine fear in his voice.

I folded my arms across my chest and issued a dramatic groan. "She treats me like a damn toddler," I grumbled. I took a few steps toward the blacksmith, my mouth set in an irritated frown. "Is there anything here I can buy?" Lifting both hands, I gestured toward the entire shop.

The blacksmith lifted his hammer from the sizzling metal plate and pointed it towards the far-most corner. "You are free to peruse our selection of horseshoes."

I dropped my arms, letting my hands clap noisily against my sides. Rolling my eyes, I whirled toward the exit and marched out of the forge. "Farewell," I heard Mary call out toward the blacksmith. I was too far to hear his response, already stomping stubbornly along the cobblestone path. I was so tired of being some sort of first class prisoner, of playing Ingrid's games just to keep my people alive. I was trapped in a place I no longer belonged, a home that was no longer mine.

Mary's light tread grew louder as she jogged to catch up to me. Since Ingrid had declared my visits to the servants' floor unsuitable, we had been searching for more creative ways to meet. The bailey was an obvious choice. The circular courtyard encompassed the palace, containing workshops, stables, and gardens. It was not the optimal location as we occasionally came across a band of patrolling guards who would eye me suspiciously until I caught them in my death glare. But we made do. It was better than the alternatives: lounging awkwardly with Ingrid's court or sitting in my bedroom all day.

We were passing a narrow pen filled with sheep and goats grazing a small field. A pair of young girls carrying baskets of bread strolled by us with a respectful grin, pausing beside me to dip into a low curtsy. I did the same despite the angry pout that lingered on my lips. My thin sandals thumped along the bumpy trail as we continued onward.

From the corner of my eye, I saw Mary holding me in a persistent stare. For a while, I ignored her, peering intently at the trio of Kreagan knights chatting along the castle wall. But when they were out of view, I finally met her gaze, a sly smile now formed on her lips. "What?" I blurted.

She raised her eyebrows. "Are we not going to talk about it?"

I crinkled my forehead. "Talk about what?" But before the words could escape my throat, I felt the sides of my lips sneaking upward against my will. I coolly angled my head away to hide my unruly mouth, but it was too late. I had already been caught.

Mary tightened her lips and nodded, a thick coat of sarcasm in her eyes. She let out a breathy chuckle. "You could not keep a secret if your life depended on it."

The smile overtook my cheeks, and I forfeited my efforts to contain it. "I don't know what you are talking about," I said through a wayward giggle.

"Oh, for the love of God." Mary rolled her eyes, unfooled by my poor attempts to mislead her. "Why don't you just admit it already? You slept with Prince Rune!" I flinched, spinning my head around to ensure no one was within earshot then spun back toward Mary. "I could tell from the moment I saw you this morning."

I laughed aloud. Leave it to Mary to catch me in one of my dirty lies. "I did not sleep with him," I replied softly.

Mary furrowed her eyebrows. "You didn't?"

"No." My grin was now immovable. "We just…fooled around a bit."

"Wow," Mary said as they passed a small hut smelling of clay. We both turned and waved at the lone potter seated in the shop, her hands tinted gray as she worked at her wheel. "All that build up and you didn't even do the deed? That is unlike you." She eyed me sideways.

"It's not that simple," I said under my breath. A Kreagan soldier walked opposite us, approaching with a leery glare. I stared back with my own unmasked hatred. "He…" I hesitated, cringing inwardly. "He has never been with a woman before."

Mary scoffed. "Anyone with two eyes could have guessed that," she snorted. "So what?"

"So," I continued, "these things take time."

Mary gawked at me, her eyes narrowed in disbelief. *"These things take time?* Who am I speaking to? The holy virgin?"

Now I was the one who scoffed. "This is different," I tried to explain, although I could hardly convince myself. "He is a prince. And we are married."

She said nothing. The only sounds were the mumbling of nearby servants and the beat of our footsteps against the stone. Before long, Mary's questioning squint converted into an insightful smirk. My chest tightened. "What?" I asked, desperate to break the silence.

Her eyes clasped onto mine with a knowing glint. "You have feelings for him."

"What?" I exclaimed. The defensive tone in my voice surprised me. "I do not!"

Mary nodded, slowly growing more confident in her assertion. "You have feelings for him," she repeated with more vigor.

"That is absurd," I said a little too forcefully.

"If it is so absurd, then answer me this." She lifted her chin and placed her hands on her hips. "Are you going to see him again?"

I swallowed. She had me cornered, and there was no way out now. I looked down at my feet as they traipsed along the stone path. "Probably," I mumbled under my breath.

Mary shook her head at me, her nose scrunched in amusement. "You cannot escape reality, Evangeline. Eventually, the truth always wins out." She halted, and I paused beside her. She turned away from the path and glimpsed at a nearby shop. "I'll be right back. I need to purchase some new fabric." She sauntered toward the wooden shed and spoke to me over her shoulder. "Maybe when I return you will not be in *denial*."

I rolled my eyes. "I doubt that!" I yelled back. Mary shook her head again, turning to flash her sparkling grin before disappearing into the shop.

Now alone, I scanned the area. We had made it to the end of the bailey. Our current section of the path empty save for a few maids milking cows in a nearby barn. I strode toward the tall iron gate at the edge of the road, one of the only transparent sections in the massive rock wall that enveloped the palace. Through the grooves in the metal, I saw the village. Although the spot may not have matched the stunning acrial view from the north tower, there was something about this ground perspective that made the town feel more personal, more real. I could see the winding dirt trail that led into the village, spanning the rolling hills that separated the castle from the rest of the kingdom. From where I was standing, I could just make out the townspeople. They wandered about, speeding between the cottages like ants.

I let out a long breath and slumped a few inches closer to the ground. *Had it really been over a month since I visited the village?* I asked myself. Guilt swelled in my chest, making my heart ache. I knew it was my own pride that kept us separated. And yet, I still felt knots in my stomach when I thought about taking a trip to the town. I was their greatest disappointment, a complete failure in their eyes. How would they ever respect me again?

My jaw tightened and I swallowed. There was only one option left for me now. I knew it was time for me to accept the truth. Vitalia was gone. I would never again serve as its fearless knight or its noble leader. If I truly loved my people, I had to let those dreams go. It was time for me to surrender to my fate.

Just then, a dark, hooded figure appeared beside me. My body tensed, my instincts preparing me for action. With my fists clenched, I dared a sideways glance at the stranger. I could not make out their face, shadowed beneath a woolen cloak. Only their hands were visible through the thick gray coat, their fingers wrinkled and covered in dirt. They stood tall, several inches above my own head.

"We need to talk," the mysterious figure mumbled. At his words, I relaxed my shoulders. I recognized that voice. It was Benedict Walters, the village cobbler who had made my cherished leather riding boots. I gradually let my guard down and turned to face him fully.

He spoke fast, his tone urgent. "Try to be discreet." I promptly swung my head back around, my vision directed toward the village but my mind focused only on the sound of his voice.

"There is a meeting in the village," the man continued. "Tomorrow night." I detected a subtle shaking in his voice, a tone of urgency with a hint of fear. "You need to be there."

Before I could fully comprehend what he was telling me, I felt him slip a folded sheet of paper into my palm. I hastily wrapped my fingers around the note and stuffed it stealthily into the top of my dress. "What is this about?" I whispered through the side of my mouth. I waited in silence, receiving no response. Finally, I dared a cautious glance his way. But to my surprise, he was gone.

I twisted my neck around, turning my back to the iron gate to inspect the area. It was now completely vacant, not a soul in sight. My heart pounded rapidly in my chest, the sobering interaction throwing me off guard. I had no clue what he was referring to. What kind of town meeting would I possibly need to attend?

Cautiously, I ambled back to the weaver's shop, keeping an eye out for any suspicious characters. A few servants were passing by, holding stacks of hand-woven baskets. I hurried through a curtsy then quickened my steps. Across the path, a Kreagan soldier guarded the castle entrance. He was glaring at me through tight eyes, a severe expression on his face.

I froze, feeling my stomach drop. I could only pray he had not seen me talking to the cobbler. I bit my lip and tried to look natural as I strolled casually by him, careful not to make eye contact. The hairs on my neck prickled as I felt him stare into the center of my back. A thick drop of sweat dribbled down my spine.

At last, I turned the corner, the rest of the bailey coming into view. I felt my body untense, then quickly shuffled the rest of the way to the weaver's workshop. When I arrived, I snaked around the outside of the building and crept behind the rows of square huts. Certain I was now alone, I plucked the crumpled note from my bust and hastily unfolded it. With my chest still thumping fiercely, I peered down at the scraggly handwriting:

Wilhelm's Granary
Midnight

Chapter 17

Rune

She woke me at midnight. Her hands gripping my shoulders, she swiftly shook me from my sleep. My eyes shot open to find her standing over my chest, her feet bordering my sides. She stared down at me in silence, speaking only with her eyes. They glowed dimly beneath the faint moonlight bleeding through the window. She lifted one hand, her palm facing upward, and curled her index finger inward. *Come*, it said.

Wordlessly, I rose from the floor, carefully rolling the wool blanket aside. Evangeline straightened and backed away, closely watching my every step. I felt the pounding of my heart in my palms as I inched toward her. When I met her by the door, she took my hand. Hers was surprisingly warm in the cool of the night, drawing me swiftly from the room. I hung my arm limply, letting her drag me along behind her.

Her brisk footsteps made no sound as she padded down the long hallway. My feet were not so nimble. They clomped loudly against the stone floor. No quieter were they when I walked on the tips of my toes. She pulled me onward nonetheless, ignoring my thumping gait, both of us speeding through the dark corridor.

We hadn't passed a soul since we left the bedroom. I began to wonder if the halls were empty at this hour.

But upon rounding our first corner, the princess spiraled backward and threw my shoulder blades into the wall. She pressed her palm to my mouth, stifling my startled cry. I stilled myself beneath the pressure of her hand and breathed through the space between her fingers, flattened against my lips. She tilted her head and peeked back around the corner. Before long, I heard the plod of approaching footsteps. The sound slowly intensified, and I held my breath. I bit into the sides of my cheeks as the uniformed guard casually strode by us, coming within inches of Evangeline's shoulder. She pressed me tightly against the stone, not even flinching when the soldier paused to take a quick scan of the area. When he turned his head away, traipsing a few feet past us, the princess spun around the corner and dashed into a hidden stairwell.

I raced after her, sprinting as I struggled to maintain her speed. Panic rose in my chest as I watched her rapidly descend the stairwell then slowly fade from view. I worried I would get lost in this unfamiliar part of the castle without her direction. When she reached the base floor, she threw open a tall wooden door and disappeared through the other side. I skipped the last few steps then bolted through the faint doorway, scrambling after her.

A cold breeze rushed over me. As I caught my breath, I looked upward, surprised to find we had made our way out of the castle. The darkness finally subsided, and we were showered beneath the full light of the moon. The stars danced in the sky above us. I stared in awe at the infinite galaxies that speckled the heavens. I had never seen the stars this close. In Kreagan, the sky had always been hidden by a blanket of thick storm clouds, but here, the entirety of the cosmos willingly revealed itself.

Taking hold of my hand again, Evangeline yanked me from my trance. We flew around the castle's edge and came upon the training fields at the back end of the palace. I gaped out at the barren plot of land and the all-encompassing forest beyond, wondering where she was taking me.

But the fields were soon stripped from my view. With a firm tug, the princess pulled me into a small wooden structure hugging the palace's back wall. She swept the creaky doors closed and reset the lock with a nimble flick of her finger.

The first thing I noticed was the smell: the woody scent of hay and the unmistakable odor of horse dung. I glanced down at my feet. Even in the darkness, save for the few channels of starlight that seeped between the wood panels, I could just make out the clumps of straw littering the floor. They crackled lightly beneath our feet as we wandered farther into the room. I turned my head and saw that we were surrounded by stables. Some of the horses had woken from their slumber when we hastily barged into the dingey barn. A few whinnied in complaint as we strolled by, tossing their manes through the air in protest. The night's chill wind forced its way through the barn's rickety walls, making me shiver beneath my thin night clothes.

The princess led me deeper, her pace now slow as we neared the far end of the stables. Beside the back wall, I noticed a distinct plot of hay on the ground, more illuminated than the surrounding area. The bundle was stacked a few feet higher than the rest and caught the moonlight at the perfect angle. I felt my limbs start to thaw as we ambled closer to this seemingly sacred place, my lower half tingling in expectation.

I was surprised to find her movements much softer than they had been in the library. She seated me on the hay with a gentle press, not a hasty shove. She eased herself into the space beside me with her fingers still entwined with mine. Then, gradually leaning her chest forward, she snuck her lips around my own. I was not used to this kiss, this long, drawn-out caress of her mouth, patiently consuming me. Her fingertips drifted down my arm unhurried, like she knew she had all the time in the world. There was no rush, no restless urge, only her tender touch. She was slow and thoughtful. A holy goddess of time.

When her fingers sank into my hair, I released my first sigh, this time making no attempt to hold it back. Since our first touch, I had dreamed endlessly about her hands, about the silky texture of her fingertips, and now I savored every second they brushed against my skin. They swept through my curls, separating the locks effortlessly as she pressed her tongue into the depths of my mouth. I leaned my head back, letting it slide deeper as I dared to connect it with my own.

I reveled in the taste of her lips, just as succulent as I remembered. Between each prudent kiss, she hovered her open mouth over mine. I waited restlessly for her to return, but she would linger there, just a whisper away, until I ached to sink her lips between my teeth. Her fingers twirled along my scalp, slowly migrating toward my bare neck. I slumped my upper body lower so that our faces were even, yearning for her to thrust my back into the hay. But she did not succumb to my desires. Instead, she kept me seated upright. Abandoning my frenzied efforts to rush her, I yielded to her pace, granting her full control.

She pressed her taut breasts into my chest, her hands traveling calmly down my arms. I quivered as they inched lower, desperate to hurry them to their final destination. Before they could, however, she eased them away. I opened my eyes and searched her face avidly. She pushed her thumb against my bottom lip and pulled down slightly, letting her nail rest against my teeth. "Strip for me," she whispered. Her breath washed over my cheeks like a warm wave.

My stomach tightened. Taking in a shaky breath, I nodded obediently. I angled my chest back and took hold of the bottom of my tunic then pulled my shirt over my head. Standing to my feet, I loosened my breeches and let them fall to the floor in a messy clump. I bit my lip, my hands shaking uncontrollably. I held them behind my back and looked down at her awkwardly, the tips of my ears burning. For the first time, she saw me in my entirety, fully exposed. I stood high above her, and yet I felt indescribably small.

From the square bale of hay, she gazed up at me, completely disrobed before her very eyes. I recognized their hunger, but this time she held back, not yet letting them partake in their feast. Sliding seamlessly onto her knees, she crawled forward, her widened pupils still pouring into mine. Her hand dashed suddenly to my thigh, granting herself one forceful squeeze around my leg before restraining herself once more. Then, holding both hands loosely around my hips, she slid me into her mouth. From the base of my throat, I let out a violent moan. My knees shook, straining to keep me upright. She softly gripped the sides of my legs until they stilled. I felt myself throb between her wet lips, her tongue running smoothly up and down my shaft.

Too soon, she released me. She leaned back and stared up into my face. Sensing her teeming lust, I sunk down to my knees beside her. This time, I was the one who waited eagerly on the ground while she stood to undress. Her turquoise nightgown slid off her shoulders with ease. There was nothing to restrict her form tonight. Her breasts plunged outward and bounced before settling back into place, her pink nipples hard. Her waist curved inward to display the fullness of her hips. She displayed herself openly before me, and I sighed aloud. The sight of her body alone made my head spin.

She took a nimble step forward then reached her fingers around the nape of my neck. With a gentle tug, she pulled my face toward her bare hips. I flashed my eyes up into hers, sensing her growing expectation, then sunk my lips into her delicate flesh. I sighed as my tongue stretched into her sacred space. I savored the taste collecting on my tongue, moaning within her before she could let out her first breath. As her exhales turned to groans, my chest fluttered with longing. She desperately pulled my face closer, sharply crying out toward the ceiling. When I felt her body start to tremble, I pressed my tongue deeper into her tender vault, reveling in the violent quiver of her hips as she gasped into the darkness.

After she finally caught her breath, she pressed my lips away with a palm to my shoulder. I sat back and looked up at her through blurred vision, still reeling. Crouching back to the ground, she crawled forward like a cat on all fours. Placing one hand against my chest, she thrust me backward, sending the back of my head crashing into the hay. I toppled flatly onto the earth, the straw catching me like a soft pillow. She slunk on top of me with an agile slither, hovering her chest and stomach just inches over mine.

I could feel the heat emanating off of her, burning my skin. I felt the thumping of a nearby heartbeat and wondered absentmindedly if it was hers or mine. Her irises shone iridescent under the faint light as they studied my nakedness. I held my breath as the space between us diminished, releasing the air in my lungs when she finally closed the gap.

My soft groan was released in time with hers, a long-held tensity finally freed as our bare chests connected. We readily breathed each other in, our hearts joined and then our mouths. She plunged both hands into my hair now, lightly rubbing her thumbs against my temples. I tugged eagerly at her lips and graciously accepted the warm liquid that dripped from them. Lifting one hand, she took up my arm and placed it gently around her waist. I willingly complied, wrapping both of my hands around the small of her back. I rolled my fingers up and down her spine, memorizing the texture of her skin.

When she pulled away, a knowing smile had overtaken her face. The look thrilled me and unnerved me equally. She grinned wider. I swallowed.

Carefully, she elevated her hips, floating them in the air as she slid her body back. When she settled them down again, she delicately took me within her, transporting me into a universe of unknown pleasure. My throbbing surged when my fullness was within her, for the first time conjoined with her inner flesh. I felt her slick lips soften around me as she sunk her body closer to the ground, pulling me deeper.

With long, slow strokes, she rode me. I watched eagerly as she skillfully rocked her hips. It was celestial, a moment of divinity I had never experienced. I tried my best to keep my eyes open, to watch the steady bounce of her breasts as she glided forward and back, but my eyes plunged helplessly to the back of my head as she slowly drowned me in ecstasy. When I finally managed to regain my sight, I found her watching me through drunken eyelids, her mouth hung half open.

I swept my hands up and down her sides, taking hold of her luscious curves. My fingers tingled, craving more. Before I knew it, I succumbed to my forbidden desire. Easing my hand upward, I rested my palm against her cheek. Her eyes widened at my unsolicited touch, her movements slowing, and her eyes sharp. My wrist tensed, and I readied myself for her forceful swat. But instead, she cautiously let her face drop into my hand, releasing into me the weight of her head.

Without warning, her speed increased. The entire room began to blur. My pleasure climbed to levels beyond any I had ever imagined. At long last, I burst within her depths. I cried out wildly, arching my back and letting my hair submerge into the pool of hay. Pressing both hands into my chest, she forced my back into the ground with a savage energy. She took my mouth in hers and inhaled my cries, drinking me into her until I had nothing left to give.

Chapter 18

Eve

Lying restlessly in my bed, I stared out the window at the alabaster sheen of the moon. If you looked at it for long enough, it was nearly blinding. It had been approximately three hours since sundown, since I had lain upon my mattress and feigned sleep, listening only to the sound of Rune's snores. I would have to get up in just a few minutes to start my long walk to the village, that is if I chose to attend the mysterious town meeting.

With a long sigh, I dropped the back of my head onto my pillow and gazed up at the ceiling. For the hundredth time that night, I considered my perilous situation. Sneaking out of the castle in the middle of the night would be highly suspicious, and if I was caught, the queen would surely have me flogged until I revealed the reason for my midnight voyage. And even if I made it to the village undetected, I would finally be forced to face the commoners. My former subjects would no doubt eye me with disdain, would glare in disappointment at my failure to defend them, and that was something I was not yet sure I had the strength to face. My stomach had been in knots all afternoon, mostly because, despite the dread I felt, I knew I would go to the village that night.

Of course I would go. Regardless of how I felt, I was still Evangeline, woman of the people.

Dismissing any lingering fears, I rolled off the side of my bed. I quietly slipped out of my nightgown and threw on some beige trousers, a pair of leather riding boots, and a long black cloak. All I had to do now was tiptoe out of the room without waking the sleeping prince. As I crept by his spot on the floor, I took a quick glance over. He was curled up on his side, buried beneath the navy blanket, and, just as I expected, fast asleep. Creeping gingerly past him, I eased the door open and slipped out of the room without a sound.

It was much easier sneaking through the castle halls tonight. Without lugging Rune along behind me, I did not have to worry about his heavy trod giving away my position. Suddenly, memories of the previous night flooded my mind, and I tried to suppress the smile that spread across my cheeks.

Our night in the barn had been thrilling—there was no denying it. I had spent many nights with countless men in those stables, but being with Rune was different. There was something unique about him. Maybe it was the way he looked at me, with both awe and lust. Maybe it was the softness of his touch, the tender way he traced my skin. Or maybe it was because even though he gladly surrendered to my every wish, somehow I knew he would never let me fall.

I felt my body warm as I relived our first night of passion. It was clear the physical connection we had was rare. And I had to admit, even though I could not curb the grating feeling that I was betraying everything I believed in, I knew our secret relationship was far from over. There was something more between us I had yet to discover, something I had never experienced. And even though I knew it was wrong, I was eager to find out what it was.

I made my way out of the castle in minutes, skillfully evading the gaze of each guard I came across. But when I arrived at the bailey, I knew it would not be so simple. A lone figure circling the exterior of the palace in the dark of night would no doubt set the queen's soldiers on high alert. Rather than risk detection by walking down the middle of the path, I pressed my back against the chill stone wall and shimmied along the castle's edge. Before each blind turn, I glanced around the corner to ensure no knights were waiting for me on the other side.

Finally, sidestepping all the way through the bailey, I made it to the front of the palace. I studied the tall iron gates from behind the nearest straw hut. It was the most highly guarded area on the castle grounds. Standing before the doors and manned along each northward facing window were ranks of soldiers, armed and at-the-ready. No way could I pass by unspotted, not unless I could make it through the gates in the blink of an eye.

I steadied myself with a deep breath and reviewed my escape plan. Searching the ground, I soon found a perfectly sized stone. I picked up the round rock, fitting neatly in the center of my palm, light enough to hurl a few dozen feet but heavy enough to turn heads. Crouching into my ready position, I thrust the stone across the courtyard. It landed opposite the main gate, thumping loudly against the cobblestone path. As the crash reverberated throughout the bailey, I dashed toward the nearest exit, one of the small, metal-grated doors beside the larger main gate, and prayed that my diversion would be enough to distract the guards. I did not wait around to find out.

I shot down the dirt path, running toward the village at top speed. I did not slow my pace until I descended the first hill. Sprinting behind the nearest tree, I waited. My heart was beating furiously through my chest as I peered anxiously around the trunk, scoping out the path I had just crossed for any trailing soldiers. When several minutes passed and not one of them appeared, I let out a sigh of relief and hiked back to the trail, slowing to a quick walk for the remainder of the journey.

I arrived to find the village streets empty, which was unsurprising considering the late hour. Few candles remained lit inside the wood-framed cottages, homes, and shops bogged down by bulky straw-thatched roofs. Nevertheless, I crept along the barren roads as quietly as possible, hunching my body low whenever I passed an open window. I may have evaded the castle guards, but there was no need to announce my arrival to the entire town. Who knew what eyes were watching?

The granary stood at the backside of the village. The building was raised over the tall grass on wooden stilts, and the area surrounding it contained vast, open fields where cows, horses, and sheep usually grazed. A ray of artificial light seeped from beneath the front doors, and a low buzzing of voices drifted from within. When my fingers connected with the door handle, I froze, once again wrestling that nagging voice of dread. All it took was the memory of my father's dying words, and the voice fell mute.

I shoved the doors open and marched into the granary with a powerful strut. The wide storage area was brimming with men of all ages dressed in dirt-covered tunics and well-worn breeches. They were huddled together in small groups, each holding their own lantern or candlestick as they mumbled to each other beneath their breaths. It took a few seconds for the mob of anxious villagers to notice my entrance. But once I removed the dark hood from my head, the slew of conversations turned to whispers, and the whispers soon hushed to silence. I ambled toward the center of the room then stopped, holding my chest tall and my head upright. My hands shook imperceptibly by my sides. I did not meet their eyes, too afraid to see what was going through their minds. Instead, I peered aimlessly into the center of the crowd.

The painful stillness finally broke when a shorter man, tucked within the enveloping mob, scrambled into an open aisle and hurried toward me. "Princess Evangeline!" the man said in an over-zealous tone. "We are so glad you've come!" He raised his lantern to illuminate his face, but there was no need. I recognized his voice—the same one owned by the mysterious hooded figure outside the castle.

"Good day, Mr. Walters," I said with a shallow bow of my head. But when I lifted my chin, the cobbler was no longer standing before me. He was kneeling. The congregation of men followed his lead. All across the room, the villagers sunk to the floor and humbly lowered their heads.

I was shocked. The last thing I expected upon my long delayed return was a heartfelt welcome. Not once when I ran my mind through this dreaded night did I imagine a reverent greeting. They honored me as they would a trusted ruler even though I had relinquished my power. I did not understand it. How could they have any respect left for me?

"Please," I stuttered, not sure how to respond to such

undeserved praise. "There is no need for that." The men hesitantly lifted their gaze from the floor. Eyeing each other uncertainly, they slowly stood back to their feet, the cobbler the last to do so.

"Princess, I would like to—"

"What is this all about?" I interrupted before he could offer me any more unwarranted cordiality. "Why did you invite me here?"

The cobbler paused, his hand frozen in the air. "Of course," he said, bending into another low bow. "I shall get right to the point, your majesty." Spinning on his heels, he scuttled toward the back end of the granary where a short podium had been erected. Once positioned atop the stand, he cleared his throat then raised his arms skyward.

"Friends, brothers, fellow Vitalians!" My heart leapt at his simple form of address. I hadn't heard my kingdom's name spoken aloud in what felt like ages.

"We are gathered here tonight because we are being oppressed by a vicious parasite. It has been three fortnights since the honorable King Ricard was brutally murdered by a band of northern thieves." He spoke with both bitterness and fortitude, stirring the pent-up fury of the crowd. I swallowed, clenching my fists to stifle their trembling. "It has been forty days since the great name of Vitalia was wrongfully renounced, traded for the wretched title of Kreagan." The men's faces wrinkled with disgust. A few of them hissed angrily.

"For far too long, we have suffered the injustices of this foreign power. For far too long, we have endured fear, hardship, and grief at the hand of these ignoble knights." He paused for a moment and carefully lowered his upraised hands. "So many loved ones have been lost.

227

Too many." A deafening silence. Shared sorrow flowed through the room.

The cobbler suddenly turned, staring straight at me. My stomach clenched. "And none of us understand this pain more than our princess." The mass of commoners shifted their gaze from the podium, now gaping openly at me. Still standing in the middle of the room, I held my breath. I stared in confusion at the horde of steady onlookers then peered back at Mr. Walters with a questioning look. "Which is why," he said, his grin returning ever-so-slowly, "she is the one who will lead our rebellion to victory."

The men bellowed heartily and raised their fists in triumph. The cobbler was smiling ear-to-ear, relishing in the roaring fanfare. The villagers turned toward me again, this time with a spirited vigor, waiting expectantly for my reply. But I was speechless. The blood had drained from my face. My chin hung low to the ground, my mouth wide with shock. The energy of the crowd gradually subdued, and the townsmen stared at me blankly.

My lips moved frantically, but no words escaped them, only unintelligible sputters. Eventually, I shook my head, clearing my stiff throat with a humorless laugh. "You cannot be serious."

"Of course we are," the cobbler announced, his confidence slightly fading. "We want you to command the insurrection."

"*The insurrection*?" I exclaimed, dumbfounded. "The Kreagans killed half of our soldiers, and the rest were forced to swear their undying loyalty to the queen. How could you possibly hope to overpower an army of trained men?"

The corners of the cobbler's mouth curved upward once more. "You."

"Me?" I asked incredulously. "You think I can take on the entire Kreagan guard?"

"We want you to train us. To lead us." He swept his open hand across the granary. "This is your army." He closed his fist and rested his forearm against his chest. "We are your soldiers."

"But," I stuttered. "I cannot—"

"We know you, Princess." His tone was somber, pressing. "We have all heard of your legendary battles. You are undoubtedly Vitalia's finest warrior, our greatest leader by a landslide. If anyone can train us to wield a sword and shield, it's you."

"It is not that simple," I said with exasperation. "Learning proper swordsmanship can take months, even years."

"Then we will train hard," the cobbler declared with a hopeful lift to his voice. He looked out at the men with encouragement, as some had started to lose their resolve. "We will do whatever it takes to drive these villains from our land."

I sighed and shook my head despairingly. What they were suggesting was absurd, impossible even. "It is a death sentence," I mumbled, rubbing my palm against my forehead. "Think of your families." I pivoted to face the crowd, imploring them to heed my warning. "If we were to fail, Ingrid will surely have each of you executed without a second thought. And even victory would mean the death of many."

The room was quiet as the men considered this. They knew I was right. Their chances of surviving a battle against Kreagan were slim, and many of them would be leaving behind wives and children.

"Then it is a risk we must take." This time, it was not the cobbler who spoke. Instead, the voice came from somewhere within the crowd. The swarming sea of villagers parted to let the unnamed speaker through. Limping slowly toward me was a shorter man with thinning brown hair. He hobbled forward with the aid of a wooden cane. Strapped tightly around his knee was a leather brace. It was Herbert Manfield, Mary's father.

I followed his movements as he struggled toward the center aisle with a wince. He gazed at me through weakened eyelids. There were more wrinkles along his forehead than the last time I saw him, likely formed from several weeks of grueling labor. I noticed a similar heaviness among other men in the granary. Time under Ingrid's rule seemed to take a greater toll here.

"I think I speak for everyone when I say we would gladly sacrifice our lives for a chance to restore our kingdom." He peered down at his crippled form. "I may not have much to offer," he said lowly, "but if you command our rebellion, I will be marching on the front lines."

I squeezed my lips together and exhaled through my nose. I was humbled by their passion but still feared the disaster that I knew awaited them. "Do you really trust me to be your leader?" I asked, my shoulders hunched forward. "I am wife to the prince of Kreagan." I stared down at my feet, the heavy weight in the room making my chest sag.

"Princess," Mr. Manfield said. I looked up to see him smiling warmly at me, the hateful disappointment I expected nowhere to be found. "You have always been our greatest protector. You surrendered your freedom to save our families. I trust you with my life."

Once again, I was at a loss for words. I gazed out at the crowd. Each face offered me its own genial grin. Thin pools formed in my eyes. Mr. Manfield softly set his free hand on my shoulder. "You are and will always be the heart of Vitalia." I saw the gratitude in their faces, the undying loyalty they had held for their country since before I was even born. But more than that, I saw their courage, their bold sacrifice that meant everything and more.

Blinking back tears, I straightened, adopting a more serious expression. "Then I suggest we get started," I said, my heart fluttering with new expectation. "We have work to do yet."

Chapter 19

Rune

Her hands were clasped around my waist, her fingernails digging into the small of my back. It was their normal placement when she was guiding my hips. But this time, I was in control. I directed my own spear, rhythmically gliding within her. And it was like I was enveloped in the gardens of paradise.

Her moans were more urgent than usual. Her arms were taut, tugging at me with a desperation I had yet to see in her. I tilted my body forward, my chest slanting over her. The skin of my palms rubbed harshly against the rough bark, forming blisters as I thrust my weight forward. But I knew my pain was minor compared to hers. The whole of her back was pressed into the tree, her spine scraping against the coarse wood.

It had all happened so fast. I barely had time to process what we were doing. One moment we were strolling through the palace orchards—admiring the scarlet fruit hanging from the branches, the apples ripe for picking—and the next I was hardily entering her against the nearest tree trunk. She had not even taken the time to remove her gown. Hidden within the thicket, she had clawed at my trousers like a starved animal, lowering them to just below my knees before pulling me toward her. She hitched up her skirts and spread her legs wide to prepare for my entry. There was no need to stroke me between her fingers first. We both knew I was already hard as stone.

Sinking her nails into my sides, she maneuvered my hips with precision, skillfully conducting the pace and pressure. She angled her pelvis upward, allowing me to slide with ease. The motion soon became natural, and I began to apply my own momentum. Suddenly, I was the one who governed the speed of our movements, who directed the tempo of each steady pulse, her grip loosening as she reluctantly let me lead the way. It was more control than I had ever been granted. It frightened me, this sense of power that I had never known before.

But I liked it.

As the heat of anticipation spread through my core, I quickened my pace. The princess set the crown of her head against the bark, whimpering into the clouds with sharp gasps. Her cries invigorated me, and I felt my legs quake as I lunged faster still. My hands tingled with a want that was all-consuming, an insatiable desire to fill my palms with her curves. I knew it would not be long before my euphoria crept in and overcame my restraint. Peeling my hands from the tree, I wrapped my fingers around her slender waist and drew her hips forward ever so gently.

Our combined forces soon became too much to sustain. I came with an unbridled groan, my low howls projecting through the orchard. The princess took my chin in her hand and tipped my face downward, quieting my unruly cries with a fervent kiss. I flooded her open mouth with the last of my irrepressible moans as I poured myself into her.

When I finally released the tension in my limbs,

letting my forehead go slack against the apple tree, she kept her hands folded around my sides, slightly easing her grip. My chest fell forward, my knees weak. She pressed her brow into the front of my tunic, resting against my pulsating heart. We stayed there as we slowed our breaths, our bodies lightly pressed together.

"Why did you do it?" she suddenly whispered between pants.

I furrowed my eyebrows and lifted my chest to look down at her face. "Why did I do what?"

"Why did you stand up for me? Why did you let her punish you in my place?"

I studied her eyes, her deep brown irises searching mine with genuine interest. "Because I could not watch her hurt you anymore." She stared into me with her lips slightly parted. "I know what it's like. She has locked me away many times before, and I never left the same. I could not stand the thought of her breaking you too."

She peered up at me in astonishment. For once, all her defenses were down. Her ever-present shield was lowered to reveal a more tender sentiment. I shivered beneath this unfamiliar gaze, her radiant eyes like melting icicles dripping onto my exposed skin. Slowly, she took her hand and set her palm along the back of my head. She gently pulled my face downward and caught my lips with hers. Her kiss was slow, soft, gracious. An armistice.

****

Things started to feel different after that. There was no doubt that she was still the same Evangeline who demanded her way, never taking no for an answer. But something was changing.

Per my mother's orders, we continued to meet every

morning and evening at mealtimes, sometimes with her advisors and sometimes alone. These awkward encounters remained as tense as ever. The three of us dined in silence, completely ignoring each other's presence so as not to spark any persisting animosity. But every once in a while, when my mother was looking down at her plate or peering thoughtfully across the room, I would catch Evangeline staring at me. Each time, she wore a mischievous smile, sharing through her playful gaze our darkest secrets. I couldn't help but smile back, my cheeks warm and my body tingling with a sinful thrill.

She grew less cautious about keeping our relationship hidden from the castle residents. Occasionally, as we ambled together through the halls, she would swing her head around, checking that no servants or vassals were in sight before dragging me aside. She would always catch me by surprise, eagerly tugging at my lips in the few seconds we had before the nearest maid rounded the corner. Then, she would saunter away as if nothing happened. I, however, was not so slick. After regaining my bearings, I would walk onward in a daze, guards and attendants staring at the foolish grin on my face.

I could feel something shifting in me, too. The unease that normally weighed heavily upon my shoulders while I was in my mother's presence seemed to lighten when Evangeline was around. She was like a fortress, an impenetrable shield that sheltered me from the cruel world I had been born into. She was the singular ray of light in the painful darkness of my existence. When I was with her, my relentless worries washed away. She freed me not from my fate, but from myself.

And when we had sex, I could sense something new unfolding, something warm and bright and electrifying. Any uncertainty or discomfort that existed between us was long gone. I learned all the right moves, the right times to touch and the right times to submit. I knew the motions that made her gasp with profound pleasure, the ones that softened her taut limbs. Her tight grip was loosening. Not as commanding as she used to be, she would gently guide me into the position she desired rather than force me there. She would rarely push my hands away when I reached out to touch her, something I now did often when the seductive shape of her body was too tempting to resist. She let my fingers explore her most sacred spaces.

There was something else too, something I could not see or touch but could sense only in the air we breathed. We had been possessed by a foreign desire, a new passion. It was different than the urgent craving that had first brought us together. It was not a spark of intensity but of tenderness. Her fingers no longer grabbed at me like they hungered for my pale flesh, but like she could finally rest when they were placed along my abdomen. The unquenchable lust that had once filled her eyes was fading, and in its place, I saw a more intimate yearning, a need I could satisfy only when I settled my chest on hers and plucked delicately at her soft lips.

I felt it in the way she used her hands. Before, she would fasten them tightly around my waist, steering me to her liking. Other times, she would anchor them to my wrists, pinning me to the ground. But now, she slowly grazed her fingers up my side, up the length of my arm and wrist, across the skin of my palm, until finally they were intertwined with mine. Sometimes she would grip them desperately. Other times, she would soften her embrace, allowing me to rub the tip of my thumb over the back of her hand. I was often the one to reach for her, but she never refused me when I gently clasped my hand around hers, when I studied the steady beat of her heart in her palms and invited her to feel mine.

One night, I was entangled in them both. She rode me in the darkness of the castle halls, her pace so quick I had to bite my tongue to keep from groaning aloud. She pressed my hands into the floor and leaned her torso over me, her face just inches from mine. When I felt the brush of her loose waves against my cheeks, I knew I could hold it in no longer.

"Eve."

The word carelessly fled from my lips without thinking. The name had been circling my mind for weeks like a song lyric on repeat. It felt so natural, so right. But I never dared say it aloud, too afraid of how she might react. I had let down my guard for one second, and the name had escaped, now a heavy weight hanging in the air between us. She hovered over me, gazing into my eyes with a stunned look.

My chest tightened, and I held my breath. I knew I had crossed a forbidden line. "I'm sorry," I whispered nervously. "I won't say it again."

She was as still as sculpted marble. For a moment, she looked like she was somewhere far away, her mind off in the distance as her gaze flowed through me. Finally, she opened her mouth, a new glimmer in her eyes.

"No," she said. "Call me Eve."

Chapter 20

Eve

After the midnight meeting in the village, sneaking out of the castle became a regular affair. Most nights, I would slip out of my room after the last torches were extinguished and creep toward the exit. I found it much easier to evade the Kreagan guards when I took the longer route to town, a path that started at the backside of the castle and circled the surrounding foothills, out of sight of even the tallest watch towers.

Each night, exactly two hours after sunset, I would meet the Vitalian rebels in the village granary. I broke the men into groups, pairing them with those of similar ability to rehearse each dueling sequence. At the top of the hour, the groups would switch. My first set of pupils would leave the granary, and I would be given a whole new squadron to train. The village carpenter had hastily crafted a set of thirty wooden swords, which we used to master the basic positions.

The townsmen were eager to learn, and I was surprised to find them quite trainable. With each session, I could see their gradual improvement. I cringed at first when a few of them displayed a particular ineptitude with a sword, worried that no amount of training would rectify their poor form. But I was impressed by how rapidly their technique was developing. I admit, I had serious doubts about the ragtag band of commoners, but now I was starting to think that perhaps the cobbler was right about them. The men were learning the fundamentals of combat much quicker than I expected. However, they were still a long way from ready to defeat an entire army of knights.

"Stay light on your feet!" I ordered a middle-aged man, the ends of his tunic frayed beneath his belt. "How will you leap out of the way of a hurtling blade if you are anchored to the ground?" The man nodded and uprooted his heels from the floor.

The short man opposite him, sporting a long beard and bald head, crouched a few inches lower and angled his sword rigidly in front of him. "Your wrist is too stiff," I said. Stepping behind him, I wrapped my hand around his arm and compelled him to loosen his grip.

From the other side of the granary, my eye caught a wayward sword swinging wildly through the air. The weapon was held by a younger man, his long hair tied back in a ponytail. His biceps flexed as he recklessly flung his wooden saber around like a windmill. I hurried over and halted him, pressing the palm of my hand flatly into his chest. He paused his frenzied movements and dropped the sword to his side, seemingly troubled by my abrupt interruption. "Let's go back to square one," I said gently. Lining myself beside him, I modeled each of the basic positions, pausing to let him mimic my stance before moving on to the next one.

Once he achieved the perfect placement, I complimented his efforts with a pat on the back. He smiled, pleased by my approval. "Thank you, Princess."

Each training session brought back memories I had almost forgotten, back when I battled armored knights on open training fields, not aging commoners in dim storehouses. Before Ingrid or Rune had entered the picture, when my principal role was to lead the undefeated Vitalian brigade to another victory. Back when I was more than just a royal hostage in a besieged castle.

It had been so long since I held a sword in my hands, and it had been even longer since I was tasked with training a team of rookies how to fight. I had forgotten how good it felt to watch a beginner slowly master the art of swordplay, the satisfaction of watching their confidence grow. More than that, I forgot how exhilarating it was to prepare for war, how invigorating it could be to develop the perfect battle strategy. For the first time since Kreagan had invaded my kingdom, I felt like I had purpose. *Maybe this was the battle I was born to fight.*

Guilt often crept in when I thought about how long I had waited before returning to the village. I could now tell how much I had hurt them by my absence. I berated myself for letting my own shame get in the way of my duty to my people. In spite of my own grief, they still needed a princess, someone to guide them when they had nowhere else to turn.

This whole time, I had isolated myself in my misery. The townspeople had welcomed me with open arms the moment I returned to the village, and I immediately found the kinship that I had long been missing. It was obvious that I belonged here, among my people, not locked away in my own tower of sorrow. I just could not believe how long it had taken me to realize it.

"What do you think?" The cobbler had walked over when I was not looking, pausing by my side as I observed the novice swordsmen from afar. He looked out at his battalion with pride then turned toward me with a hopeful grin.

"They are doing well," I confessed, performing another detailed scan of the room. "But they are far from ready." I twisted away from the drilling villagers to meet his eye, a staunch expression on my face. "We need real swords. Wooden weapons are great for building a foundation, but if we are going to have a fighting chance against experienced knights, we need to start training with true blades."

"The blacksmith has been working tirelessly to forge our weapons," he assured me, "but it will take more than a few weeks to make enough swords for an entire infantry."

I sighed. Ever since I had agreed to command the rebellion, I was becoming more and more anxious to move us along. I was growing increasingly tired of living under Ingrid's rule, and now that the villagers had rekindled the possibility of freedom in my mind, I was becoming restless. The thought of seizing my revenge on the queen excited me. It resurrected a hope that I once thought I would never unearth, arresting me with a thrill that I could hardly contain.

It was during these times, when I struggled to suppress my burning lust for vengeance, that I was thankful I had Rune. Only with him could I ease my restive mind. I found myself craving the high his body gave me, and I began drawing him out to our secluded areas of the castle more often. Unsurprisingly, he was always more than willing to comply. Once there, I could lower my cold veil of indifference and let my passion run free.

I could sense his confidence growing. His movements were becoming bolder, more daring, more independent. And to my surprise, I liked it. The ways he held me, the ways he moved me—it was something I would never consent to with another man. But it was like his fingers knew me better than I did. Like his figure was specially molded to fit mine. So when he roamed my body at will, tenderly caressing my breasts or sweeping his tongue across my skin, I did not stop him. I relented, letting the foreign pleasure rush through me.

Then came the late night in the corridor. When I heard that name—Eve—I knew I had let it go too far. All my life, I allowed no one to call me anything besides the name I was christened with at birth. No one but my father. But Rune had his own name for me now. It gave him a kind of ownership over me that no one else had.

It was my greatest fear, the pit of subjugation I had sworn I would never fall into. It made me feel trapped, like I was bound to him as we sank toward the bottom of the ocean. And yet, all I wanted was to hear him say it again.

Chapter 21

Rune

I knew she was leaving at night. I could hear her sneaking out the bedroom door when the sky was still pitch black, long before any light leaked through the window. When she left, I would lay on the floor for hours, wide awake, staring at the ceiling. Each minute felt like an eternity as I pondered where she might be. Just before sunrise, she would return, smelling of sweat and earth as she quietly slipped beneath her bed sheets.

She never mentioned these absences. Come morning, she would act as if nothing happened, like she had not crept out in the middle of the night without explanation. That was when I started to worry. It was her secrecy that scared me most.

No way could I bring myself to confront her, too afraid of how she might react. I knew she would criticize me for being possessive, for crossing the strict boundaries she had set between us. She might have even accused me of trying to control her. And if I misspoke or offended her in any way, I feared she would never speak to me again.

Besides, her secrets were no business of mine. At least, that was what I told myself to allay my crippling fears, to avoid discovering the dreaded truth. Before long, her outings became more frequent. She would rarely return before dawn. Not once did she confess to her late night ventures. An incessant sinking feeling had developed in my stomach, worry gradually creeping to the surface of my mind.

After all, I was not stupid. I knew that I had none of the qualities a prince should have, that I rated well below the standards she deserved. I was no doubt on the low end of her long list of eligible bachelors. I would not even be surprised if I was ranked dead last. So why would I expect her to stay loyal to me? How could I possibly satisfy a woman who held the world in her hands?

I would try to clear these anxious thoughts from my mind when she pulled me away from the rest of the castle, dragging me into an abandoned stairwell or empty closet. I tried to focus on her face, on the modest curve of her lips, the syrupy strands of hair that escaped her braids, perfectly framing her cheeks. But the vexing questions would reform in my mind without fail, piercing my abdomen with the sting of a thousand needles. Who else had seen her teasing smile? Who else had heard her tantalizing moans? Who else had felt the melting heat of her breath on their neck?

Not too long ago, I had started to believe there was something more forming between us. The way I felt about her was unlike anything I had ever experienced, a force so strong I was defenseless to its power. And I thought maybe, just maybe, she had felt it too. But I soon realized how foolish I had been to think I could ever be more than her plaything, a momentary diversion from her grief, a passing hobby she would eventually grow bored of. Did I actually believe she could have feelings for someone like me? I was a pale, stalky, pathetic disgrace, a total joke to my own kingdom and a complete waste of a prince. What could I possibly give that she could not find in someone else?

So when she left each night for who knows where, crawling back into bed at God knows when, I did not say a word. *I should feel lucky she wanted anything to do with me*, I reasoned. She was not mine, and I had been a damn fool to ever think otherwise.

****

She had been missing for most of the day, nowhere to be found since breakfast. Perhaps I was being paranoid, but I felt like she was growing distant. I spent the morning ambling through the gardens, trying to lose myself in the orange and brown mosaic of the trees, the frigid morning temperatures gradually withering their leaves. But my efforts were futile. I knew of only one thing that could get me out of my own head: my drawings.

As I trudged up the long set of stairs toward my room, now more of a personal studio, I felt a slight flutter in my chest, picturing my latest sketch in my mind. It was my proudest work yet, a piece I had been toiling over for weeks. It was a still-life, an image, not yet finished, of Evangeline perched by her window. Her sun-kissed skin was bare, and she stared out longingly at the mountains in the distance. I caught her this way often, quietly observing the world beyond the castle walls. I wondered what she was thinking about in these moments. Her father? The village? A far-off land I could not see? I hoped that if I drew her here, if I meticulously reconstructed the scene in perfect detail, then perhaps I could read her thoughts. But the sketch was almost complete, and I still had no clue.

Rounding the final corner, my stomach dropped. My bedroom door was open. I had never let a soul enter my room for fear of anyone discovering my private artwork. I quickened my pace, struggling against the despair that filled my chest. *Maybe I forgot to close it when I left*, I thought frantically, searching for any explanation that did not end in my utter humiliation. But when I reached the door, the horrifying truth revealed itself.

By my desk stood a lone figure, a different sketch gripped in each hand. She studied the pieces intensely, slowly shifting her gaze from one to the other. Hearing my footsteps, the intruder turned, and my greatest fears were confirmed. "What are you doing here?" I uttered, my hands trembling by my sides.

Ignoring my distress, Evangeline looked back down at the drawings she still held between her fingers. I had to stifle the urge to rush forward and rip them from her hands. "Did you draw these?" she asked without peering up from the parchment.

I swallowed then nodded. She lifted her head and caught my eye, her forehead crinkled. I held my hands behind my back, digging my nails into my palm. This was it. This was where it would end. And all because I left the damn door open.

Glancing down at them once more, she squinted. "They are good."

I bit my lip as I peered down at my toes in shame. "They are likenesses of you," I mumbled, bracing for her furious eruption.

"I know," she muttered. I swung my head up and gaped at her in disbelief. I had expected her to be furious, outraged by the way I had depicted her. "I like them," she said, finally gazing up at me, a soft smile on her lips.

Carefully setting the parchment back onto the desk, she began to slowly amble about the room. I had crafted so many sketches of her by now that there was no point trying to hide them. Dozens of my drawings were pinned to the walls. Most of the sketchbooks lining my shelves were filled with her, each page consisting of yet another portrait I had casually rendered. She paused by one piece propped against the wall and traced a finger along the thin pencil strokes. "Beautiful," she breathed, almost to herself.

Unrooting my feet from the floor, I slowly stepped toward the corner of the room where she stood. She was observing an impression I had made of the forest surrounding the castle, the browning leaves of the trees hinting at the coming of autumn. It was a familiar scene to us both: a dirt trail cutting across a field of thick brush, leading to a clear, rolling stream far in the distance. My heart beat faster as the memories of each place returned to me, the untold secrets each image held.

"You are very talented," she said, pulling me from the daydream.

I let a cautious smile creep up the side of my mouth. "Thank you," I whispered, heat traveling to my ears.

She chuckled, her laugh instantly easing my tension. "No wonder you are always looking at me so strangely." She rotated around, briefly scanning the rest of the parchment hanging around the room. "You were studying your model."

"That is not the only reason." I timidly moved my hand from my side and dared to wrap my clammy fingers around her palm. She tensed but did not pull back.

"Is that so?" she asked teasingly, carefully slipping her fingers between my own. "And what would the other reason be?" She gingerly pulled me closer, dissolving the last of my reserve.

"Perhaps because," I began as I leaned into her, our bodies so close I could feel the heat through her clothes, "you are the only thing I want to look at." I took her other hand. She accepted readily this time. "And maybe," I whispered into her hair, slowly pulling our chests to touch, "because I can never get enough of you."

I angled my chin downward to find her lips, but she caught mine first. They were like sleek rolls of velvet. Sensing my body growing more eager, I gently pressed my tongue within her open mouth. She greedily linked mine with her own. I welcomed her moisture, swallowing her as though starved. Slipping her hands from mine, she carried them up to my face, pressing both palms against my cheeks. Their warmth relieved me, and I settled my head into the smoothness of her skin. My hands now free, I slid them around her waist. How I yearned to grab the flesh held taut beneath her lacy skirts.

But, as if summoned by the lustful thoughts, my lingering dread returned. Images of her late night excursions suddenly reformed in my mind, and I stiffened. My lips stilled, rigid despite the sensual brush of her tongue. My hands froze against her sides. Sensing my tension, she paused then slowly pulled her face away. "What's wrong?"

I sighed, letting my hands fall. "I hear you leaving at night."

Her eyes widened, and her face grew pale. "You do?" she asked breathlessly.

I nodded, peering down at the floor so I would not have to meet her gaze. "But I understand."

She squinted at me questioningly, her brow

furrowed. I clenched my jaw and pushed the bubble of emotion back down my throat. "I do not claim you. You deserve more than I could ever give you. So if you would prefer to spend your time with someone else, I respect your choice."

Still eyeing me suspiciously, she shook her head. Then, to my utter disbelief, she laughed. *She laughed.* An airy chuckle leaped from her throat, slicing through me as it bounced from wall to wall. A string of knots twisted in my stomach. "You think I have been sneaking out to meet with other men?"

I threw my head upward and ogled at her. "Well, yes."

She crossed her arms, her smile still intact. "Why would I do that?"

I shrugged. "I don't know." I rubbed the tip of my elbow with my thumb. "I just thought maybe I wasn't—"

"Stop." She shoved her finger onto my lips, stilling them instantly. "If I did not think you were worth my time, I would have had nothing to do with you from the beginning." Dropping her arm, she let out another half-hearted chuckle. "You really think I would have gone through all this trouble sneaking you around the castle if I did not believe it was worth the effort?"

I pressed my lips together. "No, but—"

"Good," she said, refusing to let me complete a sentence, "because I would not be standing here right now if I wanted someone else."

I let out the breath I was holding. A wave of relief rushed through me. "Then," I started again, "what have you been doing each night?"

Evangeline's smile vanished. She was silent for a

moment, her expression severe as she contemplated her answer. Finally, she sighed. "Close that door," she commanded under her breath.

Puzzled but unwilling to question her, I twisted around and tiptoed toward the hall. I carefully pressed the door closed, this time waiting until I heard it click. When I returned, she sat me down across from her then found her own place on the floor. "You have to swear not to tell a soul," she said with a stern glare.

I nodded fervently. "Of course."

She took a deep breath. I held mine. "The villagers are planning an uprising, and I have agreed to help them."

My heart jolted. With quick thinking, the princess pressed her palm flatly against my mouth, stifling my shocked exclamation. "Hush!" she ordered.

When she was sure I was calm, she slowly pulled her hand away. "What do you mean an uprising?" I asked in a frenzied whisper.

"We are going to drive out Ingrid and her army," she said, undeterred by my hysterics. "She has taken my father and my kingdom. Now we are taking Vitalia back." There was no questioning her determination, but my pulse still raced in alarm.

"Do you know what she will do to you?" I couldn't restrain the frantic shake in my voice. "She will order every rebel killed and subject you to the most gruesome death she can devise!" Lurid images shot through my mind: the sight of blood, the sound of screams, scenes I was far too familiar with. But when I pictured Evangeline's wounds, imagined her desperate cries, the vision became too much for me to bear. "No," I said, shaking my head vigorously. "I cannot let you do this."

Her eyebrows scrunched together dangerously. "That is not your choice to make," she said in a warning tone. "Sometimes, you have to make sacrifices for the greater good. I would rather die fighting for the freedom of my people than to live my whole life under her finger." I could see the fury burning in her eyes, their flames igniting the space between us.

"But how? No one has ever gotten past my mother's guards."

"We outnumber them three to one." She was insistent, deflecting my every attack, refusing to exhibit any doubt. "I am training the townspeople for battle, and if we have to, we will fight to the death."

I bit my lip, still in disbelief. I was not sure if there was anything I could say to change her mind.

All of a sudden, her expression changed. She dropped her defenses and stared at me through sparkling eyes. "What?" I asked.

"You can help us," she murmured, as though the idea was still forming in her mind.

"Me?" I asked incredulously.

She nodded, slowly at first. Then with more conviction. I opened my mouth to object, but no words escaped my swollen throat. "Don't you want to be free from her?" she implored, softly setting her hand on my knee as she searched my eyes. "Don't you want to know what it's like to not be constantly under her power? This is your chance to finally escape."

I paused as I considered this. The thought of a life without my mother brought a soft flutter to my chest. "But what if we fail?"

Evangeline pursed her lips, thoughtful for a moment. At last, she sighed. "Then, we go down together." Gripping me tighter, she regained her firm resolve. "This could be our only chance, Rune," she said, pleading me with a slight rattle.

"So what do you say? Do you want to learn what freedom tastes like?"

I looked down at my hands. They were trembling. I hated that. I closed them into fists, squeezing them until their shaking ceased. "Okay," I said. "I will help you."

Chapter 22

Eve

When my feet reached the town's edge, I stopped. I was standing at the end of the dirt path leading from the castle, where the primitive trail turned to cobblestone streets. As always, I had waitcd until a few hours after sundown to make my leave, ensuring the palace residents had all turned in for the night. As always, I had crept through the back doors and taken the long way to the village so not even the night watchmen could spot me. As always, I arrived just before midnight, the full moon hovering midway through the dark sky. But this time was different. This time, I had Rune.

It took a bit of convincing to coax him from my bedroom. "They need to see that they can trust you," I had told him. We were seated side-by-side on the foot of my bed, my fingers wrapped tenderly but insistently around the back of his stiff hand. "You have to show them who you are, to prove that you are nothing like her."

Nevertheless, he remained hesitant, reluctant to leave the safety of the castle walls. "They will never trust me," he mumbled hopelessly, his body turned opposite me. "They believe I am the reason their king is dead."

"Not if we show them otherwise." I lifted his chin, forcing his eyes to meet mine. "They trust me, and if you come with me and let me explain the truth, I know they will trust you too."

He was nervous, there was no doubt. Hell, even I was nervous. By the time we reached the village, I could see him shivering beneath the folds of his thick cloak. "I cannot do this," he said in a breathy voice, halting a few feet behind me. I turned to find his shoes glued to the muddy path, his face ghostly pale as he stared at the village through petrified eyes. Steam poured from his mouth with each quick breath, and I worried he would faint.

"Yes, you can," I said, moving toward him with an outstretched arm.

He leaped back, evading my reach. "I'm sorry Evangeline, but I cannot be part of this," he stuttered, his chest moving fast. "I will go back to the castle and pretend you never told me a thing."

I took another step forward, but he twisted his shoulder away. I sighed, growing frustrated. "So you are going to let fear control you your whole life?" I could tell by the pain in his eyes that my words hurt, but I knew they needed to be said. "If you want things to change, you cannot sit idly by and wait for it to happen. You have to stand up and do something about it." I held out my hand once more, giving him the choice to take it. My palm floated in the air, my fingers outstretched. This time, he did not back away. "No more hiding."

Rune bit his lip. An invisible barrier stood between us, binding him to his place in the dirt. I could see him straining to push through it, his forehead wrinkled from the effort. Finally, he took my hand in his. My lips peeled into a gentle smile. I nodded, gripping his fingers tightly as I drew him across the threshold.

I had called for a full town meeting that night. I wanted everyone in attendance when I presented Rune and unveiled the latest part of my plan. I knew they would be wary of this new addition to our rebellion. After all, Rune was right: it would not be easy to convince an entire kingdom that the son of their self-appointed queen was actually our ally and could even be our key to victory. It was a risk that I was not sure they were willing to take. Even if he vowed his loyalty to our cause, what proof did they have? For all they knew, he could be acting as Ingrid's spy, ready to run back to the castle and reveal our plans to the Kreagans. It was up to me to convince them otherwise. Somehow, I had to assure them that he was on our side.

The commoners were already assembled in the village center when we arrived. It was the only place large enough for the whole town to meet. Gathering in such an open location was a risk, no doubt, but a necessary one. The men were improving quickly, and as our army grew in size, the space in the granary was becoming too tight for adequate sword training. And since I was expecting more than our typical squad of soldiers tonight, I thought it the perfect time to move our meetings to a more fitting area. I could see the light of their torches from afar, reflected on the rows of cottage walls. Their faint whispers echoed through the streets, their quiet voices audible before I could see them clustered by the narrow town chapel. I could feel the prince slightly pull back as we made the last turn into the plaza. I gripped his hand tighter.

When we stepped into the firelight, the full crowd came into view. A flock of nearby children shrieked excitedly and scurried toward me. "Princess

Evangeline!" they cried as they encircled me, their faces gleaming. I chuckled lightly, their joyful spirits refreshing after so many somber months in the castle. I knelt to the ground as they embraced me within their little arms. "We missed you!" one boy said, his curly bangs bouncing above his sparkling eyes. The other children hopped about giddily and nodded in agreement.

"I missed you too," I said with a grin, letting the boy rest the side of his head against my chest.

Upon hearing the cheerful commotion, the villagers turned, donning their own merry smiles. But they quickly dissolved when they noticed Rune standing beside me. Sensing their parents' unease, a few of the children started to back away. "Who is that?" asked a young girl, lifting her hand to point at the ashy prince.

The commoners watched me closely. The skin on the back of my neck prickled under their fearful gaze. I reached my arm back to grasp Rune's hand. He took it without a word.

Lifting my chest, I strode forward. Rune stayed close behind. I kept my eyes straight ahead, ignoring the nervous frowns of the silent villagers. As we passed, they leaped a few paces back as if the prince carried some terrible illness. We walked onward, crossing the deserted aisle and nearing the set of elevated stairs leading from the chapel. I calmly climbed to the top step, tugging Rune along behind me, then turned to peer out at the throng of villagers. They were quiet, watchful, eagerly awaiting an explanation for this unwelcome visitor.

I gave them a moment to take in the scene: their long-honored princess hand-in-hand with the prince she was ordered to wed. They stood perfectly still, gawking at us incredulously. A few of the men pulled their loved ones close, guarding them behind an outstretched arm.

Suddenly, a familiar figure pushed through the crowd. "Princess Evangeline," Mr. Walters stammered anxiously. "What is the meaning of this?" He tilted his head to the space where Rune stood beside me. "Why have you brought him here?"

I shifted my gaze from the cobbler and looked outward to address the townspeople. "Prince Rune is with me," I declared, my voice resolute despite the rapid pounding of my heart. "He is here to help us drive out the Kreagan army."

The crowd burst into an uproar of confused murmurs. "Him?" yelled a man in the front row. Behind him was his wide-eyed wife, their auburn-haired daughter tucked timidly beneath her skirts. "He is the son of the queen!" The villagers mumbled their agreement.

"He is nothing like her!" I called out, my tone defensive. "He is one of us." I gripped Rune's hand tighter. It shook between my fingers.

"How do you know?" a petite woman shouted as she stepped into an open aisle. "What makes you think he is not deceiving you, that he will not go back to Queen Ingrid and tell her everything?" A low rumble swelled through the crowd, the restless murmuring of the villagers erupting into chaos. The town swarmed with violent protests, a sharp panic edging their voices.

I took a deep breath and searched for the words to soothe their distress. But just as I was about to speak, a deep voice bellowed out from beside me. "I am her slave!"

The village fell mute. I spun my head around and stared at the prince in disbelief. His jaw was firmly set, his eyes filled with a resolve I had never seen in him. "I may be her son, but I am no prince in her eyes."

I was astonished by the power in his voice, not a stutter or shake to be heard. "I know what it is like to be threatened and used by her," he continued. "I have been the subject of her tyranny my entire life." I knew the words were ones long left unsaid, words he had been too ashamed to admit before. "For as long as I can remember, she has forced me to be a pawn in her endless conquests. But no more!" He slammed his fist into his open palm, the smack resounding through the plaza. "I refuse to let her rule over me any longer."

His lip twitched. "I know I have been a coward. I should have stood up to her long ago." He glanced down at the ground, his words clearly paining him. "The only way to redeem myself now, to become the man she never wanted me to be, is to rise against her. So, please." His eyes were glossy, fervently pleading with the crowd as he spilled out the last of his dignity. "Give me a chance."

The townsfolk, still unsure, peered at each other questioningly. Gone was their anger, and in its place was a wavering uncertainty. "He speaks the truth," I insisted, finally breaking the silence. "He has been forced to serve the queen for longer than any of us." I veered my head downward to face the cobbler. "Mr. Walters, you know we have been searching for a way to distract the guards when we make our first move." I placed my hand on the flat of Rune's back and pushed him a few inches forward. "He is our answer. He can be our ally from the inside. He is the missing piece we have been looking for."

The commoners rotated their gaze from the prince to the cobbler as they considered my proposal. A few, still unconvinced, shook their heads skeptically. "But how do we know we can trust him?" asked a man I could not see, enshrouded within the masses.

"You cannot," I admitted with a sigh. "But I can tell you this: if we want to win this war, he is the best hope we have."

Again, the villagers were quiet. None of them liked what I had to say, but they all knew it was true. Defeating the Kreagans through combat alone was a mere fantasy. If we wanted a real chance at victory, we needed to outwit Ingrid and her men. And who better to play the deceiver than her own son?

"She is right," Mr. Walters said. Separating himself from the rest of the townspeople, the cobbler marched up the chapel steps to stand beside me. "We have all been praying for a miracle, for God to give us an advantage over our enemy." He threw an open hand toward Rune. "Perhaps this is him!" The prince gazed out at the villagers, a pink hue in his cheeks. "We have never had any reason to doubt our princess, and we certainly will not start now. If she trusts this man, then so do I."

Twisting away from the crowd, he gave the prince a slight nod. Rune responded in kind, his eyes lit with gratitude. "And now that we have the allegiance of the prince," Mr. Walters continued, "we shall not fail!"

At the cobbler's contagious enthusiasm, the energy in the town surged. The villagers shouted their approval with raised fists. "Now men," Mr. Walters said, sticking out his chest proudly. He shifted toward me with a hopeful lift to his lips. "We have a battle to win."

Chapter 23

Rune

Only when we descended the church steps could I properly breathe again, when the stark tension in the air finally dissolved. The second we touched ground, Evangeline was swept away by a mob of villagers. Her hand was stripped from mine as they besieged her. Each of them regarded her with a deep admiration. The men flashed their toothy grins as they cordially shook her hand. The women, their cheeks blushed beneath the torch light, curtsied low as she passed. And the children wore their brightest smiles as they zealously tugged at her pant leg.

Their adoration came as no surprise to me. If anyone could bring a broken kingdom together, it was Evangeline. What surprised me was her response. She readily accepted each and every outstretched hand. She offered her own genial bow to the women with a graceful bend of her waist. And when the children ardently tapped on her shins, she knelt low to meet them face-to-face, returning their lighthearted smiles and pulling them into a gentle embrace. Never had I seen her so alight, her face radiant beneath the faint glow of the moon.

The townspeople had an uncommon effect on her. They brought out a side of her that she had kept carefully concealed beneath a harsh exterior. Until then, I was clueless to its existence. I knew what I saw in her eyes was the gleam of an undying devotion, a heartfelt affection that she saved for her people alone, or perhaps for Vitalia itself.

"We are grateful for your decision to join our cause, Prince Rune," a man said into my ear. I peered over my shoulder to meet his gaze. It was the man who had addressed the village alongside Evangeline, the first one to vocalize his trust in me.

"Do not thank me. Thank her," I said, nodding in the direction of the princess. She was laughing along with one of the townswomen, the skin of her nose scrunched together as they watched a young girl spin around in a dizzying jig. She was happy, happier than I had ever seen her, exactly where she belonged. "It was all her idea."

As if she could sense us talking about her, the princess turned. She soon caught my eye, and I shifted my lips into a humble grin.

When she smiled back at me, it was a smile I knew, one that had often made me ache and shudder. But now there was a new arch to her lips, a flicker in her eyes that did not make me hunger but made me whole. Her beaming smile permeated my soul. It washed away all the hurt, all the grief, all the self-loathing, and in its place left a soft blanket of comfort.

It was there, wrapped in the sheets of her serenity, that I knew that if this was her home, then she was mine.

****

We returned to the castle well past midnight. The sky was still the color of ink, but in the distance, I could just make out the first hint of sunlight creeping over the horizon. I had not slept in nearly twenty-four hours, but I knew that when we made it back to her bedroom, sleep would elude me once more. Ever since Evangeline had revealed her secret plan to me, adrenaline had been racing through my limbs, still pumping through my veins at full speed. I had spent my whole life trying to hide within the icy fortress my mother had built, but now everything I had ever known was about to change. The mere thought of this uncertain future left me wide awake.

The palace halls were vacant, which made it easy to slip into the princess's room undetected. Once the door was softly closed behind her, she stripped off the thick cloak that weighed upon her shoulders, then the cream-colored tunic along her front, then her wool trousers. She reached for a fresh nightgown hanging from a dresser drawer then threw it over her mess of brown waves. The chill breeze had flung her mane wildly through the air until each strand looked like a thin strip of lightning. Now it floated above her cotton dress in a tangled mass of frizz. After a quick look in the mirror, likely considering an attempt to brush out the turbulent knots, she shrugged, turned from the vanity, and headed toward her bed.

Still standing by the door, I watched the subtle movements of her skirt. I studied the simple pattern of the fabric, tossed through the air with each step. I was transfixed by the wave-like motion of the gown as she compelled it forward. Despite the chill wind still streaming through the window, threatening the stability of the mighty castle, her feet were bare.

"You are stunning." The phrase had been floating through my head for hours, dancing on my tongue, urging me to set it free. And now, as I watched the grace of her stride, the perfect cadence of her feet upon the ground, I knew it would be impossible to keep it to myself any longer.

She turned, frozen in place just inches from her pillow. "What?" she asked, her forehead furrowed.

"I said you are stunning." Heaving my legs forward to hide their shaking, I circled the edge of the bed. Normally, this kind of boldness would shock me. But the words spilled from my mouth like warm honey. And as I glided around the bedpost, the steady movements of my legs felt effortless. My heart felt like it was beating out of my chest, but my breaths kept their easy rhythm. It was like I was high on the energy of the night: the jovial village, the venerable townsmen, and Evangeline, her lustrous smile lighting the streets on that cold autumn night.

The princess chuckled awkwardly, tucking a loose lock of hair behind her ear. "Why do you say that?" Her chin was slightly tucked, but her sparkling eyes gazed up at me.

"Because for the first time, I can see the real you. The compassion you have for your kingdom, the selflessness you have kept so secret. And now there is no doubt in my mind. You are stunning, every part of you." Her mouth twisted into a nervous grin. She bit her cheek as she toyed with the cuff of her sleeve.

"Evangeline." I cautiously slid my fingers over the back of her hand, softly gripping her palm. "I love you."

Her bottom lip dropped. Her stunned eyes fixed onto mine. Her mouth hung slightly open, speechless. I seized the opportunity and dove forward.

Compelled by an invisible force, I plunged my lip into the depths of her mouth. I buried my fingers in the thick of her hair and pulled her tan face against mine. I heard her gasp as I tugged eagerly at her lips, my hands clasping her head. For once, I did not worry about her rules, disregarding the lines she had carefully drawn to keep us apart. I had recklessly crossed them long ago.

I readied myself for her reproach, for her to shove me away and reprimand my thoughtless act with a firm slap. But she didn't. Once she overcame her shock, she threw her arms around my neck and pulled me closer. Her lips responded with their own fervent kiss, and I slid my tongue between her teeth. Her feverish moans echoed through my throat, drawing a deep hunger from within me.

Without thinking, I grabbed the hem of her dress and yanked upward. She did not resist, lifting her arms as I tore the fabric over her head. She hastily clawed at the buttons lining my tunic, but I shoved her hands away. Resting my palm against her chest, I pressed her naked body backward, leading her to the bed. She collapsed onto the mattress then propped herself up on her elbows, watching me through awestruck eyes. I jerked my tunic over my head and tossed my hair to let it lay down my back at its full length. I dropped my breeches to the floor, hastily kicking them aside. There I stood before her, my hardness on full display. She stretched her hand toward me, but I snatched her wrist before she could reach.

With my free hand, I pressed my palm into the space between her breasts and pushed her flatly onto the bed. I hurriedly crawled over her. I hovered above her body on all fours, my knees sinking into the mattress. Staring into her shimmering eyes, I paused, suddenly realizing what I was doing. I was already pulsing violently, my pelvis floating precariously above her. I was anxious to enter her, to slide within her slick warmth, to see the unbridled pleasure in her eyes. But I waited, studying her face, giving her a chance to deny her consent.

Heat radiated from her chest, and I could see a thin sheet of sweat already forming on her forehead. I silently wondered if she would stop me, if she would flip me over and have her way, punishing me for trespassing on her forbidden territory. She answered my questions with a tender kiss. With her fingers wrapped around my neck, she drew my face downward and pressed her soft lips to mine. Then, sliding her hands down the dewy skin of my back, she placed them around my hips and gingerly pulled them downward. Creeping her wet lips to my ear, she whispered her sweet submission: "Take me."

And so, digging my hungry nails into her waist, I did.

Chapter 24

Eve

I woke to the first ray of morning light streaming through my window, glowing upon my ebony sheets. When I turned to find Rune still lying beside me, my face warmed. Memories of the previous night rushed through my mind. I welcomed the tingling feeling in my core, allowing myself to sink into the flashback.

I had been hesitant at first. My arms stiffened when his hands snatched my wrist, and I held my breath as he ripped off my gown. But there was an unfamiliar authority in his gaze, a dominant energy that unsettled me, making my knees weak. And when I saw the flare in his eyes as he thrust me onto the bed, I found myself craving his rule. I wanted him to take control.

So I let him have his way. I let him move at his pace. I let him sink his fingernails into my back. I let him drive my shoulders deeper into the bed. And when he finished, I reveled in the way he yelled my name. I yearned to hear that three-letter word when the tension in his body finally fled, still pulsing as he gasped for air. "Eve."

He caught me off guard. There was no denying it. The last thing I expected was for him to take me in my own room, the one place I had forbidden his touch. But now, still naked as I lay on my side, watching the slow inhale and exhale of his breath, his eyelids softly sealed shut, I wondered if I had been anticipating this moment all along.

What surprised me most was how natural it felt. My greatest fears had been realized, and yet I was calm. Once, I promised myself to never let a man take over me, to never let him think he held any power. And when Rune and I started fooling around, I swore I would never let him think there could be more between us.

Yet here I was. I had let him steal my reins, let him overpower me in my most sacred place, then hold me close as we fell asleep. I had closed my eyes and drifted off to the heat of his breath against my neck. And somehow, I did not feel ashamed. I felt complete, like the part of me that died with my father was finally coming back to life.

With a soft gasp, I remembered his words. He told me he loved me. That was the part that made my stomach twist and churn. It was ridiculous, impossible even. I had called him a coward and a fool. I had threatened his very life. I made it clear from the beginning that our marriage was nothing but a sham, an act for the public and nothing more. I sighed. How could I have let it get this far?

Nothing would ever be the same—that I knew. What happened last night made whatever this was between us real, and I was not sure I was ready for that, or if I would ever be, for that matter. What would he expect from me now? To tell him the same? It was something I could never do, a line I would never cross. And even though his words made me feel like I was floating, I could never love him. I could never love anyone.

Before long, Rune began to wake, his eyelashes slowly fluttering open. When he saw me, silently watching him from across the bed, he smiled. I bit my lip, but despite my best efforts, my own mouth peeled into a grin. "Hi," he whispered.

An airy chuckle blew through my nose. "Hi," I whispered back.

Sliding his hand from beneath the sheet, he caressed my cheek, his fingers combing through my hair. I flinched. His touch was automatic, uninvited but not unwanted. Inner strife ate away at my chest, a conflicting desire to both shove his hand away and cover it with my own. Instead, I relaxed my face, allowing myself, if just for a moment, to relish the tenderness of his touch.

"Eve," he started. I exhaled, the name melting away my every inhibition. I closed my eyes and let my cheek sink deeper into his palm.

When I peered up at him again, his expression had changed. His face was white, his lips pale, and he eyed me with unspoken dismay. "What's wrong?" I asked, my own smile fading.

He parted his lips and took a shaky breath. "I'm afraid." His glistening blue eyes poured into mine. "What if the queen learns of our rebellion? What if someone tells her what we are planning?"

I shook my head. "That will not happen. If all goes to plan, we will storm the castle before anyone knows a thing."

"But what if it does not go to plan?" he asked fearfully, a slight tremble in his voice. "Do you know what she will do if she finds us out?"

I swallowed. I had often contemplated Ingrid's merciless wrath if she ever learned of our plans to dethrone her. But I had not considered the risk I was asking Rune to take by joining our cause. I had been sure the queen would never deign so low as to kill her own son, but if she learned that he was aiding a revolution against her empire, I knew she would not hesitate to strike him dead. I could sense the fear in his eyes, so palpable that I felt it seeping into me.

"Then, we will fight."

Rune's eyes widened. "Fight?" he asked, growing hysterical. "I have never held a weapon in my life."

"I can teach you," I said.

The prince's forehead furrowed, and he gaped at me through squinted eyes. "You are going to teach *me* to wield a sword?" he asked, his voice dripping with disbelief.

Quickly wiping away my own skepticism, I nodded. "Of course," I replied as I plopped myself up on one elbow. "What? You think I can't?" I asked defensively.

"I have no doubt as to *your* abilities," he replied. With a long exhale, he sat upright, pulling his legs to his chest.

I lifted my upper body off the bed, my breasts suddenly exposed to the chill morning air. "Rune, I have trained more men than I can count, and no matter who they are or where they come from, they all have one thing in common."

The prince twisted his head toward me. "What's that?"

I curved my lips into a sly smile. "After they train with me, they never lose."

****

Finding a few wooden training swords was the easy part. Sneaking them through the castle in the middle of the day was a different story. When I met Rune in my room with the weapons, I handed him one before starting back toward the hall, expecting him to follow. But the prince was static. He stared down at the sword like it was a cryptic text, written in a strange language he did not understand. He awkwardly wrapped both hands around the dull blade. With a sigh, I returned to his side, taking back the sword. Then, I gently folded his fingers around the hilt, dropping his left hand so it hung loosely by his side. At my touch, I saw the tension in his shoulders release.

Before stepping back through my bedroom door, I twisted my elbow over my head and tucked the wooden sword beneath the folds of my tunic. Rune copied my movements, carefully concealing his own weapon along the length of his spine. Together, we strolled into the passageway, hiding within a swarm of footmen. The halls were bustling with Kreagan servants going about their morning duties. A few guards were stationed by each door, scanning the corridor for suspicious activity. I tried to act casual, keeping my back straight to avoid drawing any attention to the wooden plank protruding from my shirt. I could only hope Rune was doing the same, but I had a feeling he was having a harder time passing as a cursory pedestrian. A few nearby maids threw a quizzical stare my way. I responded with a friendly curtsy which they promptly returned before scuttling off.

When we finally made it to the nearest stairwell, I removed my sword from my tunic and hugged it close to my chest. "Follow me," I whispered. "I know the perfect place."

We climbed the long spiral staircase until we reached the very top of the north tower. Stepping out into the open air, I led the way onto the balcony. The clouds were sparse this morning, allowing the sun's warm rays to shower over us, a welcome relief from the biting wind. Rune ambled past me, his mouth agape as he neared the tower's edge. "Wow," he breathed, staring out at the village sprawled before us then peering upward at the distant mountain tops lining the horizon. "The view is magnificent."

I smiled, mostly to myself. "You should see it at night."

Turning from the ledge, the prince looked down at the foreign object still clasped in his hand. "So," he began, peering nervously back up at me. "What is our first lesson?"

"Defense," I replied. Without warning, I lunged forward, jabbing the edge of my sword toward his chest.

Rune gasped then frantically leapt to the side, barely catching himself before toppling onto the cobblestone. Once he regained his footing, he swung his head toward me. "What was that for?" he demanded, bewildered.

"If I am not mistaken, you are the one who wanted to learn to fight," I teased him with a mischievous grin as I ambled toward him.

"I thought we would start with some basic moves." He bent down to pick up his sword, having dropped it during my surprise attack.

"We are," I said. With his attention diverted, I struck. I flung my sword in a wide arc toward his exposed waist. At the last second, he caught sight of the wood whirring through the air. He ducked, the dull blade just missing the nape of his neck. He spun back around and glared at me with an irritated frown.

"Use your sword to deflect the blow," I instructed, struggling to keep the amused expression from my face. I hurled my weapon forward once more, this time from the other direction. He let out a high-pitched squeak and squeezed his belly inward. The tip of my sword just grazed his abdomen.

"How am I supposed to do that?" he asked in a frenzied voice, his sword fumbling in his palm.

"Angle your blade to block my strike." I lifted my own sword over my head, pausing it in the air to give him enough time to react. Finally, I sent the saber hurtling downward. He thrust the flat of his sword upward and turned his head away, his eyes pinched shut. With a dull clank, our weapons made contact. The power of my blow was stalled, eventually coming to a halt. Cautiously, he peeped one eye open. When he realized he had successfully blocked my hit, his face brightened.

But I did not let him dwell in his victory for long. Seconds later, I hurled my sword toward his hip. He acted fast, throwing his weapon to the left and perfectly parrying my attack. I retracted my sword immediately and drove it up toward his chin. Once more, he deflected my strike, his confidence swiftly building.

He was beaming now, his eyes glowing with pride. "This is not so bad." I could tell from his smirk that he was growing cocky, a fatal mistake for a novice swordsman. Before he had time to counter, I jabbed the tip of my blade into his stomach. He wheezed as the air fled from his lungs, falling to the ground with a loud thud.

"You were saying?" I asked with a sneer, propping the flat of my sword onto my shoulder. Rune's ears were bright pink as he picked himself off the floor, softly chuckling at his own impudence. Suddenly, he charged at me, emitting a deep grunt as he swung the edge of his sword toward my ribs. I dodged it easily. The prince's footing was poor, and the momentum of his swing flung him sideways.

I was merciful this time, giving him the chance to regain his balance rather than punishing him for the mistake. "You have to keep your feet grounded," I told him as I modeled the stance. "Keep your knees slightly bent. Remember, your power comes from your base." With my core tight, I demonstrated the proper technique, hurtling my sword through the open air with a powerful crosswise swing.

Rune settled his own feet into the ground, trying to copy my movements, but his rotation fell short. He knit his eyebrows together in frustration. I set my own sword on the ground. "Follow through with your hips," I explained as I approached. I gently placed my hands along his waist. I felt him shiver beneath my touch. "Now try." This time when he swung the sword forward, I guided his hips with my hands. The wood whooshed as it sliced through the air, completing its full arc.

"There," I said, my lips skimming the edge of his ear. At my praise, the prince turned, our faces just inches apart.

We paused, both our bodies frozen as our eyes connected. Hastily, I shifted my gaze toward the ground and removed my hold on his waist, taking a small step back. But when I chanced a glance back upward, I found him watching me, his lips curved in an easy grin.

There was something new in that look. Maybe it was the way he tucked his chin a bit lower to meet my eyes or how the left corner of his cheek curled upward when he smiled. His confidence was growing by the day, his touch more adamant, his words more certain. And now, there was something new in his eyes, something more enduring. His gaze was fixed, not wavering for even a moment.

An anxious prickling began to form in my stomach. *Last night was a mistake. I should have never let him take my control.* The Rune I knew had been trampled by his mother his entire life, ordered to act in complete subservience and forced to succumb to her every command. But now I wondered: when she was gone, would he change? Would he be the same Rune who had followed me to the stream, who kissed me in the dark of the stables, who whispered my name when we made love? Or would he be different?

When I peered back up at him, his smile remained. "You are scared, aren't you?"

I paled, my cheeks cold. "Scared?" I asked, clasping my hands nervously behind my back.

Rune nodded. "Scared I will soon become a better swordsman than you."

I let out my breath with an airy chuckle, restoring my carefree grin. "In your dreams," I said with a playful shove to his chest.

The prince lifted his eyebrows. "My lady." He lowered the tone of his voice, drawing out his words to mimic a noble aristocrat. "I challenge thee to a duel." He tucked his sword beneath the crease in his arm and rolled his chest downward in a dramatic bow.

I shook my head, rolling my eyes in amusement as I reached down to retrieve my weapon. "I accept your challenge," I said smugly, folding my arms over my chest. "But I warn you, I take duels very seriously. Do not assume I will take it easy on you."

The prince laughed aloud then carefully retook the ready position he had just learned. "I would expect nothing less."

Chapter 25

Rune

I woke one morning to find her bed cold. I was used to the feeling, having slept for so long on the icy floor. But since the meeting in the village, I had been spending my nights beneath her obsidian sheets. With the princess tucked in my arms, my chest pressed to her bare back, I no longer had to endure the bitter chill of the bedroom floor. But when I opened my eyes now, I shivered, suddenly taken back to the memory of those lonely nights on the ground. There could only be one explanation: the princess had vanished, disappearing from her place beside me.

Sitting upright, I scanned the room. She was not seated by her vanity or standing by her dresser. Her nightstand was empty save for the most recent volume I had swiped from the hidden library, a favor I now did for her regularly. I rose from the bed and meandered across the room, my bare feet traipsing along the cold stone floor. The room was dark, the princess nowhere to be found.

A fearful knot twisted in my stomach. It had been weeks since she had risen before dawn, since she had departed the palace with the first light. After a full night of sword training with the villagers, she would often sleep through the morning, not leaving the comfort of her bed until well after sunrise. But the sun was just cresting over the mountain tops, and she was gone.

I swallowed. The aching feeling that bloomed in my stomach now spread through my limbs, making my fingers twitch. Something was wrong, and I was not sure how, but I thought I knew exactly where to find her.

****

I peeked around the trunk of a thick pine, scoping out the scene before I made my approach. But the tree's leaves had fallen long ago. All that was left was the bare branches, making it a poor source of camouflage. She was sitting atop a flat rock, her back hunched forward. Her legs dangled over the water, the tips of her toes slowly inching along the surface. Despite the morning frost, she wore only a thin cotton tunic, her boots discarded by the riverbed. Part of the stream was frozen over, but she dipped her bare feet into the water nevertheless.

With a deep breath, I stepped forward. A loud crunch emitted from the ground as my shoe made contact with a pile of fallen leaves. I winced at my carelessness, freezing in place as I waited for her to confront me. But the princess did not even turn. She was completely still, apart from her copper waves tossing in the breeze. At first, I thought I had gone undetected. But I realized the foolishness of my assumption at once. Evangeline was as keen as a fox. Of course she did not turn at my blundering misstep. She already knew I was here, likely from the moment I arrived.

Nonetheless, I tiptoed as quietly as possible as I approached her place by the water, reluctant to disturb her peace. When I made it to her side, my jaw tightened. She was staring out into the forest, her lips pale, her face blank, motionless. Not once did she turn to acknowledge me. I could see a subtle quivering in her shoulders, a small patch of goosebumps along her neck.

I started removing my cloak at once, surprised by the sharp bite of the wind along my arms. I carefully wrapped the fabric around her shoulders. She did not thank me. She did not say a word. The only sign of life in her was the mist that flowed from her mouth with each breath.

I knelt down beside her, gently taking her hand. My knees stung against the sharp pebbles, but I ignored the pain. I squeezed her fingers tight, gazing anxiously into her eyes. "What is it, Eve?"

She exhaled. Another trail of steam poured through her nose. Her lips were as white as a ghost, and I wondered if, perhaps, their ashen hue was not from the cold at all. I squeezed her hand tighter, bracing myself for whatever came next.

"I'm pregnant."

The words left her mouth in no more than a whisper, but I jumped like her voice was made of thunder. My bottom lip dropped open, and, for a moment, I forgot how to breathe. Each time I tried to speak, a sharp wheeze rose from my chest. I fought against the lump in my throat, still mute as I grew desperate for oxygen. Finally, forcing myself to settle, I regained my senses. "Pregnant?" I stuttered, pressing my nails into the backs of my arms to ease their shaking.

Evangeline nodded, her lips sealed. She was still watching the slow-moving current as if transfixed.

The pain in my chest was unbearable, like a pair of hands squeezing my heart. My mind raced as I restlessly combed my fingers through my hair. "Are you certain?"

She nodded again, her lips slightly parting. "I missed my period," she said toward the stream. "I knew it was late after a few days, but I thought perhaps it was only a fluke." She swallowed and stared down at her knees tucked tightly into her chest. "But that was weeks ago. There is no denying it now."

As reality set in, my eyes glazed over. The world around me started to spin, its color slowly dissolving. I thought about dunking my head in the freezing water. Surely that would wake me from this nightmare. But I could tell from the violent trembling in my legs that this was no dream.

"Do you know what this means?" I sank back to the ground, suddenly shivering harder. "This is exactly what she wanted. Once my mother finds out, she will keep you locked away until the child is born. And then…" I paused, too afraid to speak the words aloud.

"I know," she replied flatly. She lifted her head back up to face the water. It was as if the energy had been sucked from her body, leaving her a cold, lifeless shell. "She will kill me."

"No," I breathed.

"It's over, Rune," she continued, ignoring my panicked denial. "There will be no rebellion. Vitalia is dead."

"No," I repeated more adamantly, lightly shaking her arms. From the ground, I gaped up at her with pleading eyes. "We cannot give up. What about the townspeople?" I bit my lip. "What about us?"

The princess finally turned to face me. She pinched her brow, her eyes stern. "There is no us," she growled, her cold tone making me flinch. "There never has been, and there never will be." Seeing the pained expression on my face, she tore her eyes away, looking down at her lap. "We failed."

"We can still fight!" I insisted, rising to my feet. "We still have time."

She shook her head. "The queen will never let me out of her sight once she learns the truth."

"She does not have to find out."

Growing annoyed, she rolled her eyes. "It will not be long before people start to notice, and I am certain Ingrid will be the first to know."

I paused, racking my brain for a solution. Evangeline was right. A few weeks would be enough time for my mother to grow suspicious, no matter how hard the princess tried to hide. Soon, the truth would come out, and when it did, all hope would be lost. Once the child was born, Evangeline would be executed. My mother would fabricate some story for the townspeople about labor complications, and the Kreagan Empire would ascend to its full power.

Suddenly, the answer came to me. My heart racing, I peered down at her with new resolve. "What if we fight now?"

She lowered her forehead to rest on her knees. "They are not ready."

"Yes, they are," I said, leaning closer. "I have seen the villagers train with you. They are as ready as they will ever be."

Throwing her head upward, she met my eyes with an exasperated glare. "That is not good enough!" Her voice was sharp, like knives piercing my chest. "I cannot ask them to risk their lives unless I know they have a fighting chance."

"They do!" I was surprised to find my own voice

rising to rival hers. "This could be the only chance we have. No matter the odds, we have to take it."

She shook her head again, her cheeks twitching as her eyes turned glossy. The pain I saw in them made my heart ache. Slowly, I returned to my knees, settling into the space beside her. I squeezed her hand tight, willing her to meet my gaze. "Please," I begged. "I cannot lose you."

When she looked over at me, her anger was gone, and for the first time, what I saw in her eyes was not the fierce confidence she always wore so well. It was fear. "It's not possible," she muttered, her voice shaking.

I wrapped my other hand around hers, encasing it within my own. "Are you kidding me?" I asked with a gentle smile. "You are Princess Evangeline. You can do anything."

Chapter 26

Eve

The mob of angry villagers roared in protest. The tension in the town center had been steadily growing since we arrived, finally culminating in all-out turmoil. "Three days?" exclaimed an indignant voice, yelling over the chaos. "We cannot possibly be ready to storm the castle by then!" Meanwhile, I stared miserably down at my feet, too ashamed to meet their petrified gaze.

"We are finished!" another man shouted frantically. "No way can we defeat them now!" I could hardly stand to listen. Each cry of despair weighed heavy on my already sunken heart. I wanted nothing more than to relent, to call off the battle and simply accept my fate. Yes, the people of Vitalia would be bound under Ingrid's wrath, forever subjected to her ruthless power, but at least they would live.

Pulling me from my misery was a light brush against my arm. I turned my head to find Rune a few inches closer, his elbow lightly skimming my shoulder. It was no accident, I knew. It was a message, a gentle offering of courage. I took a deep inhale then clenched my fists tighter.

"I know it is not an ideal situation," I began, willing my sagging chest upright. "We could all benefit from more time to prepare, but it is time we do not have." I bit my lip, trying desperately to stifle the guilt that threatened to drive me into the ground. "If we wait much longer, we risk the news going public, and once the queen learns the truth, there will be no rebellion." The townspeople shifted their heads toward each other, mumbling in consternation. "I will be constantly policed by the Kreagan guards until the child is born." I swallowed. "Then it will be too late."

The men quietly contemplated my words, but they were still not convinced. "What if we wait until after the birth?" suggested a low-toned villager hidden within the large assembly. "We could take the next few months to perfect our strategy and then attack when the time is right." A few men around him nodded in approval, but I shook my head.

"We can't," I sighed, letting my head drop back toward the chapel steps. "Once the queen has her heir, she will have me killed."

A low gasp shot through the crowd. The panicked rumble of the townsmen surged anew. "How can she do that?"

"She can and she will," I muttered. From the corner of my eye, I saw Rune inch his hand toward mine, his knuckles tenderly grazing my palm. "She will have no need for me anymore, not once her lineage is secured."

The town fell into a painful silence. "Then that's it," said a younger man, his arms wrapped tightly across his front. "It's over. We will never win without our commander." A troubled commotion again began to swell. I bit down on the inside of my cheek, willing myself to stay strong as their anxious chatter grew hysterical.

Suddenly, the prince took a step forward, bringing

their frenzy to a halt. "You are right," Rune muttered. The townspeople froze, gaping up at him in astonishment. It was the first time he had spoken since we arrived in the village. He had stood faithfully beside me as I labored through my speech, watching in humble silence as I delivered the fateful news to the commoners. So when his fixed stature suddenly shifted, all stopped to listen.

"You are right," he said again into the stillness. Baffled, I stared over at him, my mouth agape. Peering sideways, he caught my eye. In his gaze was not the dismay I had expected, not a somber resignation, but a quiet boldness. "We cannot win this war without her." He lifted his chin, growing a few inches taller. For once, he appeared as colossal as he truly was. "If we wait for the perfect moment, for the day all the stars align, we will undoubtedly fail. None of us are fit to command an army, let alone lead a rebellion. If we attempt to charge the palace ourselves, we will surely be defeated."

He shifted his shoulders my way, shamelessly meeting my eye. "That is why we must act now. We must take what may be our last chance at freedom." I gulped down the lingering nerves that stung the back of my throat. "The odds may be against us, but if we do not stand now, we will be forced to live under the queen's tyranny for the rest of our lives."

The villagers eyed each other skeptically, silently reflecting on the prince's words. Still, no one dared voice their agreement. Rune released a long exhale, letting his shoulders drop. "We have to face the truth," he declared, appealing to them with his most sincere gaze. "A life enslaved is simply not worth living. I know what it is like, and believe me, it is a fate worse than death."

I dug my thumbnail into my palm in an effort to hold back the tears I had long subdued, tears that now hovered dangerously close to the surface, as I watched Rune with wide eyes. "You have been training under the greatest warrior this world has ever seen," Rune continued. "No one is more qualified to lead this war. Without her, we are all doomed." There was a small shake in his voice, the faintest hint of uncertainty. But he pushed onward. "So if you want even the slightest chance of victory, you must fight now."

Turning my way once more, the prince entwined my hand in his with a tight squeeze. His gaze was so genuine, so vulnerable that it made me shudder. "Princess Evangeline has risked her life on the battlefield for us countless times. Now it is time we return the favor."

****

"We will start at the granary." I pointed toward the top right corner of the thick parchment splayed out on the table. It was a detailed map of the whole kingdom, a comprehensive rendering of the village along with the entirety of the castle grounds and the fields and pathways in between. Rune and I had spent all afternoon working on it. In the seclusion of his room, I had envisioned every twist and turn in Vitalia, relaying them aloud as the prince masterfully transferred them onto paper. After hours of work, the sketch was complete, just in time for the last of our secret midnight meetings. All that was left was to solidify our plan of action.

"The moment the sun rises, we march," I said, facing the gathering of townsmen closely clustered around me. I could not quite read their expressions under the faint candlelight. It was a rare moonless night, cloaking the village in an eerie darkness. "We will take on the guards stationed in the village first." I directed my finger along the bold line depicting our war path. "We will charge forward en masse. The soldiers will not stand a chance."

A few of the rebels grinned, eyeing each other with an air of self-assurance. "Do not be too confident," I warned with a frown. "Making it through town will be the easy part."

The men swallowed, restoring their sober expressions. "By the time we reach the castle gates," I continued, "the bailey will be mostly empty. Prince Rune will have lured the knights into the palace, giving us a clear path through the front gates."

The villagers turned, now setting their gaze on the tall figure standing beside me. The prince lifted his chin an inch, trying to appear undaunted. But I saw the light trembling of his knees, the gentle shake of his hands kept carefully tucked behind him.

"Our front line will break down the doors," I said a bit louder to regain their attention. One-by-one, the villagers turned to look back at me. Rune released a long-held breath, his tension dissipating. "And once they do, all hell will break loose."

A unified shudder traveled through the tight room. A few of the villagers fidgeted uneasily. "What if they overpower us?" asked a plump man in the front row.

I let out a long sigh. "Then all will be lost," I began, ignoring the anxious groans of the villagers. "That is why we cannot surrender. You must trust your training, and you must trust each other. We will not stop until this battle is won."

A few of the men nodded reluctantly, but a nervous

tension still hung in the air.

"You need not defeat them all," Rune interjected. The restless villagers stared up at the prince once more. "As long as we capture the queen," he continued, pointing toward the skillfully drawn copy of the throne room, "her knights will have no choice but to concede."

The townsmen mumbled quietly to one another. "He is right," I said. I looked over at Rune, impressed by his perceptiveness. For someone who had never fought in a war, he had proven himself quite knowledgeable. "Once we seize Ingrid, our uprising will be all but won."

I could feel the spirits of the villagers starting to rise. "In twenty-four hours, our battle will commence," I said, sensing my own excitement growing. "Today, we make any final preparations. Tomorrow, we attack."

Turning my head, I gave a slight nod toward Mr. Walters, standing along the far side of the crowd. The cobbler walked forward, separating himself from the masses. "You heard her, men," he proclaimed. "Time to get some rest." His mouth curved into an eager smile. "We have a battle to win tomorrow."

Their confidence now secured, the villagers gradually scattered, abandoning the room in small groups, until finally, only Rune and I remained. As I rolled our map into a tight scroll, I felt my stomach churn. Whether the feeling was the bubbling of excitement for the coming battle or a painful tangling of nerves, I did not know. One thing was certain: whatever happened tomorrow would change our lives forever.

"Evangeline," Rune said lowly, interrupting my racing thoughts.

I twisted my head around and peered up at him, the parchment now held tightly in my grasp. "Yes?"

"Is there anything more I can do?" he stammered, anxiously fingering the cuff of his doublet. "I know I am no expert with a sword, but I can still—"

"You are already helping us," I interrupted, taking a few steps toward him. "In fact, you might have the most important role of all." I placed my hand softly upon his shoulder. "It is your job to make sure no Kreagan soldier is prepared for our attack."

"But I want to fight," he cut in. "I want to battle alongside the townspeople. I do not want to be the coward who stands aside while you all risk your lives."

"And you won't." I wrapped my fingers around the top of his arm and squeezed. "Rune, you are our front line. Before we make it to the castle, it will be up to you to take out as many of Ingrid's knights as possible. You could be the difference between victory and defeat."

The prince stared into my eyes with both determination and fear. I could tell he was trying his hardest to push away the uncertainty, to shove down any doubts that he still held inside. At last, he took a deep breath, his features stark and resolute. "Then, I guess I will just have to become my mother's worst nightmare."

****

I twisted my head around to stare out the small window, its glass panels nearly fogged over. There was still no sign of the sun, but it seemed like the black sky had grown a shade lighter. Or was it only a mirage?

With a shaky exhale, I turned back toward the crowded assembly of townsmen. They were clustered about the small granary, speaking to each other in low whispers. My own movements were stiff beneath the thick layer of armor piled upon my shoulders. Every inch of skin, from my neck to my toes, lay buried beneath a heavy sheet of metal. Covering my chest was a sparkling silver breastplate. A sturdy pair of sabatons enveloped my feet, and two leather gauntlets concealed my callused hands. All that was left to don was my iron helmet. It was leaning against the podium at the end of the room, shining beneath the faint glow of the hanging lanterns.

The villagers were similarly clad, huddled together in a tight mass. Clutching their shields to their chests, the men fidgeted within their rigid armor. I could hardly blame them. Ages had passed since I had felt the stiff pressure of chain mail upon my shoulders or the irritating scrape of metal against skin. But I was comforted by the familiar weight of my sword settled in the sheath upon my hip. It was a newly crafted broadsword, a double-edged blade three inches wide with a wooden hilt. It was the same sword my father had gifted me when I first learned to fight. *How fitting*, I thought, running my fingertips along the grip, *since it could be the last I ever wield.*

My hands had been tingling all morning, my heart thumping out of my chest. But I did not mind it. How I had missed the feeling, the surge of pre-battle jitters pumping through my veins, the thrilling rush of adrenaline. But I knew these villagers, men who had spent their whole lives farming or crafting, were unlikely to feel the same way. The air around me hung thick with their restless energy.

I made another quick scan of the horizon. The sky may have still been shrouded in darkness, but I knew our time was running short. Before long, the first ray of light would illuminate the hills, signaling the dawn of our rebellion. But at present, the townsmen were pale and shivering, huddled together in silence. I could see the unease in their faces, the ghostly sheen of fear that obscured any conviction they might have held within. No way could we go into battle like this. If we wanted to make it out of this war alive, we had to fight with passion. We had to be animated, inflamed, our blood flowing with rage.

Shifting my armor around, I marched toward the end of the granary. The men stilled at once, their eyes watching me expectantly. I rested my hands on the podium and gripped its slick wooden edges as I searched for the words to turn these commoners into warriors.

"Today, we are not fighting for ourselves." I lifted my head and stared out at the anxious knights, a great sea of amateur swordsmen, desperate for escape. Despite the chill of the winter morning, their foreheads were drenched in a sheet of nervous sweat. I cleared my throat and stood as tall as I could muster. "We are not fighting for our freedom, not even for our wives and daughters." A few of the men turned to peer at each other, clearly confused.

"Today, we fight for those we have lost." A low mumble of understanding swept through the room. "We fight for the men, for the women and children, who were ruthlessly murdered by the stone-hearted Kreagan army. We fight for the brave Vitalian knights who selflessly gave their lives to defend our kingdom."

Their impassioned murmurs grew louder, and I sensed the fire in the room would soon ignite. But before I could continue, a sharp pain bloomed in my chest. "Today, we fight for King Ricard." The townsmen let out a heavy sigh, their own grief evident. But their anguish soon shifted to anger, the uncertainty in their eyes turning to fury.

"Today, when we charge the castle, the one wrongfully taken from us, not only will we expel the corrupt empire who unlawfully stole our land, but we will avenge our people." As the intensity of my voice increased, my body began to shake with fervor. "Today, we fight in their honor. We will not let their deaths be in vain."

The villagers hollered with enthusiasm, their cries filling the dim storehouse. Every fear, every doubt, was dissolved as the bitter flames engulfed the horde of angry men. "Today, we fight for vengeance, for the pride that Queen Ingrid has savagely stripped away, pride that some will never reclaim." I was shouting along with the crowd now, stirring myself into a frenzy as the heat within me surged. "Today, we fight for Vitalia!"

Raising their fists, the villagers cried out as one. Their fervid cheers bounced from wall to wall. An untamable blaze burned bright in their eyes, and I knew that Rune had been right after all. They were ready. Now was the time for a revolution.

Once more, I peered out the window. There was no denying it now. The sky was growing lighter, gradually transforming into a cool morning blue.

Squeezing my eyes shut, I sent a pleading whisper into the frigid mountain air. "Come on, Rune. It's up to you now."

Chapter 27

Rune

Her fingernails beat against the table with a dangerous click, making my heart jump with each sharp tap. My own hands were out of sight, tucked beneath the long dining table, my forearms lying restlessly on my lap. My fingers were weaved together so tightly that I could feel the quick beat of my pulse through my palms.

It took everything I had to keep my breath steady, to keep the faint color in my cheeks. Although I felt like I might hyperventilate at any moment, I knew I had to stay calm. Evangeline and all of Vitalia were depending on me. I had to be alert, and most importantly, I had to ensure my mother and her guards did not expect a thing.

I dared a quick glance toward a nearby window. A faint, iridescent ray streamed through the stained glass onto the floor of the dining hall, illuminating the space in a vibrant prism of light. Morning had come. The rebellion had begun. The townspeople were approaching the castle.

Suddenly, the queen banged her fist onto the table, rattling the silverware and making me flinch. She groaned aloud as her lips twisted into a malignant snarl. Flattening her hand, she pressed all five fingers into the wood. "Where is she?" my mother growled. Her silvery hair hung flatly against her back, her violent outburst sending a few strands floating upward before they settled back into place. Her sapphire gown left not an inch of skin uncovered. The cobalt sleeves enwrapped her arms like snakeskin, their fabric stretched to the base of her thumb. Her lacy neckline clung tightly to her throat, so high it nearly hugged her chin.

"She was supposed to be here a quarter hour ago." She flexed her jaw as she jammed her knuckles into the table then turned her menacing gaze toward me. I swallowed. "Why didn't she arrive with you?"

I cleared my throat, tucking my chin to stare down at my thighs. "I'm not sure," I mumbled. "She was gone when I woke this morning."

The queen released an exasperated sigh and rolled her eyes in irritation. "She was gone," she repeated dryly, her rigid glare locked on my pale face. Lifting her palm, she folded her hands before her and pressed the tips of her elbows into the table. "Rune, how many times must we go over this? The princess is your responsibility. Her disobedience is your misdoing."

I did not respond, too distracted by the nervous ringing in my ears to hear a word she was saying. "Are you even listening to me?" she shouted. I popped my head up and turned toward her with petrified eyes. She shook her head, growing increasingly frustrated. "I don't know why I even bother with you." Folding her arms in front of her, she slumped back into her chair. "You are just as stupid and useless as she is."

A dagger twisted in my stomach. It stung just as it always did when my mother flung her brutal insults my way. But I knew from the dull flutter in my chest that something had changed. Normally, her attacks made me fold into myself, but not this time. Clenching my fists, I let them drop to my sides.

"She is not useless," I spat through gritted teeth.

The queen swung her head toward me, her eyes wide. "What did you say?" she muttered.

"I said she is not useless." Slowly, I lifted my head and met her with my own stern glare. "And neither am I."

Her brows furrowed, her eyes squinting into slits. "You dare contradict me?"

"And she is not stupid either," I said, lifting my chest taller and ignoring her ominous tone. "In fact, she is the most intelligent woman I know, far wiser than you will ever be."

Her jaw dropped open, but only for a moment. Hastily pulling her lips back together, she tightened her mouth into a thin line. "I suggest you watch yourself, Rune," she said lowly. "That girl makes you careless. She has filled your head with lies." Leaning forward, she caught me in her most piercing glower. "Must I remind you of the penalty for slander against your queen?"

"You are no queen of mine," I said. My chest began to shake with anger as I rose to my feet.

"Sit down," she said firmly, but I could hear the subtle unease trickling through her voice.

"You are no more than a tyrant," I continued. I lifted my chin an inch higher, doing everything in my power to keep my quivering knees from buckling.

"That is enough!" she roared, her dark eyes turned venomous.

"Tell me, Mother," I said over her bouncing echo. "How did you do it?"

"How did I do what?" she asked lowly.

"How did you kill my father?"

She stiffened, her eyes going cold. "You wanted all the glory to yourself," I continued. "There was not enough power for the two of you, so you got rid of the only man standing in your way." My fingers were trembling violently. I squeezed my fists tighter. "You murdered him." One look and I knew she was ready to erupt. The fuse was lit, and I was about to suffer the blast.

With one quick shove, the queen thrust her chair back and surged to her feet. "How dare you speak to me in this way!" She was gripping the edge of the table so tightly that her knuckles turned white. Her face twitched as she revealed her fangs. My hands and feet went numb, but despite the dread that coursed through my veins, I did not cower.

"Guards!" the queen shrieked. "Remove him at once!" Her shrill was like the cry of a siren, her voice cracking with her delirium. A trio of knights standing along the wall started marching toward me. Pushing my chair aside, I shuffled away from the table. Now was my time. No matter what obstacles she threw my way, I would not back down.

As the first guard approached, I squatted low to the ground, assuming the fighting stance the princess had taught me. With my knees bent, I lifted my forearms to guard my face. The knight lunged for me, his closed fist barreling toward my ear. In a flash, I dodged below his arm and scurried out of the way. Without hesitation, the second guard advanced with both hands outstretched. I quickly stepped to the side, narrowly evading his clutches. Then I drove my fist outward, knocking him away. He stumbled to the floor, landing on his knees with a loud thump.

Astonished, the third knight approached with more

caution. I returned my shaking arms to my chest and waited for him to make his move. He pounced without warning, leaping through the air in an attempt to tackle me to the ground. Quickly, I shuffled to the side and ducked. The guard flew through the space beside me, landing flat on the other side.

I made a swift glance toward my mother. She was stunned, momentarily frozen as she witnessed the impossible. But soon, she shook the baffled expression from her face and let rage reclaim her features. "I said get rid of him!" she screamed. She was growing hysterical, digging her fingers into her hair and tugging violently, ripping a few strands from her scalp. "Take him to the Reflection Chamber!"

The remaining guards along the edge of the dining hall came rushing toward me. At the commotion, a few knights raced inside from their posts flanking the castle. Before I knew it, the entire squadron had me surrounded. I had been lucky so far, but there was no way I could escape the queen's entire army. Still, I had to try. With a deep grunt, I charged forward and sent the crown of my head into the stomach of the nearest knight. We crashed to the ground, the man's armor clanging against the stone floor. Before I could hop back to my feet, a pair of gauntleted hands seized my wrists and yanked my arms behind my back. I wriggled and writhed to escape their clutches, but it was no use. Several guards now had a hold on me, their grip too strong to evade.

When the remaining knights reached my side, they each took turns bashing my defenseless body. One sent a gloved fist into my stomach. I groaned aloud as I doubled over. I would have collapsed to the ground, but the guards held me firmly upright. Before I could catch my breath, another fist came hurtling toward my nose. My head flew backwards, my neck nearly snapping from the impact. My world went black and regained its color slowly, stars twinkling at the corners of my vision. But the steel knuckles returned, this time sinking into my right eye socket. My neck twisted sideways, causing a sharp pain in my spine. My consciousness was wavering, but I refused to let the darkness overtake me.

Suddenly, the punches stopped, and the guards clasping my wrists began dragging me away from the dining table, lugging me toward the door. In a panic, I resumed my frenzied squirming. "Admit it!" I howled over the violent pounding of my heels against the floor. "Admit you killed my father!"

"Get him out of here!" the queen yelled over me.

"You killed him!" I squeezed my eyes shut and pulled at my bound arms with all my might. "You killed him!"

"Of course I killed him!" she screeched with the ferocity of a mountain lion. "And I'll kill you next!"

All at once, the chaos stilled, interrupted by a loud banging on the castle doors. The guards froze, still holding me in the air as they stared in confusion at the palace entrance. Even the queen paused, breathing hard as she gazed across the room, open-mouthed.

Another powerful thump erupted through the hall, making the walls shake. The knights turned toward the queen in puzzlement, awaiting her next command. Releasing the tension in my body, I let my back slump into the floor and dropped my head. With my face toward the ceiling, a flood of laughter fled my throat. The sound traveled skyward and rained back down in an ominous echo.

"What is this?" the queen demanded. There was no denying the fear in her voice now, the slight shake in her words oddly reminding me of myself.

I spat a thick glob of blood from my mouth then laughed again, a blaring cackle that turned the throne room to ice. Twisting my neck to face her, I smiled a cold, vengeful smile.

"Restitution."

Chapter 28

Eve

With a third and final heave, the castle doors broke open and the legion of commoners plunged into the palace. "Brace yourselves!" I warned. The men lifted their shields before them, positioning their swords at the ready. But not one of the queen's guards was stationed at their normal post by the door. Instead, we charged inside without resistance.

As I led the rebels into the throne room, I quickly scanned the area. The Kreagan knights were all clustered a few feet from the dining table, stupefied as they gawked at our assembly of armored townsmen. Ingrid was standing at the far end of the table, her chair toppled to its side by her feet. Her hair was disheveled, her dress tousled and pulled to one side. Pure terror shone through her eyes.

My heart raced with furor. The last leg of the battle was upon us. Everything was going according to plan, but something was wrong. Worry flooded my veins as I flashed my eyes about the room, frantically searching for Rune.

Our two armies stood at a stalemate, each one carefully watching the other. Only a few yards separated the confused guards from the armed villagers, but not one man dared move. All waited for their leader's command.

As expected, the queen spoke first. "Arrest them!" she demanded. I had never seen her so rattled, so wild and perturbed. Her jaw was clenched so tightly that her entire body shook. Whatever the prince had done to divert his mother's attention had worked.

The Kreagans finally snapped out of their stupor and began their careful approach. I could delay my men no longer. "Attack!" I called out, lifting my sword skyward. The townsmen bellowed as they charged forward, racing toward the queen's battalion with their weapons outstretched. Slipping off to one side, I watched as the embittered mob of men poured into the castle, quickly overwhelming their adversaries. On the other side of the madness, I saw the queen fling her head from side to side, scouring each door for the rest of her reinforcements. I smiled to myself. No one would be coming to her aid this time. Little did she know that my army had already taken out her first few lines of defense while marching toward the palace gates.

I was still slinking along the walls as the hordes of men converged. I desperately scanned the wide room, looking for any sign of the prince. But I could see nothing around the hectic collision of knights. "Rune!" I shouted over the sound of clanking swords.

Then I saw him: a pale, crumpled body splayed on the ground amidst the surrounding chaos. I ran into the carnage without hesitation. Ducking beneath the swarm of flying blades, I dodged each pair of dueling swordsmen. As I came closer, I started to make out a small puddle of blood gathered around him. My stomach dropped in despair. I dashed the rest of the way through the mass of fighters before dropping to my knees beside him. The left side of his face was swollen, battered beyond recognition. A steady stream of blood poured from his misshapen nose. It spilled freely down his temple, collecting in a pool beneath his hair. I knew he was breathing by the subtle rise and fall of his chest, but his hands were growing colder by the second. "Rune!" I yelled, shaking his shoulders frantically.

He slowly rolled his head toward me then cracked open his uninjured eye. "It took you long enough," he groaned with a playful side smile.

I sighed aloud, relief sweeping through me, but I did not let my guard down for long. "Come on!" I exclaimed. "We have to get you out of here!" With one quick tug, I pulled his arm around my shoulder and hauled him to his feet. He winced as he tried to stand, pressing most of his weight into me. Grabbing his limp hand draped over my shoulder, I trudged forward. Some of the townspeople caught sight of us struggling through the crowd. One by one, they shoved their Kreagan foes aside, clearing a path. I pushed onward, not stopping until we made it to the furthest corner of the hall, far from the nearest brawl.

Carefully, I lowered Rune to the floor. He collapsed onto the ground with a pained wheeze, resting his back against the stone wall.

Once I was sure he was out of harm's way, I stood and unsheathed my sword. "Stay here," I instructed. Twisting toward the warring men, I took a deep breath. But before I could dive into the scuffle, I heard the low sound of Rune's voice.

"Evangeline," he breathed. His tone was weak but insistent. He did his best to focus his gaze on me through his wounded eye, using all his strength to lift his head. "Be careful."

I nodded. Gripping my sword tighter, I took one last look at his soft blue eyes, his bruised cheeks, his light blond hair dyed red with the blood still pouring from the gash in his forehead. Finally pulling myself away, the shape of his features still lingering in my mind, I charged into the disarray.

As I made my approach, I was astonished to find the number of Kreagan knights slowly dwindling. The battle raged on with no sign of stopping, but the queen's men were falling fast. I raced into the fray to aid their efforts. With a swift kick, I punted the nearest Kreagan to the ground. His back knocked flat against the stone, his weapon flinging from his hand. Before he could even catch his breath, I plunged the tip of my sword into his chest. A torrent of blood burst from the wound, showering me in crimson.

I perked my head up, detecting the footfall of another guard rapidly approaching. With his teeth clenched and his eyes red with fury, the man swung the edge of his sword toward my hip. I parried his strike easily, driving his weapon upward with such force that he stumbled backward. While he struggled to regain his balance, I sunk my saber into his leg. He howled wildly and shot his hands over the deep cut. Leaned over and distracted by the stream of blood gushing onto the floor, he did not see the flash of my blade. This time, I was not so merciful. The edge of my sword connected with his open neck and sliced his throat in two. The knight's head flew through the air, spinning in space until it plopped to the ground beside the rest of his lifeless body.

Wiping his blood from my forehead, I lifted my gaze and glimpsed over the commotion. I spotted Ingrid at once. She was whiter than I had ever seen her, her cheeks ashen as she watched her glorious empire collapsing before her. While her army withered, she stepped slowly back from the swarm of soldiers, inching away from what she knew would be her certain end. I bolted around the last of the men with my sword clung tightly to my side. The queen was running now, sprinting toward the safety of the north tower. But before she could reach the door, I seized her forearm and flung her back. She swung around, stilling at the cold iron of my sword against her throat.

"It's over, Ingrid," I said between breaths. I tugged the blade an inch deeper, making her flinch. "Surrender."

She chuckled coldly, her body still frozen. "Too afraid to kill me, are you?" She tried to appear unfazed, as calm as she could be with my steel sword pressed to her neck. But I could feel the rapid pulsing of her heart against my arm, could see her hands quivering by her sides.

Tightening my jaw, I felt my forehead burn with unfiltered rage. I gripped my weapon tighter and readied my wrist to finish the job, to bury my blade into her meager flesh. I would slice through her fair skin and watch her bleed out onto the floor, the same way she had watched my father die. And I knew I would enjoy every second of it.

But before I could, I noticed a flash of movement from the corner of my eye. It was the prince, hastily limping across the hall. Despite my orders, he had risen from his place against the wall and was now scurrying toward us. I looked back at the queen, her helpless body trembling in my arms as she prepared herself for my fatal slash. This woman had oppressed him his entire life, had broken him down for her own gain, had torn him to pieces for her own sick pleasure. She had done everything in her power to destroy him, to turn him into a frail, lifeless slave. And although ultimately she had failed, Rune would never be the same, forever scarred by her cruel abuse. For him to truly live, I knew she had to die.

But she was still his mother.

I peered back at the prince, reading the alarm in his eyes. I saw the quiet desperation that begged me for no more hurt, the silent pleading for an end to the ceaseless string of heartache that had been ripping him apart since birth. And I knew I could not be the cause of any more of his pain.

Slowly, I eased my sword from Ingrid's throat, letting it hover in the air before her. She gradually softened her limbs before letting out a bitter laugh. "You two truly are perfect for each other." Rune made his final labored steps toward us, stopping just a few yards away. "You are both weak, too weak to yield any real power."

Rune eyed me uneasily then turned his gaze back to the queen. "It's time to go, Mother."

She was silent for a moment, her eyes curious as she studied her son. Then, she twisted her head toward me. "You are pregnant, aren't you?"

My body stiffened.

She laughed again, shaking her head as her cold cackle grew. "You think you can deny me my heir?" I frowned, my eyebrows furrowed. "That child belongs to me," she said, pointing a bony finger at my abdomen. "I am the one who brought you together. That baby is the heir of Kreagan."

"You are wrong," I said lowly, clenching my open hand into a fist.

The queen glared at me with a sinister smile. "You may have won this battle, but the war is far from over. One day, I will return, and I will take back the child that is rightfully mine."

My heart stopped. My vision went red. I drove my sword back into the fold of her neck, just enough to break the skin. She gasped. Pulling her body closer, my breastplate crushing the bones in her back, I pressed my lips to her ear. "If you ever show your face in Vitalia again," I growled, my spittle spattering her cheek, "I will kill you myself and display your severed head for all to see."

She swallowed, staring ahead nervously. "We will see about that," she mumbled.

In the tense stillness, my fingernails digging into her skin as I longed to rip her heart from her chest, I suddenly noticed the hall had gone quiet. I shifted my gaze upward and realized that the chaos in the room had dulled. The fighting had ceased. The battle was over.

The floor was littered with bodies, the remains of a bloody massacre. Groups of surviving villagers hobbled toward us. Some winced as they gripped fresh wounds. Others ushered the last of the Kreagan knights forward, men who had dropped their weapons in surrender. The rebels watched me closely, approaching the tense scene with caution.

With a long sigh, I released my tight grip on the queen. "Take her away," I commanded. A group of townsmen marched over and took Ingrid by the elbows. She kept silent, her face set in a cold sneer, as they pulled her arms behind her back and escorted her from the hall along with what was left of her army.

As soon as they were out of sight, the Vitalian

soldiers started to cheer. They threw their helmets in the air and shouted in triumph. In an instant, I found myself tossing my sword aside, letting it clang to the ground. I shot across the hall without thinking, racing toward the prince at full speed. I crashed into him with such force that he stumbled backward, undoubtedly caught off guard, but I threw my arms around him to keep him from tumbling to the floor. Squeezing him tightly, I buried my face in his chest and let the tears fall. I wailed into the folds of his doublet, the safest place I knew. At last, recovering from his shock, he returned my embrace, dropping his nose into my neck and pulling me even closer. "You are free," he whispered in my ear.

I pulled back, holding him at arm's length. "No," I said with a grin, gazing into his misty eyes. "We are free."

Chapter 29

Rune

There is something so surreal about watching as your whole world is ushered away, when everything you have ever known is driven from your life forever.

My mother was loaded into the same cart she had ridden when we first arrived here, the same velvet litter she had traveled in since we began our spree of invasions years ago. What was left of her guard trudged along the path before her, their garments now tattered and torn, their heads hung low in disgrace. All was the same as the day we first came to Vitalia, all except one thing: this time I stayed behind. I was not dragged along at the back of the procession as a second thought, a necessary inconvenience. This time, I stood beside Princess Evangeline, watching from afar as all that remained of the Kreagan Empire faded into the distance.

As the villagers escorted her to her cart, the queen had halted her march then turned to face me. Her stony features were hardened in place. She glared at me through menacing eyes, two shards of broken glass that threatened to slice my skin.

I did not drop my gaze. I did not even flinch. Her murderous look had lost all power over me.

The villagers eyed the princess uncertainly, anticipating her next command. She lightly flicked her wrist and nodded. The men carefully released the queen's shoulders and moved a few feet back.

My mother took a small step forward and lifted her chin, staring at me down her pointy nose despite the fact that I stood a whole head taller. Her lips curved into a sneer, the shape they had always held best. "I would never have expected my own son to betray me," she said, her forehead crinkled in disgust. "But I should have known all along. You have been nothing but a curse from the day you were born." She turned to glare at the princess through piercing eyes before flashing them back to me. "I assume you will be staying here, abandoning your own kingdom, your own family?"

I swallowed, not saying a word but never once letting my gaze fall. Instead, I welcomed the gripping tension in my limbs, the growing warmth in my chest. I embraced the anger.

The left side of her mouth peeled upward in an ominous grin. "You will never last. You are just as feeble as your father was."

At the mention of his name, my hands twitched. Blood rushed through my veins anew, and a fresh wave of heat spread through my cheeks. "Goodbye, Mother," I mumbled, wrestling to keep my voice steady.

She set her face back into a grimace, her lips parting to show her teeth, but before she could reply, the princess gestured toward the townsmen who swiftly reclaimed their grip on her arms. Twisting her back around, they lowered her head and guided her into the cart. The maroon door was hastily shut behind her, the gems along its edge glistening in the evening light, and the knights were directed to commence their shameful march. They plodded back through the castle gates, back through the emerald valley, back through the village streets, leaving the same way they came.

And just like that, she was gone. It was not quite like I expected, not like the final chapter of a long tragedy but like a page turning, like a new story beginning.

Shifting away from the setting sun, I turned to look at Evangeline. She was staring intensely toward the end of the dirt path as if unsure they had truly gone, as if she was already planning for the queen's pledged return. I knew she would never stop watching, not until my mother was dead and Vitalia was safe from her wrath for good.

"What now?" I asked gently, easing her from her watchful state.

When she turned her head, her face had changed. Her features grew soft, and for the first time, her eyes were full of hope. She enfolded her hand in mine, her lips curved in a soft smile.

"Now we rebuild."

****

Evangeline retook control of her kingdom the moment my mother fled from view. She picked up right where her father left off, putting the valley back into order in a matter of days. Gone were the guards patrolling the village. Gone were the dark Kreagan flags shadowing the town streets. All sanctioned labor assignments were abolished, and for the first time in months, the castle staff could return home to reunite with their families and commemorate their newfound freedom.

The celebration lasted for weeks. There were open markets in the village, musicians playing in the streets, and dancing in the town square. Once the castle had been restored to its former glory, the princess invited the whole kingdom to a feast, promising a royal banquet like no other.

On the evening of the grand reopening, the villagers entered the tall castle gates with their mouths agape, as did I. The great ballroom was even more spectacular than I remembered. Light poured through the newly paned windows, the marble floors glowing in a mesmerizing hue. The walls, once dark with the somber colors of the Kreagan Empire, had been brought back to life with glittering gold and violet Vitalian banners. The hall was spotless. No one could have expected that, just a few days before, a revolution had been waged in this very room. The spacious stone floor was cleared of the battle's bloodshed and was now covered by countless rows of tables and chairs, each place set with the most elegant dishware.

When the guests arrived, there were no seating arrangements. The entire kingdom was free to sit wherever they pleased: cobblers with merchants, masons with nobles, farmers with knights. It was a sight to behold, a grand conglomeration of Vitalian citizens relishing in each other's company.

Once everyone found their seats, I pulled myself from the dreamlike atmosphere and turned my head toward the end of the hall, expecting to find a pair of thrones against the far wall. But even those were nowhere to be found, replaced by yet another set of tables with high backed chairs, already filled to capacity. I searched the room with furrowed brow, scouring the hall for Evangeline, suddenly aware that I was the only one left standing.

"Rune!" a voice called from behind me. I spun

around and found the princess seated at one of the center tables with an open chair on her right. Relieved, I hurried over and took my seat. Dining across from us was a group unfamiliar to me. To my left sat an older man holding a cane, his hairline slightly receding. Beside him was a thick woman with flushed cheeks and a pair of young girls, their hair tied back in silver ribbons.

Upon observing the guest seated on Evangeline's other side, my puzzlement dissolved. "You have met Mary, haven't you Rune?" the princess asked.

"Of course," I replied, lowering my head in a modest bow in the direction of the lady's maid.

The girl twisted her lips into a knowing smile then ducked her chin. She hastily cleared her throat before gesturing toward the other side of the table. "I would like to introduce you to my family."

The plump woman across the table promptly stood, taking her skirts in one hand and sinking her chest to the ground. The two young girls hastened to their feet, imitating their mother in a low curtsy. "A pleasure to meet you, your highness," the woman said with her head still bowed, her mouth set in a firm line.

The man, on the other hand, did not make such a dramatic display. Laboring to his feet, he simply reached a long arm across the center of the table. "It was an honor to fight with you, your majesty," he declared with a humble grin.

"You as well," I said, swiftly grabbing his large hand and returning his genial shake. From the corner of my vision, I could see the princess beaming, her eyes fixed on the side of my face. But when I turned to meet her gaze, she quickly pulled her head away, hastily resuming her neutral demeanor.

Without warning, Evangeline sprang to her feet. The legs of her chair scraped noisily against the floor, silencing the crowd in an instant. The visitors twisted in their seats to face the princess.

"Thank you all for coming this evening," she said with the wide grin of a lively hostess, her hands folded delicately before her. It was a new side to her, this regal chieftess. A role that fit her well.

"Tonight, we are here to celebrate you. All of you." She paused briefly to peer around the room, ensuring that every corner of the hall was properly acknowledged. "I cannot thank you enough for your loyalty and sacrifice during our most trying of times." For a moment, her eyes dimmed and she withdrew into herself. "I know that if my father was here today, he would be proud of us all." I felt the weight of the room grow heavy, a few eyes dropping to the floor.

It was Evangeline who finally broke the silence, bending over the table and grabbing her drink. She lifted the goblet, letting it twinkle in the fading evening sun. "Long live Vitalia!" she declared, raising her arm heavenward.

At once, the entirety of the kingdom rose from their seats, their faces alight as they hoisted their own glasses toward the sky. "Long live Vitalia!" they repeated ardently. They each took a hefty sip of the dark wine before returning to their chairs.

With her amicable smile restored, the princess clapped her hands together. "Let the feast begin!" she exclaimed.

Without missing a beat, a long line of servers marched in from the far end of the hall. They traversed the maze of tables with haste as they delivered the diligently prepared food, carefully placing the impressive platters before the guests. When the lids were removed and the dishes revealed, the citizens moaned with delight. Even I was awestruck by the lavish spread: cauldrons of grilled white meat stew, buttery fish pies of salmon, trout, and mackerel, split pea soup still steaming from the bowl, and countless loaves of fresh bread stacked beside piles of jam and butter. The villagers wasted no time digging into the hearty fare. They filled their plates with the savory cuisine and dove into their meals with fervor.

I was unsure where to begin. Finally, I reached a hand toward an inviting mountain of roasted chicken legs, but before I could grab a piece, I caught sight of Evangeline. She had yet to move an inch since returning to her seat, her plate empty, her silverware untouched. I paused my hand in midair and turned to study her. She was not even contemplating the extensive feast. Instead, she watched the villagers. I followed her gaze and watched with her as the guests filled their plates with pleasure. They heartily munched on the seemingly endless trays of food as they talked and laughed along with the people beside them.

"Are you all right?" I asked gently.

Pulling herself away from the merry commotion, she peered at me through glistening eyes. "This is what I always wanted," she said just loud enough for me to hear. She shifted back toward the joyful party, her face as bright as the sun. "A banquet for the whole kingdom. All of us together in one place. What could be better than this?"

But I was no longer watching the villagers. My eyes were drawn to the princess, to the subtle lift in her cheeks, the glossy copper of her waves, the powerful light she radiated through the palace, more vibrant than the North Star.

Nothing.

****

As time slowly passed and life returned to normal, Evangeline began to grow, her belly expanding by the day. At first, her sprouting bump frightened me. I was the last man on earth fit to be a father, let alone to the heir of Vitalia. But from the moment I first rested my palm on her swelling womb, I was transfixed, enchanted by the tiny human that was slowly budding within her. I would lay for hours with my fingers resting over her abdomen, feeling her powerful heartbeat in my hand, trying to make out two.

And when we made love, I would hold her gently, careful not to put too much pressure on her stomach or rock her too roughly. I would kiss her ever so softly as I rolled my lips down her body, placing gentle pecks along her neck and blooming breasts then tenderly pressing my mouth to the tip of her belly.

But when she rolled her own fingers over the growing bulge, when she studied her evolving womb in the mirror, I saw no fascination or fervor in her: only uncertainty.

"I was never meant to be a mother," she whispered to me one sleepless night. Her eyes were wide with dread, their whites gleaming under the glow of the moon. "I was born to be a warrior. A killer. How could I care for a child?"

Pulling her close, I lightly rested her head against my chest. "You are going to be a great mother," I assured her, softly brushing my fingers over the stretched skin of

314

her abdomen. "You are Princess Evangeline. You can do anything." I lowered my lips to graze her ear. "Never forget that."

Then, I lifted my mouth to her temple. I kissed her forehead until the tension in her arms fell away, until her breath slowed and her heart softened and I knew she had finally found rest. This is how we slept most nights: she curled up on her side, her knees tucked to her chest, her cheek pressed to my ribs; and me coiled around her, my lips to her forehead, my nose buried in her amber hair.

Until the night the baby came.

Lady's maids scrambled purposefully around the bedroom. Some hastily stripped the sheets from her bed, setting fresh towels beneath her legs. Others stood beside her pillow, wiping the sweat from her forehead. I heard them whisper anxiously to each other as the time quickly drew near. I stood nervously by her side and gripped her hand tightly, not letting go when she shrieked in agony, her fingernails digging into my skin. I held on until she released her last wail and I heard a piercing cry.

The maids wrapped the baby in strips of cloth before handing the tiny bundle to me. Unprepared, I stretched out my stiff arms to catch the weeping swaddle. It barely exceeded the length of my hands, weighing little more than a dinner plate. My forearms were rigid, my entire body frozen in place as the child cried, its face a dark red.

Stepping beside me, one of the maids lightly pressed on my elbows and shifted my arms back. My shoulders loosened, and the frail head rolled into my chest. "It's a girl," said a voice I could not see, my eyes consumed by the baby's tiny fists.

My heart fluttered in my chest, and for a moment, I forgot how to breathe. *A girl. A daughter. Our daughter.*

"How is she?" Evangeline asked, still catching her breath as she pushed herself upright.

I strained to pull my gaze from the scrunched up fingers, my eyes eternally fixed to the stubby little hands. I felt like I was hovering above the floor, like in my arms I held the most divine of creatures. "She is beautiful," I said breathlessly. I blinked, sure that when I reopened my eyes she would be gone, that she was merely a hallucination, a rose-colored dream of a life I would never know. But there she was, cradled in my arms, her crumpled face wet with tears, still as dazzling as ever. I held my breath a little longer, worried that even the subtle rise and fall of my chest might disturb her.

"What is her name?" another voice asked through the haze. Her impossibly small toes were curled up and kicking about wildly.

"Her name is Sky." I flashed my head upward and stared at Evangeline with my mouth slightly ajar. She was gaping in awe at the small human tucked into my chest, this pure being we had made together. Any trace of the fear she once held was gone. All that was left was wonder. "Princess Sky."

Once more, I peered down at the frail infant. She was no longer fussing or rattling her slender limbs. Instead, she rested her soft cheek against my ribs, her body calm with sleep. Before long, my own eyes grew damp, but I quickly shrugged a shoulder to my face and wiped them clear. I would not miss a single second of her.

****

After her recovery, Evangeline spent every waking moment with baby Sky. She refused to let our newborn daughter out of her sight, often staying awake throughout the night to watch over her as she slept. Before the child could let out a cry, Evangeline was there, ready to cradle her in the comfort of her arms.

The princess remained vigilant, keeping a close watch of the infant's every breath. It was soon clear that her careful surveillance was driving her to exhaustion. She permitted herself to rest only if I promised to watch over Sky in her place. Then, she would collapse into bed and promptly fall into a deep sleep.

The reason for her excessive protection was not lost on me. I too could not help replaying my mother's ominous threat: *One day, I will return, and I will take back the child that is rightfully mine.* With Evangeline in power, her soldiers ordered to be on constant high guard, I knew it was impossible for the queen to pass even a single foot through the palace gates. But I also knew my mother. When she wanted something, she would do anything in her power to obtain it. No sacrifice was too great, no act too cruel.

So Evangeline never took her eyes off the child. She would not let a soul near unless they were one of her most trusted servants. Most days, the only other person she allowed in her room was Mary.

The lady's maid was huddled close to the princess one afternoon, the two of them seated on the edge of our bed, completely spellbound by the tiny figure pressed to Evangeline's chest. The baby was lost in a peaceful slumber. The two women giggled quietly to themselves as they watched the quick flickering of her eyelashes, like the swift flap of a hummingbird's wings.

I was sitting on the floor, my back propped against the bedroom wall. What used to be the cold sleeping quarters I had been banished to each night had become my favorite place to rest. Here, I could observe unhindered the two creatures I admired most in the world: the meager infant swaddled from head to toe, a thin patch of auburn hair sprouting from the center of her head; and the woman who held her, who tucked her sleeping daughter into the crook of her elbow, who still held the lighthearted smile that had taken over her features since her daughter's first breath. During the few brief moments when she lifted her gaze to catch mine, I sensed us both thinking the same thing: it was all too good to be true. She was too perfect. Life was finally going our way, and we had both seen far too much to believe it could last.

Suddenly, Mary cleared her throat. She wiped away her joyful grin and adorned a more serious expression. "Now that we have a new princess," she said, lightly pressing her thumb into the center of Sky's palm, "I believe we need a new queen."

Evangeline twisted her face around. She was still for a moment, silently contemplating Mary's words. Gradually, a heartfelt grin worked its way across her cheeks. When she turned toward me, her features were brilliant, her face gleaming like the morning sun.

"I suppose it is time for a coronation."

Chapter 30

Eve

First came the sound of trumpets. When I heard the horns blare, each note in time with the pounding of the drums, I recognized the melody immediately. It was the song of Vitalia. The anthem of a queen.

The palace doors tore open, knocking me backward with a cool rush of wind. As the path cleared before me, the music surged anew. The powerful waves of sound collided with my body, shaking the ground beneath my feet. Despite the evening's late hour, the hall was bursting with light. Hundreds of burning candles were scattered about the room.

Every Vitalian was in attendance. The long aisles were filled with the immeasurable crowd of citizens. Most of them had squeezed their way into the towering ballroom, wedging themselves into the tight assembly to get the best view possible. Those who could not fit inside stood behind me, forming a semicircle around the open doors as they gaped into the elaborately decorated throne room. Along the center of the floor was a long violet carpet. It spanned the entire length of the grand hall and ended at the feet of the three priests lined at the other side.

I paused in place and took a deep breath. Then, I stepped forward.

Every eye was fixed on me. I felt each one, pinned to me like thistles lightly prodding my skin. My arms felt stiff by my sides, but my legs flowed effortlessly forward. They glided me across the room as if controlled by some unknown entity, pressing me gently onward.

My light cotton robe brushed against my shins like tall blades of grass. And suddenly, I was five years old again, running through the thick fields behind the palace, racing toward the forest with abandon. My long hair flew behind me, loose and untamed. The heat of the morning sun warmed my face, and I smiled, welcoming the feeling as I tipped my chin upward to catch the light.

I was not the same girl I was then, and yet I was. I might have been a few years older, might have grown a few inches taller. I might have acquired more scars, some wounds that would never heal. I might have been a wife and a mother. But I was still her, that same princess who used to run recklessly through the castle halls. Who used to pout and gripe when she did not get her way. Who used to beg her father to let her fight. Despite everything, I was still that same little girl, now walking toward her destiny.

It felt like years before I reached the end of the long carpet and met the priests face-to-face, adorned in their most holy vestments. They watched me silently and I them as I slowly knelt to the ground. Lifting my head upward, I let my bronze waves fall down the length of my back. The middle priest took a step forward, closing the space between us. In his hands was a small metal plate. I could not see its contents from below, but I did not need to. He dipped his fingers into the dish then rolled the edge of his thumb down my forehead. Cool oil dripped down my face, collecting in a small pool at the tip of my nose. I closed my eyes and focused on the steady drizzle. It was a sensation I would never know again: the feeling of anointment.

Two servants rushed to meet the priests in the center aisle and delivered the royal garments. As the men sauntered toward me, I rose to my feet. The first placed a vermillion surcoat over my plain, white robe. I extended my arms outward as he slid my hands through the sleeves. The second draped a long velvet mantle upon my back. I recognized it instantly. It was the same royal cape my mother wore in her portraits, the same vestments she was clothed in the day she became queen.

For the first time, I allowed myself a quick glance toward the audience, finding what I was looking for within seconds. Rune was stationed at the front of the crowd. His smile was soft, but on his lips I read the words left unspoken: the affection, the reverence, the pride. I saw all the things he left unsaid now pouring through him, the sentiment that needed no words, and I smiled.

When I turned again to face the holy men, I found the third priest had returned. In his arms was a shimmering crown plated in pure gold. Its band was patterned with sparkling amethyst and crystal, and its edges jutted upward like the tall castle towers. Bowing slightly, I felt the wild beating of my heart as the crown slid over my hair, finding its place of rest upon the center of my head.

Excited murmurs finally broke out from the silent crowd as I regained my full height. I turned to face my people with my chest high, my heart overflowing. The congregation began to cheer unprompted. I heard a light chuckle from behind me. Even the priests knew they could not keep the citizens solemn and orderly for long, not when their esteemed leader had just been crowned queen. Breaking the suspense at last, the men joined in their lively praise. "All hail Queen Evangeline!" they proclaimed.

The crowd erupted with jubilation. "All hail Queen Evangeline!" they repeated zealously. The assembly clapped and jumped about with renewed gaiety. A joyful laugh escaped my throat, and my lips spread into a wide smile. I was practically soaring, my chest brimming with honor and my heart swelling with elation.

Before the applause could die down, I turned toward Rune, brushing my mantle aside. With a subtle wave of my hand, I motioned him over. His smile fell instantly, his face suddenly pale. Ignoring his wide eyes, I repeated the gesture, offering him a comforting grin.

Hesitantly, he took one step forward then another. When he drifted into the space beside me at last, the crowd had grown quiet, staring with interest at the anxious prince. Twisting my head over my shoulder, I beckoned forward a hidden lady's maid concealed within the masses. When she stepped out into the open space, the townspeople gasped. Ambling steadily toward us, she held before her another gold crown set upon a dark satin pillow. The audience murmured to each other in hushed breaths as the maid gradually approached.

When she halted beside me, Rune's mouth was wide with shock. His eyes flashed from me to the servant then back to me again. I took the crown in my hands and held it lightly before me. Rune ogled at me in astonishment, his body rigid, his features frozen in place. My lips curved slightly upward as I leaned my mouth toward his ear. "Kneel down," I whispered.

He hastily dropped to his knees, staring up at me in

wonder. Gently, I brought the crown downward and slipped it over his thick locks.

When he stood again, he wore a smile like I had never seen. His eyes were so full of joy that I felt my own grow misty. Suddenly, he took my hand. His excitement finally spilling over, he shifted us back toward the masses and lifted both of our arms skyward. "Long live Vitalia!" he exclaimed.

"Long live Vitalia!" the crowd echoed. Their roars of adoration resurged, and the castle boomed in exultation. Shouting along with the crowd, Rune squeezed my hand tighter. He was beaming toward the large assembly with such ardor that it made my heart flutter. It was a side to him buried so deep that I had never known it existed, concealed beneath countless years of torment and self-hate. But seeing the light emanating through him, I knew that the man who now stood beside me had been the true Rune all along. All it took was some time to dig him from the pit he had lost himself in.

A year ago, I met a tall, fragile boy petrified of what the future held. But today, I stood beside a new man.

A king.

****

The celebration lasted well into the night but still ended too soon. The valley was lit only by the glow of the moon when the townspeople finally made their way home, stuffed and drunk and teeming with bliss. Mary had been kind enough to watch over Sky during the evening festivities, but when I came to take her back, fast asleep in a cotton blanket, Mary refused.

"I will watch her tonight," she said. "You two could use some time alone." Peering at me with a sly grin, she ushered me away with a loose flick of her wrist. Despite my persistent protests, she would not take no for an answer. Eventually, I relented, knowing well enough that Mary would not be swayed, no matter how insistent my objections. Bending over the tiny bundle in her arms, I gently pressed my lips to Sky's forehead. She did not fuss or move an inch, lost in a dream.

I found Rune standing across the great hall, conversing with a few lingering townsmen. He spoke loudly, his empty goblet wavering dangerously between his fingers. The villagers were laughing heartily, clearly enjoying the effects of the wine. When I reached his side, wrapping my hand around his, their conversation ceased. Pausing midsentence, Rune turned to face me with a clumsy smile, his drunken eyes dancing in the firelight.

"Come," I told him, the corners of my lips helplessly pulling upward. Tightening my grip on his hand, I eased him away from the remaining guests then dragged him out of the hall.

We were both giggling madly by the time we made it to my bedroom. The door had barely closed when I spun myself around and pulled his face to mine. I pressed my mouth into his, ardently driving my tongue between his teeth. His lips found their rightful place with ease. He tugged eagerly on my bottom lip, stretching my neck upward to get a better taste.

Without hesitation, I began unbuttoning the front of his doublet. He emulated my movements, tearing the heavy cape from my shoulders and throwing it carelessly to the ground behind me. The weight of his body compelled me backward, hastily urging me toward the bed. Not once did I separate my lips from his, not when I jerked his shirt from his arms or when I lowered my fingers to loosen his breeches.

Before I knew it, each of my royal vestments had been strewn about the floor, and all that remained on my otherwise naked body was the towering gold crown upon my head. For just a moment, Rune paused his hurried fingers, taking the time to carefully remove my crown and place it gingerly on my nightstand. I did the same. Plucking the sparkling metal from his curls, I let his hair drape like curtains around his indigo eyes.

Rune's smile was so wide I could see the dim candlelight reflecting off his teeth. I laughed again and wrapped my hands around the nape of his neck, dragging him back toward my open mouth. One more step and the backs of my legs crashed against the side of the bed. I collapsed onto the mattress. Rune crawled on top of me zealously but not quickly enough. Gripping my hands around his ribs, I thrust him onto his back, his body gliding through the air. His backside struck the mattress with a heavy thump, and he stared up at me in a daze. Straddling his hips, I shot my lips toward his, sinking my fingers into his hair as I drank him in.

I could feel him pulsing against my abdomen in time with the quickening beat of my heart. I reached one hand down and took him between my fingers, stroking him tenderly. He groaned into the depths of my mouth, making me shiver.

He labored to lift his back from the bed. Once upright, he twisted his head and buried his mouth in my neck. His soft lips traveled hungrily down the side of my throat then fed greedily on my firm breasts. I released a heavy sigh, moaning desperately as his tongue swept across my nipples. Beneath my high-pitched cries, I heard him growl, devouring my body as if starved.

He swiftly wrapped his fingers around my waist and whirled me onto my back. I landed with another sigh, unprepared for his sudden attack. Pitching his head downward, he plunged his mouth roughly onto mine. I wrapped my fingers around the sides of his face, pulling him closer still.

The night was like a cloud-covered rapture. We were two lovers floating through space, drifting weightlessly among the stars. The brush of his fingertips, the heat of his chest, the low groans that slipped from his throat—they were like celestial orbits in a universe of our own. It was a place with no time, no doubts or restraints. It was ours, this world we created, this galaxy we would dwell in for eternity.

****

After, when our heads rested just inches apart, when our eyes were heavy with drink and sleep, I lay still, savoring the subtle warmth of his skin. His firm chest was like a comforting flame against my back. His knees were tucked in the folds of my legs. His arm was wrapped tenderly around my waist, his fingers forever entwined with mine.

I felt the air steadily leaving his nose as he exhaled, pouring against the back of my head. I tried to listen more closely, unsure whether it was the even breath of sleep. He was motionless apart from the slow beating of his chest. I felt my heart quicken. My stomach tightened with restless anticipation as I parted my lips.

"I love you," I whispered into the night.

I did not know if he heard me or if he knew I had spoken at all.

But I knew.

Chapter 31

Rune

I woke to the sound of a piercing scream. It burst through the walls with an earsplitting shrill, a bloodcurdling shriek that made the hairs on the back of my neck stand on edge. At first, I was paralyzed by the deafening cry, my body rigid as my eyes shot open in terror. Evangeline sprang from the bed without hesitation, racing from my arms and propelling me out of my fear-induced coma. Hastily rubbing the sleep from my eyes, I darted through the door behind her.

The scream grew closer as we tore through the hall. An icy chill rolled down my spine. Evangeline was far ahead of me and gaining distance. I moved my feet quicker, pumping my arms to close the gap. At last, she turned into a room at the far end of the hall. I sprinted as fast as my legs could carry me, ignoring the fiery pain in my lungs, and charged in behind her.

When I saw what waited for me inside, my stomach dropped. My limbs stiffened back into their frozen state. My bottom lip fell open and quivered with dread.

Evangeline was already on the ground, kneeling beside Mary, frantic and bleeding, crumpled in a tight ball. She was bawling uncontrollably, tears pouring from her eyes as she flailed about helplessly. Her frail arms shook as she tried to push her bruised body upward. But her thin elbows buckled and she collapsed, her forehead crashing against the stone. Only then did I notice her legs. They were completely disfigured. Her knees were twisted at unnatural angles that no joints should ever go. Large, swollen welts had formed on her kneecaps, the skin purpling by the minute.

"What happened?" Evangeline took hold of Mary's wrists and yanked her upright. The maid howled in pain, her seated position adding an unbearable amount of pressure to her battered legs. She did not answer right away but continued to sob wildly. "Where is Sky?" Evangeline yelled, gripping her by the shoulders and rattling her violently.

Finally, between feverish pants, she spoke. "She…took…her."

My heart stopped. An instinctive tremor shot through my knees, and the tips of my fingers turned frigid, a feeling I knew all too well.

Evangeline was growing delirious. "Where?" She looked deranged, her eyes darting madly about Mary's face.

The maid lifted a quivering hand toward the door and pointed unsteadily at the staircase across the hall.

As I turned to follow her finger with my eyes, Evangeline flashed by me like lightning. She was already tearing up the steps when I spun myself around to chase after her. I hurtled up the stairs three at a time, worried I might lose her in the great maze of the palace. "Where are you going?" I yelled after her. I was gasping for air but did not dare slow my climb.

"I know where she is!" She was already too far ahead for me to see her. I could only hear her rapid footsteps, her voice raining down from above. As her words showered over me, my entire body began to shake. Only one person would go to such lengths to take our daughter.

Evangeline did not slow until she reached the highest point of the tower. I increased my speed as I reached the final level and, by some miracle, arrived only a few seconds behind her. By the top step, she stopped, standing as still as death. Her face had gone white, her gaping eyes like glass as she stared out over the balcony.

Standing by the railing was my mother. Her face was shadowed beneath an obsidian cloak, a dark cape that hid the shape of her gaunt features. Her smoky hair fluttered about her, the high winds tossing the strands violently through the air. I could see the shape of her bones through her cheeks, her body even more skeletal than I remembered. She squinted to keep the tousling hair out of her eyes, but I could still make out the dark shade of her pupils, like deep beads of fresh ink.

In one arm, she held Sky. In the other, a dark silver longsword hovering precariously outward.

"Let her go!" Evangeline thundered. Her hands were fixed by her sides and clenched in tight fists, her knuckles a ghostly white.

"She belongs to me!" my mother screeched. Her arm was shaking, struggling under the unfamiliar weight of the sword, making the blade wobble in the space before her. "I brought her into this world. If it was not for me, she would have never been born." I thought I had witnessed the most demented side of my mother, but I had never seen her like this. Her normally spotless appearance was wild and unkempt. Harsh red lines scraped across the whites of her eyes, making her look crazed. Her sparkling teeth had turned dull and grimy, and her forehead was caked in a thin film of dirt.

"You banished me from my own kingdom," she hissed maniacally, "and now, it is time to take back what is rightfully mine." Sky was wailing frantically into her chest, her puny fists shaking helplessly through the air. A surge of wind struck my mother from the side, and she teetered dangerously toward the edge.

"Please," I pled through a panicked crack in my voice. I took a cautious step toward her. "You do not have to do this." I had promised myself that I would never beg my mother for anything ever again. But in her arms, she held my whole world, and I would fall to my knees and submit my life to her if it meant I could get my daughter back.

"Get back!" my mother screamed, shifting the weapon so it pointed toward my chest. "Not another step, Rune!" Her entire body was trembling now, and I did not know if it was from rage or fear or the chill of the wind. She flickered her eyes back to Evangeline, her chattering teeth on display. "It is time for you both to get what you deserve."

Slowly, she twisted the sword and pulled it inward. She brought the blade closer and closer until the edge was just inches from Sky's throat, the weapon wavering unsteadily before her squirming body.

I heard the harrowing roar first. Then, I saw her flash by me. She bellowed out like a raving barbarian, gnarled like a rabid beast. It was the deep growl of a wolf braced for slaughter. The fierce cry of a mother.

Evangeline shot forward with her arms outstretched, her teeth bared and her forehead wrinkled with unfiltered hatred. The blaze in her eyes burned with the heat of a thousand embers, a fire that could have melted the earth.

She flew unbridled, unrestrained, so quickly that my mother barely had time to react.

With one hand, she seized Sky, swiftly tearing her away from the raised sword and wrapping her tightly to her chest. With the other, she drove her palm between my mother's ribs. Plunging her hip in a full arc, she thrust the disgraced queen back.

I heard a loud crack as my mother's back connected with the stone railing. Her head swung back, and her feet floated from the ground. Flailing her arms powerlessly, her body tilted over the edge. It was as if she had offset a perfectly balanced scale, her meager weight tipping her backward. Through horror-struck eyes, I watched her fall: first the tips of her graying hair drifting toward heaven, then her arms reaching helplessly upward, then her legs, her slender ankles bare as she vanished from view.

All that remained was her hair-raising scream, her voice gradually dwindling until the gushing wind made her no more. She was gone, lost in the oblivion with only her sword and her dishonor. And even they would turn to nothingness when she reached the bottom.

I stood frozen as I watched the scene from afar. When Evangeline turned, our daughter was gripped tightly in her arms. I sighed aloud and searched for the reassurance in her eyes, the relief that could clear the crippling ache in the pit of my stomach. I scanned her face for the soothing warmth I always yearned for to make me feel safe.

But it was nowhere to be found. Instead, her features were flat, her cheeks pale, and her eyes wide with terror. I furrowed my brow in confusion as I took my first step forward, wondering what could possibly make her gaze so chilling, shaking me to the very bone.

Then, I saw it. It bloomed through the cotton of her dress, a bulb that swiftly blossomed into a scarlet rose. Thick drops trickled down the side of her leg. They drizzled onto the floor, quickly dying the cobblestone red. As the ground grew darker, her lips grew whiter, her arms, her chest and neck, losing their lustrous color.

When her knees gave out and she toppled forward, I was already there. Her forehead collided with my chest, her faint hand pressed weakly to my shoulder. As she collapsed to one side, I caught her in my arms before slowly easing her to the ground. Instantly, I ripped the dress from her body to find the source of the dark flower. Through her abdomen was a gaping hole, a grim void, the sight of which sent sharp pains through my chest.

My lips began to tremble. My eyes darted from the wound to her face then back again. I had not seen the sword pierce through her, had not heard the metal slice through her skin, but there it was nonetheless: a deep, bloody cavern.

With shaking hands, I pressed my palms into the red crater, willing the bleeding to slow. My arms quivered so violently that I could hardly keep them in place, the blood splattering onto my tunic. I could hear her mumble something, her voice gravelly and muffled, but I was not listening. I was tearing off my shirt, hastily tying the cloth around her stomach. But it was completely drenched before I could fasten the knot, the fabric just a sponge to carry the spill.

She spoke again, this time lifting a frail hand to my shoulder. I stopped my frenzied movements and gazed up at her, my hands still submerged in the bottomless red pool. Her mouth was slightly ajar, her breaths shallow.

"Take Sky."

I turned my head. The baby was still tucked in the crook of her arm. Her small head was buried in her mother's neck. I brought my hands toward the child, my fingers tainting her blanket with blood. Pulling her to my chest, I quickly peered back down at Evangeline and gasped.

Her abdomen was now completely submerged in blood, the color of her skin slowly disappearing. "I have to get help!" I croaked through my swollen throat. But when I leaped from my knees, I felt her fingers brush my side.

"Don't go," she breathed.

I turned toward the stairwell then back to her, my heart beating rapidly in my ears as I struggled to comprehend what she was saying. Suddenly I understood, hearing the words she had left unspoken, and my legs went numb. I sank back to the ground and took her hand in mine, delicately wrapping my quivering palms around her limp fingers. "I am here, Eve," I choked, my eyes growing cloudy.

"Listen," she grunted. A tear slipped from the corner of her eye and rolled into her hair. "Don't you dare let them tear her down." I lowered my eyes toward the weeping bundle in my arms then brought them back to Evangeline's pasty lips. "The world will try to suppress her. They will try to mold her as they see fit, but you cannot let them."

I gritted my teeth so tightly I could feel my gums shake. Squeezing her hand tighter, I nodded. "Please," I gasped between sobs. "Please don't leave."

She ignored my pleading but kept her fading gaze fixed on me, refusing to pull her eyes away. Another thin stream rolled down her cheek. "You must lead Vitalia now."

I squeezed my eyes shut and let the rivers of tears run down my face as a sharp wail escaped my throat. I shook my head, barely able to catch my breath. "I can't."

Raising her hand from the ground, she lightly pressed her palm into my wet cheek, her fingers as cold as ice. "You can," she whispered, gently brushing at my tears with her thumb. "You are ready."

I lifted my hand and laid it over hers, holding it against the side of my face. "Please don't go," I said again. "I cannot live without you." I impelled my own warmth to seep into her, to refill her empty veins. I wanted to give her every breath I had. I wanted my life to be the one draining out onto the ground.

Soon, I noticed that her fingers were no longer pressed to my cheek. Instead, I was carrying the weight of her palm in mine. When I withdrew my hand, her lifeless arm fell to the ground, splashing into the lurid pool of blood. Her open eyes had lost their focus, peering through me, peering through this world into that which I could not see.

The palace walls were burning. A rush of frost and flames blew through me with the changing wind. She was there and then she wasn't, this dissolving ghost that stained my fingers an eternal crimson. The world lost all sound. All I could hear was the fire waging.

The palace walls were burning. I took her icy cheeks in my palms. Shaking her head, I yelled her name again and again. I let my tears rain down on her, rolling along her cheeks as my helpless cries poured endlessly from my throat.

The palace walls were burning. Two hands found

my shoulders and tried to pull me away. I tore my arms back with a primal shriek and threw my head onto her chest. I listened for a beat that was not there. Then, I sank into her, and together we took one last swim. I held her so close that nothing could ever rip us apart. This time, I would keep her head above the surface. This time, I would not let her drown.

The palace walls were burning. Sky was crying. And down fell the ashes.

Down fell the ashes.

Down fell the ashes.

Chapter 32

Rune

I was never meant to be a king. I was never meant to lead anyone. So when I became the sole ruler of Vitalia, I knew it was just another one of God's cruel tricks, some kind of twisted joke that I would never understand.

I did not leave her bedroom for days. Not for her burial. Not for meals or mass. Not even when the citizens begged me to speak, to grant them the faintest glimmer of hope.

Different servants came to my door each day to urge me out of bed. But I disregarded them all, too lost in my misery to even lift my head from her pillow. I knew before long I would die there, and perhaps then, the heartache would finally end.

One morning, it was Mary who came to me. I was weak and sickly, a pile of bones on a cold mattress. She rapped her knuckles so lightly that I could barely hear the knock. When she eased the door open, I was buried beneath a mass of sheets with my back to her and my face hidden in my burrow of darkness. I heard her pause by the side of the bed. "Rune." She hesitated, carefully considering her words. "We need you."

I said nothing, feigning death as I lay motionless.

She sighed. "I know what it is like to lose someone

you love, but you must—"

"You know nothing," I growled, my voice muffled through the thick layers of linen.

She swallowed, ignoring my sudden outburst. "I know how hard it is. God knows I miss her too, but—"

"But what?" I roared, suddenly wrenching my head upward. "I should just forget about her?" I shouted. "I should just move on?" I flung my hands to my face and scratched at the red bags beneath my eyes. "I cannot walk out of this room and act like none of it ever happened. I cannot just pretend that all is well because it isn't."

A new flood of tears was spilling from my eyes. Mary was stunned, gaping at me with her mouth hung open. I bit my lip. "Before her, I was nothing. I had no will to live. I was waiting for the day my mother would get rid of me once and for all." I hugged my elbows into my chest. "But when I met Evangeline, everything changed. I changed. She made me someone. With her, I was free: free from Kreagan, free from my mother, free from myself. She was the reason I finally fought back. She made me realize that my life might finally be worth living if I could live it with her."

I paused, gasping for breath. Mary watched me with a shaking hand over her lips, her own tears streaming down her face.

"So what's the point?" I yelled. "What's the meaning of anything anymore?" I wanted to scream, to snatch each of her books from the shelves and hurl them across the room, to take every trinket upon her dresser and crush them with my bare hands. I was bursting with a rage I had never let myself feel, a fury that now spewed out in full force.

I was sure Mary would soon run out, defeated like all the rest. But she stayed.

"You cannot give up!" She wept, rubbing at the streaks along her cheeks. "This kingdom needs you!"

I scoffed, rolling my eyes bitterly. "You do not need me," I spat, wiping the snot from my upper lip. "No one needs me."

She shook her head, her chin trembling. "You are wrong," she said. "Evangeline believed in you. She trusted you to stand up and lead in her place."

I laughed humorlessly as I sank my face into my knees. Mary inched closer, carefully reaching for my hand before gently laying her fingers over my closed fists. I stifled the urge to tear them away. "I know how hopeless it feels right now, like you would be better off dead." She sniffled, struggling against the tremble in her voice. "But this is not what Evangeline would have wanted." Her glossy eyes desperately pleaded with me to see the light. "She wanted you to stand up for her people. To be there for your daughter."

I squeezed my eyelids together, the rest of the tears dripping down my face. "How?" I sobbed. "How am I supposed to live now that she is gone?" I lifted my chin and hopelessly searched her face for an answer.

Mary sighed, holding my gaze despite the pain, despite the uncertainty, despite the grief that would never fully disappear. "One day at a time."

****

Only when they brought me Sky did I find the strength to pull myself out of bed. I was too weak to lift her from her crib, my body too frail to even stand after so many days without food or light. Staring into her perfect face, I knew that somehow I had to pick myself up. I had to put myself back together, even if it was just so I could hold her in my arms again.

As I cared for my daughter, I relearned how to care for myself. She became my purpose, my sole reason for rising each morning. She was the thin ray of light at the end of my harrowing black tunnel. And when the sorrow threatened to overtake me again, I would pull her close. I would press my ear to her chest and listen to her heart because that soft, steady beat meant everything. It was living, breathing proof: proof that it all really happened, proof that this woman I loved had truly been, that part of her was still here.

Several weeks passed before I found the courage to face the townspeople. I was petrified, sure that when I saw them all gathered before me, I would feel it happening all over again. I could not bear to relive it, and yet I did every day. Every waking moment, I saw the gaping wound, her pale face, the pool of blood, her fading lips. Every living second, I saw her tears fall, replayed her final words.

So when I walked out onto the castle terrace, the entire kingdom assembled before me, I did not know what I would say. I was hardly one for speeches. I could never find the right words, let alone the boldness to speak them aloud. What could I even say? Could any words mend this brokenness?

But to my surprise, I did not have to say a thing. When I reached the end of the balcony, placing my shaking hands on the cold stone railing, my anxious thoughts were interrupted by a cool rush of wind. I glanced upward, expecting to be hit by a heavy gust of air, but instead, I saw a living current. Like the swell of the ocean, the sea of people sank to their knees. They floated downward like a wave, like an endless tide sailing across my vision. Every head was bowed, every eye lowered, the entire congregation kneeling in solemn silence.

As I witnessed their wordless tribute, this small act of shared reverence, I felt her. Her spirit was permanently embedded in this place, her memory living forever. But this time, the aching in my chest was more than the misery and heartbreak. In this quiet moment of somber respect, I saw the first spark of hope for tomorrow.

We had lost our greatest treasure, our bravest warrior, the very heart of our nation. But together, we could learn to live another day.

****

A dim ray of light finally returned to Vitalia with the birth of spring. Fields of gold and green dotted the horizon. The forest bloomed with apple blossoms, their drooping branches given new life, now stretching toward the sun. And as the morning frost was traded for the warm glow of daylight, Princess Sky grew.

She was like a wildflower, growing with no bounds. Her fragile limbs turned to strong legs that raced her through the castle grounds. Her hair grew long like vines, twisting down her back in caramel-colored waves. And her small voice swelled like the vibrant color of new life, her booming laugh just like her mother's.

Fathering a child alone is hard enough. Raising the daughter of Queen Evangeline was a much more challenging affair. Princess Sky was furiously independent and tremendously stubborn. She knew the soft spots and pet peeves of all those around her and never hesitated to use them for her own interests. She knew exactly what she wanted and did not stop until it was safely within her grasp. And yet, everyone in the palace loved this remarkably headstrong girl.

She spent most of her time in the village, the place she swore was far more interesting than the dull castle halls. There, she would play with the other children uninterrupted, cavorting with the sons and daughters of local farmers, shopkeepers, and masons. She would sprint with them down the town streets, would frolic alongside them through the nearby fields. She would return home covered in dirt and sweat, brandishing a score of scrapes and bruises and wearing the widest of smiles.

Those of us old enough to remember saw more than a lighthearted young girl. We saw that familiar fervid spirit, one that we would not soon forget. Often, I would try to make out the small hints of Evangeline from within her, tiny flickers that were easy to miss if you did not look closely enough. I saw it in the way she lifted her chin a half inch when she spoke. I saw it in the scrunch of her nose when she became angry. I saw it in her smile, in the perfect curve of her lips and the soft indent of her dimples along her cheeks. Sometimes, I would see her mother there, living on in the daughter she left behind.

Never did I sense her spirit more than on Sky's sixth birthday. The two of us were in the library—she dancing around the room while I poured over my latest sketch. My pencils were scattered upon a nearby table as I traced the hair rolling delicately down her front. She pranced around the towering bookshelves despite my protests, twirling merrily about the furniture. "Stand still, Sky," I instructed, peering up at her from the parchment.

"Look, Father!" she exclaimed, ignoring my

direction. I watched as she leaped through the air and whirled her skirt in a wide arc. Her violet gown was incandescent, glistening despite the dim light of the library.

I rolled my eyes in an amused grin, more interested in her beaming smile than her graceful spin. Setting the paper aside, I gently patted the empty space beside me. She scampered over and plopped onto the cushion, her honey curls blocking her vision until she blew them aside.

"What would you like for your birthday this year?" I asked, tucking a few loose strands behind her ears. She pursed her lips and stared thoughtfully toward the ceiling.

Suddenly, her face brightened, her cheeks spread into a wide grin. Her green eyes sparkled like emeralds, their effect entrancing. She bounced onto her knees and brought her mouth close, her lips grazing my ear. "I want a sword," she whispered eagerly.

My stomach tightened. My chest throbbed with the pain of a memory now distant but never too far. She must have seen the uncertainty in my eyes. Sticking out her bottom lip, she sat back on her shins. "Please, can I?" she begged, gripping my hands and shaking them fervently.

Behind my eyes, I saw her once more, that ghost from my past, and I remembered what she told me. I had always known this day would come. But now it was here. It felt so soon, too soon.

Releasing a long exhale, I pulled myself back to the present then softly lifted the corners of my lips. "Of course you can."

I was there when she skipped out onto the training field for her first lesson. She was clad in a specially made suit of armor, clutching her brand new wood sword by her side. She swayed about giddily as she scurried behind her new instructor, her stiff chainmail practically devouring her small figure. Before she could get too far, though, she spun around, her eyes searching for me. When she saw me leaning over the edge of the balcony, she waved.

I waved back, my heart fluttering. She was buzzing with excitement, so full of energy that she could hardly stand still. Turning back around, she sped onto the training field unrestrained, almost like she was running toward a long-lost friend.

"Do you really think I can do it?" she had asked me just moments before. Staring anxiously at her wooden sword, her nerves had finally started to show. "Do you think I can be a warrior?" It was a rare moment of doubt in her, an uncommon shift from the confidence she always wore like a crown.

Placing my fingers beneath her chin, I eased her head upward and held her eyes with my most sincere gaze. "You are Princess Sky," I said, my mouth curling into a wistful grin.

"You can do anything."

Acknowledgments

It took me four years to find the courage to write this book, a story that has been on my heart since I was eighteen. I did not think I would ever be able to put Evangeline's story on paper, and never did I imagine it would be published for the world to see. I spent three years pouring my heart into this book, and I am so grateful to you for reading it.

I have so many people to thank for helping me make *Some Call Me Eve* a reality. Mom and Dad—you have been my biggest fans from day one. You always told me to follow my dreams, to work hard, and to never ever quit. This time, I didn't give up, and I am so thankful that I have parents like you who have supported me every step of the way.

To the Fisheries—Camryn, Haley, Kara, and Jing— you taught me the true meaning of friendship. You helped shape me into the fierce, persistent woman I am today. Without you, I would never have met Evangeline. I am eternally grateful for your endless encouragement and your unwavering loyalty.

Bethany—I am forever indebted to you for the unconditional support you have shown me from the moment I started my very first draft. You believed in me before you even knew me. You read every chapter as I worked through my manuscript, and if it wasn't for that, I'm not sure I would be able to call myself an author today. Thank you for helping me be true to myself and to find the strength to pursue my calling.

To my wonderful law school friends—Bre and Haley—thank you for sticking by me as I trudged through the final edits of this book. You stuck by this crazy JD student/romance novelist, and you didn't let me back down. Thank you for believing in my story and my writing.

To my editor, Ally Robertson, and the rest of the staff at The Wild Rose Press—thank you for taking a chance on this unknown girl from a little Arkansas town who longed to share her stories with the world. You turned my wildest dreams into reality. This opportunity has changed my life, and I am so grateful to work with such a fine publisher.

Finally, to my amazing fiancé—from the day we met, I told you I wanted to be a writer. It was a bumpy road along the way, but you never stopped believing in me, not even for a second. You could see my passion, and you didn't let that fire within me go out. You could sense the joy that writing brought me, and you pushed me to keep pursuing my dream. I love you so much, Will.

A word about the author...

T. Pike grew up in Northwest Arkansas where she swam competitively for more than 17 years. After graduating from Texas A&M University with an English degree and All-American honors, she returned home to pursue her master's in English and write her debut novel: *Some Call Me Eve*. Now a law student, she enjoys running and hiking with her dogs and exploring the mountains with her partner.